M000288362

Mooncallers
Shadows Burn

Edited by Losse Lorien and Leda C. Muir.
Proofread by Losse Lorien.

Fonts created by Peter Rempel and Manfred Klein.
Cover illustration by Theodore Tryon.
Back cover illustration by Leda C. Muir.
Chapter illustrations by Leda C. Muir and Theodore Tryon.
Maps by Leda C. Muir.
Book design by Leda C. Muir.

ISBN 978-0-578-41196-5

*For all those who love this world like I do.*
*You know who you are.*

# My Words to You

There's A world in every head, in every heart. We visit them in dreams, in memories, and in nightmares. Because of that world, all of us, at some period in all of our lives, experience a feeling.

*"I want to go home."*

That is from whence Amniven came. A yearning for escape that grew so real that it now exists for at least one person. This is a plane in which souls from any walk of life are welcome.

On this journey, you may meet friends, lovers, guardians, and enemies. Believe it if you will, every inhabitant of Amniven is as alive as you or I. They live within me, and my greatest wish is for them to live within you too. That being said, do not expect this land to be any kinder than the one in which you currently live. I will not promise you a safe haven, for only you can provide that for yourself.

Amongst these pages, you might discover hope, humor, joy, insight, strength, and perhaps even love. You might also discover poverty, inequality, hierarchy, war, hatred, judgment, and all else that is universally feared. Just like the world of humankind, this world suffers, its people suffer, and while reading, you may suffer too.

But without pain, this story never would have come to be.

# Synopsis

This is the second part of the Mooncallers' story.

It began with a woman pulled out of Tal Am T'Navin River and taken to the infirmary in Tel Ashir, the home of the Speaker of Oscerin the Moon Goddess, Prince Ares Lavrenthea. When she woke up, stars were in her eyes, and she had no memory of her past except for her name: Luxea Siren.

One year later, Luxea and her mentor, Avari, were sent to Lor'thanin where they discovered a massacre brought upon by Widow, a fabled goddess. To warn Prince Ares, Luxea broke into Castle Lavrenthea. Soon after, Oscerin then sent Ares message pleading him to "keep the stars safe." Trusting in Oscerin, he brought Luxea to the royal chamber of the castle to live.

The two spoke seldom until Ares conversed with Luxea about her magick and an oddity in his own blood. Draconism, a curse placed upon the first Tzapodian people, granted them a dragon's abilities with the price of insanity and eventual entrapment in a dragon's body.

The Prince later received a missive from the Lady Peyamo Nelnah, inviting him to a gala in Solissium. As Ares' lover of yore, Annalais, was the Empress of Goldenrise, he would only attend if a woman went with him. He chose Luxea.

En route to Goldenrise, the Mooncallers were captured and brought to Blackjaw Hollow by the Riders of the West. The Chieftain Gajneva chained them out of hatred for the Lavrenthea family, but the Mooncallers escaped when her counterpart, Veshra, killed her and herself. A rider named Brielle Joined the Mooncallers with her wolf brother Ruka.

The Mooncallers traveled to Solissium to attend the gala where, in Haven de Asrodisia, Luxea Siren met a ten-year-old courtesan named Unblossomed and promised to help her and her mother escape.

Halfway through the gala, odd happenings began. Ares received another message from Oscerin, and he and Luxea left to a House of Worship. Shortly after, the villa was bombed, the attack brought on by Sun Chief Garamat un Gatra who was Widow's devotee.

After the Mooncallers slew Garamat, Ares and Peyamo faced Empress Annalais. She admitted to signing a contract with Widow and handing over Goldenrise to the Brood. Before leaving Solissium for Tarot, the Mooncallers freed the slaves of Haven de Asrodisia.

They rode south to the Wraiths but got lost on the Riddling Roads. For the night, they stayed in the town of Witchsleep where Luxea and Avari met a sorcerer named Cherish Ven'lethe.

In Anathema, Ares discovered that Cherish was Widow's servant, and his purpose was to kill Luxea — the greatest threat to Widow for reasons he wouldn't confess. Cherish inflicted Luxea with 'nightmare venom' and revealed to her that he'd been her magick instructor before she lost her memories.

In Tarot, Luxea hallucinated about a little girl who looked just like her. To save her, the Moon Goddess willed Ares to carry her to a forgotten island within Sh'tarr's Iris, the eternal storm, called Mythos.

When the Mooncallers boarded the Lady's airship destined for Tel Ashir, the little girl showed herself to Luxea once more — this time to kill her. She screamed, 'Anzthoraz' and threw Luxea off the airship. Ares jumped too and carried her to the Iris in the form of a dragon.

Luxea's soul was caught by Oscerin. While Ares fought with Sh'tarr the Storm Goddess and Alatos the Sea Goddess, Oscerin revealed to Luxea that She had taken her memories and sent her to Tel Ashir to meet Ares. Together, they were Her chosen.

As Ares nearly drowned, Oscerin used the gravitational pull of the Irestar to control the tides. Ares and Luxea were delivered to the shore of Mythos by Oscerin's hand.

In the second part of the story, Ares' past is brought back to life, and many of Luxea's questions about her own are unraveled.

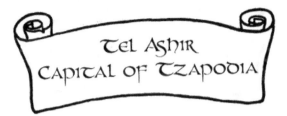

# Tel Ashir
# Capital of Tzapodia

# ANUNARU

# TABLE OF CONTENTS

# SHIR

## 1.SNOWHOWL.25.OSC.3
### MYTHOS

FAR AWAY, across the ocean and through the storm, there was green. Then came white, and nothing else. At last, there were stars.

The galaxies in Luxea Siren's eyes churned. Something about that sleep felt longer, deeper. Where was she? Why, when she'd kissed the mouth of the end, had she woken up?

She lay in a patch of grass so thick that she wondered if the blades had bones. The earthen scents of moss, orchids, and rain brushed up the length of her nose. She lifted herself onto her elbows, expecting to feel heavy, but she was weightless — brand new, untouched, and unfettered.

Ten feet away, something shifted. Between the curled spears, Luxea caught sight of a shade of black she'd seen many times before; she'd never realized how dark it really was.

Crawling silently, just as Avari had taught her, Luxea made her way to a dip in the meadow beside the black mass. It was hair, lank but tangled. She reached out and touched honey brown skin. A groan came from the body as it turned onto its back.

As if there wasn't enough of the color, Ares' green eyes opened.

The last time they'd been face-to-face, they'd fought and never come to a resolution. Luxea's thread of life had been stripped bare, and Ares had taken action with the belief that only one or neither would survive. Now, as alive as alive could be, there was no longer a point to their quarrel.

He exhaled. She inhaled. In that breath, they forgave each other.

For the first time, Luxea hugged Ares. With her arms around his neck, his head snared to the damp soil, it dawned on him that the stroke had been reversed. His promise to Oscerin had been fulfilled, Amniven would have a chance, and Luxea was safe. Hope was restored to a state where such a thing existed at all.

Luxea backed away, and Ares sat upright. Open-mouthed, they examined the white-barked trees and turquoise leaves around them. In the eye above them was a cyan sky. Crystals with frosted edges circled their meadow, a faerie ring of minerals and light; pure energy lived within their shells, coursing and pulsing as they breathed. The stone sang inside their ears, as deep but shrill as the vestigial hum of a bell after the ringing stopped.

"Where are we, Ares?"

"Mythos," he said. "Oscerin bid me to bring you here. Creatures live on this island, the Mythics, *Sil'simani*. They saved you."

"*Sil'simani* means *'Sacred Children'* in l'arian elvish," mentioned Luxea. "I haven't had more than two years to study Amniven's history, but I've never read anything about Sacred Children."

"This place was left behind in history, long ago. We may be the only ones alive who know about it," said Ares, in awe. "The Mythics once walked this planet like us, but the divines hid them from modern man to keep their purity intact."

As Ares relayed what the Moon Mother had told him about Mythos, Luxea sat cross-legged and wrapped blades of grass around her fingers. It wasn't a simple concept for her, or him, for that matter, but he gave his best effort. She felt like he was telling her a fairytale.

The Mythics had been born from the womb of Sirah the Crystal Spire, one of Amniven's natural towers, six of which drilled into the core of the planet and scraped the highest layer of the stratosphere. As long as the Mythics' purity remained intact, they could transcend time, space, and reality. Nature adhered to their will, and their vision of energy was so excellent that jumping from locus to locus was as simple as ascending a staircase.

Most importantly, they could absorb maladies from other living things. That is why, when Luxea would have faced death by any other means, Ares threw away his own future to bring her to Mythos.

Once Luxea had grasped enough understanding for this lost world, she and Ares slunk through the woods. The land stole their breaths as they moved along. Transparent insects the sizes of cats and dogs rested on bouncy leaves and buzzed around the branches. Deer, snakes, and bears lay on the terrain, but none fled or attacked; all animals on Mythos were frugivorous, at peace with no need for fear or violence.

Time spun by an hour ere they found a shore with black grains of sand, as plump and shiny as beads. Foam sloshed to their toes, bright blue with bioluminescent plankton. No wind raged where they stood, but half a reach from the shore, the white caps turned the waves into snowy plains. Not far above them, branching down from clouds as dark as soot, were silver cyclones and purple lightning.

"So that's Sh'tarr's Iris. We're inside of it," whispered Luxea.

"It's much lovelier in the eye than out there," said Ares irately.

Off the coast, a palm frond from some distant shore flew into their line of sight. The wind bit the leaflets from the rachis and spat them into the sea, leaving nothing but a bare spine until that too was eaten.

Had Ares been any less careful in his endeavor to Mythos, had the Goddesses of Storm and Sea been any more merciless, he and Luxea might have been a pair of skeletons on the seafloor.

"Why did you do it? Why did you jump?" She watched as the splinters of the frond were hammered into the ocean. "You nearly drowned fighting Sh'tarr and Alatos. Those are *goddesses,* Ares. Were you thinking at all? Why would you put yourself through that?"

In truth, Ares had wondered the same thing every other blink during his flight to the Iris. He was equal parts grateful to Oscerin and his own thick skin for breaking the storm, but it had been Luxea's voice in his mind that night that had urged him to breathe. He might have imagined it, but that inner plea was what had saved him.

*'Ares, don't give up! We have to go home!'*

Her voice was all he'd heard in his last moments of life . . . but could he tell her that? No. Such a confession would be pitiful.

Instead, he asked, "I said that I owe you my life, did I not?"

The urge to wrangle Ares to the ground in an embrace put up a good fight, but Luxea won by clasping her hands tightly behind her back. "Thank you, Ares."

"Thank *you* for not dying before we made it here," he laughed.

Luxea grinned. "That would have been a disappointment."

It was becoming habitual for Ares to replay his conversations with Luxea in his head. This time, he uncovered a troublesome detail.

"How did you know I'd fought Sh'tarr and Alatos?" he asked.

Luxea wasn't sure. Only the waves spoke for minutes and minutes. Staring at sea foam didn't help, so she turned her eyes to Ares. The starry, silver pendant that dangled over his broad chest twinkled.

The Felastil — the Moon Mother's relic.

It all came back in a deluge. She had to sit down. "I still see Her."

Ares sat too. "See whom?"

"I met Her. I was with Oscerin." She started to giggle. "She caught me before I was lost to Eletheon. She had a Felastil too. *That* is what allows Her to speak with you. She told me that She gave me a piece of Herself, Her eyes, so that She can view the mortal realm. But that's not all. She sent me to Tzapodia to cross paths with you. Like She chose you, She chose me. She said we're Her holders of the keys to fate, that you're the Parallel, and I'm the Divide . . . but I don't know what it means."

This account was a twist to Ares' arm. His greatest wish had forever been to meet the Moon Mother — but Luxea hadn't believed in the divines until recently! Instead of being excited for her, he was painfully envious as if he'd suffered a loss.

Pretending not to want to hear more, he asked, "Is that all?"

"No. When I was returned to the mortal realm, She poured moonlit water into my mouth. As I disappeared, She said, *'Never can shadow touch you with moonlight in your veins.'*"

Ares had never wanted a cigarette more. He mulled over Luxea's words for a breath before asking, "Oscerin, how does She look?"

Luxea eyeballed the Felastil. Within it, she saw Oscerin smiling at her. "She's stunning. Huge, bigger than anybody else. She has dark skin like you, white hair like me, and eyes like mine too — stars. She wears black, but She's so bright. She looks like . . . love."

As Ares envisioned the Moon Goddess that he'd heard since his childhood, he wished She'd show Herself to him too. But while he couldn't see Oscerin and maybe wouldn't until his death, Luxea's description restored to him some peace.

"Thank you," he said softly.

A ground-shaking rumble woke up Luxea the next morning. She froze, wondering if a lion had crept into their meadow.

*Grumble.*

Oh. It was only her stomach.

"I'm starved as well." Ares had been awake for twenty minutes listening to her guts whine. He shook the stiffness from his arms and legs. "I've no clue how to hunt without a weapon, but we can capture a grouse if we're patient."

It wasn't that Luxea wasn't salivating at the thought of cooked grouse, but killing anything on Mythos felt wrong. They differed from the animals on the mainland; their populations were balanced.

"How about fruits or vegetables?" she hinted.

"If you'd like," said Ares compliantly.

Following the fungi that grew on the northern sides of the tree trunks, they set off through the rainforest. It wouldn't be challenging to find their way back to the meadow — they hoped — but it would be lovely to get lost anywhere on this island.

They discovered fascinating beasts and plant-life on their walk, fruits and vegetables too, but were wary of touching them. Anything that might have been edible looked a bit too alien.

Ares probed a tree with bulblike roots and branches that expanded and contracted like they were breathing. Although disturbed by the fruit it bore, which looked uncannily like a human heart, he picked one off the stem.

"I've not studied much about comestible plants, but I don't think this is one of them," he said uncomfortably.

"Avari taught me about vegetation when I was her apprentice, but none of these are recognizable." Luxea twisted her face at the heart-fruit. "I imagine they must be native to Mythos. I'm not sure what's safe to eat."

The heart pulsed. Ares flung it. "We'll keep searching."

Their hunt for food proved to be, quite literally, fruitless. After scaling plains of shuddering grass and pulling each other up quartzite paths, they stumbled upon a lightless cave.

"Let's see what's inside." Ares took a step, but Luxea stayed back. His dimples appeared. "Afraid of the dark?"

"No. Unfriendly with the dark," said Luxea defensively.

He smiled but not enough to embarrass her. As she scooted along elsewhere, he crooked his arm for her. If she were to be mauled by a creature, having a dragon at her side would make it less terrible, wouldn't it? Albeit reluctant, she clutched his sleeve and inched into the cave.

That unfriendly darkness didn't linger. Ten feet from the entrance grew a ceiling of light-shedding pods with glass shells. They must have been some species of fantastical bean.

There was a *clack*. Saving herself, Luxea dove under Ares' arm and hid behind his curtain of hair. But there wasn't anyone else in the cave. Nothing moved, no fearsome, glowing eyes stared at them.

"I think it was a rock," she sighed.

He retook her arm. "If one comes for you, I'll fight it."

She pouted. "How noble."

Deeper inside, a few more *clacks* were heard, along with Luxea's startled peeping, but the two were doubtlessly alone. After a while, they met another noise. Running water — lots of it.

The cave opened over a cliff beside a waterfall. The ledge was shockingly high up, but neither Luxea nor Ares feared heights. And, yes, they hadn't found food, but this view of Mythos gave meaning to their aching legs.

For an island that had been omitted from every world map, it was extensive; the western shore must have been ten reaches away. Not an inch of the terrain was less heart-stopping than the last. The colors of the leaves, crystal towers, and twinkling rivers and lakes were so vivid that Ares and Luxea learned a few new shades. Canyons of ruby, sapphire, and jade squiggled through the earth like they'd been carved by giant termites. In the spring below was a white turtle the width of a ballroom floor. Beside it swam three hatchlings, splashing their feathery fins and popping their bulbous heads in and out of the water.

The serenity was broken by a *grumble* quite like the one that had woken Luxea from her dreams — but it hadn't come from her this time. Ares crossed his arms over his stomach, appearing as grouchy as he had on a daily basis in Castle Lavrenthea; there, he'd rarely had gaps in his schedule to enjoy meals.

Luxea was about to suggest that they continue their hunt for food when another, more frightening noise filled the cave.

*Clack!*

"What was that?" she gasped.

"One of those ferocious rocks again?"

Ares had expected Luxea to make a sour face like she usually did when he cracked jokes, but from the corner of his eye, he saw that she was gawking at something.

"Is that a carrot?"

His eyebrow hiked. "Is *what* a carrot?"

Luxea spun Ares around by his forearm, and he made a squeak that she'd never heard from him before. Poking up from the soil were carrot greens, five in a row with fluffy leaves — and, oh, were they succulent.

"Where did those come from?" asked Ares quietly.

"I don't know, but they're here now."

She dropped to her knees and dug. The first carrot was long and fat with hairlike roots. The second was skinnier but brighter in color. The next three were stunted and shiny.

One at a time, she handed them to Ares — who wasn't pleased with dirtying his palms. When she was done, she brushed herself off, reclaimed the vegetables, and scampered to the ledge to rinse them in the waterfall.

"Which one would you like?" she called.

"Whichever you don't want."

Luxea had never *loved* carrots but had been eying the skinny, bright one. She handed Ares the heftiest. He spent a while picking flecks of dirt from the scars, but Luxea dove right in.

The carrot was crunchy and sweet, the most scrumptious thing she'd ever tasted! Her arms and legs melted as she munched. Through a mouthful of orange shreds, she said, "I'm so happy."

Ares leaned against the cave wall and bit down on his carrot. Before his teeth could snap it, the rocks to his right moved.

*Clack!*

He did a double-take, and his carrot almost fell out of his mouth.

"I see a tomato plant."

Luxea's crunching and gulping ceased. She propped her half-eaten carrot on a rock and got to her feet. Indeed, across the cave was a tomato plant with the plumpest, reddest, juiciest tomatoes. They must have been as big as cantaloupes, these things!

If there'd been an award for *'Amniven's Fastest Tomato-Picker,'* Luxea Siren would have won it. Her arms moved at the speed of light as she gathered.

She heard another *clack!*

To her left were strands of velvety pea pods she could have bet her life hadn't been there before. Sprouting from the cave floor below them were wide-brimmed mushrooms without a scratch on their caps.

"Peas and mushrooms!"

*Clack!*

"Luxea, is this a potato?"

With an armful of tomatoes, pea pods, and mushrooms, she swiveled to face Ares. Swinging from his closed fist was a flowery stem with three potatoes dangling from the bottom. They admired each other's harvests with silly, ravenous grins on their faces. She swiped his potatoes and scampered to the waterfall.

"Wash these off, please!"

She left the stack and dashed away. Humming what sounded like a lullaby, she picked up a bunch of rocks and positioned them in a circle on the cave floor.

Rinsing a tomato, Ares asked, "What are you making?"

"A fire pit," said Luxea inattentively. "What do you say to stew?"

"I say I don't know how to cook stew."

"I'll do it. Avari trained me in areas other than combat. Cleaning, dying clothes, skinning, building fires, fixing shoes, cooking — all without magick too. Although it does make it easier."

Thanks to that very magick, Luxea wouldn't need kindling for the fire. She felt so refreshed on Mythos that she was confident she could conjure an entire wildfire. All preparations for the stew went smoothly until she remembered that if you're going to cook, a bowl might be necessary.

"Bowl, bowl, bowl," she mumbled to herself.

Shaking water droplets off a mushroom, Ares suggested, "What about those pods? Their shells might serve well as bowls."

"How innovative," purred Luxea.

Ares smiled to himself.

She ventured to a light-shedding pod, one not too far into the darkness of the cave, and jumped a few times to pick a pair. One was small. Luxea decided that the bigger shell would be their pot, and the others would be bowls. She knocked the pods against a rock, and they cracked open, spilling gooey sap that smelled a bit like cinnamon.

Once the vegetables had been washed, Ares cut them into slices with his talons. He'd never imagined that dragon blood would make for a decent culinary trait.

Luxea scrubbed the large shell until it was crystal clear and filled it with water one-third of the way. She set the shell on the rock circle and said, *"Yeth'lavren."*

A blue arcanan fire crackled. She dumped the chopped vegetables into it with one hand and spouted flames with the other. As they waited keenly for their stew, she and Ares snacked on pea pods.

Soon, the water was boiling. Chewing on about twenty peas at once, Luxea ceased her magick and stirred their meal with a piece of wood she'd broken off the wall of the cliff. Ares didn't appreciate sticks in his food, but Luxea was working hard to feed him, so he didn't complain.

She dipped the small shells into the stew. The water dripped down the outside as she handed it to Ares. His eyes floated around to the right; he was searching for a spoon. It occurred to Luxea that, as a part of a royal family, he'd never eaten soup without utensils.

Giving him an example, she brought the lip of the shell to her mouth. Ares hadn't wanted to be rude in front of a lady, but if she drank her stew, so would he. They gulped. The broth was sweet from the residue of the cinnamon sap, the tomatoes gave it thickness, and the vegetables were soft and flavorful.

Luxea's stars sparkled into an adoring, pink shade. This taste was the closest thing to falling in love she could get. Ares had a similar critique. Maybe he was just starved, and maybe they were guzzling it from shells in a cave, but this was the best stew he'd ever had.

"You're a magnificent cook." A smirk arose. "It makes me wonder what other talents you might be hiding."

She slurped. "Wonder away."

Once their bellies started to fill, something dawned on Ares. He glared at the vegetables at the bottom of the cooking shell and then at the ceiling.

"Do plants of this sort not require sunlight to thrive?"

Mushrooms, at times, grew in caves; carrots, tomatoes, peas, and potatoes, however, didn't. Yet here they were, eating a stew made with fruits and roots and vegetables that had appeared miraculously. Luxea was suspicious too, but that didn't stop her from enjoying her meal.

It was midnight when they found their meadow. Their stuffed bellies had sent them into a stupor and gotten them lost.

This evening was frosty. Ares' dragon blood heated him, but Luxea was trembling without proper warmth. She shuffled outside of the crystal ring and collected offshoots — tiny stick, thorny stick, just a leaf. The wood was lightweight and papery, so she wouldn't have trouble starting another fire.

As Ares lay supine with his eyes on the stars beyond the trees, Luxea positioned the wood into a cone. It was exemplary; she wished she could show Avari how much she'd learned about campfires.

*"Yeth'lavren."*

Dark blue flames illuminated the grass in a cold, eery glow. The crystals surrounding them let off rays of pink, yellow, and orange, turning the meadow into a watercolor painting.

She flopped onto her belly with her head on her arms. The hotness of her cheeks softened her gooseflesh and made her hairs lay flat. Soon, Ares fell asleep with one hand behind his head and the other clutching his Felastil. His eyebrow twitched. If he was having a dream, Luxea hoped it was a good one.

The wood in the fire pit had lit easily but was so thin that it turned to ash in mere minutes. Luxea was once again plunged into a bout of shivers. Not wanting to wake Ares, she unbuckled her sandals and slipped them off. Her knees cracked as she stood. She winced. Her ankles cracked too. Stupid joints!

In the rainforest, she snapped branches off the trees and hummed the same melody she had in the cave. She couldn't say where she'd heard it . . . but she knew it so well. It wouldn't leave her alone.

She circled a grove and swiped sticks off the forest floor. From a trunk grew a skinny, tapered twig. It was at a downward angle, which

Luxea thought was odd, but she grasped it anyway. The second she did, a shockwave coursed through her.

*What kind of a feeling is this?*

Then the twig whisked out of her hand, and a gigantic humanoid outline appeared. It wasn't a twig — it was a finger.

Ares woke up to the sound of Luxea screaming. He leaped out of the grass and bolted into the woods where he found her with her back pasted to a tree. He followed her gaze and blenched.

Cowering there was a nine-foot-tall creature, white and crystalline. Upon its narrow head was a crown, not the sort worn by royals but part of an exoskeleton. Within it was a strand of light, bifurcating between its opalescent eyes to its nape. It was unclothed which wasn't a shame, for its flesh was stunning enough to have brought Ares and Luxea to tears had they not been scared out of their wits. The body was willowy, two legs, two arms, but reproductive bits were amiss. Nothing about this creature's form could determine it as one thing or another.

This had to be one of the *Sil'simani* — a Mythic.

Translating peace, Ares put up his hands. The Mythic took two giant strides back, not frightened but conflicted. As softly as he could manage, Ares asked, "Mythic? *Sil'simani?*"

The creature's eyelids crackled as it blinked. It rubbed its graceful hand in circles over its middle. Ares and Luxea contemplated if it was going to eat them until it made a motion as if it were lifting a ball.

Beneath it sprouted carrots.

"Carrot . . ." Luxea's stars exploded into color. "It was you, wasn't it? You planted food for us because we were hungry!"

Painstakingly slow, the Mythic picked one of the vegetables. With its crystalline fingers quivering, it held it out.

*A gift?*

Luxea scooted forward and took it, and the Mythic shied away. "Thank you," she said softly. "May we speak?"

The Mythic didn't know the common tongue but plainly wanted to converse. With its glinting stare switching between the two of them, it crouched and laced its rocky hands into the grass —

Then the impossible happened.

Its fingertips sank into the dirt, and veins of white light appeared in the soil; Ares and Luxea shuffled back as they spread to their feet like roots. The voices of everyone who had ever lived echoed in the air, bouncing off invisible barriers and swimming through their heads. The Mythic absorbed the sounds trapped within the earth, learning as it listened. It removed its hands, and the rainforest went silent.

In a breathy voice, indistinguishable between male or female, the Mythic said, "We may speak."

But now Luxea was speechless. She'd previously been sure of her ability to take in high volumes of information at once, but everything the Mythic had just done proved her very wrong.

Ares stepped in. "You grew us the vegetables, but you also rescued us, didn't you? You picked us up on the shore and healed her when she was sick."

"Us, not I," corrected the Mythic.

"Where are the others?" questioned Ares.

The Mythic passed a look over its shoulder. "Everywhere."

With the grace of falling feathers, tens of figures stepped away from the trees and the rocks, lifted up from the tall grass, and crawled out of the winding rivers. They were as transparent as glass until their

15

splashes of color returned — garnet, lapis, agate, fluorite, zircon, citrine, amethyst, obsidian, selenite . . .

Alien ringing sent chills darting up and down Ares and Luxea's backs. The Mythics said thousands of words to each other within a second's time in a tongue without tongues. In sync, they turned to the humans. The first blinked at the carrot in Luxea's hand.

"Are you . . . friends?"

Ideally, Ares would have discussed this with Luxea before giving a definitive answer, but she had a different agenda.

"I'll be your friend!"

The crystal strangers all grinned, their lack of teeth making them look happier. Luxea ignored Ares' ocular requests for reconsideration as she asked, "You trust us? We've just met."

"No, you have just met us," said the first Mythic.

Ares scanned their faces. "You've been watching us?"

"Yes," said the Mythic honestly.

The Prince had been trained well to sniff out hidden forms, and Luxea, previously the apprentice of a ranger, had learned the same to a lesser degree. But the Mythics had followed them for two days without either of them having the slightest idea.

Luxea stepped forward, but the Mythics moved away. She set down the carrot and extended her arm. "If we're friends, would you like to shake hands?"

The Mythics' heads tipped right and left, and the first wiggled their fingers. "Shake? For what purpose?"

"It's a greeting for humans — oh, but only if you're comfortable touching me," blathered Luxea. "Would you like to see?"

A thought passed through the Mythics. "Yes," said the first.

Smiling as if she'd been tickled, Luxea faced Ares and held out her hand. Putting on his best example, Ares performed the shake. Looking into her eyes, he said, "It's lovely to meet you."

The crystal strangers were fascinated. Meeting someone new was so simple! The first gingerly reached for Luxea; its hand was so enormous that hers looked like a newborn's.

Touching a Mythic was somewhere between sucking on an ice cube and having a wonderful, wonderful night in bed. Keeping herself together, Luxea shook their hand. When it was finished, she was sweating, and her cheeks were flushed. But then the Mythic took back her hand. She whimpered.

"I neglected to say, *'It is lovely to meet you,'*" they hummed.

The Mythic let go. Luxea's knees buckled, and she plopped into the grass, quivering. Ares' eyebrows raised. Whatever the Mythic's contact had done to her, it looked enjoyable. Briefly, he felt it himself.

They shook the crystalline hands of sixty Mythics, heard, *"it is lovely to meet you,"* and experienced feelings equally exhausting and fulfilling. After ten minutes, they were lying flat on the grass with their wet clothes sticking to their bodies. The Mythics were beyond human, mineral, or object. They were electricity, pleasure, hope, purity. A single touch activated the five senses to an extreme.

The first Mythic knelt in front of them. "We enjoy you."

"We enjoy you too," panted Luxea. She forced herself upright. "Since we've met, I suppose we should share our names. I'm Luxea Siren, a student of the arcana. This is Ares Lavrenthea, Speaker of Oscerin and Prince of Tzapodia. What are your names?"

The Mythics harmonized with one another, ringing in varying tones and volumes. When they were done, they looked proud.

"Are those your names?" asked Ares.

"We think so," said the first Mythic.

Luxea bit her lip. "There seems to be a language barrier. Is there anything else we can call you?"

"No."

It seemed like a lost cause to call to these creatures individually. Ares was about to say, *"it's all right,"* but noticed how eager the first Mythic was to delve into the world of these things called *'names.'*

"What if we give you a name?" he suggested.

The Mythic twinkled. "Yes."

What, of all names, would fit a Mythic? Something so inhuman, living in a land where nothing visits and nothing leaves. Ares and Luxea considered simple options — Halthric, Ferensa, Qyarra — but none suited the Mythic's elegance. It wasn't until Luxea visually inspected the creatures that she cupped Ares' ear and mumbled an idea.

He nodded and whispered to her, "Beautiful."

Luxea boosted her shoulders. In an involuntarily excited pitch, she said, "In l'arian elvish, the word for *'glass'* is *'shir.'* Do you like that?"

If it were anatomically possible for Mythics to shed tears, the first one would have. The power of a name made them feel invincible.

"Shir. Shir. Shir." Their crown gleamed. "My name is Shir."

# The Speaking Tree

## 3.Snowhowl.25.Osc.3

### Mythos

Darts of violet ash pelted his scales, and hot wind gusted from under his wings. Towers were smashed, and ashlars and silver bells were hurdled into the scorched streets.

Black and crimson dragons bit and scratched with claw and fang and dressed each other in fire. The black cast down the crimson, and his weight left a scar in the earth that would never heal. The black fell too, and his veins netted him down as they emptied. His scales were shredded and lapped away by the slate ocean waves that spilled into the new rift in the world.

A silver crown lay before him, steepled, faceted with gems of blue and white, and stained by smoke. Human once more, he reached out — but he could not claim what was his. His foe stole the heirloom, for he was the King of Tzapodia, and so he would remain.

The crimson took flight, wounded by cut and curse, over the sea.

Ares choked on his breath. When he realized he was in the meadow, not in flames, his violet eyes flickered back to green. Luxea was fast asleep close by with her hair and face freckled with shreds of moss; she must have tossed and turned. Seeing her resting brought Ares' pounding heart back to a steady pace.

He rolled his shoulders and gazed skyward where through a break in the trees was blackness sprayed with stars. It was the middle of the night, but he couldn't fall back asleep.

Trusting that Luxea would be safe alone, he went for a walk to a spring they'd passed while searching for fruit. The water steamed, and plants of sable, ivory, and scarlet swayed along the bottom.

As he undressed, the scar on his back ached. He hadn't thought about it for years, but after that nightmare . . .

The water was startlingly hot, even for a dragon. As much as Ares had foreseen enjoyment in a rinse, it wasn't so. For the first time, he laid eyes upon a full arm of scales. He ran his fingers over the shallow grooves between them; they were smoother and shinier than the ones on his hand.

He hated them.

The Prince had sworn never to let his draconism spread this far. Now his life had been shortened, and his sanity had been lessened. He'd known when he'd jumped off *Matha ou Machina* where his wings would take him, that sharp, stinging darkness that wouldn't let him go. But he'd furthered his affliction for Luxea's sake . . . and that alone felt like forgiveness.

A pin was pressed into Ares' thoughts when the transparent outline of Shir popped up out of the water. He nearly jumped right out of his skin — scales too.

The Mythic blinked. "It is lovely to meet you."

"You only say that once. Hello, Shir," sighed Ares.

Humiliated, the Mythic shivered. "You had a nightmare — you lived it. It lingers yet in your head and in your flesh. You think more than most humans, in the day and the night. What is on your mind?"

"Things I would rather forget," said Ares vaguely.

Waiting for a more descriptive answer, Shir glinted at his scales. Ares supposed there was no hiding the truth from a Mythic. He pulled his flat, wet hair over his arm to hide the corruption.

"I'm thinking that you healed Luxea's wounds but not mine."

The Mythic's shimmering crown dulled. "It was attempted."

"But it didn't work?"

Startling Ares, Shir snapped off their forefinger; it crumbled into pebbles which *plopped* into the spring. "Injuries, diseases, poisons, and addictions cannot affect us. We do not have brains whose chemicals can become imbalanced. We do not have veins through which substance can run. We do not have cells open to invasion. And our bodies . . ." their finger regenerated, ". . . our bodies will burgeon until the planet itself ceases transition.

"But the ailment from which you suffer is unlike any of these. You are cursed, and a curse is not limited to human biology. Curses devour all; they *too* can change us. Our genetics do not permit us to take it from you because it would threaten our survival."

Ares shouldn't have hoped. "I see."

"I am sorry we could not help you."

Although disappointed, truly and truly, Ares understood. "I came here for one purpose, and that purpose has been fulfilled. You don't owe me anything, Shir." He felt another question arising. "If the *Sil'simani* can remove psychological maladies, why did you not relieve Luxea of her amnesia?"

"What lives inside her is not amnesia," said Shir, suddenly grim. "Her memories have been caged by a divine force far more powerful than that of my kind. We could not cure her mind because there is nothing to cure. The barrier was erected by *Her,* and it will remain a part of Luxea only until *She* removes it."

"She?"

Shir pointed at Ares' Felastil as its starry jewel rippled under the water's skin. "The Moon."

At dawn, Luxea was shaken awake by crystal hands. It made her heart swell twice its size. Shir wasn't aware of what touching the Mythics did to humans; it wasn't exactly a sensation she wanted to experience first thing in the morning — or maybe it was.

"Shir, what's the matter?"

Her voice woke up Ares who'd fallen back asleep after his bath in the spring. "Are we in danger?" he asked sharply.

"Danger? No. But we must hurry." Shir dusted Luxea along the forest floor like a maid with a broomstick. "There is a tree that wishes to speak with Luxea."

"A . . . tree?"

They hiked behind Shir who had much less trouble scaling the terrain. They passed trees ornamented with lamp-like chrysalises, tunnels sheeted with puckering flower buds, and a crystal bridge that arched over a whirlpool. Along the way, Shir grew them fruits and vegetables; they simply popped into existence in the palms of their hands whenever they wished it. Ares and Luxea devoured three each, having been famished.

The three came to a cliff that overlooked a reaches-long ravine, filled continuously by salt waterfalls from the ocean; they were towering and crashing but didn't make a sound. Through curtains of flying, tropical birds, Ares and Luxea beheld a blackwood tree that stood larger than most of the sort.

The tree's branches were springy with bark that wound to the ends like a croissant. It was so black that it looked as if it had survived a forest fire or two, and the leaves, as with all blackwoods, were lavender with white tips.

Shir trod down a rocky path beside Ares — who was very unhappy with the goopy mud on his boots. After twenty minutes, they arrived at the foot of the tree where several other Mythics rested. They shook hands with their human friends and said, *"It is lovely to meet you."*

Luxea's mouth opened wider the higher her eyes rose up the tree trunk. "This is the one that wants to talk to me?"

"It has a message," said Shir thinly.

The Mythics blinked at the tree as if they were waiting for something. Luxea scratched her forehead and tossed an unsure glance at Ares. "Has it said anything yet?"

"Touch it," said Shir without looking at her.

Why was Luxea hesitating? She was skeptical that this tree had anything to say at all, but she feared it. It was just *wood!* But if it did speak to her . . . what would it say? How had it known she was there, and why was it so pressing?

Noticing her trepidation, Ares said, "I'll go with you."

Abreast, they drew up in front of the massive, cavernous trunk. The hollow was so dark that they couldn't see the other side. Ares set his hand on the bark and motioned for Luxea to do likewise. She laid her palm flat beside his.

The blackwood tree did more than speak. It gave Luxea a memory.

## 16.Duskriddle.6.OSC.3

### Nav Amani Forest

*It was twilight. Luxea would miss dinner — again. She veered off the trail in front of her manor to a tall blackwood tree. Staring up the trunk, she kicked off her tiny, blue sandals and gripped the coiled wood. The tread would have been better had she not bitten off her fingernails.*

*She ascended to the crown and threw her leg over a branch. It was so high up! Her father would be furious with her if he found out, so she would have to keep her mouth shut. Giggling mutinously, she scooted forth. But then the nerves on her back tingled.*

*Was someone . . . watching her?*

*Luxea glanced over her shoulder. Behind her, swinging her legs, sat a shadow with stringy hair that rippled upward, unaffected by gravity. Her rawboned body was bound in moth-eaten, black fabric, and her limbs were disproportionately long.*

*In her smallest voice, Luxea said, "Hi."*

*The Shadow wiggled her rootlike fingers without saying a word. Keeping her balance, Luxea shifted to face her headlong.*

*"Are you a faerie? Is this your tree?"*

*Laughing without volume, the Shadow's shoulders bounced, and her head shook. Luxea said, "Okay. We can share it then! I don't mind. What's your name?"*

*The Shadow's hair jolted as she turned away. She covered her mouth, refusing to answer. It was just a name, what could be so bad about it? Was it ugly? A silly, laughable name?*

*"Why won't you tell me?"*

*The Shadow dashed her forefinger across her twiggy throat in a slitting motion.*

*"It will hurt you?"*

*The Shadow nodded, and bugs crawled down her cheeks through the tears in her bandages.*

*Luxea stopped smiling.*

*Don't be scared, she thought. Butterflies are never scared. What do butterflies do? Father dresses her in pretty gowns of silk and pearls with puffy sleeves and shoes just like a princess. He tells her that she makes everyone feel happy. Maybe that's what butterflies do; they bring cheer.*

*"Do you want to play?" suggested Luxea.*

*The Shadow tipped her head. She must have never played with anyone even though she was as big as a grown-up — no, bigger!*

*Accepting the offer, the Shadow leaned in and covered her face. Luxea waited eagerly. The Shadow lunged out of her hands, startling the little girl. But this was so fun!*

*"Again! Then I'll go!"*

*The Shadow hid her face once more. When next she sprang forth, she was much closer. She pointed at Luxea; it was her turn.*

*Luxea mimicked her actions, concealing her face and popping out again with her baby teeth showing. The Shadow pretended to be afraid. Luxea was proud of how scary she was.*

*"One more time!"*

*Grinning behind her fingers, Luxea inhaled and leaped free. The Shadow's black bandages then peeled open into a mouth full enough to swallow Luxea, and she exhaled an oppressing, inescapable breath.*

*A sickness took Luxea at once.*

*As she fell down from the tree, she thought she saw the Moon.*

Bracing for impact, Luxea swiped her hand away from the tree.

Ares stepped back as well. "What did you hear?"

Shaken up, Luxea muttered, "I saw . . ."

"A vision?"

"A memory. I was small, five or six years old, perhaps. There was a shadow . . . but she was a woman too. She made me ill, and I fell out of a blackwood tree."

"A shadow? You're sure it wasn't a vision?"

"Positive," said Luxea thickly. "I remember the sandals and dress I wore that day. Blue leather and white satin with matching stockings."

A breeze went by, something unusual for Mythos. Wind roared all around the island, but today it gushed through the ravine. The blackwood's lavender leaves shuddered and danced down from the branches, and the Mythics looked off in the same direction.

"What's wrong, Shir?" asked Luxea gently.

Shir stayed worryingly still. "There was a feeling. It is gone now."

That evening, Ares and Luxea lay in the meadow with an arcanan fire flickering between them. They'd been quiet since returning from the blackwood tree, and the Mythics had receded, suddenly refusing to interact with their guests.

Owls with flashing feathers swooped around in the branches above. As Luxea watched them, she started to miss Tel Ashir. Mythos was a fantastic place — near perfect — but Tzapodia was home. It was too hot in sunrae and too wet in redrift, but that's what she missed the most: those days she'd wish for the next season to come, the chatter in the castle halls that woke her up ten minutes earlier than she'd wanted.

She wondered what Avari was doing right now. Knowing her, she was likely eating. Oliver Kross too. He loved nighttime because it didn't hurt him, and working girls were an easy find. And Brielle and Ruka . . . she hoped they felt accepted in Tzapodia.

Then there was Unblossomed — Runa. Luxea hadn't spent much time with her, yet she'd become one of the most important people in her life. At ten years old, she'd experienced the closest thing to Hell and survived.

But what about the rest of the children in Goldenrise?

"Ares?"

"Yes?"

"On the airship, you told me that we would go back to Solissium to help the people," said Luxea thoughtfully. "Did you mean it?"

The notion of returning to the capital of Goldenrise for any reason at all made Ares go numb, but he'd promised to reverse the dangers in which he and The Six had placed the citizens.

"Yes, I meant it." Ares shielded his eyes with the crook of his arm. "Annalais won't be willing to let us take her people, but it's no longer her choice. We'll recuperate in Tel Ashir first. After that, a promise is a promise."

The arcanan flames in the fire pit vivified when Luxea smiled. "When will we go home? I'm sure the others think we've perished — including your people."

Ares expelled one of his signature drawn-out sighs that meant he didn't want to talk. "I don't know how to get off the island."

"Shir could help us."

"Possibly."

Luxea rolled onto her side, and her white hair bunched up under her cheekbone. "You don't want to go back to Tzapodia, do you?"

His lip quirked down a bit. "Do I have to? Yes. Do I want to? No."

"Why not?"

"I'm . . . tired."

In Tel Ashir, Ares had worked nonstop with hardly a moment to recoup. When last they'd been in Castle Lavrenthea, he'd had dark circles under his eyes, and their green had been lackluster. On Mythos, he was bright, and his countenance was brighter.

However, he had responsibilities, and so did Luxea. Oscerin had chosen them to ward away the Widow and change the course of fate. If they stayed on Mythos forever, the world outside Sh'tarr's Iris would wash away.

Luxea wouldn't let that happen.

"Do you think I can convince you to want to go back?"

"You may try," drawled Ares.

It wasn't difficult to find a starting point; there was just so much to love about Tel Ashir.

"Where I live, there's one of everything. Each boundary leads to something new. Moonpass, the road. Woodpass, the forest. Riverpass, the river. Sandpass, the desert. What's most memorable is the ocean. The waves aren't as tranquil as they are here, they're angry . . . but it's the sort of anger that lulls you to sleep at night."

Ares envisioned his kingdom through Luxea's eyes.

"The exploration never ends in Tel Ashir. The Court of Light is a circus! It's swimming with parents and their children, and you could trip over an Ashi priest at any hour of the day, any day of the week. The barracks, well, if you want a dirty pint of ale or a punch in the face, that's where you go."

The smallest laugh escaped Ares.

"There's the Sapphire Bazaar — one of my favorite haunts. Anything you've ever wanted, you'll find it there. Dancing girls marketing their beaded belts, circles of wrinkly men peddling canes.

Some merchants have options that don't make the teensiest bit of sense. A man once tried to sell me his baby teeth for six sterling."

"Quite the bargain," said Ares lightly.

Luxea grinned and went on. "Then there's where I stay — Castle Lavrenthea. The highest ceilings, one too many staircases, silver and blue tassels swinging above every portal, stained glass casting colors on the floor. . . . The building is a city on its own. If you don't know your way, you'll get lost. Sometimes, that's a good thing.

"But the loveliest part is the people. There's an old, old woman who runs the infirmary with an obsession with herbs and linens, Mollah. A seroden elvish ranger with the biggest mouth you'll ever see, Avari. An aestof lord from the Isle of Varnn who says the wrong things at the right time, Oliver. There's Ruka, a wolf the size of a carriage. His rider, Brielle, who would fight anything, even a dust bunny. Right now, there's Peyamo Nelnah, a woman made of metal who might have a drinking problem."

More quietly, she said, "And a little girl who grew up not knowing what it means to be free. She loves songbirds, and her name is . . ."

". . . Runa," whispered Ares.

Luxea nodded. "As for the city folk, there are no two alike. Some are wise, some are shallow, some eat too much, others not enough. There are fire-breathers, thieves, candlemakers — even architects and locksmiths. But inside them is something that can be felt, a characteristic they all share: faith in their leader.

"Perhaps he doesn't hear it, but the people in Tel Ashir are always talking about Prince Ares. I've heard a number of rumors. Some say one lock of his hair is worth a fleet of ships — but others say it's worth *two*. There are dazzling maidens who'd never wish for anything else if they got to stand next to him. From experience, I've learned that he's a bit snappy and could use a flick on the wrist every now and then."

Ares turned on his side to face her. He wanted to steal a glimpse of what hid in her head, and watching the rosy stars swaying in her eyes was the closest thing to it.

"What I've felt the most is, *'we need him.'* Whether to heed their complaints, approve their requests — or reject them — to listen to their prayers, or simply to be a symbol of guardianship . . . without Ares, there is no Tzapodia."

The dark blue fire trembled. Luxea watched the flames, but Ares watched her. She noticed his stare and met it. His expression was unreadable until the corners of his eyes crinkled with a smile.

"I want to go home," he told her.

# CITY OF MOURNING

## 4.SNOWHOWL.25.OSC.3

### CALDAVAAN COVE, TZAPODIA

The sheet of paper on Oliver Kross' lap bore the weight of the world. After Luxea had fallen off Peyamo's airship, *Matha ou Machina,* the Mooncallers had discovered a stack of farewell letters in her satchel. They were crinkled and hardly legible, but Oliver hadn't put his down once.

"Do you think they're alive?" he murmured.

You would have thought there was a lemon in Avari's mouth with the face she made. Her head bent low, and she gave a superb example of how to angrily lace your vambraces.

Brielle twisted one of her red locks around her finger. "Every eve when Starlight was dying, the night glittered. After Dragon took her into the storm, I've not seen stars at all."

"I saw a star last night," said Oliver optimistically. "Do you think it was Luxie? Maybe she and Ares made it to . . . wherever they went."

"There must have been some reason behind Dragon's actions. The Goddess of the Moon whispers in his ear. Mayhap She shared with him secrets we cannot yet learn," offered Brielle.

He'd already read it more times than people normally read letters, but Oliver trailed his eyes over Luxea's again. Amidst the lines of *'I'm sorry'* and *'take care of the Usinnon,'* he saw traces of Ares too.

The Prince wouldn't have allowed Luxea to die, Oliver was sure. Ares had never voiced it, but his care for her was different — the sort of care for which you'd give your life.

"I think they're all right," said Oliver inwardly.

Avari couldn't handle another word about the lost. She stood up, kicked over a stool, and stormed out of the galley. Oliver and Brielle's stomachs vibrated with each furious stomp she took up the staircase.

Sky-sailors chattered on the weather deck as they steered into Tel Ashir, the capital of the Kingdom of Tzapodia. The serodens relished the warmth of the south, but the dread of returning without Luxea Siren and Prince Ares Lavrenthea quickly snipped the wings that had kept the airship afloat.

Avari shoved past Peyamo Nelnah and dislocated the Lady's shoulder plate. Peyamo didn't admonish her, for she was just as heartbroken. She popped her metal arm back into place and limped to the bow.

The silhouette of Castle Lavrenthea grew, that polished mountain of a landmark with knifelike turrets and pennants of ultramarine. Tel Ashir glowed against a vast, golden backdrop. The city of dragons, fashioned from silver, blue, and black, was the royal medallion worn by the sands of the Aratoia Desert. Palms swayed, flocks of many-colored cranes soared, and the air itself twinkled.

When last the Lady Peyamo had sojourned Tel Ashir, it had been her thirty-fifth lifeday. Ares had taken her riding to Samsamet's Roost in the mountains where he'd gifted her five bottles of her most favorite spirits. They'd spent all evening sitting there on the edge of a cliff, their legs swinging, their guts filling with liquor. Today, at thirty-nine, Peyamo yearned to see her dearest friend waiting for her at the dock. But he was gone.

"Nika," she said to her helmsman. "Initiate descent, but leave the alarms cold. We don't got to let anyone know we're comin'."

This had been the first time Peyamo had given Nika Lecava an order in a few days. Careful not to bump the airship's alarm button, he tugged a lever and pecked out the command to decrease energy usage. Steam sputtered from the vents on the hull, the propellers slowed, and the stomachs of the passengers drifted around in their ribcages.

Peyamo didn't want to attract attention. If the citizens of Tzapodia were informed of their leader's disappearance, the outcome would be anarchic. But, unfortunately, the glint of her shiny, bronze airship by the loading dock above the castle was an aerial magnet for all eyes in the capital. In minutes, crowds swarmed the Steps of Sevinus to welcome their Prince.

As soon as *Matha ou Machina* was close enough to the platform, the Lady kicked open the gate. It walloped the slate rampart with a *clang*.

Before her stood five familiar faces, those of the Mooncaller Council whose presence had been expected but not appreciated. Four of the fifteen members awaited — Wing Regent Isaak, the placeholder of the throne of Tzapodia, General Skythoan, the head of the military, Lieutenant Claymore, Skythoan's second-in-command, and Spymaster Ruri, the Black Ghost of Tzapodia. From the Ghost's arm hung Mother Mollah, the infirmary's head sage.

Oliver and Brielle exited the galley with Luxea Siren's spellbook, the Usinnon; it was wrapped in a cloth, for spellbooks couldn't be touched by non-magick users. The two tied their satchels and petted Ruka. The wolf's ears hadn't pointed upright since the disappearance of their companions, making his frosttear coat look even puffier.

The Lady Peyamo trod down the ramp behind Avari onto the castle roof, but the ranger was eager to reach solitude. As the Wing Regent moved to salute, Avari dashed by him and vanished without lifting her sopping, brown eyes from the ground. Oliver knew that she would be bothered if anyone came within ten feet of her, but he felt obligated to offer his company and went after her.

With two fewer people to welcome, the Wing Regent proceeded. He and Peyamo clapped hands, but her usual, knuckle-snapping grip was weak.

"Amo, it's been a long time," he said respectfully.

"It has," mumbled the Lady.

The airship groaned as Ruka stepped onto the platform. Three of the council members shuffled back, fearful of a wolf of such a surreal stature. Claymore, however, bowed his head, for he had grown to know Brielle and Ruka well on their journey to Solissium in Redtail. No one else proffered a greeting to the rider or her beast, for they were too busy searching the ramp for a sixth and seventh pair of feet.

Isaak clutched his broadsword's grip. "Where is Ares?"

The Lady Peyamo's arm whistled, warning her that her heart rate was increasing. She banged on the meters, and the alert fell silent. "I don't . . . I don't know where he is."

"You don't know?" laughed General Skythoan.

"That's what I said, ain't it?" snapped Peyamo.

From a distance, Brielle felt a secondary sting in her eyes, a suppressed anguish that Peyamo refused to show. She slid off Ruka's back and palmed the Lady's shoulder.

"You, go. Mourn and recover. I will talk to them."

Mourning sounded tempting to Peyamo. Sucking up her sniffling as if a single tear would kill her, she trudged to a red and yellow stained glass door and vanished into Castle Lavrenthea.

The Mooncaller Council and Brielle were equally wary of each other; they stood utterly still with only their fingers tapping pommels and brushing bow feathers. To the royal servants, looking into the wolf rider's eyes was looking into a predator's.

"You wish to hear what befell your Speaker?" asked Brielle lowly.

"We do," answered Spymaster Ruri.

"We've never seen the likes of this woman," said General Skythoan secretively. "Why should we believe the words of a mongrel like her?"

Not even a whisper was quiet enough to counter Ruka's acute hearing. He bared his teeth and huffed a fiery breath. It took that one glimpse of the beast's bone-grinding jaws for General Skythoan to think twice about insulting the wolf twins.

"Speak with care, General," warned Claymore. "Brielle and Ruka are not mongrels, they are the saviors responsible for Garamat un Gatra's death. The Sun Chief's life was taken by the wolf's teeth and the rider's arrow."

For such a small group, the council members' murmurs were noisy. Brielle grew impatient. "Your Prince is missing. You will listen to me now!" The members shut their mouths. "Good. We traveled south to Tarot after our parting in Solissium. In the Wraiths, we encountered a sorcerer by the name of Cherish Ven'lethe. The knave lured Starlight into the night and forced upon her nightmares — ones that promised to kill her."

"What is this wild-woman saying?" scoffed Skythoan.

"Silence!" hissed Ruri.

As the Mooncaller Council members squabbled without allowing Brielle to finish her recapitulation, Mother Mollah let go of Spymaster Ruri and inched forward. Something about the old sage intrigued Brielle. She was frail, utterly ancient, but she bore the aura of a warrior. Not only that, but her eyes were inhumanly large behind her spectacles.

Surmising that the rider didn't know what eyeglasses were, Mollah plucked them off her wrinkly face. "These are glasses, dear. They help me see."

Brielle took them and blinked through the lens. The world got fuzzier as if it were made out of cotton. What a dizzying, unpleasant sensation! She held them up to Ruka's eyes next, and he sniffed curiously. Brielle met Mollah's stare. Without this contraption of metal and magnifying glass on her nose, the sage looked much less threatening. The rider returned the eyeglasses, and Mollah slipped them back on.

"Rider?" she whispered.

"Brielle — with an 'E,'" corrected Brielle.

"Forgive me, Brielle. I must ask . . . I've once called a woman 'Starlight' too. But the rest, do they know her as 'Luxea?'"

Skythoan tilted his head. "Siren?"

"Yes, Luxea Siren," said Brielle, aching on levels beyond physical. "Skin and hair of snow, magick blood, stars in her eyes. In her final breaths, she fell off the sky ship. Your Speaker jumped with her."

Mollah's bones turned to mush. Ruri kept her standing as she sniffled, "Ares . . . and my little star . . ."

Drops of sweat slipped through Skythoan's greying brows. "Did I not say that Ares leaving Tzapodia was a terrible idea?" He muttered curses about the Prince. "Who will guide us now? Widow's forces have surrounded Tzapodia, north and south. Who will be our guardian?"

"Isaak has experience at the throne," reminded Claymore.

"And he too will be dead before we know it," snarked Skythoan.

The Mooncaller Council was deeming Ares and Luxea as lost causes, and that did not sit well with Brielle. She pointed and asked, "Are you fools, all of you? Have you forgotten what your Speaker is? A curse lives within him, one that, in this instance, was a blessing! Never have I feared any beast, but since that day, I've feared dragons. Black scales, violet eyes. . . . But the monster that dwells within your Speaker is also a protector. Had he not shown his true face, he and Starlight would have met their ends. He caught her — she didn't fall."

"And where are they now?" asked Ruri tensely.

Brielle knew where but not why.

Ares had carried Luxea northwest to the world's most violent natural landmark, Sh'tarr's Iris — the eternal storm, the dark cell of the planet. Not a soul had entered the Iris and lived. Ships ground to dust, feathers stripped from the wings of birds, death to all.

"Dragon's wings carried them into the storm . . . Sh'tarr's Iris."

Skythoan threw up his hands. "Then Ares is gone. Fantastic."

"You doubt your pack leader?" growled Brielle.

General Skythoan guffawed. "You believe anyone could survive those winds, dragon or man? The Storm Goddess resides in those clouds, wolf rider. Ares and Luxea's doom is indisputable! You and that mangy mutt must've been in a hole a few years too long."

Just to scare Skythoan, Brielle slung an arrow from her quiver and aimed it between his eyes. He gulped at the arrowhead and waited for a council member to step in for his safety, but no one did.

Two days had the Wing Regent wondered if he would become the new ruler of Tzapodia. Some men would do worse than kill to fill such a position, but Isaak would have done the same to escape it.

It wasn't the paperwork or the schedule packed with meetings, it was the emptiness of the chair in the Ruby Bureau where Ares usually sat, the lack of roseleaf smoke staining every curtain. The Prince had left many times in the past to travel the Joined Hands for business or for pleasure, but he'd never failed to return.

Since the news of Ares' demise, Isaak had spoken daily to the late Queen of Tzapodia Manalaei Lorcé-Lavrenthea. *"I'm a guardian, Mana,"* he would tell her, *"but I have not the wings to chase him."*

Queen Manalaei would have been enraged to learn that Ares had put himself in danger's way. She'd once had as hot of a fire in her soul as her son — hotter even. Isaak was in no doubt that, given a chance, she would have flown into the Iris after him.

As the Wing Regent strode through the Emerald Wing, his armor closed in on him. His heart was the most caged of all, and he couldn't rule without it, so he turned back to hide in his bedchamber —

Until he heard shouting through the window.

*". . . a traitor!"*

*". . . Lavrenthea . . . !"*

*". . . we've been left to die!"*

Isaak dashed to the nearest brattice. Stories below, a wave of Tel Ashians rolled over the Steps of Sevinus. Fire lilies and lune lilies were piled outside of the portcullis which had been shut for the first time in a decade. Men, women, and children wept and fought over theories, Ashi priestesses and thurifers chanted and burned herbs, and some civilians bellowed political slander.

The secret was out. The ripple effect had begun.

With all speed, the Wing Regent descended the western stairwell to the vestibule. He shoved past keepers and serving girls and seized a sentinel by the arm in the Porranim Courtyard.

"What is all this racket? Why are these people here?"

Giving a Tzapodian salute, his thumb and little finger pointed in the same diagonal direction, the sentinel declared, "They're grieving, Wing Regent. Some have come to pay their respects . . . but others think His Highness has forsaken us."

"Who told them about Ares?"

The sentinel glanced at a platform outside of the barbed portcullis where stood a man that Isaak was weary of seeing. General Skythoan, who was avowed to protecting Tzapodia, had taken advantage of the Prince's disappearance.

"Ares Lavrenthea leaped into affliction to save *a girl!*" yowled the general. "He deserted his people — deserted you! I warned him that he would never return, but he refused to listen! Tell me, citizens of Tel Ashir, what kind of leader must he have been to abandon us when we need him the most? He, the son of Heavens Devil, will be the driving force behind our deaths! He is a tyrant, a monster like all dragons!"

The Wing Regent's sword ached for his hand. He cleared a path and twisted the portcullis capstan with the help of two sentinels. When the bars lifted, Isaak ducked under them. His sabatons bore the force of a landslide as he crushed the bouquets and plowed through the mobs. He gripped the general's cape and threw him off the pedestal.

"Enough! Until the Prince returns, you are under *my* command, Skythoan. And this? This is slander!" Isaak revealed his broadsword and pointed it at the rioters. "I was Ares' guardian before any of you people had a clue he existed. If you wish to challenge my faith in him, speak now. You will meet the tyrant you have deemed him to be!

"Never has Ares acted without a purpose. Have your hearts lost their vision? Have you forgotten that Oscerin chose him? The Moon Mother would not leave him unsheltered, for he is Her child! We must believe that he will come back to us. If we don't, he may never!"

Some few families and Ashi priests knelt to offer their support to their leader — wherever he was. The rest, corrupted by the general's words, glared silently.

Isaak tore Skythoan off the ground and kicked him under the portcullis. The sentinels shut it, and the crowds picked up their yelling as the council members made for the castle.

In the vestibule, Isaak slammed Skythoan into the wall and gripped the neck of his breastplate. The general didn't retaliate, for initiating a fight with the Wing Regent would send his head rolling.

"Doryan Skythoan," seethed Isaak, "if I hear another word of disrespect from that piggish mouth of yours, I'll cut out your tongue and feed it to you on that gold platter for which you so long."

The general's eyes darkened to slits. "Yes, Wing Regent."

# DEATH OF
# THE STORM

## 5.SNOWHOWL.25.OSC.3
## SH'TARR'S IRIS, ETERNITY'S OCEAN

THREE SHIPS crashed over the waves and through the furious winds that threatened to crack the palm wood and tear the red sails into ribbons. Two of the fleet and twenty-four men had been sucked down to the depths by Alatos.

Seaspray needled the remaining sailors, making fabric of their rocky skins. A cloaked rishja stood at the stern with his golden braid tucked under his crossed arms, watching as a mast *cracked* down the center and splashed into the sea. The sail was devoured by the undertow.

"Sh'tarr's Iris will kill us all. Tell Her we must turn back," said the braided man to the nearest crewman.

*"Aku, Yaz Magia,"* said the sailor; *'yes, Sun Chief.'*

The ship rocked wildly, throwing racks of battle axes across the main deck and casting the crewmen to their already splintered knees.

The sailor gripped the broken mast as he stumbled to a hooded figure at the bow.

Gales sank their claws into Her black raiments, but She was unfazed. This was why She was followed and feared. Turned weak by no enemy, neither man nor divine. A woman who falters not loses not.

"Mother!" shouted the sailor, spattered in the face by foam. "We must surrender. Sh'tarr has taken many and will take more! Please, the Sun Chief insists we end this mission. It is suicide!"

The hooded woman barely turned Her head. Her four black eyes were coals with eight white diamonds for pupils — ones that cut. She calmly pulled down Her hood, revealing an elongated skull and a bald scalp. On Her forehead was scarred a symbol, a circle with a horizontal line through the middle and two inverted, diagonal prongs on the ends.

Whispers filled Her ears. Not those of the sailor or the sea, but from a mouth unseen. *"We mustn't fail,"* they said. *"Raise your hand, Child, and let me in. Together, we shall capture the storm."*

From afar, the bald woman sent a smile to Sun Chief Ralvesh, a smile like that of an angel in a graveyard, a lover, a mother, and a friend — but also a killer.

Her voice was heard by all ears as She said, "We go on."

Ralvesh couldn't show his disagreement. She was his master, and he was Her champion, but his ships were sinking, and his men's souls were becoming food for Sh'tarr and Alatos. His doubt in Her grew in strength until the next terrible gust arrived.

Her hand raised.

With a dark and chilling grace, She snatched the wind right out of the sky. What was She doing? That wind belonged to the Storm Goddess Sh'tarr, yet She reeled it in like a rope!

The Iris lost its force in an instant. Tears appeared in the sky, revealing the bright blue that the sailors had gone days without seeing.

From a long way away dinned a bone-chilling scream. It was everywhere, every intonation. Then a woman's figure manifested at the bald woman's fingertips.

The Storm Goddess, bending to the will of another divine? How?

Sh'tarr's only defense as She was dragged nearer was to cling to cirrus and stratus. "No! Who are You? *What* are You?" She squalled.

The bald woman clutched Sh'tarr's face in Her hands, the Storm Goddess' eyes shedding tears of hail. Voiceless and powerless, She dwindled into a misty orb, and the bald woman dropped Her into Her pocket like a little marble.

And so commenced the enslavement of Sh'tarr.

For the first time in millennia, the Iris stopped permanently. Along the coast of L'arneth, eyes who thought they saw a dream were met with a cloudless day. The crash of rain against the stones of the Great Bridge, Tarhelen ceased. An eery quiet was spat into the ears of travelers. Heads poked out of carriage windows, flaps of canvas tents, and weathered raincoats. Whetstones scraped to halts on blades.

The ocean, that too fell flat.

The bald woman shook rainwater from Her hands and heavy, black earrings. Oh, She was being watched, wasn't She? In the sea in front of the ship were the two aqueous eyes belonging to Sh'tarr's sister, the Sea Goddess Alatos.

"Good morning, Alatos," said the bald woman devilishly.

Since Her creation, the Sea Goddess hadn't once wondered if She was in danger. She didn't wonder now either — She *knew.*

The bald woman poked Her little finger on a splinter from the handrail. Black, inky blood swelled on Her grey skin and dripped into the water. Alatos let out a gurgling scream and plunged beneath the surface.

As shadows pursued the Sea Goddess, She wished there were someone to whom the divines Themselves could pray. That fabled devil divine that Alatos had doubted, until now, had trapped Sh'tarr.

All the way to the Southern Pole of Amniven, Alatos swam at the speed of sound, but the speed of light would have been preferable. She slithered through an arch of stinging anemones and into the Coral Spire Tsrei, the sanctuary where She'd been born. Darkness couldn't enter such a sacred place.

She was safe — for now.

The Mother of the Sea curled up, and eels, rays, and schools of fish suckled at Her feet and whorled through Her kelpy hair. She cupped Her face in Her webbed hands, and bubbles blipped from Her gills as She wept. Her cetacean cries mirrored off all surfaces throughout the oceans of the planet, telling the marine life that the Goddess of Storms had been taken and that, soon, She might be taken too.

Luxea Siren wasn't sure how, but Mythos became more fantastical every morning. Sparkling fog rolled over the flowerbeds and swelled up her legs as she and Ares strolled to the beach.

Along the eastern shore, arches of crystallized stone dove in and out of the water like a sea serpent, and grass grew in perfect circles in random spots on the black sand. How incredibly kind of nature to give them such a splendid place to sit and enjoy breakfast!

The Mythics had been unusually reclusive since Luxea spoke with the blackwood tree. To not starve the mortals, Shir taught them about the vegetation on the island — which they claimed was all edible. Ares wasn't opposed to trying some exotic produce as long as he wouldn't have to put that pulsing heart anywhere near his mouth.

Dotted across the crowns of the tropical trees were fruits of every color. Shir said they weren't called anything, so Luxea named them. A green one with bouncy, yellow antennae became bugfruit. One that tasted like a grape but was the size of a watermelon she called a grapermelon. Ares admired her effort but gave them better, more creative names in secret.

For her meal, Luxea chose a pink fruit that was fuzzy like a peach with a flavor like sweet cream — which she named 'milkball.' It was too high for her to reach, so she hoisted herself onto a branch. But she'd never had excellent upper-arm strength. She was swinging her limbs and sputtering curses when a large hand picked the fruit for her. She released the branch and plopped onto the ground. Smiling subtly, Ares handed it to her.

For himself, he harvested two dark red fruits with a tang not too far off from red wine. Everyone in Castle Lavrenthea, and probably the world, knew that the Prince of Tzapodia would accept a glass of wine at any time of day, any day of the week, for whatever occasion or non-occasion. Mythos didn't have a winery, and Ares couldn't make it himself, so this non-alcoholic fruit would have to suffice.

The two sat on a grassy circle with their bare feet in the sand and their shoes stacked between them. As they ate, Luxea lay on her back and watched Sh'tarr's Iris twist in a funnel above her. Maybe she was getting used to seeing it up close, but the storm looked less calamitous today.

Ares sucked juice from his thumb and started on his second serving. He was content observing a pair of chromatophoric crabs clack about in the sea-foam until Luxea sat up and dropped her fruit.

Ares didn't like her expression. "What's wrong?"

Her stars went out one by one. "Is the storm . . . stopping?"

Sh'tarr's Iris, the most deadly natural force on the planet, was indeed stopping. For millennia, it had hovered over Eternity's Ocean to ward off all intruders who dared come within one hundred reaches of Mythos. The only instance in the history of man that the barrier had been breached was a week ago when Ares had carried Luxea into it. Oscerin, a greater divine, had suppressed Sh'tarr and Alatos' powers long enough for them to pass to the island safely.

Now the storm was dying again.

In minutes, all that was left of Sh'tarr's Iris was a thin layer of clouds.

From the depths of Mythos came the barks and roars of deer and bears. Frightened chatters of birds fluttered through the leaves of the forest. Then came the ringing of the Mythics, their many voices vibrating the grains of sand on the beach.

"Something's not right. We have to go!" said Luxea urgently.

She put on her sandals and started to run, but Ares grabbed her.

His jaw was clenched as tightly as his fingers around Luxea's arm as he moved her behind him, away from the ocean. Snaking through the teal water was fluid darkness; it bled into the foamy waves and killed the glowing plankton. The blue light flickered out bit by bit, and the tides turned as black as the sand. Offshore, the flying fish melted to bones and flopped, lifeless, onto the surface.

Bumps rose on Luxea's skin and spread to Ares' when faint, ominous chanting floated over the still air. Booming voices, blaring horns, and percussive thumps.

"What is that? Over there!" she gasped.

In the distance, pointed, red shapes glided on the water.

*Ships . . . so close to Mythos?*

Ares' eyes narrowed and then opened as wide as they would get. He swiped up his shoes, yanked Luxea behind a fading crystal, and crouched. Stuffing his feet into his boots, he panted, "Those are Ank'tatraan sails."

"The desert rishja? What are they doing here?"

His thoughts rewound a fortnight. The more Ares came to realize how doomed they were, the less he felt like he could explain. Oscerin had told him how to get to Mythos, but he hadn't told anyone else.

So how were they followed?

"The Sun Chief is Widow's servant," he said. Luxea fell onto her side. "In Tarot, Peyamo warned me that Ralvesh un Gatra tricked us in Goldenrise — his own father too. He and Widow conspired to rid of Garamat so that he could become the Sun Chief. He belongs to Her, to the Brood."

As the Ank'tatraan ships sailed nigh, Ares and Luxea made out warriors rowing and striking beast-hide drums with their long braids flinging around. One rishja emptied his lungs into the mouth of a war horn, hollowed out from the tusk of a mammoth.

Luxea covered her ears. "But why would the Sun Chief send men here?" she asked during a gap in the clamor.

"For us . . ." Ares faced her, ". . . or for you."

The first ship made landfall. Rishja wielding scimitars, crossbows, and spears poured over the rails and smashed into the black sand.

They hadn't seen Ares and Luxea just yet, but Ares had a feeling that they would.

The Phoenix Sons, the soldiers of Ank'tatra, were the purest of the half-giant descendants of Xeneda. They were ruthless, bone-eating men with a leech's thirst for blood. If one of their whiteless eyes spied them . . .

The Phoenix Sons slashed their left palms and smeared dark red across their faces. As if that wasn't nerve-wracking enough, what Ares and Luxea saw next filled their hearts with poison.

Standing at the bow of the last ship was a woman in a strapped, black cloak with an elongated head and the Brood's symbol carved into Her scalp. Her four soul-scoring eyes shifted right to Ares and Luxea in their hiding place.

And then She *smiled* at them.

Eight spider legs erupted out of Her back and raised Her twenty feet in the air. She crawled up the one unbroken mast and rested Her chin daintily on the masthead. Pointing directly at them, Ares read on Her black lips, *"I see you."*

This woman wasn't a servant of Widow — it *was* Widow.

"Run!"

With Luxea's arm shackled by his fingers, Ares vaulted out of the sand and disappeared behind the trees. The commander of the Phoenix Sons rose his golden blade high above his head.

*"Ganac naaj!"* — *'get them!'*

The Phoenix Sons sprinted into the brush, weapons thirsty.

Sun Chief Ralvesh strode down the ramp of his ship and halted beside the grass circle, his already crinkled nose crinkling more. Out of spite

— out of *loathing* — he squashed the fruit that Ares had been eating beneath his sandal.

Widow climbed down from the mast and hovered over him. "You mustn't forget, Champion. The dragon stays alive. The girl is mine."

Stone-faced, Ralvesh said, "Yes, Mother."

Widow brushed Her fingers down his face, nicking his pristinely shaved jaw with Her nails. "Go, go. Have fun," She said cheerily.

Ralvesh ran into the rainforest after his men. Widow's knees slipped through the cuts in Her robe as She knelt and gathered a scoop of sand from where Ares and Luxea had buried their feet. She felt their presences so strongly that it made Her ill.

But hatred is the best fuel, no?

She grinned and threw the sand. Her spearlike legs unfolded and chipped the trunks of trees as She skittered into the canopy.

The rumpus of rishjaan feet pounded to the rhythm of Ares and Luxea's hearts. They bolted across their meadow and wished it farewell between breaths, but then a quiet *snap* and a flash of light stopped them in their tracks.

It was Shir, locus-jumping to their rescue.

The Mythic pulled their human friends behind a tree, and their skin camouflaged to the bark. Ares and Luxea covered their noses and mouths as the Phoenix Sons ran past them.

"Who is here?" asked Shir, crystals trembling.

"The rishja of Ank'tatra . . . and Widow," huffed Ares.

"They stopped the storm?" asked Shir frightfully. "What do they want from us? They are not like you, not at all. These men, they are tyrants — murderers. Why come to our land?"

Luxea shut her eyes tight. "Because of me."

Ares would have given anything to tell her that it wasn't because of her, but he knew as well as she did that it was. Widow had yearned for Luxea's death all this time, and She was acting on that yearning once again.

Shir placed their hands on Ares and Luxea's shoulders. "We will protect you . . . but we cannot fight with you."

"We have to fight," said Ares curtly.

The Mythic swiveled their head madly. "It is against our nature! We are purity, and killing is impure. If our purity dies, we die."

"Fantastic," spat Ares. "Then what do we do? Luxea and I can't hold off against the Phoenix Sons *and* Widow!"

"Come with me." Shir stepped away. "We shall hide."

The three fled to the cave where Ares and Luxea had made stew. Her throat knotted. She wished she could go back to finding vegetables and clinging to Ares like a scared child, but she couldn't. The thundering of rishja war cries was nearing, and it wouldn't be long until blood was shed, and Widow got what She wanted.

It was all over.

Shir joined the other fifty-nine *Sil'simani* inside the cave. Louder and louder they rang. It sounded to Ares and Luxea like they were communicating their goodbyes, and they were right. The Mythics knew they wouldn't survive Widow's assault. They could leave but would have just as scarce of a chance off of their island.

The Mythics then did something quite peculiar: they chipped tiny pieces off each other's crowns. As Shir gathered the shards in their hands, they pulsed with light and sang a sad, sad song.

It was too much. Luxea couldn't stop herself from crying. She dropped to a squat and held the balls of her wrists to her eye sockets, sealing away the darkening starlight.

The Mythics would die, and the fault was hers. She would never forgive herself — how impossible a thought!

Ares' fingers brushed over her hair as she wept. His eyes faded to that dull, grayish green they'd been before Mythos, but not because he was heartbroken. He was *wrathful*. On all layers of his being was stacked rage and hate and regret.

"Luxea," whispered Shir.

She stood and sucked on her bottom lip to stop her teeth from chattering. With their hands cupped above hers, Shir spilled the Mythics' crystal shards into her palms. Their energy made her feel all things at once. She thought she would scream, she thought she would shatter.

"We have no place in the outside world, but you do," said Shir sorrowfully. "We will send you home where you can be safe . . . but we must ask you a favor. Plant our slivers in the soil within the Heart of Sirah. Do this, and we will meet one day again."

The slivers were weightless; Luxea was surprised they weren't floating away. Her black and red cosmos spilled sparkling tears down her cheeks, but she couldn't hide them now that her hands were full.

Neither she nor Ares accepted or denied the Mythics' request until he shuffled at his waist and removed a leather bag from his belt. He overturned it, and hundreds of shiny, gold coins clanged to the cave floor. Luxea had never seen so much money, but he was just giving it up.

He held the bag open, and she filled it with the Mythics' shards. He tied it shut and handed it to her. She unsurely hooked it to her hip.

"Luxea will take them," he said sternly, "but I'm not leaving."

"Ares?" she whispered.

He didn't look at her; he wouldn't suffer her to see what he was feeling, not right now. "Shir, you stay here. Luxea is an adroit sorceress and will fight those who threaten your lives. All I ask is that if Widow shows Herself, you send Luxea back to Tel Ashir at once."

"And you?" asked Shir breathily.

"I can take care of myself."

"You can't," hissed Luxea. "What do you plan to do?"

"Must you ask?" bit Ares. "The rishja are terrified of me. Dragons, the Lavrentheas, are responsible for the loss of half of their population. They should have known better than to taunt one."

"No! Your affliction will spread, it will —" Luxea then realized that, having carried her here in the form of a dragon, it must have already consumed him. "Where do your scales end now?"

"It doesn't matter."

"It does!"

Ares turned to leave, but Luxea nabbed his arm. The collar of his shirt rode down and revealed the curve of his shoulder. Black scales, hundreds rode up the length of his left arm when, only a week ago, they'd been on his hand.

Luxea only knew as much about draconism as Avari and Ares had told her. The further the curse spread, the more Ares' mind was broken. Eventually, he would be trapped inside the body of a dragon. With any less care, his life would be much shorter than was merited.

"Why didn't you show me?" she murmured.

Ares hadn't even wanted to show himself. He gently took his sleeve out of her hand and tried once more to leave the cave, but Luxea pulled him back.

"Stop it! You're not going anywhere!"

"This isn't up for debate! You're the one Widow wants, Luxea, but I'll be the one She gets." His tone was threatening, but his malice wasn't directed toward her; beyond that fire was a dragon protecting its treasure.

Luxea hated it — hated *him* for giving her such unfair demands. She wanted to hit him!

All Ares did before he left was wipe a tear off her cheek. Luxea was devastated. Her arms and legs turned to glass as his silhouette grew smaller.

When he was at the cave entrance, an arrow came flying.

# Scorched Skin

## Mythos

A Mythic's forehead shattered, and its crown slowly drained of light. They stared with dying, ruby eyes at the palms of their hands as they turned to stone. In seconds, its body crumbled.

One Mythic had perished. Fifty-nine remained.

*"Aim for their heads!"* came a shout from outside the cave.

Their heads? But Ares was right there. Why target the Mythics and overlook the greatest threat?

Another arrow slipped from the nock and drilled closer, but Luxea wouldn't wait for more Mythics to die. She shouted, *"Sheishan'in!"* and a shimmering arcanan shield flared out in front of her. The arrow's shaft snapped in two and clattered to the ground.

The shot had come a little too close to Luxea for Ares' taste. The desert rishja had a saying: *"The best way to kill a dragon is to make it angry."* Speaking for all of his kind, he disagreed. The best way to *be* killed by a dragon is to make it angry.

He leaped out of the cave and landed in a line of Phoenix Sons who marched up the path. On the ground, he slashed a soldier's waist with his claw. As entrails gushed onto the dirt, Ares stole the scimitar from the fallen's scabbard and sliced through the neck of a second man. Two kills, and he was drenched in rishjaan blood.

Holding up her shield with one hand, Luxea told Shir, "Stay where you are. Do *not* leave the cave. I'm fighting too."

Shir was petrified but joined the others against the wall.

Luxea skidded outside. On the path below, she saw Ares slicing necks and clawing faces; however, none of the Phoenix Sons attacked him unless he attacked them first.

A soldier spotted her. He roared, and ten more rishja ran after him.

She heard Ares shout, *"Luxea, they'll kill you!"*

Did he not remember what she could do?

Two soldiers lunged. Luxea threw out her hands, and a torrent of arcanan fire devoured them and four others. Instantly, they turned into pitiful piles of blue ash and gold trinkets. She flipped her hands over twice. It seemed she too hadn't remembered what she could do. Her magick had *never* been this potent.

One of the surviving Phoenix Sons lashed at her. She rolled out of the way, and his scimitar left a crack in the ground. Like a toddler, she crawled between his veiny, rock-hard legs and kicked him in the groin. He dropped his weapon at once. Luxea kicked him there once more, just to be a pest, and then the back of his knee. He fell flat on his face.

Two more came for her, but then their heads went flying in different directions, and their bodies were shoved aside. Somehow, Ares had already cut down the twelve or so Phoenix Sons who'd stood between himself and Luxea. Another enemy came. Ares flung his scimitar and pinned him to a tree. Luxea had never seen him fight with a blade. He was skilled — more than skilled.

"Get out of here *now!*" His irises were violet, and his pupils were in vertical slits; he was trying to scare her into retreat. "I didn't fly you all the way here to die!"

"Quit it!" Luxea burned down a Phoenix Son without so much as looking. "I'm growing weary of this one-or-both-of-us nonsense!"

As Ares and Luxea argued and decapitated or scorched incoming foes, a band of rishja assassins sneaked into the cave. The Mythics were frightened but had been told to stay.

Dagger by dagger, the killers struck the Mythics' crowns. Not one of them fought back. The cave rang with melancholy as the Sacred Children died.

With only four surviving Mythics, Shir realized that they couldn't kill, but they *could* defend. Three Mythics were left. Shir camouflaged to the cave wall. Two remained. Shir sneaked to the exit. One now. Shir left the cave. None were left. The last Sacred Child threw up their arms, and a wall of crystal in every color sealed the entrance, trapping the assassins inside.

"Tell me that all you want, but — !"

"Luxea, I don't want to hear another word. *Go!*"

The altercation between Ares and Luxea was cut short by a godly voice in the woods. "The Last Dragon Prince and his starry-eyed lamb! What a delight!"

It was, most unfortunately, the Sun Chief Ralvesh un Gatra, sauntering nigh and flipping his twin swords in his hands. The blades were newly burnished and blinding, and from the pommels came sharp, eye-gouging spikes. The soldiers fell back. That worried Ares.

If the Phoenix Sons had enough faith in their leader's ability alone, that had to mean Ralvesh was dangerous.

"Just this once, take cover," Ares whispered to Luxea. "This is *my* fight. Stay behind that tree until I win it. Move."

He pushed her away. Luxea stumbled but decided to abide. If Ares found himself in trouble, she'd be able to step in. She scurried to the trunk and squatted.

Ralvesh had seen her but not gone after her. He approached Ares, towering seven and a half feet. The Prince was extraordinarily tall, but the Sun Chief's half-giant blood gave him a twelve-inch advantage.

"Who do you think is a better fighter?" asked Ralvesh with a ready gleam. "My father, or me?"

Ares wrenched a scimitar out of a Phoenix Son's skull. "For your own sake, pray for the latter."

The Sun Chief laughed hard. "I am not meant to kill you. The Brood Mother wants you alive. But that does not mean I cannot hurt you." He slit his left palm and watched the beads form. "In rishjaan, my name means *'Snake.'* I've never liked that translation. Can you guess why, Your Highness?"

"I've been dying to know," said Ares, humoring him.

The Sun Chief smeared his blood across his mouth and licked the excess from his plump lips. "Because I am no snake. I am a *viper.*"

He lunged, and their swords clashed. As Ares had feared, Ralvesh was much stronger than he looked — and he looked plenty strong. Ares' muscles quivered under his sleeves, and his feet skidded inches at a time. Ralvesh threw Ares and aimed for his legs. Ares leaped over the blade and thrashed back, leaving a deep cut across Ralvesh's chest.

"You're better than I'd imagined," panted the Sun Chief.

"Your imagination must be bland," quipped Ares.

That comment wasn't appreciated. Ralvesh wrested Ares' long hair and chopped with full force at his left arm. Luxea clapped her hands over her mouth.

But . . . Ares wasn't hurt. His sleeve was torn, but his arm was entirely attached. His new scales had stopped the blade and cracked it down the middle all the way to the hilt.

Perhaps curses had their perks.

Ares grinned fiendishly and rolled his shoulder. "Know better. A snake cannot slay a dragon."

Enough! Ralvesh threw his blade and rushed Ares head-on, pinning him to the ground in one swift movement. He gripped the Prince's claw, forbidding a counterattack.

"You aren't as ruthless as they say." Ralvesh twisted Ares' arm. "The viper coils, and the dragon submits. Is this all you can muster?"

Behind the tree, Luxea's stars lit up.

*Dragon . . . dragon? Oh, dragon!*

Thinking on her feet, she muttered, *"Nav'in ei th'luneth."*

Ares struggled to free himself, but Ralvesh was twice his weight and twice his strength. There wasn't a chance. Humiliating him, Ralvesh slammed the Prince's head against the ground. Through Ares' dizziness, he felt the bones in his wrist scrape; they would snap soon.

But then —

"Dragon!"

*"Int na dracona!"*

*"Gavo!"*

The last of the Phoenix Sons screamed and left their leader to deal with the new threat. Maybe they hadn't held much faith in Ralvesh. The Sun Chief showed his oversized teeth and glanced over his shoulder. Then his grip on Ares' wrist loosened, and his blue, whiteless eyes quivered. He fell away, fearing for his life.

Stomping nigh was an azure dragon. The razor-sharp spines riding down its neck brushed the canopies of the trees, and its massive, clawed feet created fissures in the ground.

Clutching his whirling head, Ares looked up and spotted Luxea's pale hand poking out from behind the tree, controlling the dragon. Her illusions had improved immensely. Maybe he shouldn't oppose her participation in his battles.

*"Get up, Ralvesh,"* sighed a voice from the trees. *"It's a trick."*

The Sun Chief ceased his scrambling. A trick? But this dragon's slitted, violet eyes looked so real, they were as much of a death omen as his ancestors had described! He steeled himself and swished his hand . . . and it phased right through the creature's hide.

So it *was* a trick.

Ralvesh glared at Ares but was resistant to attack. Why?

The tree branches above Luxea's head groaned. As much as Ares loved that disparaged look on the Sun Chief's face, he had to see what was making the sound. What dangled up high obliterated all remnants of possible victory there had been. Ares' lip bent down, showing his bottom line of teeth. He tried to stand but fell to his shoulder in a daze from the blow to his head.

"Luxea, come to me! Run!" he screamed.

Hand dropping, dragon vanishing, Luxea peeked out. Ares appeared desperate, horrified. She moved, but her blouse was stuck.

It felt as if someone was . . . holding onto her.

Slow as slow could be, she turned.

Hanging upside-down from a ropey web was Widow.

An evil, evil grin stretched across the Brood Mother's face. "Oh, those eyes *are* so pretty, aren't they?"

Her web snapped. She dropped onto Her legs and lifted Luxea by the shirt. As she dangled above the ground, Luxea could only stare at Widow.

This abomination, this genocidal divine who was hatred itself —

She was beautiful.

Ares propped himself up with his right arm, swiped a scimitar from a fallen Phoenix Son, and sliced it into one of Widow's spider legs. The blade shattered upon impact.

"You're wasting your breath, Ares." The Brood Mother fluttered Her free hand at the Phoenix Sons in the line of the trees. "Chain the dragon. He is ours now."

Giant rishjaan hands cast Ares to the ground and wrangled his arms behind his back. His horns carved lines in the earth as he punched, bit, cut, and thrashed. His head was stood upon while heavy chains were wound around his neck and wrists.

"Let go of me!" The green of Ares' irises was vibrant against the growing redness of his whites. "Please, don't hurt her! Let me go!"

His pleas were sugar to Widow. She turned back to Luxea and said, "You've been so irritating. I should do this quickly, no? I wouldn't want you scampering off again, you little *rat.*"

Ares' screams and Ralvesh's laughter were drowned out. Luxea might have allowed herself to die right then, but there was one question she had to ask first.

"Why are you doing this?"

Widow's wicked grin flattened, and then something else appeared. Pain. Human pain. "Because I hate you," was all She said.

That statement would forever weigh on Luxea. Something within her felt like she deserved to be hated, to be destroyed. Should she let Widow kill her? If she did, would it be done? Would this end?

Widow's scalp peeled back into four sects like a flower. Beneath it was a spider's face, riddled with black eyes and wet with fluid. Her clacking fangs neared, ready to consume Her starry-eyed prey, at last.

But then a tiny rock hit Her in the forehead.

Widow's appearance reverted to a human state. She glared at the silenced mouth of the cave where stood the last Mythic. Shir threw another rock. It thunked off the Brood Mother's skull.

The Brood Mother scampered to Shir and pouted. "Thousands of years, and yet so naive. You think stones will hurt me, Sacred Child?"

Shir couldn't be afraid. "Hurt you, no."

Oh, how poised Widow was to crush the Mythic, to wipe them out for good! But Shir was too quick. They touched one of Her legs, and crystal formed around all eight.

Stone couldn't hurt Her, but it *could* trap Her.

Widow struggled to move. While She was distracted, Shir yanked Luxea out of Her grip and ran across the clearing.

"Don't let her escape!" She screamed, retracting Her legs.

By the mob of Phoenix Sons, Shir set Luxea on the ground. The Mythic had seen what she could do with magick and hoped she would do it again now. To their delight, she did.

Luxea threw out her hands and shouted, *"Vastal'hel ma!"*

The rishja were blown into the forest, their heads smacking on tree trunks as they tumbled down the rocky hills. Luxea knelt at Ares' side and cracked the chains on his wrists with magick. She'd reached for the one around his neck when Widow ran to her on foot and kicked her over.

She sat astride Luxea and shook her, pulled her hair, and beat her chest. Luxea might have reacted had she not been mesmerized by the droplets leaking down Her face.

Widow was crying. This goddess, this tyrant, longed for Luxea's death so strongly that it brought Her to tears.

"You will not evade me again! You *have* to die!" Shaking with ire, She grabbed Luxea's throat. "I'll kill you, I'll kill you, I'll — !"

The Brood Mother floundered and gaped at Her palms. Before Her eyes, Her skin burned down to Her bones — from touching Luxea. She reeled, screaming like She'd never felt such a pain.

Widow was a murderer, a monster. So why did Luxea feel guilty?

Before she could fall further under Widow's spell, Ares dragged her to Shir. The Mythic's eyes trailed across the sealed off cave where their kind had perished. They touched their friends' shoulders. There was a flash, and then they were gone.

Widow was left alone to suffer in the haven She'd destroyed.

# WEOREM

## ETERNITY'S OCEAN

THEY FLICKERED into existence in the middle of Eternity's Ocean, atop a rock blanketed with popping barnacles and tresses of seaweed. Having never teleported, neither by magick nor by Mythic, Ares doubled over and heaved.

Still awestruck from her experience with Widow, Luxea sat down and harked his spitting and the chain on his neck scraping the stone. Shir perched beside her and watched a nacreous sea snail inch into a groove, leaving a shiny trail of slime behind it.

Luxea made fists on her knees. She hurt but was sure that Shir hurt more. "I'm so sorry," she whispered. "The rest of your kind are gone because of us . . . because of me."

The Mythic looked pensive. This emotion Luxea was portraying, contrition, it hadn't occurred to them how harmful it was to humankind. But Shir's perception of life, death, and all in-between was far more expansive than hers. They started smiling.

"They are not gone." Shir pointed at the bag that drooped off her hip. "They are right here with us."

Luxea squished the Mythics' shards through the supple leather; they *crunched.* Even without direct contact, she felt their energy. "All we have to do to bring them back is plant them in the Crystal Spire?"

"Yes," said Shir unambiguously.

"Then I'll help you plant them," promised Luxea.

Ares wiped his mouth on his sleeve and plopped onto the rock beside Luxea. "We'll go together. En route to Goldenrise, we can enter Sirah," he said, tugging frustratedly on the chain against his throat.

"Let me," offered Luxea.

She reached for his neck. He pulled his damp, bloody hair out of the way, and she saw a few black scales poking out from the collar of his shirt. That felt like her fault too.

Unable to meet his eyes, she snapped the links with magick; they fell onto the rock with a *clang.* Ares massaged his neck, his golden flesh now scratched and crimson.

"Thank you," he sighed.

Luxea was about to mumble a pathetic reply when a wave of fizzing water swooped tens of feet in the air and crashed over them. Shir didn't react, but Ares and Luxea were drenched to their skins.

They coughed and wiped their faces. Luxea glared at the ocean but then forgot about the salty wetness in her clothes. In the dark beyond the drop-off of the stone were two enormous eyes. They flitted back and forth and then submerged.

"Th-there's something in the water!"

Angry wavelets and endless strands of kelp rushed toward them. Ares and Luxea slid back, afeared of whatever was approaching. The seaweed was sucked beneath the rock. Seconds after, a woman with clear globules for eyes arose.

Ares recognized Her — Alatos the Sea Goddess, the one by whom he'd nearly been drowned. Although She was thousands of times smaller today, She was as menacing as ever.

Alatos' webbed feet *slapped* nearer. She scowled at Ares. An eel slithered from Her eye socket into Her finned ear as She said in a low-pitched, burbling voice, "I am not here for *you,* boy."

Kneeling before Shir, Alatos told them, "We have failed you. Had these insects and the Moon Mother not been so insolent, reality would be more forgiving. But the *Sil'simani* are gone . . . and my Sister."

Shir tilted their head. "Sh'tarr?"

"Yes. The Widow came, the sky was stolen, and my waters were corrupted. The darkness reached for me, but I evaded." Alatos' spiny eyebrows jerked. "But Sh'tarr . . . I cannot find Her or feel Her."

Luxea felt that speaking to a goddess without Her blessing might be sacrilegious, but she did so despite herself. "Excuse me, Alatos?"

Is that how you address a goddess? Likely not.

The Sea Mother's muddy lips raised to show Her rows of serrated teeth. Luxea gulped. "May I ask how Oscerin was able to suppress the power of You and Your sister when Ares flew me to Mythos?"

"Because Oscerin is one of the *greater,"* said Alatos derisively. "The Lemuria made Her, and She made us. That night you trespassed by wing and scale, the Irestar was in perigee. Oscerin was close enough to our world to take from us the gifts She had bestowed."

"But Widow did the same," said Luxea studiously. "Correct me if I'm reaching, but wouldn't that have to mean that She is *also* a greater divine? That Widow, like Oscerin, came before You, Sh'tarr, and the five others of the mortal plane."

Alatos' kelpy hair shivered with rage. "There are three greater — only three!" She made a face like She didn't believe Her own words.

"But Widow . . . She has to be one of the greater. She took Sh'tarr. She sealed Her away."

Ares spoke next, his usual peremptory tone dwindled to a sheepish mutter. "Is it possible for the greater divines to be harmed?"

"You have the Moon to answer your questions," spat Alatos.

Shir looked depressed. "Please, Alatos. Be kind to them."

Never would She, the Sea Goddess, take the words of lesser forms of life to heart. But She'd spent thousands of years watching over the Mythics, and that flake of a motherly figure housed within Her reacted. She resistantly complied.

"It is possible for any of us to feel pain," She told Ares through a snarl, "but only if we inflict it upon each other."

"That can't be right," murmured Ares. Alatos *hated* that statement. "I mean not to belittle Your words, but it can't be. If Widow is any divine at all, why was She burned when She touched Luxea?"

Alatos was listening now. "Burned . . . by a mortal?"

Out of a new, dangerous curiosity, She brushed Her slimy hand across Luxea's cheek. It left a streak of mucus, but Luxea wouldn't insult Her by wiping it. The contact didn't hurt Alatos. She bristled and said nothing more about it.

"If I may speak again," said Ares, stealing Alatos' glare. "We will search for Sh'tarr, I promise You. Widow cannot have that kind of power at Her disposal, and Sh'tarr wasn't made to be confined. When Shir returns us to the mainland, we'll help You find Her."

Shir's eyes sank low. Luxea asked, "What is it?"

"I could do anything and go anywhere when the others were with me, but . . ." The Mythic stuck out their arms to show the fading light under their crystal flesh. "I am alone. I am tired. I brought us here but can go no farther. Not yet."

"How will we get back to L'arneth?" whimpered Luxea.

"I am sorry. I feel weak," muttered Shir.

Alatos' gills flapped about as She sighed. "These mortals, are they of import to you?" She asked the Mythic.

Shir stared at Ares and Luxea's hands; they'd shaken and told each other it was lovely to have met. "Yes. They are my friends."

The Sea Goddess scoffed. *Friends.* She was visibly irritated but felt indebted to Shir after having failed to forestall their endangerment. Wearing a rending glower, She faced the ocean and whistled so shrilly that it nearly sent Ares and Luxea to sleep. Alatos' hair spilled tiny crabs and slugs as She waited.

In mere moments, a second whistle from the lowest fissure in the sea responded, loud enough to crack the rock. Then a towering fin like a manta ray's, carved with swirling, green scales, flopped out of the water. A swell came over the stone and soaked Ares and Luxea once again.

A pearly white eye poked up through the surface and blinked at Alatos — the eye of a whale, but not any sort the world had ever seen. This whale was massive enough to swallow ten, perhaps twenty other whales and still have an appetite.

Alatos petted the creature's fin. "This is Weorem, the King of the Abyssal Plain. His speed is unmatched by any of my creations, as he was the first. Tell me where you wish to go — but not you nor you, only them," She said to Ares and Luxea.

The Mythic didn't know where they needed to travel, so they gazed at Ares expectantly. The Prince cleared his throat and whispered, "Caldavaan Cove. It's in Southern Tzapodia. Tel Ashir."

Shir passed the message to Alatos. "Caldavaan Cove in Tzapodia."

After a curt nod, Alatos whistled to Weorem. Water sprayed out of his blowhole. Alatos' anemone lashes swayed as She spat, "Go."

With a thankful expression, Shir stepped onto Weorem's slippery fin. They sat down cross-legged on his back and admired the pulses of light coming from his embossed skin. Luxea shuffled past Alatos. She was as hated by the Sea Goddess as Ares, so she mounted Weorem without a word.

The Prince took a step, but Alatos snatched his arm and burrowed Her chipped fingernails into his skin. It took quite a lot of force for Ares to feel pain, but this hurt him. The spiny fins on the sides of the Sea Goddess' head flared out, and Her nose wrinkled.

"Find Sh'tarr," She rasped. "Fail me, and you shall be forever cursed by the sea. You have one too many curses already, don't you?"

He was released with a hateful thrust. "We'll find Her."

Weorem moaned and splashed into the water with three passengers on his back. As they rode the ocean, Luxea looked back at Alatos. The goddess faced the sky with a lonely air until She leaped, transformed into a four-headed shark, and swam away.

Ares, Luxea, and Shir had been scudding along the waves for close to three hours. Each time the great whale splashed over a swell, their bellies jumped up into their throats. Ares couldn't wait to get back to Tel Ashir now. Sailing the ocean had never been an activity he was against, but this was too rocky for his liking.

Luxea crouched on her hands and knees and reached for the dolphins that swam under Weorem's wings. She was too distracted to notice Shir falling increasingly silent. The Mythic drew circles in the mucus on Weorem's back and frowned as the designs glistened away into shapeless droplets.

Ares scooted closer. "You're upset."

"No," said Shir. "I am afraid."

"Of?"

"Your world," replied Shir. "Long ago, men coveted us — but not to spare us. They saw money in our skin, so we were hunted. You and Luxea accept that we are more than riches, but others do not. I am a walking treasure, Ares, not a life. I surmise that greed has only worsened since that time."

Ares counted the turrets on his castle as its silhouette came into view atop the sea cliffs. "Greed is eternal, but we will protect you, Shir. You and your kind have spared my life and Luxea's. I'll give all in my power to keep you untouched. If they make you suffer, they will suffer tenfold.

"But if it's estrangement you fear, there may be a remedy for that as well," he added, lighter in the face. "When Mythos was still a part of L'arneth, did you hear of the Riders? Tribesmen with a soul shared between man and beast."

Shir twinkled. "The practice of division has lived nearly as long as I. These Riders, their customs survived the growth of civilization?"

"They've avoided civilization as you have," corrected Ares. He motioned to the castle in the distance. "Unless she and her brother have chosen to leave, there's a pair from the western tribe living on my land. You'll meet them. Brielle and Ruka are their names. One is a woman dark of skin and red of hair. The other is a wolf — a large one at that. They taught me about the *Sil'simani* and the Stag God Wynd. Is that story true?"

"We have crossed paths with Wynd. He would have lain there until every one of His thousand lives drained had we not given Him new antlers. There are a few divines we have met. Wynd, Mamaku, Raveth,

Alatos, Sh'tarr, and N'ra." Shir lightened. "A wolf. This makes me happy. I feel like smiling. I would like to meet Brielle and Ruka."

Luxea grew teary-eyed as they neared home. She'd missed Tel Ashir since before she'd left in Redtail. It was where she'd woken up without memories, seen her eyes for the first time, met Mollah, Avari, Ares, Oliver, and so many others. She imagined the scent of jasmine and sandalwood, the softness of her bed covers, and the morning warmth spilling through her balcony doors.

Beside her, Ares had thoughts too. When last he'd seen his home from the ocean, he'd sailed on fancy boats, surrounded by dancers with bare, toned bellies, tables of Tzapodian delicacies, and the most expensive wines in the world. It had been a superficial life. He'd had an expectancy for servitude, a longing for everything that didn't matter and nothing that did.

Back then, he hadn't deserved the title of a Guardian of the Joined Hands. The most he'd done was clash claws with the King of Tzapodia, but that was only for himself and his mother.

Today, he'd stared into the eyes of the most terrible threat Amniven had ever seen and been ready to relinquish himself to stop it for the sake of the world.

He looked at Luxea. She was smiling. What if she hadn't shown up in Tzapodia? He would have been as shallow, hard, and detached if that were the case. But she was here, and she was *smiling*.

Suddenly, he was smiling too.

In Caldavaan Cove, Weorem moaned. Colorful birds flew out of the tall palm trees, fleeing from the sound. From afar, Ares saw workers in the royal harbor dropping ropes and hammers to run for their lives. Well, Weorem was gigantic and thusly terrifying. Additionally, his right fin was coming dangerously close to the docks.

Ares tapped on the whale's back. "Do *not* destroy the harbor."

"I don't think Weorem understands common," gulped Luxea.

The whale had responded to Alatos, so Luxea tried to mimic the tones. She whistled high, her lips cracking it every few seconds.

Weorem's pearly eye shifted to her. He picked up speed.

Two of the eight royal docks were obliterated. Ashlars and planks of wood soared and crashed through the lower windows of Castle Lavrenthea. Weorem's belly scratched up the side of the sea cliffs. He moaned, and more of Castle Lavrenthea's windows broke. Ares was going to hear a spiteful word or two from his treasurers.

The Prince was snarling and wringing water out his hair when Luxea spotted the glows of flaming arrows in the loops on the castle's rampart. It was no surprise that the sentinels aimed at them; they *had* breached the royal perimeter on the world's biggest marine mammal.

Luxea pointed at the archers. Ares glanced upward and whispered a word in draconic that she was sure was a curse. It had been some time since the Prince had exercised his autocratic nature, but with tens of arrows on him, he felt now was the time.

Slipping on his feet to Weorem's head, he held up his arms and shouted, "Shoot at me, and it will be the last shot you ever make!"

The flaming arrows disappeared, and a line of helmets popped over the parapet. They were staring, so Ares pulled back his sleeve and flashed the Tzapodian military salute with his claw.

This gesture confirmed that he was, in fact, their leader.

Several figures disappeared — because they fainted. All mouths were robbed of words until one sentinel managed to announce, *"His Highness lives! Get to the boats!"*

A train of men ran out of view. The last remaining sentinel held a dracas horn to his lips and blew melodic, wobbling notes.

This was the song of the dragons, the song of the kings and queens and princes of the past, all of which had died —

Except for the one who returned.

Wing Regent Isaak darted through the Obsidian Wing of Castle Lavrenthea. His leather boots crunched upon glass, embedding the broken faces of gods and demons into the rug. He took hold of the first keeper he could find.

"You! Are we under attack?"

The keeper was as white as baby powder. "The harbor is ruined, but, no, Wing Regent."

"Well? Won't you tell me what happened, or will you stand here with your damned mouth hanging all day?" spat Isaak.

In Castle Lavrenthea, the keepers, sentinels, and the like were afeared of the Wing Regent. But not today. For today, the figure of just power overshadowed him.

The keeper said, "It's His Highness."

A boatswain docked nearby with some trouble, for Weorem wouldn't quit flapping around. Ares hitched his fingers in the grooves of the whale's skin and worked his way to the bottom of his fin. He stood tall and met eyes with his sentinels through his dirty, black hair.

All of the slander that General Skythoan had spread mattered no longer to the sentinels. The survival of the Speaker of Oscerin and Prince of Tzapodia was the only truth. They saluted, maintaining straight expressions, but Ares caught tears streaming down a few of their broad, rugged faces.

This was what Luxea had meant. The Tzapodian people *did* hold unshakable faith in the Prince. He'd always taken their gestures as a mere obligation and never seen the wholeness of it — not until now.

He saluted them too.

Luxea began her descent but noticed Shir curled up on Weorem's spine. They refused to look at the castle, to face the steel and silver and blood that men had built and spilled.

Luxea knelt. Her stars were every color, and it reminded Shir of Mythos. "I was scared too," she whispered. "Waking up in a place like this without knowing your name, without a friend or goal or duty in the world . . . it wasn't easy. But if I could do it, you can do it."

Keeping their gaze locked with hers, Shir took hold of her sleeve and stood. Luxea led them across Weorem's back and, with her wrist still in Shir's grasp, crouched by the great whale's eye.

"You caused a lot of damage, but thank you, Weorem."

She kissed Weorem's head, and he whistled. Luxea wiped his slime from her mouth and sat next to Shir on his fin. They slipped down to the boats. The sentinels and boatswains were out of words when they saw the Mythic.

What in the world was it? A rock? A mutant? A god?

The Prince wanted the Mythic to feel safe in his kingdom, but his gawking sentinels weren't helping. From the corner of his mouth, he told them, "Shake their hand."

A line of hands shot out, which Shir recognized as a gesture of friendship. They slipped their fingers off Luxea's sleeve and into the palm of a boatswain. As had occurred with Ares and Luxea, he began to sweat, and his dirt-covered arms hardened.

"It is lovely to meet you," said Shir politely.

"A-and you," stammered the boatswain.

They were friends now, the Mythic and the boatswain.

While they were rowed to the nearest intact dock, Luxea waved at Weorem. The whale blinked at her and crashed down the sea cliff. Waves rocked the boat as he dove into the depths.

The Wing Regent rushed down the steps from Castle Lavrenthea into the harbor. His armor clanked to silence at the bottom stair. Beyond the clusters of helmets, scruffy, balding heads, and striped scarves was long, black hair and curled horns.

Once he'd helped Luxea off the boat, the Prince made his way to the castle. His sentinels created a pathway. In a trice, Ares met eyes with the Wing Regent.

Ares' dimples sank into his cheeks, and he hugged the Wing Regent as tightly as his aching arms would allow. Isaak *must* have been imagining things. The Prince hadn't embraced him since he'd been a child — six perhaps.

The Wing Regent's frosty eyes melted onto his waterline; the tears never reached his cheeks, for they were caught by the bags under his eyes. Isaak got a better look at Ares, the blood crusted on his face and in his hair, the dirt lodged in the grooves of his horns, and his clothes ripped and stained with mucus.

"I was under the impression that you flew into a storm, not a vat of fish guts," snarked the Wing Regent.

Insurgent, Ares wiped his slimy hand on Isaak's breastplate. Isaak scraped the mucus off his chest before it could crust, maintaining his stoicism until the Prince grinned. The two men clapped their hands together despite the goop.

"The others arrived safely?" asked Ares, ill at ease.

"Indeed, two days ago."

Ares couldn't see the airship. "Where is *Matha ou Machina?*"

"The Lady was beside herself with grief and couldn't stay here. She took leave for the Storm Plains just yesterday," informed Isaak.

"Badly timed impatience," sighed Ares.

While Shir shook hands with each boatswain, sentinel, and passing fisherman, Luxea hurried up the staircase. The Wing Regent stepped away from her and watched the pink and yellow stars in her eyes stir.

"Luxea Siren?" he asked contemptuously.

Her cosmos darted about Isaak's breastplate until they landed upon the Wing Regent's Seal, an upright fist with a crown around the wrist. Starstruck, she straightened her spine and saluted him.

"Yes, Wing Regent."

Isaak's stare inflicted frostbite. "Because of you, the Kingdom of Tzapodia nearly lost its leader."

The Prince openly expressed his disapproval of the remark. Isaak devoured his hotheadedness like a delicacy. His wrinkled lips showed a mocking smile as he held out his hand to Luxea. Feeling somewhat disarmed, she took it.

"I've never known Ares to do such stupid things." Isaak made a kissing motion over her knuckles. "For that, you must be worth the respect of a thousand men. Welcome home, Miss Siren."

# FORGIVENESS

## CASTLE LAVRENTHEA, TZAPODIA

SERVING GIRLS and keepers fainted in the hallways, and Ashi priests fell to their knees. All the rest gossiped about the Speaker, the woman for whom he'd fallen through the sky, and the stranger of crystal light that tailed them.

Wing Regent Isaak insisted that Ares join him in the council room forthwith, but Ares, even more adamantly, declined. He and Luxea needed a bath — badly — and refused to wait a minute longer to reunite with wine, food, cigarettes, and friends.

Shir was frightened despite the barrier that surrounded them due to Ares' presence; no one dared touch the Mythic with him nearby. In the stairwell to the Amber Lounge, Shir stopped and cowered. Ares sensed Luxea's eagerness to see the other Mooncallers, so he tapped the back of his hand on her arm and motioned up the stairs.

"Go on. I'll stay with Shir until they're ready."

"Are you sure?" asked Luxea, buzzing about. "You don't have to cater to my impatience, you know."

He playfully shooed her away. "It's an order."

Luxea grinned ebulliently. "Yes, Your Royal Highness."

Once she'd pantomimed a curtsey, she sprinted to the Amber Lounge. Her throat caught fire as she ascended. Before she'd fallen off *Matha ou Machina,* she'd written goodbye letters because she'd believed she was going to die. Now the friends she'd been sure she would never see again were one spiral away.

The walls were smears of polished stone, iron bars, and bejeweled frames as she ran. Then a door swung open, and two blonde women emerged with their sandals in their hands. Luxea wheeled herself to a halt. The blondes curled their lips at her mucus-coated attire and strutted down the hall gossiping. It wasn't ten seconds later that a half-naked man poked out of the room.

"Oi! Couldn't you broads've closed the door?" He glanced at the back of whomever's white-haired head stood before him. "There were three of you? Felt like two."

Luxea spun around. *Of course,* the man who'd been yelling was Oliver Kross. He fell back against the doorpost. "Luxie . . . ?"

Her sinuses ached. "Hi, Oli."

He almost bounced into a hug, but she was a lady — one of the few he respected — so he dressed first. Once a shirt covered his narrow waist, he picked her up and squealed things into her ear that just didn't make sense. He'd missed his starry-eyed friend so much. He'd thought she was gone forever, that she'd left him with nothing but a letter.

But here she was.

Oliver set her down. Only then did he notice that she was covered in fish muck — and so was he. He flicked his hands. "Gross, love. You could've taken a rinse 'fore runnin' at me."

"You'll find a way to cope." Luxea grabbed his hand and ran down the hall. "Will you take me to the others?"

He was too elated to see Luxea to deny her request — however smelly she was. "Aye. C'mon. They'll shite hard 'nough to send 'em through the roof!"

Together, they skidded into the lounge. There sat a ranger, Avari Vishera, bent over the arm of a sofa with her head down. Her curly hair was droopier than usual. Beside her was the wolf rider, Brielle, who had a pile of wood shavings accumulating on the rug as she carved arrow shafts. Behind the sofa, the only spot he'd fit, snoozed Brielle's animal brother Ruka.

Avari peeked up from her arm where she saw Luxea Siren standing at Oliver Kross' side. She flipped over, not waiting to process reality, and vaulted to her best friend. She was a koala bear on the trunk of her favorite tree. The pair of arms and legs around Luxea's waist sent her tipping onto the floor.

It was real. It was really, really real! They felt each other's warmth, heard the sniffles. Avari cried, first shocked and then joyous.

Ares came around the corner and nearly trod on Luxea's hair. He scooted past as she and Avari rolled around. Oliver closed in to hug him, but Brielle moved much faster. She had to touch someone — or hit them — and Ares was the most suitable candidate. She slugged him hard in the chest.

"You foolish, *foolish* dragon!"

The wolf rider mashed her face into Ares' torn up tunic and hoisted him off the ground; she was stronger than he'd expected. Ruka opened his amber eyes then; he would have rubbed them if he had hands. Tail about to fly off and out the window, he bounded to Ares and Brielle. The Prince was knocked against the wall and covered in wolf slobber.

Ares wiped saliva on his trousers. Oliver's fangs showed as he grinned and yanked him into a hug. He'd received fish slime from Luxea, so why not wolf spit too?

Once Oliver had welcomed Ares back from the land of the supposed death, he went to the sofa and shuffled around the side. He returned to Luxea with a bundle of cloth. If it was wrapped up, that meant Oliver couldn't touch it, and there was only one thing that couldn't be touched by other hands.

Her spellbook.

Luxea folded back the fabric, and there it was, glimmering at her. The gems on the Usinnon's cover were sleepy; it had been napping. She tossed the cloth and stroked it, whispering, "There you are."

Sparks fell from the Usinnon. From it came that voice that no one could understand. *"Hashi . . . ! Shasiashashisia . . . !"*

"I missed you," said Luxea, kissing it.

Ares watched her dotingly. He'd given her that spellbook a few moons after she'd moved into Castle Lavrenthea. He didn't regret having bestowed upon her such an invaluable object, for she'd used it well and would only excel as the time went on.

The rejoicing ceased when Shir peeked around the corner. The Mythic inched forth and stooped under a stone arch, absorbing new faces. Brielle yelped like a newborn puppy and strapped herself to Ruka with her arms.

"What is that thing?" gulped Avari.

"C-crystal stranger," shuddered Brielle. "So that's why you asked me about legends, Dragon . . ."

"Yes. This is Shir, a Mythic from the island of Mythos," informed Ares. "They're the last of their kind. It's up to us to keep them safe."

Shir's quartzite eyes drifted to Luxea. She fluttered her fingers to remind them how to make friends. Timorous, Shir held out their hand. Brielle was the only one willing to touch them. When she did, she and Ruka's pupils dilated, and their blood became pure light.

"It is lovely to meet you," said Shir, bowing their head.

"And . . ." Brielle let go and caught her breath, ". . . and you."

Oliver contemplated Shir.

"Are you a girl?"

"No."

"So you're a boy."

"No."

"Then what are you?"

"I am me."

After some thought, Oliver raised his eyebrows and nodded.

Ruka, having recovered from Shir's indirect contact, nudged his sister in the shoulder. *"Brie, I want to be their friend. Can I?"* he asked, his childlike voice sounding in her head.

Shir's crown lit up. "I will be your friend, Ruka."

Brielle's hundred locks almost stood as straight as Ruka's hackles. She trailed her forefinger between Shir and her brother. "You . . . Shir. You spoke to my brother. You spoke to Ruka!"

"I did. It would be rude not to respond to his question."

Interactions with animals weren't unusual to the Mythic. They'd been alive for thousands of years, learning the language of rock, water, beast, man, and mind. To them, Ruka spoke as comprehensively as anyone in the room. But this had never happened to Ruka — even the other Riders of the West hadn't been able to communicate with him.

The wolf's nails clicked on the tile. *"You can hear me, Shir?"*

"Yes," said the Mythic.

"No one can hear Ruka but me," stated Brielle.

Shir lightened. "And me."

Eyes narrowing, Ruka decided to test the Mythic. He glanced at Ares and said, only for Brielle to hear, *"Dragon smells like a salmon."*

Startling the rider and the wolf, Shir giggled. "Salmon are freshwater fish. I would argue that his scent is that of tuna or marlin."

So Shir *could* hear Ruka.

There hadn't been a moment since his freedom from Blackjaw Hollow that Ruka had felt so gleeful. Not only was the wolf no longer caged in the forest, not only were his friends alive, but now, for the first time since he'd died and been revived, he could now talk to someone other than Brielle!

He bounded in circles around Shir. *"Can we play? Brie and I have been going to the gardens every day! Will you play with me? I'll show you my favorite places! Please, Shir? Can we?"*

The Mythic was afraid of leaving but trusted that Ruka wouldn't let them be hurt, especially if Brielle was there too. Their toothless mouth formed an upward half moon.

"Are there flowers?" they asked.

*"Yes, flowers and sunshine! Trees too, and sand to roll in!"*

The grin on Shir's face stretched wider. "I will go."

As Brielle left with Ruka and Shir to the Flame Gardens, she shouted promises to the others that she would return to catch up. When they were gone, Ares mused about their conversation. He raised his forearm to his nose and sniffed his sleeve.

"They were referring to me, weren't they?"

Ares and Luxea took baths in their bedchambers. They'd been covered in blood, sweat, seawater, and mucus from Weorem, and a rinse had never been so satisfying! Luxea thanked the gods for Castle Lavrenthea's indoor plumbing — courtesy of the seroden elves.

It wasn't for two hours that Brielle bounded up the steps with Ruka and Shir. The Mythic was yet taciturn, but if they were close enough to Ruka, their crystals didn't shiver as much.

For a while, the Mooncallers reminisced about the positive bits and pieces in their past few months of havoc. It wasn't until Avari asked about what had happened after Ares had flown into Sh'tarr's Iris that the conversation diverted to a darker destination.

The Prince and Luxea, who surprised the others by sitting right next to each other, silently decided who would speak first. Ares would begin, as he'd been the only one conscious when they'd fallen. He wished Peyamo were there to listen; she'd doubted him the most.

Their tale of divines, both dark and light, seemed impossible to the Mooncallers. Ares and Luxea recounted Ares' dream, the Iris, and Luxea's encounter with the Goddess of the Moon Herself.

"The last thing She said to me was, *'Never can shadow touch you with moonlight in your veins.'*" Luxea brushed her pale fingers over her throat. "When Widow tried to strangle me on Mythos, She burned. Whatever it is that the Moon Mother fed me, it made me impervious to the Brood Mother's contact."

Ares whispered in her pointed ear, "Do you think that may be why Widow fears you?"

Brielle clapped her hands. "Secrets, Dragon! If we speak, we speak with full voices." She read the details in Ares and Luxea's faces. Something hadn't been shared. "There are words in your throats. Tell us what they are."

Ares and Luxea traded stares. It was unusual to see them communicate in such a fashion; it hadn't been that way before

Mythos. The Prince couldn't decide what to say, so Luxea gave him a hint.

He glanced at her lips as she mouthed the word, *"Goldenrise."*

The others deserved to hear it. Ares had violated the trust of The Six the night he'd told Luxea the truth and ruined whatever slight bond they'd had. His silence had annihilated her; it had jeopardized her life and thousands of others in Goldenrise. Luxea respected his secrets to an extent, but he knew she wanted a confession.

He gave in.

"The reason Widow set upon Goldenrise was Luxea," he admitted.

Avari's chubby cheeks looked gaunt as she bit them from the inside. "What do you mean?"

"The assault on the gala in Goldenrise. The intent of it was to kill Luxea," clarified the Prince.

But there was something else, what Ares and The Six had done after the attack. Luxea bore the truth and was pleading him to say it. His faith in her judgment was escalating at an alarming rate, and he wasn't sure he liked it.

"I lied to all of you," he said next.

The voices stopped. Ares thought Brielle's glare might disembowel him. "You're lying to us now, Dragon?" she hissed.

To put himself at ease, he stared at Luxea's pale hands as they rested on her knees. No, no. He was being fragile. What would her hands do to help him? He looked away and grabbed his wineglass.

"I lied about Goldenrise, for I was bound by an indenture. Peyamo, Annalais, and I swore that we wouldn't release information that would put the Empress' standing as a member of The Six at stake, that we would keep silent."

"Keep silent 'bout what?" sniffed Oliver.

"I told you that Annalais was unaware of why the attack at the gala took place. The truth is . . ." Ares finished his wine. "Widow was there that evening. She offered the Empress a contract to join the Brood, and it was signed."

"It was *what?*" snapped Avari.

"Annalais gave herself to the Brood. The Empire of Goldenrise now belongs to Widow," said Luxea when Ares didn't speak.

Before Annalais Taress had become the Empress of Goldenrise, Ares had been engaged to her. She'd been set to become the Queen of Tzapodia — until Ares had discovered her with other men and left her. Luxea and Oliver knew this. Avari and Brielle, however, had not the slightest understanding for his background with the Empress. They screamed at him, overlooking how painful it had been to trust her with Goldenrise.

"Why hide these things from us, Dragon?"

"Ares, those people aren't safe!"

When Luxea had learned the truth, she'd spouted her anger at Ares too. In sooth, she hated Empress Annalais. That woman had forced no less than fifty men, women, and children into sex work and relinquished her empire to Widow. Oh, if she could, Luxea would give Annalais a big, nasty piece of her mind. Ares, on the other hand, had been reprimanded enough. Whatever Avari and Brielle said now would cause him pain, not teach him a lesson.

The moment that she could get a word in edgewise, Luxea shouted, "Stop arguing!" It was unlike her to raise her voice, so Avari and Brielle went quiet. "I've already talked to Ares. What matters now is that he's agreed to return to Goldenrise to undo The Six's oath of silence. He wants to evacuate those people as much as any of us. If you target him, target me too. I've known about all of it since that night in Anathema."

This threw off Avari and Brielle. They realized that they'd been taking out their pent-up frustration on Ares because he could handle verbal attacks, but the notion of doing the same to Luxea wasn't as fulfilling. She was right. All that mattered was that they were alive and Ares would fix what he and The Six had done. Avari unwound, but Brielle was yet distrusting.

"I'm sorry, Ares," sighed Avari. "For yelling at you, and that Luxie hit you with you an arse-full. She can get scary, can't she?"

Brielle wouldn't apologize; the daughter of the wolf never apologized. On the contrary, the son of the wolf would. Now that his sister wasn't his only communicator, Ruka relayed to Shir what he wanted to say to Ares.

"Ares, Ruka hopes you forgive his sister," said the Mythic mildly.

The veins on Brielle's clenched fists swelled. "Ruka . . ."

The wolf wagged defiantly.

# EMPTY THRONE

## THE AMBER WING, CASTLE LAVRENTHEA

THE PRINCE'S bed wasn't nearly as comfortable as the meadow on Mythos; he'd never fathomed that he would prefer sleeping on grass to a feather mattress. He kicked about in his chambers, waiting to get tired again. His eyes shot to his door between paces. Perhaps a walk would be beneficial.

He heard a frustrated groan as he passed by the Amber Lounge. Slouched on the sofa was Luxea, using a candle to read the Usinnon and take notes. The notion of wandering the castle halls by her side tempted him; it felt reminiscent of their time together on Mythos.

"Luxea?"

She looked up from the Usinnon, her green stars twinkling in the darkness. "Good evening. Trouble sleeping?"

"I see I'm not the only one."

"You noticed," she sighed.

Ares fixed his sleeves. "Would you be willing to give your mind a rest and join me for some late-night ambling?"

Had anyone else asked her to walk, she would have said no. Ares, however, had been blessed from birth with an irresistible aura. Luxea clinked her quill into the ink pot and set down her spellbook.

Next to Ares, Luxea puttered up and down corridors and stairwells familiar and unfamiliar. Beyond the walls of the servant and kitchen quarters came the snoozing of chefs and the occasional gossip of serving girls. Luxea swore she heard a conversation about having spent a night with Oliver Kross. How surprising.

It lightened Ares' mood to see her taking in details about the castle that she'd never seen, but he'd memorized. It was the Obsidian Wing by which she was the most fascinated. She'd cut through the upper levels but had never had a reason to tour the ground floor.

Ares had an embittered look on his face as they trod over the rat-eaten carpet; evidently, the servants didn't care much for the Obsidian Wing. His boots and her flats *clacked* and *slapped* down a hall with enormous portals leading to the sea cliffs. The Irestar was bright above the Blightwater tonight. Light dribbled through the starry pattern in the latticework and turned the black stone floor into lapis.

There hadn't been doors on the left side of the hall until the Obsidian Wing met the Ruby Wing. This door wasn't one to be overlooked; in fact, it was unforgettable.

It was doubled, two stories high, and formed of silver. In it were embedded precious gems so large that Luxea would have needed both hands to cup one. A thousand dragons were engraved in swirls, drops, and sharp angles, flying toward the center and clashing at the seam. In front were two with their outstretched claws extended from the surface, creating the handles. From them dangled beads of garnet, the blood of each other forever falling.

What was most peculiar about this door were the crisscrossing metal bars blocking it and the clunky lock holding them together. It was newer than the door, more polished; it hadn't been there long.

"Where does this lead?" Luxea traced the curves of the dragons' scales and rubbed her finger on her skirt. "It's dusty."

Ares' belt rode against the stone wall as he leaned back. Through the dark, morose showed in his eyes. "It's the King's Court."

"I wasn't aware there was a court," said Luxea.

"No one is meant to be aware." He spun his rings under his crossed arms. "Some pieces of this castle are best left abandoned."

"Why is that?"

Luxea's curiosity was endless, just endless. Ares wished he'd never let her close enough to ask questions . . . but then he started *wanting* to tell her. He strode in the direction of the vestibule, hardly believing that he was about to address such a sickening topic.

The Wing Regent was right. Luxea made him do stupid things.

"Because I'll never be the King of Tzapodia," he confessed. "I refuse to take the title until I recover what's been stolen. But there's scarcely a chance that I will. This curse has spread too fast. By the time I do what must be done, I'll forever be a monster."

"You aren't a monster," said Luxea piteously.

"Don't correct me." The demand sounded like a thank you.

She nibbled her lip. "What was stolen?"

"The Crown of Tzapodia."

Luxea had wondered since the first time she'd stepped into the castle why Ares hadn't become the King. Avari had told her that he hadn't publicly addressed the issue. Never would she have guessed that one of the reasons was a missing heirloom.

"I can't imagine it was easy to steal the crown," she said, stepping into the vestibule. "How was anyone able to get their hands on it? Was it not guarded?"

"It didn't have to be."

"But it's gone now. Who took it?"

Ares stopped walking. Eyes veiled to the crimson dragon painted on the ceiling, he whispered, "The King. It was stolen by the King."

There wasn't anything more to say than that. Luxea had learned very little about Naiv Lavrenthea, Ares' father. That nightmare of a man was gone from the kingdom yet right in front of them, painted on the ceiling with his slitted, violet irises flooded by loathing. Ares' gaze was similar.

"The last time my father spoke to me, he told me that my eyes were like my mother's," he said, so quietly that Luxea had to hold her breath to hear. "But the last time the King spoke to me, someone entirely different, he said, *'Until you take the head from my neck, you will never be a king.'*

"That was the day the Queen died, and a part of me came alive that I'd never planned to touch. But to destroy the King . . . I would have done anything. The city fell because I couldn't stop myself from pursuing him. It didn't matter to me who was hurt — myself, my people. I only cared if the King died.

"Something in my blood was starved for the power that had lain dormant. But when first I allowed myself wings, I felt the hourglass tip. I was no longer human. I couldn't control that flow of rage and lust and hate. What scares me the most is that I didn't come to this realization until it was done, after I'd almost given my life to take that of the man who'd given it to me in the first place.

"What consumed me then was a monster. I could have killed anyone — I would have, for dragons see naught but death. I'll never be relieved from this fear of harming someone without intent. All it takes is one wrong move to drag me and those around me to Sithe.

"I've accepted that I won't bear a sound mind long enough to fill the role into which I should have been born. My people have suffered too many monsters on the throne, and I won't be the next. I'll end it before it begins, spare the kingdom harm, and pass my titles to the one most worthy of it. It will be up to them to decide if Tzapodia ever has a king again."

Luxea resented his words.

He wasn't a monster. Monsters don't feel. Not like this.

A sudden rattling came from outside the castle. Ares dropped the subject of King Naiv and spun around. He'd heard this only once in his life, that very day the Queen had died — the portcullis.

"Stay quiet," he said, sidling along the wall to the entrance.

Luxea sneaked close behind him, watching her footing so she wouldn't heel his boot. They poked their heads around the doorway.

Ares wouldn't be sleeping that night.

Hundreds of Tzapodian citizens hovered on the Steps of Sevinus, some shouting and banging their fists on the portcullis bars, poked back by the blunt ends of sentinels' spears. Others camped with their children under tattered blankets or knelt in prayer.

Tied in bundles and piled against the gate were mountains of bright orange and purple flowers. In Tzapodia, fire and lune lilies were hung when there'd been a death in the royal family — but Ares was the only member left.

Someone had told them he'd perished. Now to find out who it was.

# OSCERIN'S EYES

## 6.SNOWHOWL.OSC.3
### THE AMBER WING, CASTLE LAVRENTHEA

AT DAWN, Luxea was woken up absurdly early by a knock at the door. She answered, rubbing her stirring eyes and wobbling about. She looked a bit like a vengeful apparition. Her nightgown was lopsided, and her hair was a child's scribble.

The Prince, on the contrary, was prepared for something. His silky tresses were tied over his shoulder, and pinned to his black and silver suit were four badges: the Lavrenthea crest, the Tzapodian sigil, the Speaker's mark, and what Luxea guessed was the emblem of The Six. Was he set to attend a ball at six o'clock in the morning?

"Get dressed and meet me in the hall." The door closed.

"Yes, Your Highness," grunted Luxea.

In five minutes, she entered the hall. Ares almost led her away, but then his stare dropped to her feet. Luxea tipped her head down.

How had she forgotten her shoes?!

Hot in her cheeks, she reached into her bedchamber and swiped a pair of sandals. "Where are we going?" she asked as she fit them on.

"Council room." He stalked off in a hurry.

Luxea was more awake now. "The council room? I've never been there before. The council members won't like it."

"I don't really care."

*Okay then.*

They ventured up two staircases and crossed a bridge over the vestibule to the Emerald Wing. Far below, Luxea noted the crowds outside of the portcullis; they'd densified.

The council room was vacant, for Ares had called for an emergency meeting just before waking up Luxea, not giving much time for the members to gather. He pulled an extra chair to the left of his own; the spot to the right was reserved for the Wing Regent. Ares had what was virtually a throne at the head of the table.

They waited for twenty minutes. The Prince chain-smoked roseleaf cigarettes and clacked his talons on the jeweled pommel of his sword. Luxea assumed that he'd arranged this conference to address the most apparent problem: his supposed death being made public. Why he'd asked her to join him was a mystery yet unsolved.

Perhaps emotional support?

The council room door opened, and the fifteen members spilled inside. Evidently, some of them hadn't been told about the Prince's return.

Keeper Vessias fainted. His tablet soared across the room as his shiny, bald head disappeared from sight. Priestess Daiada's red veil was wet with tears as she fell into a bow and laid her forehead on the ground. The rest saluted speechlessly. The Wing Regent had his eyes on Luxea, his expression translating, *'You're brave to sit so close to Ares right now.'*

Spymaster Ruri straddled Keeper Vessias and offered him smelling salts. He blathered as he woke up. The council members stood behind their chairs around the table, but General Skythoan hadn't moved from the doorway; he was too stunned to remember how to do a thing.

Yet neglecting to meet the eyes of anyone in the council room, Ares gathered another cigarette and frisked himself for a match. The quiet moment made Luxea impatient, so she flicked her fingers and lit his roll with magick. He smiled at her, not a thankful smile — a calm before the storm smile.

"Sit down. No one may speak."

Ares barely waved his hand as he said this. The butterflies in Luxea's stomach went up in flames. The Prince of Tzapodia was much more intense in a professional setting.

It took General Skythoan's every effort to leave the threshold. Through a cloud of pale blue smoke, Ares hunted him all the way to his chair.

When the seats were filled, Ares spoke a bit sardonically. "Good morning, *hilien dam, valathes rasone, desal yajacitua.* As you can see, I'm well and alive, and Tzapodia is not without guardianship. It would have been delightful if my people thought the same — but somehow, they learned of my disappearance."

He smiled at General Skythoan charmingly. "That issue will be addressed shortly. On a more immediate note, I must introduce you all to Luxea Siren." Her fists were tight enough to pop. "Miss Siren has a brilliant mind and sound morals. I ask that you accept her, as she is the newest member of the council."

Luxea and Isaak mirrored each other's baffled expressions.

"Some of you may be familiar with Miss Siren," continued Ares. "Claymore and his troop were the first responders when she was found in Tal Am T'Navin two years ago. Luxea and her mentor were the first to discover the destruction in Lor'thanin and hear the name *'Widow.'* Had she not had the courage to break into the castle to warn me, we might not be here today."

Isaak chuckled. "So that was you. Ares gave me an earful."

The Prince didn't appreciate the interruption, but Luxea found it funny, so he let it go. "It was soon after the incident that Oscerin reached out to me to keep the stars safe. Luxea has been in Oscerin's presence. She has consumed Her, touched Her, and seen Her — and through Luxea, Oscerin sees us all." The glares and stares of the council members were on her. Luxea shrank, so Ares sat taller to make up for her meekness. "Because of that, she will be, from this day forth, the counterpart of the Speaker under the title of *'Seer of Tzapodia.'* Do you accept, Miss Siren?"

For a blink, Luxea thought Lieutenant Claymore looked proud. This should have been a history-making moment, but she could hardly pay attention because of the urgency in Ares' face.

There just wasn't a more difficult *'yes'* or *'no'* question. She would have felt less tense had a god asked her to dinner. A member of the Mooncaller Council — her? And her hair was such a mess today too. Ares could have warned her! What would Avari say? Of course, she wouldn't say anything; she'd sooner combust.

"Luxea."

Ares' voice was low enough only for her to hear. She glanced up at him, her blue and green stars frozen in their places. A tiny dimple showed on his cheek. What a provocateur. She wouldn't decline, and he knew it.

With her tongue wrung out of words, she hummed, *"Mhm."*

It was done. Luxea Siren was the Seer of Tzapodia.

"Thank you." Ares didn't seem to have as much trouble processing what had happened as Luxea and the other members. He put out his cigarette. "Then we have fifteen members once again. Excellent."

Keeper Vessias, who'd recovered from his fainting spell, tallied the heads around the table. Yes, he was an accountant, but even a pebble could have known that there weren't fifteen seated.

"Your Highness, there are sixteen now," he said sheepishly.

"No, there are fifteen. One of you has lost your position, and the only question now is: who?" Ares melted a hole through General Skythoan's breastplate with a glare. "Would anyone like to confirm who told the public I died?"

Lieutenant Claymore's chestnut eyes shot to Skythoan. Although her head was low, Spymaster Ruri's chin was pointed to the general too. Ares searched the Wing Regent's face. Isaak nodded.

The Prince swished his talons. "Everyone but Isaak, Claymore, and Skythoan is dismissed."

The lieutenant hid his fright. He couldn't lose his title now, of all times; his first child would be born so soon. The eleven members whose names hadn't been called let their shoulders rest and vacated.

Clutching her elbows, Luxea went to the door. Before she could leave, Ares called out, "Spymaster!" Ruri stopped, and her greasy, brown hair swung under her hood. "Take Luxea to the smith. Have a sigil forged for her."

"At once." Ruri pointed at Luxea and then to the door. They left.

The council room felt more like the gallows. Ares rose to his feet, rounded the table, and stopped behind Claymore and Skythoan.

"Get up, both of you."

The lieutenant followed his orders with all haste. General Skythoan stood, staring at his sabatons like a puppy who'd gotten into the garbage. Ares' black hair cascaded over his shoulder as he dipped into the general's line of sight.

"First, you slander my name, and now that I've returned from the dead, you won't meet my eyes?" he asked gutturally.

The general's hand twitched into a salute. "Your Highness, we all thought that you'd —"

"Thinking doesn't require a loose tongue," cut in Ares. "Do you realize the effect this will have on my kingdom? My people are losing their heads, and *I* have to pick them up again. The last thing we need in a time of chaos is more chaos. Is that so difficult for you to learn?"

"Your Highness, I was only doing what should've been — !"

Ares cornered him. "What did I just say?"

"Your people had questions!"

"You told them that Ares deserted us!" blurted the Wing Regent. The Prince listened attentively but didn't take his eyes off Skythoan. "You convinced them that he died because he refused to listen to you, because he cared more for a girl than his people!"

"And where is the lie in that?" roared Skythoan. "Your Highness, I warned you that Widow would come for The Six in Goldenrise. It was as I'd foreseen. You lived, but then you left us for Siren's sake!" He motioned to Luxea's chair and scoffed. "What, when Oscerin sends you a starry-eyed cunt to play with, your kingdom matters no more?"

*Fire.*

The placidity on the Prince's face was mortifying. Skythoan immediately realized the grave error he'd made. He almost took a step away, but what Ares said next reeled him back in.

"I was wrong."

The general couldn't believe it. If the Prince was going to admit to his faults, he wanted to hear every word. Ares distracted Skythoan with a yielding smile so that he wouldn't see his fingers tightening at his side.

"I was going to be civil — I was wrong to think you deserve it."

A fist crashed into Skythoan's nose. Bridge broken, another swing came. He tried to escape, but Ares wrested his cape and locked him against the wall. Another punch, and a tooth flew out of his mouth.

Another. Another. Another.

The general toppled to the floor, clutching his beaten-in face. Ares shook out his hand. His knuckles bled, but his anger had been sated. As Skythoan's mouth bubbled with red saliva, Ares knelt, hooked his talons under his badge, and tore it off.

Skythoan's life in Tzapodia was over.

The Prince faced Claymore and wiped a drop of blood off of the Tzapodian General badge with his thumb. He flicked it, and the lieutenant caught it in one hand.

With a smile, Ares said, "Congratulations, General Claymore."

The Spymaster and the Seer moved through the Pearl Alley and down the steps to the Flame Gardens. The forge was located outside the Aptuli where Luxea had first met Oliver Kross.

Avari had spoken many times about Ruri Nairn, the Black Ghost of Tzapodia. If Ruri tried, she could take down a mammoth with a kick and a slash. She was notorious for her quick feet and quicker blades. What Avari had mentioned the most was how she'd been recruited.

Thirteen years after King Naiv Lavrenthea had laid waste to Naraniv and claimed the territory, the mountain rishja had sought revenge. Rushing into a dragon's lair would have gotten them burned, but sneaking up on a dragon could result in something else.

The Chief of Nan Jaami had sent recruiters to Orchiris, the capital of Avi Tulani, where had lived a sellsword renowned for ruthlessness. She'd been a murderous whirlwind — and an expensive one.

The rishja had spent weeks searching. But no man found Ruri Nairn, she found them. She'd slitted half their throats before their commander had woken up and talked her down. Ruri had sheathed her daggers only when she'd been offered four sacks of gold coins.

Ruri Nairn had been hired to assassinate the King of Tzapodia, for she was just the sort of woman who could slay a dragon with her bare hands. Little had she known that this was to be her final assignment as a sellsword.

She'd left for Tzapodia on the last day of Blackomen and walked right into Castle Lavrenthea as if it had been a bakery. Not a soul had noticed her until she'd peeked into a chamber in the Amber Wing.

Lying on his bed with a sitar had been a teenage boy with horns curling from his black hair. There hadn't been a need for him to ask, for he'd known she was an assassin and known her goal.

Ruri hadn't wanted to kill a child, but if she had to . . .

However, the dark-haired boy had lowered his green eyes and played his instrument as if he hadn't seen her. Ruri had left him alive.

The boy's feigned ignorance had allowed for an unnoticed attack, but King Naiv Lavrenthea hadn't been an easy target. He'd left her with inches-deep cuts in her legs and chest, forcing to make a retreat. The King had chased her, but that black-haired boy had sooner pulled her into his room and hidden her under his bed. The King had entered the bedchamber but hadn't found her. When they were alone, the boy offered the assassin bandages and sent her on her way.

It wasn't for four years after Ruri had failed to assassinate the King of Tzapodia that she'd received a missive from Prince Ares Lavrenthea. That black-haired boy had become the ruler of the kingdom and hadn't forgotten her. He'd promised her coin and fame and blades of silver in exchange for her service.

Now she was his Spymaster.

"Ruri," voiced Luxea. The Spymaster didn't react. "Thank you for taking me to the forge."

"It was an order," said Ruri solidly.

Engaging in conversation with an assassin was about as fun as feeding porridge to a rock. They continued down the arched corridor without opening their mouths. Luxea had never been so aware of the loudness of her footsteps, for Ruri was a feather in a pair of leather boots. The silence was uncomfortable — until it was obliterated.

"There you are!"

Luxea leaned back and saw Avari jogging to her from behind a fountain in the Flame Gardens. She offered her a one-arm hug and mashed her face into her chest. Luxea was awestruck because Avari, the most observant, sharp-sighted person she knew, didn't heed Ruri's presence. It made sense then why Ruri was called the Black Ghost of Tzapodia. She was invisible.

"Where've you been all morning?" wondered Avari.

"Ares needed me," said Luxea imprecisely.

The Spymaster turned her head. The movement alerted Avari, and suddenly there were daggers in her hands. Ruri hadn't pulled her weapons, but it would have taken her half a blink to cut her down.

Two cats were head-to-head, measuring each other's claws. Avari's blades soon fell back into their scabbards, her arms to her sides.

"What are you doing with the Spymaster?" she murmured.

Luxea clenched her teeth. "Ruri, this is Avari Vishera. She was my mentor. May she come with us? I want to explain the situation."

Ruri's black, sawlike eyes flitted to the stars. "You don't need my permission, *Seer.*" She sneered and went on with noiseless footsteps.

"What does she mean by *'Seer?'*" whispered Avari.

Luxea imprecated and pulled her along. "This morning, Ares named me as the newest member of the Mooncaller Council."

Avari tripped. She never, *ever* tripped.

"He wanted me as the fifteenth member of the council because of Oscerin." Luxea was trying to be quiet but knew Ruri could hear her. "As he's the Speaker, he named me the Seer. Oscerin speaks through him and sees through my eyes. That's what happened. We're going to the forge to commission my emblem."

"Luxie, you're tugging my tush, right?"

They followed Ruri into the forge. A roughed-up blacksmith set down his hammer and bowed. "Spymaster."

"Pleasure, Lorith." Ruri bounced her head to the left. "This is Luxea Siren and . . ."

Avari crossed her arms. "Avari Vishera."

Ruri jerked her scarred chin at the anvil. "Leave your project. His Highness wants an emblem made for Siren. She's been made the *'Seer of Tzapodia.'*" Her last words were scathing.

The blacksmith grinned; he would have been attractive had it not been for the layers of soot on his face. After a long look at Luxea's body, he took her hand and set upon it an ashy kiss. She didn't like it.

"A delight, Seer," he purred. "How fortunate that such a stunning lady as yourself is a part of the council. You're always welcome to my workshop. I have very few visitors and would love your company."

Lorith must have had a soft spot for l'arian girls; they were a rarity now that Widow had wiped them out. Ruri and Avari exchanged distrusting looks. The Spymaster may have been a killer, but she was also a woman and could tell that Luxea was uncomfortable. She spoke up.

"I should mention that she's the Prince's favorite."

Lorith let go of Luxea in an instant.

"Smart," growled Avari.

As Lorith forged the emblem, the three girls sat on a bench at the far side of the room. Avari bounced her feet. The sound of the soles of her shoes scraping on stone commingled with the clang of the hammer on the anvil.

"Are you sure you want to be a council member, Luxie?" she asked from behind her scarf. "That's going to be a hells of a lot of responsibilities. Your position won't be a sinecure anymore."

"Yes, it will." Painted with firelight, Ruri said, "The Speaker doesn't want to give her tasks, he wants her to be closer to him." She scoffed at Luxea. "Please, the *'Seer?'* That's an excuse to cross work and play. What else could you offer us? Perhaps Oscerin sees through you, but Tzapodia needs warriors, not oracles."

Luxea didn't appreciate the denigration. Ruri saw her as a plaything, but that couldn't have been less valid. She almost didn't make a move. Reacting to provocation would be petty —

*But, oh, who cares?*

Three fingers apart from Ruri's thigh, Luxea tapped the bench. Magick snapped the wood, and the Spymaster's eyes bulged before she fell out of view. She caught herself, but Luxea wasn't done. Ruri's daggers, even the one hidden in her boot, lifted into the air. Luxea clasped her hand in her lap, and the blades clattered to the ground.

The blacksmith glanced in their direction but kept his head down. Ruri stared at her collection of weapons on the floor and then squatted to collect them with the haste of a magnet to metal.

She stood above the broken slab of the bench with her arms locked, a blade in each hand. Frowning, she said, "Braggart."

Luxea grinned. "Cynic."

It was twilight when Luxea and Avari went back to the Amber Lounge. Ruri had left, without a goodbye, to her own smaller quarter within the Emerald Wing. Avari scampered off right away to tell Oliver, Brielle, and Ruka the news about Luxea's initiation. She'd include Shir too, although they wouldn't understand.

In the meantime, Luxea went to Ares to ask why he'd chosen her. She hadn't been inside his bedchamber since the night Oliver had arrived at Castle Lavrenthea, and she hadn't felt all too observant that night.

Ares opened the door, an unsure crack and then a full swing. He held it open for her and shut it when she was inside.

The only inconsistencies between his rooms and her own were minor — if you overlooked the absurd size difference. The titles of the books on the shelves were far less mystical. The state of his bedsheets said that the servants hadn't stopped by today; Luxea always made her own bed. The butts of cigarettes in a dish on the table were a given. An emerald ring sat on the desk, surely one of his many pieces of jewelry. What intrigued her was the sitar resting against the wall beside a stack of what she assumed were music scores.

As much as she enjoyed this window into his private life, Luxea shook herself out of her spell of curiosity. She sat next to the Prince and folded her legs under her; he didn't mind her feet on his cushions. Luxea mulled over how to begin but then spied cuts and bruises on his knuckles — ones that hadn't been there that morning.

"What happened to your hand?"

Ares was yet recovering from the rush of the incident. Until today, he hadn't recognized his fierce need to pummel the general's face.

"Skythoan," he said concisely.

Luxea's stars reddened, and those in Ares' Felastil reacted to her emotions by turning a similar hue. General Skythoan was one of her least favorite people. She and Avari had once joked daily about his narcissistic behavior and stocky body. *'Skythumb,'* they'd called him.

"Skythoan attacked you?"

A rascally glimmer showed in Ares' eyes. "No. He provoked me."

Putting it lightly, Luxea was elated to hear this. It was about time someone put the general in his place. Better yet that it had been Ares, the man who intimidated Skythoan the most.

"So," the Prince switched subjects, "did the Seer of Tzapodia have a reason to pay me a visit, or was she feeling friendly?"

"Actually, I'm here for that." She timidly flattened her skirt. "I'm wondering why you invited me to the council. It was . . . unexpected."

"Would you rather not be involved?"

"That's not it." Luxea tipped back her head, and Ares saw her throat wave as she swallowed. "I don't understand, nor do the other members. Ruri seems to be categorical with her opinions."

"I assume they were negative," said Ares peevishly.

"A little. It isn't often she shows her acceptance, is it?"

"Correct."

Luxea still didn't have the answers she needed. Quieter, she asked him, "Had you been planning on asking me to be a part of the council?"

The Prince shrugged. "No, but your role isn't one that can be filled by another. What made up my mind was our conversation about the King's Court. I put my trust in you, and if that trust holds in personal affairs, it will hold in those of a professional sort."

She took the chance to make a cunning remark. "You asked me to join your council because you like spilling your guts to me?"

A smile floated over Ares' lips, too transient for her to catch. "It would be a lie if I said I don't."

# SONG OF SOULS

## 27.SNOWHOWL.25.OSC.3
### CASTLE LAVRENTHEA, TZAPODIA

THE DAY after Luxea's initiation to the Mooncaller Council, Ares made an address. It was daunting even for someone who'd spent most of their life in the view of the public eye. He'd returned from the dead more than he liked to admit but had never done so in front of a whole country.

Three weeks after the broken heart of Tzapodia had healed, the figurative devil hanging on the Prince's shoulder let him go. The prospect would have been preposterous a moon before, but he was beginning to *enjoy* council meetings. Why? Because his newest member was an industrious powerhouse.

Luxea Siren showed up to the council room ahead of schedule every day, the Usinnon under one arm, a journal under the other. During conferences, her quill moved so fast that the conversation couldn't keep up with her. She noted each upcoming appointment, major and minor, jotted down new laws and proposals, and listed the names of contractors, politicians, and financial advisors. Ares paid more attention to her work ethic than the work itself.

Keeper Vessias soon came to worship Luxea. Before now, he'd been the only scholarly member of the council. That isn't to say that all brains around the table weren't impressive, but she was the perfect balance between pedagogic and frivolous. Between topics, the two cracked spacetime jokes or exchanged theories on parallel realities.

The enchantment Luxea placed on the ewer to fill everyone's wine glasses when they were empty was a welcome change, so the Spymaster too had loosened her judgmental chokehold — oh, but just by a little.

Apart from Luxea's new workload, she spent her free time with Avari and Brielle. They introduced Ruka to the best places to run and hunt. Brielle's favorite area was the desert. *'So much sand . . . where did it come from?'*

As Ares had promised over a month before, he provided Ruka with two fresh fenlaigs daily. The flesh was fatty, the meat was hearty, and the bones — what ideal toothpicks! But the wolf had gained so much weight that Brielle had to practically roll him out of the castle every day to exercise.

Additionally, Luxea reunited with Runa Faust, the ten-year-old courtesan whom the Mooncallers had rescued from Goldenrise. The little girl became a comet the first time she saw Luxea, rocketing into her savior's arms and proceeding to talk off her ear about her new life in Tel Ashir.

It was the weekend, so Ares and Luxea finally had the time to recover from however many meetings they'd endured over the past twenty-one days.

At noon, an urgent message arrived at the Amber Lounge from the infirmary. The scroll was from General Claymore. It was simply written, which wasn't unusual for him.

*"I'm a father."*

It wasn't often that Ares failed to hide smiles, but the joy was too overpowering. He read the letter out loud. Luxea gasped and shook Oliver, and Avari laughed, "The kid'll be a sword master by the time it's six moons old!"

"We should visit them," suggested Brielle. "I enjoy the sight of new life — pups more than human children, but I'll manage."

"Can we go, Ares?" begged Oliver. "I love babes. How are their hands so small? Don't make no sense."

"Probably because they're babies," snorted Avari.

The Mooncallers ventured down the stairs, leaving Ruka with Shir. Luxea peeked into the infirmary. It looked empty, but that was only due to the mob of sages gathered around a cot at the far end of the hall who squealed and swung flowers and gifts over their heads.

Close by, Luxea spotted Runa curled up with her mother. She was too precious in her black and white sage uniform; it suited her far better than the beaded chamise she'd been forced to wear in Haven de Asrodisia. Estalyn, however, had worsened. She was thinner, and her skin was sallow and blotchy with dark purple furuncles.

Luxea whistled. "Runa!"

The little girl sucked in an excited gasp and slid off the mattress. Estalyn nudged her along, promising she'd be fine without her. Runa jumped into Luxea's arms. "Luxea Siren! You're back!"

Runa peeked past her. Seeing Ares made her mouth drop. She'd met him before but had been told about him all her life; it was unusual for her to be around someone with such a mighty name.

"Um . . . do you want to see the baby? It's small!"

Impatient, Oliver asked, "How small?"

Runa made her hands into a shape like she was holding a loaf of bread. "This small. Come with me!"

The Mooncallers followed Runa as she dragged Luxea across the infirmary floor. Mother Mollah noticed her visitors and hobbled closer, fixing her buggy glasses. She promptly swatted Ares' waist.

"You'll come here to see a babe, but not an old woman?"

Ares pecked her wiry bun of hair. "I'll visit you more often."

"You'd better." Mollah patted his cheek and chuckled at his stubble. "Shave that off, won't ya? It doesn't suit you."

Oliver giggled at the idea of the Prince with a beard. Ares rubbed his jaw and frowned as Mollah moved on to greet Luxea.

"Goddesses be good. Every time I see those eyes, I feel a decade younger! Congratulations, Seer of Tzapodia. I always knew you were a special one."

"Thank you, Mother." Luxea embraced her gently.

Claymore kissed his wife and child on their heads and verged Ares. He was . . . *smiling?* The Prince was baffled. Everyone had always wondered if Claymore had emotions in there somewhere. All it had taken to rouse them was a baby.

Ares clasped hands with him. "How does it feel?"

The warmth of his child's wispy hair and chubby cheeks had soaked deep in the general's fingers; such a sensation would never leave him. His harsh, brown eyes glinted as he said, "It feels like I have two worlds to protect now."

If Ares were a father, he'd have said the same. "Put yours first."

Mother Mollah shooed away the sages. "Go on! I don't pay you to dawdle. You can see the little moppet later. Back to work!"

The crowd cleared. In bed lay Hanalea Moots-Urius, Claymore's wife. She was a sage herself but also the woman who'd jumped into Tal Am T'Navin River to save Luxea's life when her story in Tel Ashir began. Without Hanalea, she might have never been found.

The cot was swarmed again, this time by the Mooncallers. Avari and Oliver squeaked and whispered. Brielle, also born under the sign of Fenne the Wolf God, studied the baby from afar, deciding which traits of the wolf it had inherited. She smirked. This infant would grow up to be a fighter, a pack leader.

Luxea knelt beside Hanalea. Her child had brown hair the same shade as its father and freckles like its mother. It opened its giant, hazel eyes and made a spit bubble. It was drawn in by the starlight, so Luxea leaned closer and blinked.

"Is it a boy?" she asked softly.

Hanalea's cheeks flushed. "A girl. Kalo is her name."

"Hello, Kalo. Welcome to Tel Ashir," said Luxea adoringly.

Oliver scooted to the cot and, being awfully polite, asked, "Excuse me, Miss, can I hold her? I'm real good with kids."

Adjusting herself on her pillow, Hanalea said, "Yes, you may. Be sure to hold her head."

"I will, Miss."

Oliver cradled the child. Kalo waved her tiny hands and poked him in the eye. He frowned. He'd once had a daughter named Rosamie but had only met her once because her mother hadn't wanted him around. The first time he'd held her, she'd poked him in the eye — the same one as Kalo. Rosamie was gone now, killed at age five when the Isle of Varnn had been overrun by Widow's Brood. He pushed Rosamie out of his head and went on to make Kalo laugh.

Resting her chin on the mattress, Luxea said, "Hanalea, I never got to thank you for what you did that day at Tal Am T'Navin River."

Hanalea had a smile like the taste of gingerbread. "It wasn't me," she said lightly. "I swam after you, but Lali found you."

"Lali?"

"Yes. See that small one by the window? Hair in a mess." Hanalea motioned across the hall to a sage who looked like the byproduct of a man and a mouse. Scrawny, little eyes, big ears, a bit jumpy. "It was our day off, but our colleague wrote in sick. Mollah chose us to do her chores. You floated by Lali while she picked riverroot, but she was too scared of dead people to do a thing about it."

"And she works in an infirmary?" asked Luxea playfully.

"She's only here for the health benefits," whispered Hanalea. She rested her head, and her loving eyes scanned the Mooncallers. "Who would have thought that I'd bring a girl like you to Tel Ashir. Look at you now . . . the Seer of Tzapodia. You're Mollah's favorite, you know. When she catches us sages lazing, she asks, *'Did I tell you about my patient who worked for me because she wanted to?'*"

Luxea snickered. "All I did was slice bread and cheese. Speaking of which, do you need anything?"

"Well . . . I have wanted a sandwich."

"What kind? I'll make one for you."

"Anything with bread." Hanalea became florid. "Oh, but I would like glazed ham — lots of it. Perhaps a pinch of powdered sugar too?"

"Ham and sugar?" Luxea sucked her teeth. "Okay. I'll be back."

She hurried to the counter, and Runa bounced after her to help. Hanalea observed as the Seer taught the apprentice sage how to hold a knife while cutting bread.

After Brielle had her turn with Kalo, Claymore collected his child and brought her to Ares. The Prince's cheeks tickled him when he saw that Kalo had dimples too; he'd never liked his own until now.

"Would you like to carry her?" offered Claymore.

Ares nodded. The moment Kalo settled in his arms, he came to realize that he'd never held a baby. There was a life in his hands. She wasn't his own, but he would have done anything to guard her.

Kalo reached for Ares and gripped the silver cap on the end of his right horn. Her feet kicked happily inside her blanket. Ares smiled a few times, but each one looked more unsure.

"She likes dragons," said Claymore warmly.

*'Until she doesn't,'* thought Ares.

The baby nestled her head into the Prince's long hair and started to doze. As she became still, Ares panicked. Why wasn't she moving? Had he done something wrong, had he hurt her? He almost touched her with his talons but sooner stuffed his claw into his pocket.

Claymore sensed a change in the Prince. "She's only sleeping."

That statement made Ares feel much, much worse. Teeth clenched tight, he handed her back to her father. Claymore said nothing about the Prince's turbulence as he rocked his daughter and tucked her tiny hand into her wrap.

Ares left the infirmary straightaway.

It was dark. Everyone else had gone, but Luxea stayed in the infirmary to sit by the window with Runa and teach her about the constellations.

"See that one there? That's Novis, the One-Eyed Cat."

Runa touched the cold glass. "Why does it have one eye?"

Luxea had no idea why. "She's winking at us," she joked.

Runa thought this was silly. Together, they winked back at Novis.

Suddenly, a patient spiraled into a coughing fit. Runa jumped off the cot at once, but another sage had already taken to caring for the ailing. She sat down again, shoulders dangling.

Luxea's heartstrings were taut as she asked, "Is that your mother?"

"Yes." Runa trailed her big toe over a crack in the tile. "Mother Mollah says Mama's body can't fight anymore. Her blood forgot how to protect her, so she might . . ." She couldn't finish her sentence.

Estalyn Faust wheezed and coughed. The sage at her bedside wiped the blood from her shriveled lips and blotted her forehead. The last of her golden glow, as dim as it had been, was flickering out.

With her knobby knees tucked, Runa started to cry. Luxea wasn't sure what to tell her. She'd met death, but Ares and Oscerin had been there to stop it. That wasn't so for Estalyn. She hugged Runa as she curled up on her lap and shielded her eyes with her fists.

"I don't want to lose Mama."

Three days after the birth of Kalo Moots-Urius, Ares called those who lived in the Amber Lounge to his personal office. There'd been a luncheon scheduled with the Prime Minister of Avi Yeromin, but he'd canceled, so there was no better time to make plans for Goldenrise.

Luxea and Oliver had seen the Ruby Bureau, but Avari, Brielle and Ruka, and even Shir were awestruck. The Lavrenthea family was notorious for its love of exorbitant decor, but this had to be the most glamorous room in the castle. It was also one of the few places that wasn't themed by blue and silver; it was all scarlet, the diaphanous curtains, the jewels lining the cornices, even the leather of Ares' chair.

While it wasn't the treasury, mounds of coin spilled out of velvet bags and littered the spaces on Ares' desk that weren't covered by documents. The hanging gas lamps, fashioned by diamond patterns and mosaic glass, allowed one to see everything — except for the floor. The gold and black tesserae were hidden by tasseled rugs and cushions and government files.

"Please don't play with that, Ruka," sighed Ares.

The wolf, who'd been bumping the silver armillary sphere on the ceiling with his nose, tucked his tail and scampered to the window.

"Why're we here today?" asked Avari, plopping onto a cushion.

"To discuss our return to Goldenrise. The Empire is open to assault by the Brood, and, if we tarry, Widow may begin the winnowing before we redeem anyone," said Ares gravely.

"This wouldn't have happened if you'd told us the truth from the start, Dragon," said Brielle grudgingly.

Overlooking the rider's passive-aggression, Ares unrolled a map and went on with planning. "As with our last journey to Solissium, we'll ride to the Storm Plains through Selnilar. But we'll need to delay. Luxea and I owe much to Shir and the Mythics, so we'll enter the Crystal Spire en route to replant their kind."

"That sounds like a real bad idea," gulped Oliver.

"We'd have to cut through Lor'thanin, wouldn't we? I don't know about you folks, but I'm not itching to go back," added Avari.

Shir petted the crystals of their lost family members through the suede pouch on the table. "There is no need, for I was born from the womb of the Spire. We will not pass beyond the walls of man but through the veins of the earth. Sirah will lead us."

"Thank you, Shir, that will be very helpful." Ares turned back to the map of L'arneth. "Once the shards of the *Sil'simani* are in place, we'll continue north. Brielle and Ruka, I'll need you two to navigate through the Western Woods."

"We will meet no impasses," said Brielle confidently.

"Good. Once we reach Dundis Angle in the Storm Plains, we'll seek out Peyamo and her men. The elves of Tarot will assist us with the evacuation of Solissium." He poked a silver pin into the map. "Before the incident on the airship, Peyamo briefed me on her locomotive project. Her station should be under construction roughly here, so we will meet her and —"

Three knocks, and the bureau door opened. Through the gap came a castle keeper. Typically, they required something from the Prince, but this one paid no attention to him. His round, blue eyes couldn't identify who he'd been sent to collect, so he flipped his tablet and read the title of the addressee.

"Luxea Siren?" He mispronounced her name.

"That's me, but the *'x'* is said as *'sh,'*" Luxea told him.

"Oh, Seer! I'm truly sorry." The keeper saluted her. "Your presence is required in the infirmary — with urgency."

Luxea started from her chair. "Runa? Ares, I'm sorry. I have to go. Estalyn might be gone soon. I can't leave Runa alone."

"Her mum? What'll happen to Runa?" muttered Oliver.

Ares nibbled his lip under his palm. This was sudden. "If Estalyn passes, Runa can stay with us in the Amber Lounge. I'll assign a *maolam* to care for her while we're in Goldenrise."

"I'll take her in after that. Thank you." Luxea ran past the keeper.

Shir rang lowly. Ruka glanced at them and lifted his head from his paws. The Mythic's skin crackled, and then they vanished.

Before Luxea reached the stairwell, Shir locus-jumped to her side and tailed her down the steps. "Why is Estalyn dying?"

"She's sick, Shir," said Luxea breathlessly. "She's been unwell for a long time, but she's all Runa has. I worry for her."

Shir's crown glimmered. "May I make a suggestion?"

The infirmary was deathlike. Estalyn's wheezing had weakened to slow rasps, and she couldn't keep her eyes open long enough to look at her daughter. This was it. Estalyn knew — and worse, Runa knew.

When Luxea and Shir entered, the sages in the hall dropped their bloody rags and herb pouches; one even broke a teacup. This crystal thing had legs, arms, and a head but no reproductive organs or flesh. It countered all they'd studied. Even Mother Mollah, Tzapodia's medical doyen, was baffled by the Mythic's anatomy.

Runa hiccuped. "Luxea Siren?"

Luxea knelt beside her. "I'm here."

Estalyn was falling fast; her mouth was dangling open, and her lips were blue. Luxea glanced at Shir and said, "I brought a friend, Runa. This is Shir. May they meet your mother?"

With tears dripping from her chin, Runa stared at Shir. She'd never seen anything so pristine. Even their proximity made her legs weak, and the hairs on her arms reach upward. It was an outlandish feeling, but her heart told her there was nothing to fear.

Shir honed in on Runa's hand as it twisted around Estalyn's. They smiled and said to her, "Let go."

Naturally, Runa was resistant to releasing her mother, but Luxea urged her to have faith in the Mythic. The way her stars twinkled, it said, *'This will change it all.'*

Runa unlaced her fingers from Estalyn's and crawled to Luxea.

The Mythic read Estalyn's colors. Within her were lights — red spots of inflammation, purple weakening joints, and blue failing lungs. The pain was everywhere.

Shir had never healed anyone on their own, but they had to try. They sat cross-legged on the floor, closed their eyes, and rang. The Mythic's voice brought one sage to tears, for it wasn't just noise, it was the song of souls.

In Estalyn's mind was a soft, heavenly voice, saying, *"Not yet."*

Shir extended their hand and placed two fingers on Estalyn's chest. Veins of light branched from their fingertips and soaked into her skin. The warmth returned to Estalyn's hands and face, and her expression changed; she was doe-eyed and stirred like she'd been startled awake.

Concurrently, Luxea saw Shir's crown changing. Where once had been pure white appeared a gaseous, greenish brown. It was working, Estalyn was recovering, but Shir's head was dipping as if they were falling asleep. What worried Luxea was that Mythics never slept.

Shir was weakening.

Luxea rushed around the side of the cot and tried to touch Shir. Their eyes opened at once. They weren't wrathful, it wasn't possible for Shir to feel such an emotion, but they were averse to contact.

"Stay back."

"You're killing yourself, Shir!" whimpered Luxea.

"It will not hurt me," whispered Shir.

The Mythic removed their hand, and the veins receded from Estalyn's skin. Yes, Shir had lost some vitality, but it would renew. Their crown wasn't bright, but their smile was. They'd done it.

While Estalyn blinked at the many faces standing around the infirmary, Shir asked her, "Is that better?"

Unsure, Estalyn nodded. Her pupils contracted.

She *nodded* — and it didn't hurt?

Her spine didn't ache, her brain was no longer tight with pressure. Gooseflesh appeared on her arms which were now clear of spots and bruises. She raised her hands as if they were priceless gifts. It had been years since she'd been able to move her fingers. She peeled the blankets away, and the fabric stuck to her skin where once had been bedsores.

By habit, Runa tried to help her stand. "No, Baby," said Estalyn.

Released from her agony, she rose. Her legs wobbled but didn't creak and grind. She took a deep, deep breath. No coughing; there wasn't even a tickle in her throat. She was standing and inhaling and exhaling, her eyes held life, not death, and, although they were gaunt, her cheeks were rosy.

Knees bent, skin stretching around her bones, Estalyn hooked her arms under Runa's. It was challenging and would remain so until she regained her muscles, but for the first time since Runa was a toddler, she lifted her up.

Runa's mouth opened wide. She threw her arms around her mother's neck and said, "Mama!"

Estalyn's eyelids shut tight as she cradled her baby's head.

At the end of the cot, Shir said to Luxea, "She will live for many years."

# HAPPY LIFEDAY
## 4.LIGHTSMEET.25.OSC.3
### THE AMBER LOUNGE, CASTLE LAVRENTHEA

THE NEW year began. Luxea was nescient of her date of birth other than supposedly being under the sign of Wynd the Stag, so the Mooncallers chose the fourth of Lightsmeet to celebrate her lifeday. It was a small affair in the Amber Lounge with cheese for Avari, fenlaig for Ruka, and wine for the rest.

It felt like any other day except Runa and Estalyn were present. Runa chose to wear a yellow silk dress for Luxea's lifeday; she wanted to look like a princess, and she did. Ares had said that Runa could live in the castle upon her mother's passing, but he'd given them the room between Luxea's and his own regardless that she'd been healed.

As Ruka rolled around behind the sofa, the Mooncallers drank and ate in honor of Luxea's life — however old she was. Oliver, who typically let loose with the snacks and the spirits, consumed them sparingly today. He was having too much fun giving Runa piggyback rides.

"Ready? Here we go, pretty stuff!"

He sprinted down the hall with the little girl clinging to his shoulders. Estalyn, who'd gained weight and proven to be the most breathtaking woman in Tzapodia, laughed as her daughter's peachy blonde hair flew around the corner. Minutes later, Oliver came back, out of breath, and set Runa on the sofa between Luxea and her mother.

Shir was staring at them, brighter now that they'd recovered their strength. Estalyn met their gaze, and her golden curls shone as she leaned in toward Runa.

"Do you want to give it to them now?"

Runa's eyes darted to Shir too. "Okay."

Estalyn reached around the side of the sofa and handed her daughter a parcel swathed in tattered cloth; it was the best sort of wrapping they could find. Runa hopped over Luxea and Ares' feet to Shir, who was taller than her sitting down. Red as a radish, she handed them the gift.

"What is it?" asked Shir curiously.

Luxea chortled. "It's a surprise, Shir. You open it."

The Mythic was still learning human customs. They unfolded the linen with all care. Within was a wreath of peonies tied off with string. Shir didn't have a heart, but if they did, it would have burst. They'd never received a gift.

"Flowers . . . they are splendid."

Runa giggled and scooped up the flower crown from the cloth. "It goes on your head. Let me?" The Mythic bent their neck. Runa set it atop their crest.

Shir touched the blossoms. "You made this yourself. Thank you."

Nodding, Runa scampered back to her mother. For minutes longer, Shir ran their fingers over the soft petals.

119

On the sofa, Estalyn told Runa she'd done an excellent job. Runa hummed joyously, but then she sulked. "Luxea Siren, I wish you didn't have to leave. I'll miss you."

"We won't be gone for long," assured Luxea.

"Miss Siren, why are you returning to Solissium?" wondered Estalyn. "It has only been several moons since last you were there."

Luxea passed a glance to Ares — along with the responsibility of answering the question. He was more diplomatic and less prone to stumbling on his words.

"The Empress has endangered the empire. The Six is at fault as well, myself included." Keeping his guilt a secret was painstakingly difficult, but it was made easier by the smile Luxea offered him. "If we don't act, the people will face unmerited fates. We'll go back to prevent it while we can."

Without him mentioning a name, Estalyn knew that Widow was behind the threats in Goldenrise. She kept her lips sealed for the sake of her daughter. "Your devotion to the safety of others is refreshing, Your Highness. We all make mistakes, but what sets apart a hero from a fool is the ability to learn from them."

Estalyn then noticed that Runa was frequently glancing at the Prince; she wanted to talk to him but was too afraid. "Would you like to say hello?" she asked lightly.

Runa nodded briskly.

Luxea beckoned Ares. He extended the hollow of his shoulder to receive her whisper. "She's nervous. Will you say something to her?"

The Prince peeked at Runa who looked like she was about to pop into a shower of confetti. As if he were addressing a colleague, he set down his wineglass and straightened his posture.

"Hi, Runa."

Her eyes swelled. "You know my name?"

"I do. Luxea told me that day in Solissium. You hugged me, remember?" Runa's cheeks exploded with redness. How could she ever forget? Ares had trouble concealing his smile. "Do you like living in Tel Ashir, in the castle?"

Runa fumbled with the chiffon on her dress. "Yes, Your Highness. It's warm here, and the people are nice. Mother Mollah took me to the Sapphire Bazaar in Snowhowl to buy petals for tea. It was pretty."

"I've never been to the Sapphire Bazaar. I wasn't allowed to go outside when I was your age," said Ares truthfully.

At last, Runa faced him. "Never? But you're a grown-up."

"I am, but it isn't easy for me to go places like that. I have too much work to do, and it makes people anxious." Ares' eyes found the stars. "But Luxea has shared with me a few stories about the bazaar."

It was a miracle. Runa laughed! "When she blew up the apples?"

"I wonder what else she's blown up," purred Ares.

The little girl's grin widened. "Sugar melons?"

Luxea started to look abashed, and Ares loved it. In a whisper, he asked, "Shall we find her a lifeday pastry to detonate?"

Little by little, Runa opened up to the Prince. Eventually, he and Shir took her to the Ruby Bureau to show her the armillary sphere. She never looked him in the eye but held onto the tail of his coat all the way down the hall.

When they were gone, Estalyn moved closer to Luxea.

"Don't mind Runa's moodiness. It confuses her to interact with men who don't want her as she's used to being wanted, and she began her redrise shortly after we arrived in Tzapodia." She took a breath.

"I'm thankful she no longer works for Haven de Asrodisia. Had it come any earlier, I'd have been a grandmother within a year."

"Runa is a tough girl, but it's natural for her to feel imbalanced now," said Luxea mildly. "I can't remember when my redrise started, but I do know that it hasn't gotten any easier."

Estalyn laughed. "I've heard it doesn't until it's gone. You and I have many years left to suffer well." In a tone much less pleasant, she said, "Forgive me for reviving the topic of Solissium, but I assume Empress Annalais has dealings with the Widow?"

"That's right," said Luxea spitefully.

"What a harebrained woman," snapped Estalyn. "Annalais doesn't care for her people in the way she should. This would never have happened with Emperor Rowan. Goddesses, bless him."

This wasn't the first time Luxea had heard the name of Annalais's brother and the previous Emperor of Goldenrise, Rowan Taress. She'd once crossed a headless statue inside Haven de Asrodisia with his name on a plaque. It hadn't been easy to read, for it had been scratched to near illegibility. All Luxea had gathered was that he'd died in year 18.

"What happened to Emperor Rowan?"

Estalyn held her own hand, wishing it were someone else's. "I've heard many stories — all of them suggesting that he took his own life. To me, no, to all of us, he was indestructible. The sort of person you expected to live forever, to always be there. His only enemy was hidden within him all along. Had I known he was suffering, I would have reached out."

"You were acquainted with the Emperor?"

"Acquainted?" Estalyn blinded Luxea with a smile. "I was more than *acquainted* with Rowan, Miss Siren, I was his favorite guilty pleasure. After a trying day, an argument with his sister, or even a sleepless night, he would come to me. Sometimes to use my body, sometimes merely to be held. And . . . I loved him.

"It was on a morning in year 15 that I knew he would never leave my heart. He kissed me, nothing else, and asked, *'Do you see?'* I can't tell you why I fell for him then . . . but he was the Emperor of Goldenrise, and I was a bed-cat. It couldn't be."

"If you love someone, titles don't matter," encouraged Luxea.

Estalyn smiled strangely. "Perhaps."

"What was Rowan like?" asked Luxea next.

"In public, he was confident. He would take control and cut down his enemies when he needed to." Estalyn rubbed her willowy hands up and down her arms. "When you had him alone, he was someone else. Tender, the greatest lover. But his silence is what I cannot forget. One look said a thousand words, one sigh, a thousand more. I never translated what went unspoken all those years. It's likely he'd pleaded for my help, but I wasn't listening."

"Whatever Rowan's reason was for leaving this world, it isn't your fault." Luxea's brows joined. "You worked at Heart of Haven back then? So long ago?"

"No, no," said Estalyn quickly. "I stayed in a brothel in uptown Solissium. The Emperor rode to see me every night until year 17 when he asked me to relocate to a den at Villa de Taress so he could have me whenever he wanted. I've never been so flattered, I tell you. He didn't even change his mind when I told him about my daughter. Runa was only three years old and needed support, so I accepted. I brought my baby and went to the villa. In two moons . . . Rowan was gone.

"Annalais's coronation took place on the same day as his memorial service. It was such an impertinent action, but no one

123

stopped her. She was too beautiful, too powerful to deny. It only worsened after that. Annalais's headmasters clapped me into shackles and stole my freedom. When Runa was nine, they imprisoned her too." Grateful, she touched Luxea's hand. "And then, one year later, you and your friends rescued us."

By early evening, Luxea retreated to her bedchamber to study. She didn't mind being alone on her lifeday — assuming it *was* her lifeday. Besides, she had the Usinnon to keep her company.

As she copied recipes for magick elixirs from her spellbook to her notebook, there came a knock on the door. She tossed her quill and bounced off the bed.

Ares was in the hall with a sort of *'let me in'* expression. He and Luxea seemed to be visiting each other's chambers frequently lately — if once each could be considered frequent. She allowed him in, leaving the door open, but Ares shut it promptly.

"To what do I owe the pleasure?" she asked, flopping onto her bed.

The Prince cleared his throat a few more times than was necessary. Was he . . . nervous? The idea seemed impossible to Luxea.

He unclasped his hands from behind his back. In his right was a package wrapped in paper that had been painted like the stars. Luxea just stared at it, so he readjusted his fingers and urged it toward her. Sparing him from the suffering of patience, she took it. She'd almost expected him to run out of the damned room, but he stayed.

"I didn't take you as the lifeday gift type," she said snidely.

"I'm not." Ares crossed his arms. "Open it, so I can leave."

"You're that eager?" laughed Luxea.

He barely smiled but kept his eyes low. She folded her legs and started to unwrap. It wasn't packaged well. When he'd given her the

Usinnon, that hadn't been stunning either. Amidst however many hundreds of lessons the Prince had taken in his lifetime, gifting must not have been one of them.

Within the last fold was a journal bound in black leather. It wasn't new or made to write down thoughts; this was something she recognized. She cracked open the cover where inside were pages and pages of hand-drawn diagrams of the solar system.

When they'd been trapped in Witchsleep, Ares had shared with Luxea a journal, taught her about the constellations, and told her about his childhood. This was that same journal. Under each dot, his thick, dark penmanship labeled the planets and stars.

Ares rolled his neck as Luxea absorbed his years of work. The journal was entirely filled, but the last page, what he'd been waiting for, kicked her right in the tear ducts.

This one wasn't a map; it showed trees, branches, and clouds circling the zenith of the night. In that negative space was the view of the sky from the meadow on Mythos. Ares' must have had a photographic memory, for there wasn't a single star out of line.

"Mythos," said Luxea, but it was more of a sob than a statement.

The Prince hadn't intended for her to cry. Gifts were meant to bring joy, not tears. He worried that he'd upset her until she sprang off the mattress and hugged him so tightly that he had to wonder if she really *did* have muscles in those lazy arms of hers.

"Thank you so much. I really love it."

If this was the result of giving gifts, maybe Ares would do it more often. It wasn't so bad.

He rested his chin on her head and said, "Happy lifeday."

# Grove Wanderer

## 9.Lightsmeet.26.Osc.3
### The Amber Wing, Castle Lavrenthea

The Mooncallers would leave for Sirah in the evening. This time, Luxea thought better than to pack her entire collection of mystery and romance novels and opted instead to spend time with the Usinnon alone.

*"Hashisishi . . . ?"* asked the spellbook as she hooked it to her belt.

"What? Do you want to ride in the bag?"

*"Haishi . . ."* The Usinnon twinkled.

"It is rather warm today. All right." Luxea kissed its white gold cover and plopped it into her satchel.

Oliver was seated on the floor, deciding what to bring. He didn't have much except for clothes, cloaks, and one weapon — a tiny knife.

"Avari?" he called out.

"Whatcha need?" She had a turkey sandwich in her hand.

"Does this knife got a name?" he asked, turning over the blade. "Givin' a weapon a name makes it special, donnit?"

"If you've only got one." Avari clamped her sandwich in her mouth and revealed the near-hundred knives in her bag. "When you've got an arsenal like me, naming 'em all is a waste of time."

Oliver gulped. "Blissits. Since this knife's mine, am I allowed to give it a name? It's just this one."

Avari finished her sandwich. "Why're you asking me? Go ahead."

The blade was no duller than it had been the day Avari gave it to him in Nav Amani Forest; he'd only used once before on a giant serpent in Blackjaw Hollow. He hadn't noticed how small it actually was until he held it up to his pelvis for comparison. It was about an inch shorter. He simpered and sheathed it.

"I think I'll call 'im *'Chops.'*"

Avari guffawed. "Really?"

"What? S'not good 'nough?" Oliver's attention switched to Ares as he worked a scabbard onto his belt. "Oi, Ares, does your sword got a name?"

The Prince nodded and proceeded to get ready.

"Well, what is it?" pressed Oliver.

"Sindred, Tail of Samsamet," said Ares tersely.

Oliver's eyes bugged. "How'd you come up widdat?"

"I didn't." Ares unsheathed the shamshir and twirled it twice. "In draconic, *'sindred'* means *'consequence.'* This sword was forged from the bones of the last dragon, Samsamet — a sliver of her sacrum." He brushed his finger down the fuller. "The blade was passed down from the first king to each subsequent. When a cursed child of Samsamet turns, the blade is reforged, and a scale from their hide is added to the grip."

Ares' eyes danced down the layers of multicolored scales and lingered on one beneath the pommel — gold. He sheathed the weapon with some aggression. "Two haven't been included: the last king and my own. Only then will the blade be complete, and we will have faced our consequences."

The weapon on Oliver's hip felt even *smaller* now, for it was no secret that Ares' was more admirable. "I'll think on its name."

Brielle sat outside the corral with Ruka as her comrades prepared their dracas. Silly saddle-users. Bareback was preferable and much less taxing.

Oliver had to be reunited with his dracas, Musha, which was unpleasant due to their hatred for each other. Oliver would have rather dipped his legs into a volcano than ridden that scowling thing again.

Although Avari had spent a decade training the dracas for the Tzapodian army, she was nowhere near the stables today. That was because Ares' dracas, Pveather — also known as *'finger-snapper'* — was present. That pale devil terrified Avari, so, to saddle up in peace, she led her scaly companion, Elthevir, to the Kingslane.

Conversely, Ares was delighted to be with Pveather. At age fourteen, he'd gone with his riding trainer to see the Kingsreign hatchlings. Each was unique, but a white one with red eyes stood out. She'd claimed the pen as her own the moment she came out of her egg. She was a leader. Ares' trainer warned him she was an angry girl, but the Prince wanted Pveather or nothing at all.

He ran his fingers down the spines on her neck and kissed her snout. *"Zami thois tuer valathes?"* he asked; *'have you been good?'*

Pveather trampled in circles, showing her master what a perfectly good lizard she'd been. Close by, Luxea untied her blue-grey dracas, Velesari, with a sour face. Pveather was the least bit *'good'* you could get! Yet Ares groomed her without losing a hand. How?

"You have her so calm," she said, scooting barely closer.

Cranberry eyes targeted her. Pveather galloped forth with her needled fangs snapping. Luxea ducked behind a trough and prayed for a peaceful transition into the afterlife.

Ares tugged the reigns hard. "Pveather, *dosu teille!*"

The queenly dracas whistled and slunk away. Luxea's white hair sprouted up beside an orange dracas who was munching on spring greens. Ares looked apologetic as he kept Pveather still.

"Don't mind her. She's always been hot-headed."

"Like someone else I know," she hinted. "I used to clean her stall every week — well, Avari tricked me into cleaning her stall. I've been crunched at a time or two, spat on even more. Anytime I talk to her, she attacks."

Ares glared at Pveather as she stalked around, her silver saddle and beaded trappings glistering in the dimming sunlight. "What language have you been using with her?"

"L'arian or seroden elvish, of course," said Luxea casually. "Those are the tongues we use with all of the dracas."

"I see." Ares beckoned her with a nod. "Come with me."

Albeit reluctant, Luxea followed him. Pveather snorted and scraped her claws in the dirt, ready to charge. Luxea spared herself by hiding behind Ares.

"No, no." He nudged her forth. "Go and tell her, *'Iu lemi thois.'*"

"Do you wish me to be headless?"

"You'll be fine." He faced her. "Say it with me. *'Iu lemi thois.'*"

Luxea grimaced. *"Iu lemi thois?"*

Ares started smiling. "Perfect. Don't be afraid of her. She'll be accepting of you now. Trust me."

Positive that Ares really *was* trying to kill her, she took a nervous step toward Pveather. The dracas coughed fluid on the dirt, and her spines shuddered.

*"Iu lemi thois,"* said Luxea breathily.

Pveather snorted but didn't attack.

"Again," urged Ares.

Inching hardly closer, Luxea repeated, *"Iu lemi thois."*

Then the unthinkable happened. Pveather flopped onto her back, bopped her snout into Luxea's ankles, and swished her scythe-shaped tail. She didn't want to dismember Luxea, she wanted to play with her.

Ares squatted and tickled Pveather's chin. "She hasn't listened to you because I raised her to respond to draconic."

Luxea grazed her fingers over Pveather's neck; she was colder than the other dracas because her white scales reflected, not absorbed. Pveather whistled, and her long tongue slipped past her teeth and curled around Luxea's wrist.

"What did I say to her?" she wondered.

Ares laughed when Pveather shook dust on them both.

"Something she liked."

The Mooncallers rode north. Avari, Oliver, and Brielle and Ruka were fearful of crossing enemies from the Brood; however, Ares, Luxea, and Shir weren't as afraid after having faced Widow Herself.

The sandy trails of Nav Amani Forest from Tel Ashir to Lor'thanin were pocked with reptilian footprints. To hide their tracks, Shir frequently rearranged the soil. It was rather fun for the Mythic; the forest suited them better than the castle. Every once in a while, Ruka bolted off the path with Brielle on his back to play in mud puddles.

Their plan went smoothly. They were unseen, unheard, and undetected, but only until the morning. As the Tehrastar rose, and the slate night sky lightened to velvety grey, Brielle and Ruka jolted. Shir had stopped a while back, sensing the same evil as the wolf twins.

"Enemies ahead. Less than half a reach," whispered Brielle.

Ares slowed Pveather. "How many are there?"

"I cannot see them," said Brielle timidly.

Shir stared into the woods. "Seven." The Mooncallers expected to have to reroute until the Mythic added, "Ah, but a friend is here too."

"A . . . friend?" muttered Avari.

The Mythic strode forth and placed their hand on a tree. In an immediate response, three others in the grove moaned. Four trunks tore out of the ground and stomped closer.

*Feet?*

The canopy cracked, and the leaves rustled as a skinny, wooden neck crashed down through the branches and bent around the clearing. At the end was a face with twiggy antennae, twitching and sensing. The beast was tall and treen with knots for eyes and roots for teeth. It opened its mouth, one protuberant and wide like a frog's, and fluffy, yellow spores fluttered out of its throat. If any living thing fit the description of *'woodland creature,'* it was this.

"What is that?" gulped Luxea.

Through his awe, Ares said, "A grove wanderer. I thought they'd gone extinct centuries ago. They're photosynthetic creatures, feeders of the nutrients from the daylight and the ground."

"Unbelievable." Brielle slid off Ruka's back and approached the grove wanderer with her palms upright. Its branches twisted. "All my life in this forest, and we've never crossed trails. Hello, my friend."

The grove wanderer creaked. A fuzzy leaf, the length of Brielle's arm, rolled out of its mouth and lapped sap over her swarthy skin. Brielle's amber eyes twinkled at the creature.

"Will you help us, grove wanderer?"

"It cannot hear you, Brielle. Nature's tongue is unspeakable by humankind," said Shir sweetly. "Do not worry. I will ask it to hide us."

When the Mythic rang, they became the grove wanderer's master; long had the trees lived, but the earth had lived longer. Its tubular neck squeaked as it raised its head and tree trunk legs to step over the Mooncallers. They huddled under its belly. Blotches of viridian swelled on the grove wanderer's flanks as sheets of foliage grew, and moss trickled down its wooded flesh, dense enough for the Mooncallers to be concealed from the outside world.

"Come. We will not be seen," whispered Shir.

With the Mooncallers beneath it, the grove wanderer trundled onward. For its size, its footsteps were astonishingly quiet. The dracas and Ruka trotted in the shadow at the same speed as their guardian. In half an hour, they came to a stream that ran along the outer edge of the Crystal Spire —

But they weren't alone.

A troop from the Brood was patrolling Lor'thanin's border, seven men in helmets that resembled the heads and thoraxes of various insects. They followed a dusty path on the backs of what couldn't be distinguished from a spider, a centipede, and a man. They were grotesque; Luxea briefly thought she was going to show everyone her breakfast.

Giant, childlike heads swooped from the chimeras' necks. Their mouths were open, drooling, and rowed with crooked teeth. They slunk closer, their bodies undulating on a thousand fleshy legs, all of which were torn at the bottoms to make way for the tarsus and metatarsus.

The grove wanderer didn't panic. It burrowed its head into the dirt, its legs went still, and its leaves faded to cobalt to blend in with those of Nav Amani Forest. The Mooncallers shrank low to their dracas' saddles, Brielle to Ruka's back. The Brood soldiers rode by what they assumed was a copse until there came an unlucky gust of wind.

The beasts halted, burping and croaking. They sniffed through their misshapen human noses, but the stench of intruders was well masked by the grove wanderer's pheromones. The breeze passed, and the scent was lost. The heads coughed and skittered over a knoll into a ravine.

When the way was clear, the grove wanderer uprooted its legs and proceeded. In five minutes, the Mooncallers arrived safely at the wall of Sirah.

Looking up the height of the Crystal Spire would have made anyone vertiginous. At a perfectly vertical angle, it broke the clouds overhead and pierced the sky that never ended. Within the segments of rutilated quartz were golden hairs, glimmering in the faintness of the sunrise. Woven between the strands came giant spears and circular flares of aura quartz — aqua, indigo, and opal.

The Mooncallers stabled their dracas in a wet grotto covered by vines where the pool within would provide them with water, and the moss would sate their hunger; after all, their masters would only be away for a few days.

Shir faced the grove wanderer and rang to it in thanks. The Mooncallers turned toward Sirah, but then the grove wanderer spat wood chips and lowered its head in front of Luxea; it didn't want her to leave just yet. Luxea scooted back as purple leaves with feathery tips bloomed from its snout.

"It is nature's mark. Accept it," whispered Shir.

Luxea wasn't sure how to react. She'd never encountered such a creature; maybe it wasn't carnivorous, but it could still bite. As the grove wanderer blinked its knotted eyes, she plucked a leaf and twirled the stem between her thumb and forefinger.

It was a blackwood leaf.

How had the grove wanderer known? Had Shir mentioned her memory of the Shadow in the blackwood tree?

It unsettled her, but she pretended to like it. The other foliage rotted away and fluttered to the dirt. The grove wanderer groaned as it maneuvered back into the forest, and Luxea put its gift in her pocket.

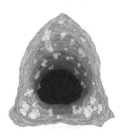

# TOMB OF VASNA LORREEN

### 10.LIGHTSMEET.26.OSC.3
### SIRAH THE CRYSTAL SPIRE, SELNILAR

OLIVER SLID down his hood. "How're we gettin' in the Spire?"

"Sirah will let us in," said Shir unambiguously.

Just as they'd done to Estalyn, the Mythic placed two fingers upon the spire. Veins spread as they sang a hymn, crystal to crystal, and, in the same haunting melody, Sirah sang back. Chimes rode the air and swirled around the Mooncallers on a breeze that hadn't been there a minute ago.

The Crystal Spire crackled. A rift in the surface arched from the ground, widening and crumbling into a tunnel, coated with minerals; the stone from which they grew was dark but somehow glinting.

Wordless, Shir entered. The Mooncallers cautiously followed.

The crystal fused shut behind them, and Luxea's frightened squeak echoed three times down the passageway. But then the shadow vanished, and rings of white and pink light appeared around their feet in reaction to the contact of their soles. Avari ran her hand along the wall, and five rainbows followed her fingertips beneath the crystal.

The seven walked for a long time, Shir leading them, Sirah leading Shir. Within an hour, the walls thinned. Through them could be seen the interior of Sirah Temple where the Light Seeker Val'noren Paah had gathered Widow's forces — where Luxea and Avari had first been exposed to the horrors of the Brood. They clung to each other, and Luxea petted Avari's curly hair, ignoring the images of her first deaths that her head wouldn't stop evoking.

Rippling through the stone were shapes of sawtoothed weapons, helmeted soldiers, and broken down cages. Black, gangling crawlers amassed in corners of the ceiling like bats, and titantulas lugged globs of flesh and bone. There weren't any corpses, for they'd been destroyed, reformed into Brood chimeras, or blended into chowders for the army.

Luxea put her fist to her mouth; here comes her breakfast again.

Farther down came a room that Ares recognized: the Shrine of *Luciem Salah*. As a member of The Six, the Prince had visited Val'noren Paah at the shrine numerous times — back when the Light Seeker hadn't added genocide to his impressive list of conquests. The place didn't bother Ares now except for the fact that it was occupied.

Within sat a felenoe man with black hair and a wiry tail. He was Tani Renayo, the Tree Warden of the nation of Drenut. Across the room, drifting about with his luxuriant, white hair in a braid, was the Light Seeker Val'noren Paah. He was no less than one hundred years old but didn't look a day over thirty; so goes the pure blood of l'arian elves.

As both Val'noren and Tani were Widow's servants, Ares couldn't dissuade himself from eavesdropping. "Go on. I'll come back to you soon," he said to his companions.

Luxea crept to his side. "I'm staying with you."

Ares almost protested, but having her close made him realize that he'd been anxious to be alone. The other Mooncallers proceeded down the passage. Brielle's lamplight stare switched between them and Val'noren, and then she wished them safety before leaving.

The voices were muted by the crystal, but Ares and Luxea could make out the conversation between Val'noren and Tani if they held their breaths.

"*. . . the Widow to control the Storm Goddess. Sh'tarr has fought, but She will be broken in due time.*" Val'noren's voice was as baritone and bittersweet as Luxea remembered it.

"*Alatos has been sighted in the Curve of Yayun and Strait of Many Eyes, searching for Her Sister of the Storm. I almost pity Her, don't you, Light Seeker?*" asked Tani, his felenoe accent heavy.

"*The Sisters of Storm and Sea will not be apart for long, Tani.*" Val'noren simpered. "*Sh'tarr is with the Brood Mother where soon Alatos will be too. Once Widow has learned to weaponize the Storm, we will move forward to leech the power of the Sea.*"

"*And what is our first course of action with Sh'tarr?*"

"*The Widow will cross the Great Bridge to Anunaru, and . . .*"

Eager to find out, Luxea pressed her ear to the crystal. In a ring, white light swelled around her; she'd forgotten that contact with the walls activated light! Ares tugged her back, but the illumination had already caught the Light Seeker's attention. Why had Val'noren lost his compassion but not his sharp senses?

The Selnilar leader slunk to their hiding place until his face was mere feet away. He was a beautiful man, androgynous and lean; his jaw was pointed and smooth, and his eyebrows were white dashes above his lively, pink eyes. Through the crystal, his stare met those of

Ares and Luxea's several times. He couldn't see them, but the wavelets of light lingered. He lifted his graceful hand and tapped his fingernails on the stone. The twisted smile that appeared then could have frozen rain.

*"Watchers in the wall,"* said Val'noren.

The train of the Light Seeker's silver raiment sailed around his feet as he rushed out of the shrine to gather his forces. Tani scrambled out of his chair, tail bristling, and bounded after him.

Ares wrested Luxea off the ground. "Run!"

Sirah sealed the way behind them as they sprinted. Luxea's heart was slamming against her ribs. "I'm sorry, Ares, I didn't mean to —"

"I know you didn't," panted Ares. "But my bigger fear is what Val'noren and Tani were discussing. Widow wishes to use Sh'tarr as a weapon . . ."

"And if Widow gained control of the Sea Goddess, we wouldn't have a chance." Luxea felt a pang of guilt. "Poor Alatos. We can't let this happen."

The tunnel ended with a cavernous room full of human shapes and a barricade of stone where the other Mooncallers awaited. But this crystal was different from the rest, not polished or carved; it was choppy with arms, legs, and the backs of skulls crowding it; while some bodies had been preserved within the stone, others had been exposed to the elements, and their bones had fallen apart.

Luxea clung to the Usinnon. The arcanan tattoo on her neck, her Magelas, stung her like the day she'd been branded. She knew where they were; Ares had taught her about it a year ago.

"This is the Tomb of Vasna Lorreen, isn't it?"

The Prince nodded vacantly.

Vasna Lorreen had been the Light Seeker of Selnilar in mid-Era Two who'd led the l'arian army, the *Leitha'maen,* into the Crystal Spire to exterminate the sorcerers within Sirah Academy. But when they'd marched forth, Sirah had come to life and swallowed them in the crystal to protect the secrets of magick. Here they stood, precisely as they had for centuries.

Half of the magick population had been stamped out that day; the rest were left inside to perish without food or sunlight. Only the sorcerers who'd managed to hide outside of the academy before the eradication lived to pass on their traits to their children.

Luxea was one of those few descendants.

Down the hundreds of steps outside the Tomb of Vasna Lorreen were clattering armors and hostile shouts. The Brood's soldiers had uncovered their location. Luxea felt Ares' fingers tighten around hers. Neither had realized they'd been holding hands. They let go.

Ares slid Sindred from its scabbard and sidestepped past the Mooncallers and crystalline bodies. "We need to move! Go, *go!*"

From the look of it, the entryway to Sirah Academy hadn't been breached since the day of the magick purge. Marks peppered the wall from the blades of looters and archaeologists with little success.

The Brood's soldiers closed in. The Mooncallers' only choices were to enter the academy or face the enemy which, in all probability, meant death. Avari struck the crystal barrier with her knives, and Ares did the same with his talons, but the stone was unbreakable; it cracked her blades and made his claw ache.

Shir locus-jumped between them. "Let me."

They begged Sirah to let them through, and Sirah responded forthwith. The Tomb of Vasna Lorreen melted like ice under a flame. Unbarred, the bodies within splayed on the ground.

"Ares," said Shir before the Mooncallers ran. "Sirah cannot let us out again, not this way. Souls other than our own are not worthy of viewing the living past."

"Is there another exit?" asked Ares frantically.

Shir shivered at the Brood's raucous chanting. "Probably."

There wasn't time to debate. Ares patted Avari and Oliver. "We'll find another way out. Hurry! Get to the other side!"

The Mooncallers were the first to pass into Sirah Academy in seven hundred years, and it felt so. The air was stale, almost unbreathable. 'Disturbing' wasn't enough to describe what it was like treading over the hundreds of corpses, their feet slipping on wads of hair and gummy flesh.

They bounded over armor, shield, and sword as thirty Brood soldiers barreled up the steps at their backs. Shir locus-jumped to the end, and Ares, again, wasn't targeted. The others didn't have it as easy.

A soldier tackled Avari and sat astride her waist. He'd planted one punch on her cheek before she flipped him onto his back as if she were doing something as simple as making a bed. She crushed his nose with the heel of her wrist over and over again until Luxea dragged her off him; had she not, Avari would have beat him until he looked like a product in a butcher's shop.

Three men climbed Ruka's flank. The wolf thrashed and killed two, but four more leaped onto him. Brielle fought to stay mounted, kicking their faces and shooting arrows at close range.

Nearby, Oliver almost kept running, but Ruka's whimpering made his feet go still. He unsheathed his tiny knife. Although he wasn't a savant of human anatomy, he figured the back of the ankle might hurt.

Ruka crushed another assailant with his jaws, and Brielle plowed an arrow through the skull of his comrade. It was then that Oliver hooked onto the last soldier's waist and stabbed him above his heel. Brielle tossed back her head and howled. Ruka bit Oliver's cloak and dragged him to the end of the tomb like a pup from its scruff.

"Not a bad cut, Kross!" complimented Brielle. She grinned at his bloody knife. "You could name your blade *'Ankle Biter.'*"

Oliver couldn't believe it. He'd slashed a man! "R-right. 'Kay."

Behind them, the Brood numbers multiplied. They crawled on the walls, cracked the floors, smashed the corpses, and released their arrows in arches. There wasn't anywhere left for the Mooncallers to run!

The enemies were no farther than ten feet away when Sirah sang.

As had happened seven hundred years ago, the legs of the soldiers crystallized, and they froze where they stood. The Brood men pleaded for Sirah to let them go, but these people and these creatures had ruined the world, and Sirah wouldn't absolve them of such sins.

Liquid crystal swelled up from the floor and crested into a wave above the Brood soldiers' heads. Shadows fell on their horrified faces as it crashed over them. Their bodies, big, small, thin, muscular, and sagging, were cleansed by the forces of the earth. Crackles echoed throughout the Spire as Sirah's crystal hardened, and a new tomb of fresh bodies took the place of the old.

Oliver dropped Ankle Biter and flopped onto his behind. He wiped back his hood and said, "I ain't never seen a rock do that."

Avari cursed and threw the haft of one of her daggers that had broken. "Anyone else getting tired of narrow escapes?"

But the others had turned around to see what lay ahead: Sirah Academy. The bodies, the tides of crystal, the elusion — it didn't matter anymore.

# The Arcanan

# Translator

## 10.Lightsmeet.26.Osc.3
## Sirah Academy, Selnilar

A STANDALONE pathway stretched for reaches in a straight line, past thousands of chambers. Windowless walls were carved with homes, shops, apothecaries, lecture halls, offices, and libraries. Curtains of ivy obscured most corridors and alcoves afar, where within were floors blanketed by skeletons in magisters' regalia.

The white stone bowed up to a ceiling so high that it might have reached into the spirit plane. Hundreds of feet below the levitating bridge was a chasm that descended into the center of the world. Curious about how deep it really went, Brielle pitched a piece of rubble into the empty space. It didn't go far. Plates of stone appeared, level to the walkway, and caught the pebble before it could fall.

Brielle's smokey, yellow eyes almost burst. She grabbed her head and gaped at the platform. "Friends, I am seeing things."

You'd have thought Luxea had stepped into a magick playground. "Amazing!" she chirped as she went to the edge.

Avari gasped, "Luxie, don't — !"

Luxea's foot fell — but an extension of the bridge flickered into view to support her weight. She balanced herself with her arms out at her sides and hopped from space to space as more tiles appeared.

"I wonder if there are stairs." As Luxea said this, a stairwell coiled upward next to her. She peeked at the others through the spaces in the steps. "Convenient, isn't it? I can do something like this in the castle!"

Ares didn't condone the idea. Someone would end up falling, and he would be left with the liability. He humored her with a *'maybe'* slant of his head.

Shir joined Luxea on the floating platforms. "Your kind are talented, Luxea. This is not Sirah's doing, this is magick entirely."

"Yes. Whoever enchanted this place had arcana potent enough to make it outlast centuries." Luxea stepped off the stairwell, caught instantly by another tile. "Ares, may we explore a while? It isn't every day we can wander one of history's most famous locations. *Please?"*

They were short on time, but Luxea's starry gaze caused the Prince to cripple. He grunted, "Fine. We'll spend the afternoon searching, but don't get lost, and don't get yourself killed. In the evening, we'll rendezvous on the bridge and proceed to the heart of Sirah."

Luxea jumped from her tile, caught by a new one left and right, left and right. Avari pranced away too. If she could find a magick blade or two, she hoped the spirit of its previous owner wouldn't haunt her for taking it. Shir sat down and spoke to Sirah, and Ares strode down the main hall with his hands behind his back, peering over the deadly edge every few seconds.

On his own, Oliver wobbled across the levitating path and jumped onto the solid floor on the other side. With his hands in his pockets, he kicked through the narrow corridors.

It took ten minutes for him to start groaning. There was nothing here but dilapidated books, scrolls inked with arcanan symbols, and a few rat skeletons. Where were the enchanted pendants, the stashes of jewels?

Bored, he turned back through a portal, but then he staggered. Seated on the cornice with her legs dangling under her scrappy, purple gown was a silver-haired woman. My, was she breathtaking with her fair skin, rosy eyes, and crooked smile.

"Hello," she said seductively. "Come to play with Sweet Salae?"

This 'Salae' didn't seem like a threat — especially not when she pulled a garter off her thigh and slung it to Oliver's feet. Maybe he'd found a treasure after all.

He straightened his dress shirt. "Sure, love. Whatever you say. Why not come down here, n' we can get to know each other betta'?"

"I wouldn't do it," said an echoey voice.

Oliver leaped when a man in a pointed hat suddenly appeared at his side. From his head to his toes, he was . . . transparent?

"She's a pretty girl, that Salae," the spectral stranger said, "but get too close, and she'll rip out your eyes and eat your skin."

The hatted man drifted away; he didn't have feet, only wispy stumps. Oliver was petrified; he and ghosts did *not* get along. Salae blinked at him, and her serene visage became that of a skull's. Another blink, and she was smiling again.

"O-oh. Maybe some other time, lovely," he whimpered.

Oliver ducked through the portal and threw himself down the stairs as they materialized under him. In the main hall, he found Ares sifting through a tome. He ran for him straight away.

"Mate! You won't believe what I've got to tell you!"

The Prince flipped a page. "I never do."

"I saw a ghost," huffed Oliver. "The lass was gorgeous, I'd've done her right! But this see-through bloke showed up n' told me that she'd —" he gulped, *"— eat my skins."*

Ares patted Oliver's shoulder. "I pray this teaches you not to seduce the undead."

Although terrified of falling, Brielle and Ruka scampered to Luxea. The three gazed at a string of tattered banners that looped around silver poles down the length of the hall.

Brielle squinted. "Starlight, I don't recognize these letters."

"They aren't letters, Brie. These are the sigils of the four magick clans. The first two are from the Greatgrace, across the ocean." Luxea pointed at a green and blue flag with a U-shaped symbol. "That's for the Hantilad Conjurers of Given. They're known for illusory magick."

Next, she motioned to a red banner with a white mask painted on it. "The mark of the Spirit Healers of Pea'natia. They're the smallest clan, but their healing is unmatched."

Third came a black, spiny standard with the skull of a banshee in a ring of orchids. "That one interests me the most. It's the sign of the Xexa Witches from The Grey. I'd have loved to meet one of them, but most who remain live in solitude."

The fourth and last was a ribbony, white pennant with a circular rune embroidered with teal thread. "This is for Encurio, the Magick Assassins. I admire the Xexa Witches, but Encurio is the most mysterious. No one knows where they're from. Traditionally, they cut out their tongues to honor the beauty of silence and master magick without speaking incantations. Because of that, some of the most powerful sorcerers in history came from this clan."

"Incredible," said Brielle dreamily. "Ruka and my ancestors are from Pea'natia. Had I been born with magick, perhaps I'd have been a Spirit Healer too."

The rider jogged to a granite statue portraying a seroden elvish man with kind eyes and a clever smile; he looked the sort to excel in sharp-witted remarks and proving others wrong. A giant feather quill floated beside him, enchanted to make swoops and scribbles above the stone book in his hand.

"Who is he?" asked Brielle. "There are others — many others."

Luxea scanned the twenty or so figures of men and women in robes with wands and canes that loomed tall over each alcove. None of them looked remotely similar to the other.

"They're effigies of the famous magisters throughout history." Luxea pointed at the seroden man's plaque. "This one says, *'Therasi Direl. Magister and Professor at Sirah Academy. Redeemer of Pixies. Designer of Homes, Lands, and Temples. Creator of the Arcanan Translator.'*" She blinked at the last title beneath his name. "He was called *'The Architect.'*"

The Usinnon, whose name translated to *'Architect,'* screamed. Brielle covered Ruka's ears. Luxea unhooked the spellbook and asked it, "What's the matter? Do you not like Therasi Direl?"

*"Hasishi . . . hisasihiasi . . . !"* The Usinnon zapped her.

"Ow! What was that for?" Luxea sucked her finger, and then her stars turned bright green. "Wait . . . are you trying to tell me that you once belonged to this man? To Therasi Direl?"

The Usinnon zapped her again. Luxea wanted to throw it into the abyss; it was right there, she could have. The spellbook sighed and flipped itself open. Had it *ever* done that before? Blue smoke puffed out from its pages and zipped into the nearest hallway. Ruka's ears flew up, and he chased it.

"What — Ruka, come back!" yelped Brielle.

She and Luxea jogged behind the wolf as he bounced down a rocky corridor, snapping his teeth at the smoke. At the bottom of the winding shaft was a grotto with a waterfall pouring the wrong way, and beside it was a monument overgrown with vines. The floor around it rolled with wildflowers, but dampening their beauty were about one hundred crumbling stone tablets. Gravestones were crammed into this space, all of which were carved with the deceased sorcerer's Magelas. This was one of the many burial sites within Sirah Academy for magisters who'd been locked inside.

The wolf chased the Usinnon's spark up the stairs of the monument and down another flight that was hidden in the floor. It led deep into a cellar full of cobwebby books, globes that spun on their own, and a copper contraption taking up the back wall; it looked suspiciously similar to early seroden elvish technology.

All the way across the chamber, Ruka knocked over candlesticks and marble busts. The Usinnon's smoke disappeared into a drawer in the desk in the center of the room, and Ruka's tail sank; he wished he still had opposable thumbs.

Brielle grabbed the wolf's pointed ears. Between each yank she gave them, she said, "Do — not — run — off — again!"

Luxea narrowed her eyes at the drawer. There had to be something in there that the Usinnon meant for her to uncover. Impatient, the spellbook zapped her again.

"Stop that! This had better not be a trick."

She set her profoundly rude spellbook on the desk and slid open the drawer. She'd dreaded a spirit emerging or a booby trap triggering, but it was a regular storage compartment. Sitting within was a flat, metal sheet with worn edges. There wasn't anything special about it other than the tiny, angular designs carved into it.

"A bookmark?"

*"Hasishiahii . . . !"* shrieked the Usinnon.

Luxea didn't have to know the arcanan language to tell that the Usinnon wanted her to pick up this bookmark very, very badly. Not giving it much thought, Luxea opened the spellbook, tucked the bookmark into a random page, and closed it.

The cellar rumbled, and dusty baubles and stacks of decayed paper fell on the ground. The Usinnon's howling began and grew cacophonous. The desk cracked. The spellbook rocked, and the gems on the cover glistered. The din ceased, the dust settled . . .

A man groaned?

"Gods be gentle with my poor soul, what a ruckus!" There was another moan. "Tell me, Miss Siren. Can you understand me now?"

Luxea and Brielle and Ruka searched the room. No one else was there — but they'd all heard that voice! A bit accented, a bit more polite, and incredibly confident. Then came a long, melodramatic sigh.

"Down here, Miss Siren. Your spellbook."

Luxea *had* to be imagining things. The Usinnon twinkled at her, and her stars shone back. "Did you just . . . speak common?"

"Thank all goodness!" said the Usinnon giddily. "I was afeared the device wouldn't be operable. It is dusty, isn't it?" It coughed jokingly. "Allow me to explain. That bookmark is the *'Arcanan Translator.'* It took decades to invent, an irksome endeavor, but the work has paid off! Although centuries late. With this, Miss Siren, the language of magick is converted through waves of sound to meet the ears of the living in the tongue they most frequent."

"A translator." Luxea picked up the Usinnon and stared at its wrinkly pages. Could it see her too? "Does this mean I can talk to you all I want? I can ask you questions and learn without having to read?"

"Yes, but — ah, no, no. I'd certainly like you to read, Miss Siren. I *did* put all of my being into these scriptures," chuckled the Usinnon.

"You? What do you mean?" wondered Luxea.

"I wrote this book," stated the Usinnon.

"Books can write themselves?" Brielle's drive to learn to read was reinvigorated. "Spectacular. You never shared this with me, Starlight."

"You misunderstand, Miss Siren and Brielle," said the Usinnon kindly. "Spellbooks themselves are not sentient, it is merely the soul of the writer within that sees, hears, feels, speaks, and thinks."

"Then you're the author of the Usinnon?" asked Luxea quietly.

"Indeed," said the Usinnon proudly. "I would bow if I could; forgive my inability. You may call me the Usinnon — by the laws of name locks, you must — but my real name is Therasi Direl."

"Ares!" Luxea ran to him covered in sweat.

He started. "What is it? Are you all right?"

"Yes, yes," puffed Luxea. "Brielle and Ruka and I found something amazing — no, extraordinary!" She held out the Usinnon. "Go on. Introduce yourself!"

The Mooncallers exchanged troubled glances. Luxea's common sense was strong enough for her to know that books couldn't talk, at least, not in the common tongue. Had she been possessed by a demon? Had she consumed some centuries-old, dream-inducing tonic?

"Hello, all of you." Oh. Books *could* talk! "We've met before in some way or another, but if Miss Siren wishes for me to give introductions once again, I will do so."

"It's sayin' things," squeaked Oliver.

"I can understand a book," wheezed Avari.

"I should elaborate." The Usinnon cleared its throat — somehow. "My name is Therasi Direl. I was a magister and professor here at Sirah Academy as well as the world's most renowned architect and the inventor of the Arcanan Translator. The process my spirit underwent is much like the ritual of the Riders of the West that put Ruka's human soul into the body of a wolf. My mortality ran out, and my spirit was therefore transferred unto the pages of my most celebrated work. My colleagues called me *'Usinnon'* to pay homage to my achievements.

"I've rested within this spellbook since Alatos.2. It was mundane, much longer than I'd have liked to sit on a ruddy *shelf!* Ares, Your Highness, your family gained ownership of me in Asrodisia.2, and I'm grateful they did. Had I not been preserved in Castle Lavrenthea, I would have been destroyed in the book burnings of the second era.

"But I digress. I led these three to my office where Miss Siren discovered my device. *My word,* it is refreshing to hold a conversation. And do not be shy. We've never had heart-to-hearts, but I have seen a good deal of your personal lives. What, did you think you could change your clothes or pick your noses without my heed?"

The Mooncallers wondered who the Usinnon had seen unclothed or with their fingers in their nostrils. The spellbook laughed. "You must be befuddled by this. If you wish to ask me questions, I permit you to do so. I'm an open book!"

"Oh, gods. It makes puns," said Avari in a whisper.

"Does it feel odd not to have legs n' arms?" wondered Oliver.

"In the beginning, yes," said the Usinnon. "But I enjoy never having the need to wash, eat, drink, or make waste."

Oliver cringed. "Oh."

"Should we call you *'Usinnon'* or *'Therasi?'*" asked Brielle.

"Please, address me as the Usinnon. Therasi Direl gives you a face to my name — that sculpture right across the hall, the fetching gentleman — but I have let go of my old life and embraced the new."

"So you're a male?" asked Avari thoughtfully.

"I was born a male and died a male, but now I'm in between. Whatever I am, I am. Shir, we are similar in that regard."

The Mythic rang. "We are."

"Ah, I'd almost forgotten!" blathered the Usinnon. "Prince Ares, may I have a word?"

Ares tried not to stammer. "Yes."

"Thank you for gifting me to Miss Siren — although it took her a fortnight to solve your riddle. I'd been asleep for centuries until she cast a spell in your bureau. Her magick woke me up forthwith. I'm delighted that you could tell I wanted her. I do love Miss Siren, truly. If I possessed the necessary parts, I'd make her my wife."

The Mooncallers snickered, but Luxea wasn't sure whether to smile or frown. Neither was the Prince.

"My, that's so nice of you," she said meekly.

# A1 FLORANA

## SIRAH ACADEMY

AFTER A short rest, the Mooncallers trekked deeper into Sirah Academy. Their search of the heart of the Crystal Spire would have been trying had the Usinnon not been familiar with the layout. A few times, Oliver saw Sweet Salae in mirrors and cracks in the doors.

By midnight, they were in a library full of cookbooks, storybooks, and volumes about potions and secrets of the ancient times. Pillars shot down from the hemispherical ceiling with strips of white silk weaving them together. From the highest point grew an upside-down tree. In the cold, dry darkness, it bloomed with scintillating, yellow poppies; its roots had spread hundreds of feet over the centuries.

Shir stood beneath it. "The heart is above us."

"Great. Any of you know how to get up there?" wondered Avari.

"The entrance is a secret," offered Brielle.

"Excellent, Brielle," said the Usinnon. "Miss Siren, take me over there, to the pedestal. Give me a look."

Luxea wandered to a stone platform where etched within was a riddle in l'arian elvish. She read as she translated.

*"My heart is a ruby, my blood is decay.*
*Trap me in darkness where there I shall stay.*
*Poor when I'm young, rich when I'm old.*
*Tell me your secrets, and they shall be told."*

"Irritating," humphed the Usinnon. "The last password I remember was *'cactus,'* but the professors regularly changed the riddle. It was protocol to protect Ai Florana."

"Ai Florana?" asked Ares.

"The realm within the heart of Sirah," answered Shir.

"Usinnon, you don't have the answer to this riddle?" sighed Luxea.

"I'm afraid not, Miss Siren. Last it was rewritten, I must not have been here — or alive, for that matter," said the Usinnon exasperatedly.

Ares reread the translation. "We'll have to solve it ourselves."

"Here I was, hopin' I wouldn't have to think today," grunted Avari.

Brielle and Ruka glared at each other. "Is it *'a wolf?'"*

The tree didn't move.

Ares rubbed his forehead. "A demon?"

"A radish?" suggested Oliver. Ares questioned him with his eyes.

"Lust?" peeped Luxea.

"Oh! A scrapbook?" gasped Avari.

The Usinnon thought. "Might the answer be *'a feline?'"*

The tree stayed where it was.

For three hours, the Mooncallers pitched their guesses. Eventually, Brielle fell asleep with Avari against Ruka's belly. Ares sat with his back to a bookshelf, and Luxea lay on the floor across from him.

"A wildfire?" he groaned.

"A picnic," she mumbled.

"Pillows," said the Usinnon.

Nothing, nothing, *nothing!*

Oliver dawdled close by. He didn't hate riddles, they could be great brain-food, but this one . . . if it were possible to kill words. He nudged a detached skeletal hand with the tip of his shoe, wondering if they'd ever get out of there.

"Come here, boy," said a whisper.

He clammed up, for at the end of a nearby bookcase hid Salae, beckoning him with her ghostly fingers. "No, thanks. You'll kill me."

Salae floated to him, her purple dress twirling around her legs. "Do not take me for a fool, Oliver Kross. I cannot kill you." Her pink eyes shot past him. "Your friends, however . . . I *could* kill them."

The timidness in Oliver's expression cracked in two, and he became something, someone new. Darker all over, he stormed to a corner, and the spirit followed him.

"Who are you?" he husked.

"Salae Haviel, daughter of Light Seeker Lorn Haviel, the founder of Sirah Academy. After his death, I taught here as a professor to aspiring magisters. Is that enough for you, or would you like to know me even better?" she purred.

"No," said Oliver sulfurously. "Why are you following me?"

"Because I see you for who you are, and not only do I know you understand me, but I know you can help me," said Salae intensely. "For a millennium, I have been trapped in these walls. I cannot suffer it any longer." She laid her hands on his chest, and he was shocked that she was corporeal. "Free my spirit. Do so, and I will tell you the password."

Oliver listened to his friends as they guessed; no one had gotten it right. "How would I go about releasing you?"

"How do you release any girl?" hinted Salae. He was unaffected by her attempt at seduction. She pouted. "I will settle for a kiss then."

Giving his lips to a woman wasn't something about which Oliver thought twice — but Salae wasn't just a woman. He was about to turn her down until he heard Luxea sighing. The Mooncallers would never uncover the answer without help.

Pretending like Salae Haviel wasn't a harvester of souls and secrets, Oliver cupped her cheeks and kissed her. Her clay-cold lips brought frost to his breath and ice to his veins. For that moment, he shared with her the sadness of a thousand years alone.

Oliver inched away. Salae smiled at him. "The answer is wine."

The image of the magistress got brighter and brighter and rippled into thin air. Oliver didn't move his hands even after she'd passed on . . . because he was missing her.

*'I see you for what you are,'* she'd said, and she'd still wanted him.

But when, in all his life, had Oliver Kross *ever* missed a woman?

He put his hands in his pockets and wished that wherever Salae Haviel went, it wasn't to Sithe or the Trihells. With his mouth chilled, he approached the pedestal and said in a drawling voice, "Wine."

Sweet Salae hadn't lied. The tree on the ceiling shivered and cracked, and shiny, yellow liquid oozed down the trunk. The branches extended to the floor, and the wood warped. From it opened a doorway leading upward.

Avari and Brielle were awake at once. The exhaustion in the eyes of Ares and Luxea vanished. The Usinnon laughed, "That's it. *Wine!*"

Ares was astonished, just astonished! Oliver could hardly solve putting on his pants in the morning let alone a riddle. "How did you find the answer, Kross?"

"Turns out seducin' the undead ain't such a bad idea." Oliver crouched next to the Usinnon with his elbows on his knees. "When you were alive, li'l mate, did you hear 'bout a pretty girl named Salae Haviel? Silver hair, li'l snarky."

The spellbook choked. "O-of course! Oh, *Salae*. Not a soul didn't fancy the beauty. My, what a sweet thing she was. The most brilliant woman of my time. Why do you ask, Lord Kross?"

"Nothin'. She's a good kisser," said Oliver remotely.

Just then, a purple light whizzed out of the tree trunk. It darted to each of the Mooncallers' faces and halted before Shir. It was a faerie, but this faerie was unlike those in picture books. She was the height of a soup spoon with a body formed of leaves, velvety petals for wings, and a hircine face.

"You?" chirped the faerie to Shir. "What are *you* doing here?"

"I must plant my kind," said the Mythic.

The faerie scowled. "These ones can't come in."

"But they are my friends," said Shir sadly.

Crossing her twiggy arms, the faerie shouted, "Ai Florana isn't for man's feet! You can enter alone, or you can all scram!"

Avari cracked her knuckles. "I'm in a squashing mood."

The faerie buzzed to Avari and slapped her on her button nose. Avari sank into her scarf. The faerie prepared to weaponize her words, but then a sigh came from within the tree.

*"Doremi, shut up. The mortals may enter."*

The faerie, Doremi, retracted her arms and legs and darted into the trunk; whoever had reprimanded her terrified her. The Mooncallers hadn't a clue what awaited them beyond that spiral of moss but were disinclined to rotting in Sirah Academy. After Shir, they ascended the upside-down tree into Ai Florana.

They emerged from a second tree, this one right-side up. Before them flourished a grove identical to Mythos, but they couldn't see the stars, and the inhabitants were plants and animals, not crystals. Clusters of faeries like Doremi peeked at the outsiders from niches in the walls. A bird with a tulip for a head swished by. It landed and bloomed where inside the petals was a crone's sour face.

In a spring to the right were men with the body of a stag and the head of a human or the body of a human and the head of a stag. Those with hands cleansed the backs of naked women with white bark for flesh and cherry blossom branches flowing from their scalps.

Far ahead, seated in the center of a tremendous stargazer lily, was a figure with minty green skin. Vines made up Her head of hair, coiling around Her feet and rooting to the floor. Pink blossoms sprouted and died on Her breasts and between Her legs. Her yellow eyes were veined like a leaf held up to sunlight.

She was N'ra the Goddess of Nature.

Brielle and Ruka dropped into a bow; the others thought it was wise to do the same. Oliver knelt, and his hand squashed a mushroom. The fungus climbed out of the soil, crying and swinging its chubby arms and legs as it ran away. Oliver felt like crying and running away too, after that.

The mushroom climbed up N'ra's hair and curled up in Her lap. She petted its cap. Over the goddess' shoulder, Doremi perched on a twig and stuck out her tongue. Avari returned the gesture.

Shir spoke first. "N'ra, it is lovely to see you."

The Nature Goddess set down the mushroom. It scampered away and jumped into a pond. "You speak the human language now?"

"Yes." Shir twinkled. "My favorite word is *'bubble.'*"

N'ra didn't care. "You've come to revive the *Sil'simani,* but it's the fault of the dragon and the stars that they perished, is it not?"

"No. It is the fault of the ones who killed them," corrected Shir.

Black flowers appeared in N'ra's hair. "What are you waiting for, *Shir?"* She asked theatrically. "Plant them. The soil is ready."

Ares unlaced the pouch from his belt and handed it to Shir. The Mythic strode to a patch of dirt by the wall and dug fifty-nine holes for the fifty-nine shards, leaving their own in the sack.

N'ra scrutinized the Mooncallers. It had been centuries since She'd seen humankind with Her own eyes; they'd changed, grown taller, less like primates and more like the divines Themselves.

The Nature Goddess' stare repeatedly flitted to Luxea as if She were expecting something. Luxea looked back. N'ra scowled at her and turned her attention to Oliver.

"Red eyes, dead skin, and fangs of a nightbird," She said to him. "You're a long way from home. Does Tirih still torment you?"

As an aestof, the Sun Goddess indeed tormented Oliver when he stepped into the light. "Aye. Wish She'd go easier on me."

The Nature Goddess laughed giddily. Sated by his answer, She latched onto Brielle and Ruka next. "You, I enjoy. You've treated my creations with respect and prolonged the practices of the first men. Rider, if you tire of these humans, I would accept your company here in Ai Florana. Consider it."

Brielle and Ruka were starstruck but couldn't accept such a sudden offer. "Thank you, N'ra," said Brielle, "but this is our pack."

Idiotic humans. Who would turn down a goddess? N'ra scoffed and moved on to Avari. "You're one of the elves who wishes for the world to be built out of metal. When Amniven dies in a thousand years, recognize that it was your doing."

"I've never built a thing. Sandcastles, maybe," huffed Avari.

"But you will."

N'ra's lips flattened out as She eyed Ares. She stood from Her throne and shrank to his size, and the flowers and vines in Her hair grasped the ground as She closed in. She slid Her thorny hand into his shirt and uncovered the Felastil.

"The Moon Mother's sigil. A powerful relic. How does it work?" It was more of an order than a question.

"It's a communicator," said Luxea for him. "Oscerin has one too."

The goddess bristled; She seemed especially wary of Luxea. "I thought *he* was Oscerin's Speaker, not *you.* "

"I am Her Speaker, but Luxea is Her looking glass," stated Ares.

The Nature Goddess broke into a million bracts and rematerialized in front of Luxea. She glared hard into her starry eyes. The cosmos switched colors as Luxea's emotions fought. N'ra's gaze darted to her legs.

"Your pocket," She whispered.

Luxea looked down and up. "What about my pocket?"

"My mark is in your pocket. Give it to me!"

What was in her pocket? She searched herself until her fingers brushed a fibrous object. Unveiled was the blackwood leaf that the grove wanderer had given her — but N'ra had called it *Her* mark. Perhaps the Mother of Nature had been the one to will the grove wanderer to offer Luxea such an obscure gift.

The goddess read the leaf like a sign, learning it from all angles. The second that She touched it, She swatted it onto the ground. "It *was* you that day. I knew it!" She poked Luxea hard in the chest. "You've touched the other side. A side I haven't."

"What does that mean?" muttered Luxea.

N'ra turned grayscale, Her eyes purple. "A blackwood tree."

Luxea understood now. "A blackwood tree and —"

"— a woman forged from the shadow."

"You can see her too?" whispered Luxea.

The Goddess wilted at the mere thought. "I made all trees, all dirt, and all flowers. I see through the eyes of bark, leaf, and petal. Through them, I saw you — and *her.* "

Luxea clutched Her arm. "Will you tell me who she is?"

N'ra threw her off. Her skin decomposed, and Her vines slouched. "I cannot, for I have not heard her name — but *you* have."

"No, she wouldn't tell me her name," swore Luxea.

"And yet, it is in your head!"

Quick on Her feet, the Nature Goddess retreated to Her throne. The stargazer lily yielded its color to Her. She drank the energy as if She'd been famished.

"You're afraid of the Shadow, aren't You?" asked Luxea quietly. "Why? How can I learn more about — ?"

"Stop talking!" The stag men and their cherry blossom lovers bounded away in fear. N'ra held Her face in Her hands. "If you seek answers, go to Anatatri. She has them all."

"The Goddess of Time? Where do we find Her?" questioned Ares.

"Within Hildre the Golden Spire," breathed N'ra. "Beyond the Timeless Mountains lies a path, and at the end of that path is the

Memory Door. Stand before it and call to mind every memory from your birth to your present. It will open for you and you alone."

Luxea's feet shuffled. "What if you don't have memories?"

"That isn't *my* problem," seethed N'ra.

Considering their current plans, Ares whispered into Luxea's ear, "We should go to the Golden Spire. If this shadow woman is as important as N'ra believes her to be, it may be worth our time to pick Anatatri's knowledge."

"I can't get in," reminded Luxea.

"Then I'll go inside for you," he promised.

By then, Shir had finished planting the Mythics' shards. Branches of crystal had already broken through the soil, and, if you watched closely, you could see them taking shape.

"Thank you all," said Shir pleasantly. "In a few years, my kind will walk this land as they once did."

Aimed at Luxea, N'ra shouted, "Good! The rest of you, leave!"

On cue, Doremi darted out from behind the throne and beckoned the Mooncallers to a passageway. "You heard Her! Get out!"

They started to move, but Shir didn't. Luxea stopped and turned around. "Shir, aren't you coming with us?"

"Of course, not," laughed N'ra. "They aren't a trinket, they are a child of Sirah. They belong in the heart of nature, not the fist of man!"

Shir was rooted to the spot by a new emotion: indecision. Their quartzite eyes flitted to their flourishing counterparts and then to Luxea's stars. Yes, they did belong in nature, but it felt as if something was unfinished. It wasn't as hard as they'd thought to choose. They strode to the Mooncallers.

"My time with these mortals is not over, N'ra. They need me yet; You see it too. I will be leaving now. Thank you," said Shir sweetly.

The Nature Goddess was jarred. She pointed at the exit. "When you are hunted for your flesh, do not expect me to take pity on you. You will die as mortals do, never to live on with the other fifty-nine."

Shir looked mutinous. "N'ra, You are mistaken. I am all sixty."

The goat-faced faerie led the Mooncallers down a path that ended with a crystal tunnel that went on and on. "Well, go!" she grouched.

"How, exactly?" squeaked Oliver.

Doremi zipped to him. "Figure it out, nightskin!"

Avari swatted the faerie and sat in the mouth of the tunnel. "I, for one, can't wait to leave." She sneered at Doremi. "So long, crapleaf."

The ranger pushed down the tube before her nose could be smacked again. Brielle leaped into the tunnel with Ruka, and the wolf's nails scratched the stone all the way down. The last three tarried. Shir went first, and then Ares.

Luxea climbed inside, but Doremi stopped her.

"Starlight."

"What is it, Doremi?"

The faerie's flitting ceased; she was utterly still in midair. When next she spoke, her voice was no longer her own — it was N'ra's.

"Remember, and we might be saved."

Remember *what?* What wasn't there to remember? It was all gone! Luxea didn't give Doremi or N'ra, whoever was speaking, a reply. She slipped into the tube.

Closing her eyes to fight back the darkness, Luxea splashed up against the curved walls like water in a straw. She heard one of two things: her friends screaming, or her friends laughing. This natural slide was delightful, the tummy swells too, but Luxea couldn't have been happier to land on a patch of grass at the end.

They were let out onto a hillock outside of the Crystal Spire. It would have been lovely to be out in the open world again had it not been for the pouring rain.

The Mooncallers helped each other to the forest floor. Most trees had cobalt leaves, so they assumed they were still in Nav Amani Forest. It was nigh impossible to see through the rainfall; the only light leading them was from Shir's crown.

They hiked with the rainwater rising up their shins. They might have reached their dracas by morning had something not sloshed from the right. Ares held up his claw, Luxea her hands, and Avari her knives. Brielle and Ruka bared their teeth. Oliver hid.

They'd expected an enemy, but it was a friend.

The grove wanderer's head poked out of the tree line, and more blackwood leaves sprouted from its snout. This time, Luxea knew it wasn't the grove wanderer offering the leaves, it was N'ra.

Even after the Goddess of Nature had banished them from Ai Florana, some part of Her wanted to guide Luxea.

It begged the question: guide her to *what?*

The grove wanderer stamped backward, and Luxea followed. Not far from the trail, the woodland creature halted by a creek and stepped aside. Luxea went still enough to crumble had she been touched.

*'Remember, and we might be saved.'*

There loomed the Shadow's blackwood tree.

# STOP SCARING HER

## 11.LIGHTSMEET.26.OSC.3
### NAV AMANI FOREST, SELNILAR

SHE REMEMBERED every branch.

Luxea splashed to her knees and scoured the flooded grass for her beaded sandals. They were long gone, but she had no doubt that this was where she'd first seen the Shadow.

The rain wasn't conducive to seeing a trail beyond the tree, but Luxea knew there was one, and she had to follow it. The others called after her, but the last thing she could do was listen.

Five minutes went by in five seconds. Luxea wiped her wet hair out of her face and stared up at the wall of thorns before her. Thirty-feet high and rectangular? This wasn't how plants grew — not without a skeleton.

She ripped through the vines. The points poked her hands and drew blood, but there was something on the other side, and she would bleed herself dry until she uncovered it.

By then, her companions had caught up with her. Shir gripped her wrist, forcing her to cease, and trailed their fingers over the ivy. The vines obeyed their command, twisting and untwisting elsewhere.

*A door.*

This door was like any other, worn oak with a rounded top rail, a decorative entablature, and a rusty bell. Luxea slipped past Shir and turned the knob. It scraped open, and rainwater gushed into the foyer.

The manor was disturbing, hellish even, and colder inside than in the rainstorm. The low ceiling, water-damaged and reclaimed by plant-life, opened up to three stories of height. The hardwood floors were ornamented by broken cups, ruined books, and blanched paintings of the sea and the woods. The air smelled of mildew, a deathly scent.

Askew above the hearth was a portrait depicting a l'arian elvish man, woman, and child. The father and mother's eyes and mouths had been carved out, and painted in black ink across the bottom was:

## I WAS HERE FIRST

The little girl in the painting was the most disconcerting of all — Because Luxea knew her.

She'd encountered this child on three separate occasions while under the effects of the nightmare venom. Once, the girl had led her to an alleyway in the Shifting City and shown her a spider eating a butterfly. The second instance, she'd tried to drown her in the reservoir in *Thali ou Tirima,* shouting, *'Stop scaring her!'* The third and last time, she'd screamed, *'Anzthoraz!'* and pushed Luxea off of *Matha ou Machina;* she might have died had Ares not caught her.

Avari trudged closer. "Luxie . . . that looks like you."

Although fifteen or so years younger, the girl in the portrait was identical to Luxea. Her hair and skin was white, her cheeks were plump, and her eyes were protuberant, but her irises were pink like all other l'arian elves'.

"It's her, Avari," breathed Luxea. "That's the little girl I saw."

The ranger grabbed the hafts of her daggers just to have something to squeeze. "Then that *is* you. Was this your house? Do you think those might be your parents?"

"Indeed, it was once her home," confirmed Shir. "There are traces of your energy in the wood, Luxea . . . in the air."

"We should conduct a search," suggested Brielle.

"I agree." Ares' eyes were hooked on the child in the painting; it was true, she did resemble Luxea, but she was sharper, emptier. "We may find information here that we can't find anywhere else. We're all tired, but this is necessary. We'll stay here tonight."

The Mooncallers split up to search the manor. Strangely, the frame above the hearth was the only portrait; the other walls were bare or smashed.

Avari and Brielle and Ruka scoured the right side of the property, Oliver took the kitchen, and Ares, Luxea, and Shir went left.

After sifting through two rooms, Ruka sniffed out an office. Inside, Brielle found a daybook in a drawer. When she opened it, a stack of four envelopes spilled out. She picked one up and called to Avari.

"Small One? This writing is difficult for me. Will you read them?"

Avari knelt by Brielle, not anticipating anything significant; business letters or recipes maybe. But what she read in the first three was outright chilling.

You've hurt her for the last time

~

166

I WILL NEVER FORGIVE YOU

~

Let me see her. Please. I'll do anything.

The fourth wasn't in the same penmanship.

You won't look at me. You won't speak to me.
But you must hear me. She's dying, and it's
our fault. I beg you to let her go.

In the interim, Ares, Luxea, and Shir found a strand of doors on the third floor. Shir entered the first, Ares the second, and Luxea the last.

The Mythic went into a room full of paintings without a subject. Art is merely a form of madness, but this was chaos. Raving smears, frenzied scratches, manic splatters — it was painful to see. Shir searched for what the artist must have been feeling, but it was too negative to translate.

The room Ares explored was a study with textbooks, journals, and workbooks heaped on a rotten mahogany table. He gathered a few and skimmed through them. Like Avari and Brielle, he found three letters, but these ones were tucked into pretty, pastel envelopes.

*Another year, and I'm more thankful for you.*

~

*I miss you, Butterfly...*

~

*I'm so proud of you. I'll see you in wolfswake.*

Ares put them aside and collected a journal. It had decayed too much to read, but he could make out a few drawings of animals; a child must have made them, for some had one too many or one too few limbs.

What came next was Luxea's diary. It wasn't all too courtly for Ares to read it, but maybe a peek . . .

The diary housed a year's worth of accounts from Luxea Siren's life. Scrawls about memorable trips with her friends to Sirah Temple Plaza in Lor'thanin, the occasions she'd bedded a boy and had her heart broken, and several pages describing her first time smoking tattleweed — which were illegible.

The middle section chronicled something Ares never would have imagined. It didn't only involve Luxea, but *him* as well. But he hadn't known her before, so how?

As he read further, it all made sense. He prayed that no one heard him laughing. This was good, so good that he wouldn't live another day without embarrassing Luxea.

At the end of the hall, Luxea found a bedroom. It had once been decorated to bring lovely dreams, but today, walking over the threshold could have induced nightmares.

A child's bed was draped in a satin, rose quilt, and deteriorating l'arian dolls crammed the shelves on the wall beneath the windowsill. A music box was on the nightstand, shining as if untouched by time.

Without inspecting the rest of the room, Luxea sat on the creaky bed and set the music box on her thighs. She opened the lid. A butterfly sprang up, spun in circles, and played a familiar tune . . .

. . . the same one that Luxea had hummed on Mythos.

When the chiming stopped, she got the urge to throw it or burn it or smash it to bits. Perhaps it had once sent her to sleep, but, gods, she wanted it gone! Even holding it disgusted her.

She set it down, poised to storm out of the room, but her knees locked by the door. On the far right wall was a mess of scratches, too dark to see clearly. She held up her hand and said, *"Amal luciem."*

An orb of light lit up the room.

There were a thousand carvings from the baseboard to the crown molding. What they said, however, that was what stole the bones from Luxea's legs. She tumbled to the floor.

STOP SCARING HER STOP SCARING HER
STOP SCARING HER STOP SCARING HER
STOP SCARING HER

Luxea had heard this saying from the little girl in her nightmares. Now she could recall hearing it many, many times before that.

## 29.REDTAIL.6.OSC.3
### SIREN MANOR

*She dreamed about a room with silks on the walls and spices in the air. The sunlight was warm on her skin, and a breeze barely tickled her cheeks.*

*In the distance, she heard a thud. She woke up.*

*At the foot of her bed awaited the Shadow. It was the fifth time she'd returned since that twilight in the blackwood tree. She'd made Luxea sick, so sick that she couldn't go outside anymore.*

*"Why are you here? I said not to come back!"*

*The Shadow's broken fingers pressed into the quilt, and her skinny neck wound about as she crawled closer. She then covered her face as she had when they'd first met.*

*Luxea's pale pink eyes watered. She was tired of the torment. She'd kept her silence and allowed herself to die slowly but refused to any longer. No more!*

*As loud as she could, she screamed, "SHE'S HERE!"*

*It was the worst mistake she'd ever made.*

*The Shadow's bandages unraveled, and she released a skull-cracking shriek that only her young victim could hear. Luxea held her dracas plushie as her consciousness wavered.*

*Was her sickness worsening? From a mere sound?*

*Just then, the bedroom door swung open. The Shadow evaporated as a man with white skin and hair fell at the bedside with a candle. He petted Luxea's sweaty forehead and made a 'shhh' sound.*

*Luxea broke into tears. "She was here again! The shadow!"*

*As she said this, the floorboards creaked, and a black mass dashed into the hall. The man's fingers tightened around the candlestick.*

*He wiped the droplets from his daughter's cheeks and said, "Stay here, Luxea. Sleep."*

*She grabbed his arm. "Appa, don't leave me in the dark!"*

*Her father's pride in her showed in his face. He set the candlestick on her nightstand and wound up her music box. With a kiss to her feverish forehead, he whispered, "Cover your ears, Butterfly."*

*He left. Although she'd been told not to listen, Luxea listened. Dancing amidst the lullaby were screams — loud, furious screams.*

*"Stop scaring her!"*

"Miss Siren!"

Luxea spun onto her back; she couldn't even recall falling or dropping the Usinnon. Once she'd returned to reality, she scooped up her spellbook.

"You were whining. It frightened me," said the Usinnon weakly.

She got up and brushed off her trousers, but she couldn't take her eyes off the scratched up wall. "Who was I, Usinnon? Was I insane?"

"Sanity is an expectation, not an obligation." The spellbook twinkled toward the door. "Come along, Miss Siren. This place is harming you. We shouldn't be here."

As she left the bedroom, Luxea heard echoes of the music box.

*'STOP SCARING HER'* was scored into her eyelids.

That night, the Mooncallers set up the best beds they could in a place like this. Brielle was flopped on Ruka's back, and the rest curled up on the floor. By the time they fell asleep, it was six o'clock in the morning. They couldn't rest long, however; a few hours, at most.

As exhausted as he was, the thoughts in Ares' head wouldn't allow him to sleep. He lay on his back and held his Felastil to his lips. Into the jewel, he asked, "May I speak with You?"

At once, his eyes rolled to the whites. Oliver woke up when the Prince's legs flopped to the side and hit the floor. Oscerin hadn't responded so promptly in years. Ares couldn't breathe but was thrilled to talk to Her.

*"You should be dreaming,"* whispered the Moon Mother.

"I can't," Ares told Her. "I have a question for You, one I should have asked sooner. After tonight . . . I can't wait anymore."

There was a pause. *"What is it, Ares?"*

"Who is the Shadow in Luxea's memories? N'ra Herself spoke about her without our mention, and She was terrified of this entity. She sent a minion of the forest to deliver Luxea to this manor, and now Luxea has recovered a second remembrance of her. You must know *something* about her. For all our safety, won't you tell me?"

The Moon Goddess' answer was too quick. *"No."*

Ares woke up gasping. He rolled over onto his elbows and covered his face. Oscerin had *never* denied him in such a way. If even a greater divine refused to address the topic, how dangerous could this shadow woman really be?

Oscerin was hiding something; he could sense it. He felt like tearing off his Felastil, crushing the jewel with his heel, and forgetting that he'd ever been Her Speaker. Since Widow had risen, Oscerin hadn't been the same. She'd been swapped with a celestial mother that cared not for the wellbeing of Amniven, but Ares' service to Her.

It stung.

It was still raining in the morning. Avari and Brielle and Ruka woke up early to hunt and returned an hour later with a wild boar. While the three could kill, they couldn't cook. Avari had learned to make stews and roasts, but turning an animal of this size into a meal wasn't as straightforward.

However, Oliver claimed to be a magnificent chef. He cleaned the kitchen as Avari and Brielle carved the boar and separated the meat from the ribs. Much to the others' surprise, Oliver really *was* skilled culinarily. New secrets about this pale, skinny lord were discovered every day. Soon, the odor of greenery in the manor was overpowered by the mouthwatering aroma of char and fat.

Shortly after waking up, Luxea went onto the front porch to watch the rainfall. Within a minute, Ares followed her outside. She didn't notice him until he started to read something aloud.

*"I pity the sorcerers in my group."* His smooth voice pulled her attention. *"They're in their beginner's textbooks, but I've been taking advanced tests since Nightspeak last year."*

"Ares, what is that?"

"Your diary," he purred.

Luxea could have kicked his head off his neck. "Reading it is a little discourteous, don't you think?"

"There's no use, princess. I've already looked through it."

*"Princess?"*

He gave her a one-shouldered shrug. "It was a slip of the tongue."

"Of course, it was. Now give me the diary!"

She tried to snatch it from him. Ares' palm made a small *clap* against her forehead as he held her back. She felt like a child begging for its toy. He kept the diary above his head as he went on.

*"We had our —"* He laughed and mashed his large hand into Luxea's face. *"We had our first rehearsal last week. The others cast illusions that looked so much like blobs that I was almost embarrassed*

173

*to give my example — which, by the way, was superb. I hope my prowess is recognized when I perform for The Six in Snowhowl."*

The pressure of Luxea's skull against Ares' fingers let up. It took her a moment of contemplation, but then she jolted as if she'd been touched by an ice cube.

"If I performed for The Six, doesn't that mean —"

"— the one time I saw magick, it was yours."

During Ares and Luxea's first somewhat personal conversation almost a year before, he told her he'd only seen magick once at a performance. Lo and behold, it was hers! She giggled, but then she recalled that he'd also mentioned hardly watching.

"It was *my* magick, and you don't remember it?"

Ares thought better than to make excuses; a woman was never to be challenged. Instead, he read her diary — as if that were any better.

*"I was right. Today was the best day of my life. The Six —"*

"— didn't pay attention?" snarked Luxea.

"Let me finish." Luxea held her tongue. Ares grinned devilishly. *"The Six loved our performance. I went last for Tzapodia, the nation most recently introduced to The Six. The Speaker left with his date early on but came back in time for my part. I think he enjoyed it.*

*"After the show, we weren't permitted to meet the members of The Six. I hate Instructor Naremi for it. All I wanted was to meet them! But I am thankful that she let us watch them from the second floor of the lobby. All the girls drooled over Emperor Rowan —"*

Ares had to collect himself.

*"— but I had my eye on the Speaker. His Highness was lucky to be across the theater. Were he any closer, he'd have been in trouble."*

He peeked over Luxea's diary and ate every spoonful of chagrin that she fed him. Had she pressed herself any closer to the wall, she would have melted right into it.

Ares closed the diary. "I didn't know you thought of me that way."

"I don't!" she blurted.

"Oh. Are you sure?"

He rolled up his sleeves halfway and tapped his fingers on the pommel of Sindred. Luxea gobbled up all of the anxiety in the world, that starry-eyed emotional glutton.

"Would you just —" She squashed her nose with her palm. Ares tried not to make a face. "I didn't write that."

He flipped through the diary once more. "No, you did. Every passage is in your penmanship."

"How would you know my handwriting?"

Pacing elegantly, he recited, *"Leaves may grow and fall away, but roots forever will remain."*

That poem about leaves and roots had been printed on the back of the farewell note Luxea had written for Ares — but she'd never had the chance to give it to him.

"You read my letter?" she murmured.

"No, I memorized it."

For an instant, Luxea was jubilant. He'd seen her dying thoughts, her last wishes — but he'd also recognized her penmanship, and that meant she really *had* written that suggestive passage about him however many years ago.

Luxea never had trouble thinking; she was a magickal genius! But right now, she was a mindless slug.

Ares stepped in front of her and gave her the diary. What a self-assured grin he had. So arrogant — but also captivating, if she was honest with herself.

"Am I in trouble now?" he asked innocently.

She shook her head.

Before he left her, he mouthed, "I think I am."

# DESHA DUNALI

## 13.LIGHTSMEET.26.OSC.3
### DUNDIS ANGLE, THE STORM PLAINS

THE NEXT day, the Mooncallers returned to the grotto where the dracas were stabled and set off for the Storm Plains. Brielle's familiarity with the Western Woods shortened their journey by one day, but at their destination, they ran into yet another problem.

The meadows had previously rolled with white and gold and green, but now they were unrecognizable. There were more military posts than trees, scraps of metal were sprawled over the barley fields, and a ladder-like track stretched to the end of the north. The once untouched land had been mowed down and plowed, drilled and paved.

Shir dipped their fingers into a puddle of oil, and purple, yellow, green, and blue slicked down their palm to their wrist. "This place drains the world. The stories within the soil have been erased."

"I don't like it," growled Brielle. Ruka barked in accord.

Avari dismounted and picked up a shard of metal. "Damn. I'm from Tarot, and it was fine when it was the Shifting City. Not here though." She slung the piece.

Ares shared a like mind. Peyamo was his nearest and dearest friend, but these lands weren't hers to modernize.

He steered the Mooncallers to the nearest guard's post where they saw a familiar face. Ordering seroden workers around was Nika Lecava, Peyamo's helmsman and head engineer. A crewman knelt, struggling to untwist a bolt from a metal sheet, and Nika insisted that he was using the wrong wrench.

The Prince put his fingers in his mouth and whistled, and Ruka bayed several octaves lower. Nika jumped a foot in the air and twirled around. His catlike eyes spun madly as he stuttered, "Y-Your Highness? And Miss Siren too! You live?"

"It's good to see you, Nika," said Ares kindly. "I'll spare you the explanations, for now. I must ask you to take us to Peyamo. I see she's taken out her grief on building, and I'd like her to stop."

Nika frowned. "Of course, Your Highness. She will listen to you. But it isn't all bad! She's been so broken up that she finished *Desha Dunali* almost on her own!"

*"Desha Dunali?* The Iron Dart?" translated Avari.

"That's right. The locomotive," clarified Nika.

"Oh, it's done?" gasped Luxea.

The engineer hopped onto the back of a saddled plainsteed. "It is. We'll be conducting a test run soon, so the timing of your arrival is impeccable. Come, come, follow me."

The Mooncallers cantered after Nika for a reach and slowed in the center of the biggest military camp; Nika said it was one of the many stations the seroden elves had built in the Joined Hands.

Due north, a cloud of white steam rose. Idle on the tracks, long and bronze, was *Desha Dunali.* To the Mooncallers, it was a demon. It had tenders, hopper cars, passenger cars, and tens and tens of boxcars. The shell was so burnished that it was painful to the eye. Supine beneath it was a body — with one human leg, one metal.

Nika bounced off the plainsteed's back. "My Lady!"

Peyamo *thunked* her head on the locomotive. "Blasted — what, Lecava? I'm real busy with this axel! Can't it wait a minute?"

Ares dismounted Pveather and leaned coolly against the car, arms crossed. "I'm not one for patience, Amo."

There was another, louder *thunk*. Peyamo recognized that voice. She slid out from under her machine, and her pair of pliers fell out of her hand with a *clang*. Ares helped her to stand up. She threw off her safety goggles and lunged to hug him, but he stepped back and pointed. The welding tool in her arm was spitting fire.

The reunion of the Mooncallers and the Lady lasted hours. She barreled Ares and Luxea with questions, but Shir enamored her the most. She conducted many scans, all of which showed incalculable results. The Mythic's production of energy was so profound that all Peyamo's lenses said was: ERROR.

When the night sailed over the Storm Plains, the Lady unlocked *Desha Dunali's* dining car; she hadn't planned to use the kitchens yet, but the day's events called for a feast. Ruka couldn't fit inside, so Shir sat outside with him to play with bugs.

There wasn't much of a selection aside from preserved beef, veggies, and plains meats. As this was Peyamo Nelnah's locomotive, there was, of course, an excess of ale. Luxea and Oliver joked that the tenders must have been full of the stuff.

It wasn't until they'd finished dinner that Ares brought up their plans to return to Solissium. He first spoke about the Golden Spire and the Goddess of Time, but upon revealing that their actual reason was to evacuate citizens, Peyamo shot him between the eyes with a glare.

"Evacuate? What for?" she asked secretively.

Luxea took the leap. "You don't have to hide anything, Amo, we all know. Ares told us about the Empress taking a bribe from Widow. I understand that he was prohibited from revealing that information, but it's too late. We can't overlook the safety of Goldenrise's people."

The Lady banged the table, spilling every plate. Her guests were shaken, but the Prince was used to her outbursts. "Dammit, Ares! Your silence was bound by the laws of the Joined Hands! Stop playin' with your hair and think 'fore you go jumpin' off ships and breakin' oaths. D'you realize how much trouble you're in? You've violated a regulation of The Six!"

"I'll violate more if need be," said Ares thickly. "We *must* reverse what we've done. If you decline, I'll leave The Six, and you can be the only member. Annalais surrendering Goldenrise to the Brood is far more concerning than my disclosure of the truth. You know this."

The Lady cleaned out her tankard, filled it, threw it, and refilled another. "Tellin' this to Annalais is gonna be a real treat, Ares."

"I'll do it. Don't worry yourself."

Peyamo tossed up her arms. "Fine then. She won't be happy with you — as if she needs more to be unhappy about."

Ares wanted to be witty, but Luxea beat him to it. "You could give Her Splendor a piece of cake, and she'd still shoot her quills."

It was exceedingly difficult for Ares not to laugh at the idea of his prickly ex-fiancée rejecting a dessert. Thankfully, the Lady enjoyed her statement too — enough so to let go of her anger.

"Bless me, Starlight, you cunning bunion." She ruffled her choppy, blonde hair. "I'm more on Ares' side than Anna's. A friend's a friend, a whore's a whore. If you go through with this, I'll stay nearby in case you need me. Stupid idiots."

"I knew you'd see reason," said Ares with a winning smile.

"Get that shit-eatin' grin off your face," snickered Peyamo.

While the Mooncallers dozed in the passenger compartments, Ares and Peyamo shared drinks in the conductor car. The Lady unbuckled her bronze leg from her hip and set it on the bench beside her. Swinging her fleshed one under the table, she clinked her tankard to his.

"You really want to do this, Ares?"

The Prince nodded. "We put those people in danger. You cannot tell me you don't regret it too." Peyamo gulped her ale, which Ares took as an obscure *'yes.'* "The Goldenrise population is higher than Tarot's and Tzapodia's, so we'll need as much help as we can get with transportation. If you can provide us with carts and horses to —"

"Carts n' horses? Please, Ares, what're we squattin' in? *Desha Dunali* was built for transportation. Listen, I'll take you to Solissium on the test run. We'll make rounds n' bring back folks little by little."

Ares pushed back his hair three times. "We'll ride in . . . this?"

"Aye. She's sturdy." Peyamo knocked on the window. "It's up to you. We can spend moons trottin' about, wastin' everybody's time — or I'll get you across the Great Bridge in a day, and we'll have Solissium clear by the end o' the week."

*Desha Dunali* intimidated Ares. He winced at the gaslights that hung from the car ceiling. What if they fell? The locomotive would explode, and everyone would die. However, taking it to Goldenrise was the most efficient option. They could get there and back in a quarter of the time and be able to move a massive number of people.

"How soon is this test run of yours?" he asked somewhat timidly.

"As soon as you need it, my friend."

Ares gave her an unsteady nod of agreement, and then they didn't speak. Peyamo even lost her words for a while; it was still fitting into her head that Ares was alive, sitting right in front of her.

"You've been fightin' death lots lately," she remarked.

"It won't be the last time." Ares hated ale but topped off his tankard. "Since last we saw each other, secrets have surfaced — horrid secrets. Ones that The Six didn't know."

"I hear you, Ares."

"Don't hear, listen." Peyamo let him talk. "This isn't only Widow and The Six anymore. This is Widow, the Joined Hands, the people, the divines, Luxea, and . . . something else. Something so dark that even Oscerin won't speak of it." He grazed the Felastil with his thumb and, scowling, tucked it into his shirt.

"The Six is finished, and we have to accept that. You don't like to break bonds, I understand, but they're already broken. If and when we defeat Widow, Garamat is still dead, Annalais is still my enemy, and the other four have still sacrificed their people for the Brood. We're in a sea of traitors and tricksters.

"I've thought about this, and it's best to put the organization on hold." Peyamo looked like she had a screw in her tongue. "You and I are the only preeminent guardians these lands have left. Our priority should be the safety of the ones who can't hold their own. The Six was for Tzapodia, Tarot, Goldenrise, Selnilar, Ank'tatra, and the Isle of Varnn, but only two of those nations are free now. The Joined Hands is being pulled apart. Our focus must be switched to all territories as one, for we all share a common enemy. Banners and titles no longer bear meaning, Amo. We preserve the world or nothing at all."

It wasn't anything the Lady wanted to admit, but she agreed. After tapping out an entire verse on the table, she groaned, chuckled, and raised her drink.

"You've grown, princeling. Seems a few years ago you couldn't tell the difference between lawmakin' and lovemakin'. Look at you now, tellin' me what's right n' wrong." Her guise became dire. "For the time bein' . . . we'll let go of The Six. But you've got to promise we'll fix up somethin' just as good when we're on steady ground."

"I promise," said Ares sincerely.

Peyamo's eye scanned the contents of her cup. There were traces of a life form in it — a bug; she drank it down. "I should apologize. When I flew you n' your friends to Tzapodia, I didn't give you my faith. I was scared of you throwin' yourself away for Starlight. I doubted you'd be able to help her without killin' yourself.

"But I also belittled her life a smidgen, didn't I? I do like her, o' course, I just . . . I couldn't stand losin' you, Ares. I was sure Oscerin pushed you but didn't care which goddess said what. I didn't want you to die — for anyone, mind you. I'm sorry. Truly."

Ares softened. "My death would have been my own fault, not Luxea's. It was *my* recklessness in the face of Sh'tarr and Alatos that put my life on the line. Not even Widow tried to . . ." He shook his head at a thought. "I don't believe She wants me harmed; She seems oddly against it. If I'm mindful, She won't target me."

As his poise rotted away, his talons scored the tabletop. "But She'll go to whatever end to kill Luxea. What She holds for her surpasses hatred. When Widow caught her on Mythos, I couldn't do a thing to stop it. I was so afraid, I've never felt so —"

Whatever he was going to say fell off an edge. Peyamo didn't have to record his vital signs to see that the prospect of Luxea getting hurt crushed him. She put down her drink and fixed him in the eye.

"You really care for that girl, don't you?"

Ares chewed his thumbnail. Of course, he cared; he wouldn't have risked his life for her otherwise. What scared him was that he would do it again and again and again.

He'd known for a while that this was more than care. He could have pushed it away, he could have buried it somewhere he would never find it again — but those who denied love craved it forever, and he knew that too.

"Yes, I do."

Peyamo's gold tooth showed in a grin.

# A KNIGHT
# IN CADLESPEAK

### 15.LIGHTSMEET.26.OSC.3
### ELDER'S EXPANSE

DESHA DUNALI'S wheels rolled two days later. High in the sky hovered the Lady's airship, *Matha ou Machina,* which would follow the tracks to Goldenrise and document the locomotive's statistics.

In the conductor's car, Peyamo wrested levers, mashed buttons, and beeped the whistle just for the fun of it. She'd waited years to experience the unhindered power of her first land-machine.

The cars jerked. Luxea's glass of water splashed into her eyes, and Ares secretively clung to the handrail at the end of his seat. Avari and Oliver, the only ones excited for it all, had been hanging their heads out the windows before the locomotive even started moving.

Ruka, who wouldn't fit anywhere but the livestock cars with the dracas, flopped onto a mound of hay. The loud noises were amplified by his canine senses, making this one of the few times Brielle wished they didn't share ears.

Peyamo had warned her passengers that *Desha Dunali* would be fast, but, apparently, they hadn't known the meaning of the word.

They were carried at such an absurd speed that they pulled into Elder's Expanse by late afternoon.

*Desha Dunali* slowed on the outskirt of Cadlespeak, the capital. Peyamo insisted on inspecting the engine before proceeding, for it would be impossible to do so on the Great Bridge, Tarhelen.

Cold wind from The Grey trickled through the pass between Calpher's Mount and the Rise of Reflection, letting out right over Cadlespeak. The Mooncallers and Brielle and Ruka spilled onto the yellow grass. Oliver engulfed himself in his cloak, and Brielle lay on Ruka's back to soak in his body heat. Luxea missed Tzapodia where it was warm and sunny. Cadlespeak felt like it was trapped in a dimension where it was eternally frosttear!

Peyamo trundled out of the conductor's car. "Ares, this might take me all night. If you n' your folks want to snooze at an inn, feel free. I heard a bit o' rattlin' when we were slowin' down. I've got to be sure *Desha's* shipshape, so we don't go flyin' off the rails."

"Take your time," said Luxea, not wanting to go flying off *any* rails, thank you very much.

Right away, Shir locus-jumped to a hill to meditate. Brielle and Ruka sped off to stretch their legs and hunt; they weren't hungry, but the wolf's belly was getting flabby from all that fenlaig he'd been eating.

The last four wandered into the city. Cadlespeak was low in population, most structures were abandoned, and only three or four old couples hobbled down each of the wide roads. It *was* Elder's Expanse, after all, the grandest locale for retirement in the Joined Hands.

Avari mashed her face against the windows of every shop. She'd never seen so many scarves! But she promised Luxea that the purple one she'd given her would always be her go-to choice.

On their stroll, Oliver convinced two middle-aged women to write to him. A third passed by, but before he could pursue her, Ares insisted that he stop giving out the address of Castle Lavrenthea.

"That's an inn," said the Prince, pointing to a two-story cabin on a knoll. "If you three have no objections, I'll reserve our rooms there."

"I'll come with. I've got to find a drink," whined Oliver.

"As long as one drink doesn't result in ten more, you're welcome to follow me," said Ares irritably.

Avari jumped onto Luxea's back, nearly causing her to face-plant. "You two can go. Starstuff and I will be on the prowl for grub."

"I ate on *Desha Dunali,*" said Luxea, working herself free.

"So did I," snickered Avari.

The sorceress and the ranger passed nine restaurants — a lodge famous for chicken steaks, a couple who cooked yulacai in a dirt pit, and a shack that sold nothing but roasted corn, to name a few. Avari, at last, selected a hole-in-the-wall cafe called *Ora Napel* which served authentic Filannian cuisine.

Luxea had never tried food from Filannia. Avari, sounding as if she were making a bet on her life, explained that the dishes had an excellent balance of sweet and spicy. Luxea had a feeling that Avari would spend all of their coin there tonight.

They slipped past the circular doorway. Inside, one table was occupied by a group of heavily armored knights; they weren't local, for Elder's Expanse didn't have a military.

The aroma of Filannian vegetable bowls could have sent Avari to Eletheon. At the bar, she practically shouted her order. The host scribbled it down and passed it to the chef.

As Luxea sat and waited, she licked her finger and dipped it into a dish of granular sugar that was on the table. It had been a while since she'd tasted it; Tzapodia was famous for spices, not sweets. Avari sauntered to her, and Luxea popped her finger into her mouth, pretending like she'd been biting her nails.

"I can't wait," said Avari, patting her taut belly. "I ordered two plates — okay, four — so, if you get hungry, you can pick off mine."

Luxea tucked her pudge into her belt. "I'm fine."

She'd missed having outings with her best friend. Avari must have been thinking the same because she said, "It's been a while since we've had a night to ourselves. So, Luxie, how're you doin'?"

"You know how I'm doing," laughed Luxea.

"But we spend time with other people now, *Seer,*" said Avari theatrically. "Won't you stop being big in your britches and tell me how you're doing?"

"I'm all right, but I do wish our lives weren't so chaotic."

"You take everything so seriously. Tell me about something saucy, yea?" Avari showed her huge, murine teeth. "You and His Highness schmooze a lot nowadays. You seem like great pals. How's that?"

Luxea swiped a sip from her cup of water. "Fine."

Oh, no. There was that classic troublemaker look Avari had.

"The *'Future Queen of Tzapodia'* sort of fine?"

"No," said Luxea tersely. "That's almost as ludicrous as calling you the *'Future Lady of Tarot.'*"

"Can you imagine?" snickered Avari. "But, really, Luxie. You've gotta move quick with Ares, or you'll be suckin' hind tit."

"I'll be *what?*"

Avari waved her hands. "Nothing, nothing. But why not? We've talked about your love life plenty before." Luxea eyebrows tweaked. *What* love life? "Did you forget about that boy you kissed after supper in Venomsnare.25?"

"That was you, and it wasn't a boy," reminded Luxea.

Avari spooned sugar into her mouth. "Shites . . . it was me, wasn't it? Well, she was tall. I like 'em tall."

"It shouldn't be hard to find you a nice someone then. Just about all of them are taller than you," said Luxea slyly.

She was about to elaborate on Avari's search for the ideal swain, but then she overheard the conversation from the knight's table.

"*. . . Western Woods . . .*"

"*. . . the Riders . . .*"

Brielle and Ruka had once been tribesmen of the Riders of the West. Now that the raven rider, Omnia, was the Chieftain of Blackjaw Hollow, the Mooncallers were sworn to protecting them. These knights, whoever they were, could put their allies in danger.

Keeping her voice low, Luxea asked, "Those people are talking about the Riders of the West, aren't they?"

Avari's playful attitude went six-feet-under. The hostess delivered four plates of steaming Filannian food to their table. She nodded her thanks and listened. The knights said nothing significant until —

"*. . . Blackjaw Hollow . . .*"

Forgetting all about her dinner, Avari left her chair with a scrape — no, she didn't forget her dinner. She swiped two plates, plopped them onto the knights' table, and sat down. There wasn't another open seat, so Luxea hovered about behind her.

The knights sliced them with four pairs of blue eyes. Three were men, two young and attractive, one with black hair, the other blonde, and a third, older with grey hair. The fourth knight was a hard-bodied woman with her wavy, auburn hair in a ponytail.

"What are we talking about?" munched Avari.

In a low, husky voice, the female knight asked, *"We?* I don't think our exchange is any of your concern."

"Maybe, maybe not."

Avari spied the crests on their unequipped helmets — a bear's skull with a mountain range painted in a toothed frame on its forehead. The men's were silver, but the woman's was gold; she was their commander.

"You're from The Grey?" asked Avari.

"The Order of the High King of Stonehall," said the older knight.

The commander disarmed his wagging tongue with a menacing glare. "Indeed. Now, if you don't mind, this table is occupied."

Avari scrutinized the commander. Her eyes were blue-green, frigid but somehow tropical like snowfall on an island. She was taller than most women — men too. She had pallor but wasn't as light-skinned as her subordinates.

"You don't look like a native of The Grey," remarked Avari.

The commander vetted Avari just as fastidiously. Tzapodian seal, short and lithe, an impressive stillness. "And you don't look like a Tzapodia native, *nasida,"* — *'ranger'* in Seroden elvish.

"Good eye," said Avari flippantly. "So, as I've asked —"

"As I've said, it isn't your business," spat the commander.

Luxea kneaded her temple. Avari had mastered many skills, but not persuasion. She scooted a plate of potatoes closer to the ranger in hopes that she would eat it and let her do the talking.

"I'm Luxea Siren," she said, extending her hand.

The commander arched her eyebrow, reclined, and spat on the floor. "What do you two want? Coin?"

"Not everyone initiates conversation for their own benefit," said Luxea sagaciously. "You were talking about the Riders of the West and Blackjaw Hollow, and we want to find out why."

The commander was pleased with her straightforwardness. "See how easy it is to be frank?" she asked Avari, who was too distracted by her dinner to notice. "Yes, Luxea Siren, we were talking about the Riders of the West. Why does that interest you?"

"It would be better for everyone if you first told us why you're looking for them," said Luxea unwaveringly.

"How are you so certain we're looking?" asked the commander.

"The Riders of the West are hiding. There isn't much else to be done besides search for them," retorted Luxea.

"Say we are tracking the Riders of the West," said the older knight. "Do you know much about their tribe?"

"Some," said Luxea minimally.

"Their location, perchance?" alluded the blonde knight.

With an unwelcoming expression, Luxea said, "Conveniently, we *do* know their location. Their tribe is allied with us."

The black-haired knight guffawed. "The Riders fight for no one."

"You sound so sure," said Avari, stirring a bowl of hot soup.

"It's common knowledge," said the black-haired knight. "Unlike their eastern counterparts, the Riders of the West show allegiance only to their own."

The commander finished her ale and shooed Luxea and Avari. "It matters not. You're meddling in the affairs of the Knights of Stonehall. If you don't wish for us to throw you out, *leave.*"

"Scare tactics won't work on us, my dear knight — especially not weak ones," said Luxea defiantly.

The older knight stood up. "Watch how you speak to her, girl. This is the High Templar of the Order. Show your respect!"

*She's the High Templar of the Order, is she?*

Luxea pulled aside her hair and flashed her Mooncaller Council member's badge, brand new and shiny. "Show me your respect, and I'll show you mine."

Avari giggled with a dumpling in her mouth.

The high templar clearly recognized the symbol and whom it was that Luxea served directly. She gestured to the sigil with a jerk of her chin. "Your position?"

"Seer of Oscerin. Counterpart of the Speaker," said Avari quickly.

Now the high templar's complexion was as white as her fellow knights' — almost as white as Luxea's. "You're close with Ares?"

That was the first time Luxea had heard a stranger call the Prince of Tzapodia by his first name as opposed to *'His Highness.'*

Avari burped and wagged her finger. "We both are, but Luxie mostly. We live in the castle with him, in the Amber Lounge."

Something told Luxea that the high templar was aware that living in the Amber Lounge wasn't the standard; that place was for royals, not council members or rangers. The high templar's distress must have been out of character, for her knights were questioning her behavior.

Luxea, although curious, wasn't finished talking about the riders. "So, High Templar, tell me: if you want information about the Riders of the West, why not ask one yourself?"

The high templar hid her thoughts behind a well-built wall. With a smirk, she said, "Show us a rider, we'll tell you whatever you ask."

The Knights of Stonehall and Avari, with her Filannian food in her arms, tailed Luxea out the door. It was safe to assume that Brielle and Ruka were still hunting, so she guided them to the forest's edge.

"Avari, do you want to call them?"

After swallowing a chunk of pork, the ranger cleared her throat and howled like a dog. The knights took her yodeling as risible but couldn't have been more clueless of its potency.

The high templar turned to leave, but then —

Another howl. The howl of a real wolf. A *huge* wolf.

Shivers made mountains on the knights' skins when two pairs of candlelight eyes shone in the brush. Ruka trotted to his friends and lapped the side of Avari's head. Brielle hopped off his back and presented a bouquet of rabbit carcasses.

"These long-ears are plump from the cold! I'll bring them onto the iron beast. My brother also caught a plainsteed but ate it. Fat, greedy boy." Brielle glanced past Luxea. "Who are these rubbernecks?"

Luxea flashed an impish grin at the knights. "They're Knights of the Order of Stonehall, Brie. They seek Blackjaw Hollow."

Brielle was about to bite. "They will not find it."

Once she'd taken her time absorbing Ruka's unnatural size, the high templar extended a well-practiced bow to the rider and her wolf.

"Miss Brie, you —"

"Brielle," corrected the rider.

"My mistake, Brielle. You're tribesmen of Blackjaw?"

"We were, but we've since chosen the path of the Moon."

"Whatever for?" asked the high templar a bit contemptuously.

Brielle nestled her head into Ruka's. "That is a story you needn't hear, Owl Child. All Duskriddle children are nosy, nosy . . ." She poked the high templar's bear crest. "Why do you seek Blackjaw? The hollow isn't for metal-skins like you."

The high templar had promised Luxea she would reveal their purpose if they showed her a rider; however, she hadn't prepared to actually meet one. She chose her words carefully. "We've been dispatched to collect arcana from the reservoir within Blackjaw Hollow. The High King of The Grey is ill and in need of it."

"Ever heard of medicine?" coughed Avari.

"Tonics do nothing for High King Urcyn," growled the high templar. "He is —"

"— a demigod," finished Brielle. "Urcyn Jjolenvaar Haldentred is a son of the Bear God Ganra, born Clawsguard.44.Himhre.2. The gods have many sons and daughters across the globe, but Urcyn is one of the few who made something of himself because of it. Most hide away, frightened of the power for which they never asked."

"You know of the High King?" The high templar's sneer said she was planning something. "Urcyn is neither mortal nor immortal, and his body is dying. If he is to continue his reign, we must find the energy to sate his form. That means collecting pure arcana from a reservoir. The Crypt of Beasts of the Eastern Riders is too far and too well-guarded, but there's plenty of arcana to spare in Blackjaw Hollow. So will you share with us the location of your tribe?"

"No," snapped Brielle. "I'm no longer a Rider of the West, but much of my family of the heart is. I'll not put them in danger's way."

"We'll not pillage your hollow, we'll collect what we need to relieve the High King of his pain and be on our way." The high templar adapted a soft, wheedling tone. "I beg you, Brielle. Urcyn is a demigod. You care for the gods, do you not?"

Brielle's pierced eyebrows raised at this sweet-talking, red-haired swaggerer. Her face twisted as she cackled, "You're just like Dragon!"

The high templar stiffened. "Dragon?"

"Yes, the one with horns and a house too big for one man. When he juices me for knowledge, he uses the same body language. A gentle voice, the most tempting of reasoning. You act the same as him."

The high templar whisked her hand at her knights. "Get back to the horses and wait for me there!" The men scuttled away. She closed in and dropped her voice to a whisper. "What *exactly* are you four doing in Elder's Expanse?"

"Do we owe you that answer?" asked Avari sassily.

"Everyone will know soon. We can tell her," said Luxea placidly. "We're en route to Goldenrise to seek out the Time Goddess Anatatri, for reasons of our own . . . and then we'll evacuate the capital."

"Evacuate Solissium?" breathed the high templar. "Why?"

Avari made a *'pbbbt'* noise with her lips. "Goldenrise is a little, eh, vulnerable. The Empress may or may not be in cahoots with Widow."

Her euphemism didn't dampen the high templar's sudden bout of fury. She mouthed what looked like hateful imprecations. "This evacuation was declared by The Six, I assume?"

Luxea grimaced. "The Six is, more or less, *'The Two'* right now."

"Which two?" asked the high templar urgently.

"You should know one, considering his Seer is floatin' right under your nose." Avari slithered her finger into the high templar's face. Her hand was smacked, and she humphed. "Prince Ares Lavrenthea and Lady Peyamo Nelnah."

"Ares and Amo are in Cadlespeak?"

That was the second time the high templar had called a leader by their first name; in this case, their nickname. From what Peyamo had told Luxea, only her personal friends called her *'Amo.'*

"Yes. Ares waits for us at the inn on the hill, and *Amo* is working on her locomotive," said Luxea emphatically.

The high templar's gaze shifted to the inn. She faced Brielle and Ruka to say hurriedly, "Thank you for speaking with us about Blackjaw Hollow. I swear we will bring the tribesmen no harm when we find them."

"They will find you first," warned Brielle.

The high templar thought it was best not to reply. Scowling at Luxea's council sigil, she said, "You other two . . ."

Her farewell was left floating. Gold armor glinted, and she was gone. Luxea, Avari, and Brielle shuddered as a freezing gale from the mountains whipped by.

"She was pretty," said Avari airily.

Through the inn window was the image of Oliver leaning over the bar, beguiling the barmaid. Ares was outside the front door leafing over the Cadlespeak news board.

Luxea jogged to him. "Ares, are you acquainted with a Knight of Stonehall? The High Templar of the Order?" she asked suspiciously.

*What a bizarre question.*

Ares thought back in time. "Not that I recall. I sojourned Stonehall once when was fifteen for the High King's two hundred and sixty-eighth lifeday celebration. I attended a feast and went to sleep early. I never spoke to the knights."

"Odd. Luxie and I crossed a few, and the High King's High Templar seemed to be *really* familiar with you," mentioned Avari.

The Prince only shrugged. Whoever the High Templar of Stonehall was, the awareness between Ares and her was a one-way road.

# FORGOTTEN FRAME

## 16.LIGHTSMEET.26.OSC.3
## THE GREAT BRIDGE, TARHELEN

CROSSING ETERNITY'S Ocean, Luxea opened a north-facing window of the locomotive where she saw, in blurs, the shocked faces of umpteen travelers. Zooming past them in the *Desha Dunali* was a powerful feeling; it was understandable why Peyamo created such machines. She stumbled across the aisle and slid down the south-facing window next. In a trice, her joy took a nosedive into guilt.

When last they'd ridden over the Great Bridge, Tarhelen, it was rainy due to its oceanicity and closeness to Sh'tarr's Iris. Today, it was sunny, and the Iris was nowhere in sight.

Luxea passed unspoken sympathies into the water. Alatos had been so afraid — and there had still been no sign of the missing Sh'tarr.

They had to find the Storm. They'd promised the Sea.

Avari tugged the train of Luxea's robe. "Come with me, pumpkin. Our favorite prince wants to talk to us in the dining car."

"What about?"

"Dunno. It sounded urgent," said Avari facetiously. "I also want to have lunch with you. It's Avari's feeding time."

Luxea shut the window. "I thought as much."

Those in the dining car had been eating for ten minutes. It took Avari only one to consume more than them collectively. She slammed a folded pot pie into her mouth, absorbed a bowl of yulacai stock, and wolfed down a side salad.

"Thank you all for coming," said Ares, stirring his black tea. "I thought it would be wise to pass along a warning before we arrive in Solissium."

"What else are you hiding from us, Dragon?" hissed Brielle.

"Nothing. My concern is that none of you have had the delightful opportunity to meet the Empress. I'm sure you will this time."

"Can I cut her hair while she ain't lookin'?" asked Oliver.

"No." Ares made a sound of long-suffering. "I'll make this simple. Annalais loves attention, flattery, and money. She hates surprises, other women, and failure. The problems with our arrival are that it's unannounced, half of you are female, and we're taking her people."

Peyamo slid open the dining car door. "You talkin' 'bout Anna? Aye, she's a harpy, that woman. Piss her off, n' she'll go to the end of the ploughin' Lemuria to make you suffer tenfold."

"And you were gonna marry this girl, Ares?" scoffed Oliver.

Avari coughed on a cracker. "You were engaged to the Empress?"

"We're not talking about that," said Ares through his teeth.

"Didn't go too smoothly," said Peyamo, earning a glower from Ares. She tossed a bronze finger at Luxea. "Sleep with an eye peepin', Starlight. Anna don't like you."

Luxea upturned one hand. "What did I do?"

"She saw you dancin' with her sweetheart at the gala," laughed Peyamo. "Called you a nasty name. Somethin' like *'that white sl —'"*

"Amo," snapped Ares, "don't you have something to do somewhere that isn't down all of our throats?"

The Lady laughed so hard that she wheezed. As she left the dining car, she said, "You catty bastard. I love ya."

*Desha Dunali* chugged into Solissium the next afternoon. Once they'd unloaded Ruka and the dracas, the Mooncallers rode up to Plateau de Taress. They cantered by the villa, their stares avoiding the ruins of the northwestern wing that had been annihilated by Widow and Garamat in Nightspeak.

Empress Annalais had watchful eyes stationed throughout the capital and had already been notified about the Mooncallers' return. She waited outside for Ares but — unsurprisingly — wasn't pleased with the sight of Avari, Brielle, and particularly Luxea.

As was the case with anyone who looked upon Annalais Taress, those who hadn't met her were breathless. There was nothing about her physique out of place. Her tanned skin sparkled through a dress that was more of an ankle-length negligee, and her eyes of aquamarine seduced and devoured. She was the sort of woman who could ruin your day with a smile.

Annalais rushed down the steps to Ares and twirled her strawberry blonde hair. "You're back so soon. You missed me that much?"

The Prince would have missed a kick between his legs more than the Empress. Monotonous, he said, "I'm sorry we failed to give you notice before coming here. I hope it isn't an inconvenience."

"You're so formal. My home is always open to you, Ares . . ." she showed her gleaming teeth, saying sourly, " . . . and friends."

"We aren't here for pleasure," said Ares diplomatically. "We have business in Goldenrise and matters of dire import to discuss — one being the Widow."

The Empress gripped her slitted skirts. *"We?* If it's about the Brood, should it not be you and me alone?"

"No secrets here," barked Brielle.

Glaring acid at the wolf rider, the Empress slunk away from the Prince. "We will address it later. Would you like to introduce me to your colleagues, Ares?"

He prayed that Brielle would behave. "That's Brielle, previously a Rider of the West. The wolf is Ruka, her brother."

As she looked Brielle up and down, Annalais *popped* her plump lips. To be a pest, Brielle *popped* her even plumper lips in response.

"I've never liked dogs," remarked the Empress.

"Then you'd better run, kitty cat," quipped Brielle.

"Brielle," said Ares seriously.

Annalais wandered to Shir next. The Mythic was leery of the reds, blacks, and violets that shimmered around her figure; it was an oppressive energy. Without moving her gaze from the crystal, the Empress said, "Ares, tell me about this one."

"Shir. A Mythic from the forgotten strand of Mythos."

"Mythos? Where on Amniven is that?"

"It's forgotten, Anna. It doesn't matter."

To break the new silence, Shir bowed their head and held out their hand to shake. Annalais took it, but the Mythic's energy jolted her. She let out a promiscuous moan and whisked away.

Shir felt ashamed. "It is . . . lovely to meet you."

All Annalais managed to say between the shudders in her loins was, "It's stunning . . ."

Wiping down the bumps on her arms, she moved to Avari. Sooner than she could ask, Ares said, "Avari Vishera, a Tzapodian ranger."

Pouting, Annalais bent her knees to remind Avari how vertically challenged she was. "Aw, that's it? A Tzapodian ranger?"

Avari squinted; she could see her own reflection in Annalais's ruby lipstick, and that was downright ludicrous. "Yup. That's all there is to me," she said with a shrug.

The Empress wasn't threatened by Avari's dull, curly bob and flat chest. She moved on, shockingly without any insults to Avari, but at the sight of Oliver, she forgot all about the other women present.

"Oliver Kross," said Ares. "Son of Masters Vesas and Levelia."

"Oh? The heir to the Isle of Varnn." Annalais feigned sympathy. "It seems you don't have anyone left to lead now. Take off your hood for me, nightskin."

Hostile emotions from Oliver toward women — particularly pretty ones — was rare, but he was repelled by Annalais. "Ask me nicer."

Holding her sides to accentuate her curves, the Empress asked again, "Will you *please* take off your hood, Lord Kross?"

Showing a sort of *'I hate this'* glance to Ares first, Oliver removed his hood. Annalais tapped her manicured fingernails on her chin and strutted around him, sucking her lip at his height and lean form. But, frankly, she didn't care; she merely wanted to see a jealous reaction from Ares. All the Prince gave her was a bored, arched eyebrow.

"Quite dashing," she purred.

Oliver crammed his head back into his hood. "Thanks."

Lastly, the Empress approached that familiar, white-haired woman who'd danced with Ares at the gala. That night, she'd been smiling — at *her* possession. Oh, how Annalais hated her. She drew in all the details: the powdered snow that lived beneath her skin, the slight pink that decorated the tips of her pointy ears. But she couldn't see her eyes, and that's what she wanted: *the soul.*

"Look at me, girl," seethed Annalais.

Oh, how Luxea hated her too. Once she'd relaxed her jaw, she obeyed and met eyes with Annalais; the stars turned a harsh scarlet without her control.

It was an impossibility for the Empress to hide her fascination with the cosmos. She wanted to rip out those twinkling eyes and set them into rings.

"So . . ." gulped Annalais, ". . . you enjoy dancing?"

Luxea could play too. "That depends on my partner."

And then they were rivals.

"Ares, who is this brat?" hissed Annalais.

The Prince almost scolded the Empress, but Luxea shot him a look that told him to save his breath. Delicate, he replied, "She's Luxea Siren, a friend, a sorceress, and a member of the Mooncaller Council under the title of *'Seer.'* While I'm Oscerin's voice, Luxea is Oscerin's eyes."

"Oscerin's eyes?" scoffed Annalais. "I won't be surprised if the next girl you latch onto is Oscerin's nose."

"Stop it, Anna," said Ares thickly.

The Empress felt like tearing Luxea to shreds with her bare hands, severing her head and hanging it by a spiked chain above the Solissium gate. She might have done it too had a disembodied voice not butted in.

"Shall I introduce myself as well, Your Highness?"

Annalais stumbled. "Who said that?"

Avari pointed at the Usinnon that hung off Velesari's saddle. "That book — shiny one."

"A *book?*" The Empress took the statement as a joke, but the straight faces around her confirmed that it was no joke at all. "Where in the Trihells did you find a talking book?"

"I am not a book, I am a spellbook," corrected the Usinnon. "My name is Therasi Direl, once a famed professor at Sirah Academy and a twice-as-famed architect of structures across the Joined Hands."

"Funny. I've never heard of you," said Annalais competitively.

"Then, speaking of books, perhaps you should pick one up, Your Splendor," said the Usinnon, verbally slapping Annalais in the face.

*No, no, no! Stop talking!*

Luxea smothered the Usinnon, but it went on babbling.

"You see, Miss Taress, *I* designed this very villa for Emperor Yerris Raleen. Are you familiar with that name? No, I shouldn't expect such cognizance from you. The Raleens were the royal family of Goldenrise before your great, great, great, great, great, great, great grandfather usurped the throne and renamed my creation, *'Villa de Raleen,'* as *'Villa de Taress.'* But don't be ashamed of the greed in your bloodline. I simply ask you to remember that I am far more celebrated in history than you — and I'm sure Miss Siren will be too."

Annalais had nothing to say. How do you win an argument with a virtually omniscient spellbook? You don't. No one spoke as they ascended the steps into Villa de Taress.

Lending bedchambers to strangers didn't thrill Annalais, but after the Usinnon's blows, she had to repair the cracks with generosity.

While the others took the evening to relax, the Prince joined the Empress in the sanctum. Annalais had wished for more intimacy than politics, but that was the absolute last idea on Ares' mind. She poured them glasses of wine and led him to the terrace where he smoked roseleaf, and Annalais drank with her heart-shaped eyes fixed on him.

"Thank you for allowing us to rest here," he exhaled.

"Always," said Annalais adoringly.

Ares ignored her intonation. "My first request is access to Hildre."

Together, they gazed at the far-off Golden Spire that towered over the skyline. "Why do you need to go there?" she asked.

"Because we have impossible questions, and N'ra told us that Anatatri can give us the answers we need," he said vaguely.

She giggled. "N'ra is talking to you now too?"

Ares showed her a glare marked somewhere between spiteful and corrective. "No, we met Her." The Empress' made a small noise. "So may I please have access to the Golden Spire?"

"How do you plan on finding Anatatri?"

"We'll enter the Memory Door."

The Empress tapped her lover's nautilus wineglass — one she'd brought out just for Ares. "You realize that the Memory Door is a myth, don't you, my love?"

"Do *not* call me that." Annalais swallowed. "I no longer believe in myths. Shir was a myth a few moons ago, and now they're here in your villa. So, no. Neither of us can say the Memory Door is a myth."

After her many years with Ares, Annalais had learned it was best not to argue. "I can't find an excuse not to, so I'll indite a writ of entry for the Timeless Mountain Pass." She chewed her bottom lip, streaking the flawless red. "Will all of you be going?"

"Yes, all of us. Within three days, at most."

Annalais was downcast that he'd be leaving and inexplicably worried that Luxea would be at his side. She could feel her emotions splitting; she had to talk about something else.

"You needed to speak with me about the Widow?"

Preparing himself for the worst, Ares drank his entire shell of wine. Annalais refilled it at once as if she'd been waiting for him to lick up the last drop.

"The agreement we made in Nightspeak is void," informed Ares. "With Peyamo's help, we'll evacuate Solissium and all other cities we can manage before the Brood Mother hears of our actions."

The Empress set down the ewer. Her emotions did more than split, they multiplied into a legion. "That's why you came," she cried. "To take the last of my power away from me."

"I came because your empire is at risk," countered the Prince. "If you had no choice when you signed Goldenrise away to the Brood, I understand. Your people, however, shouldn't suffer for your decision."

She fell onto him. "But there's been no sign of Widow — !"

"Anna, I've seen Her too, and I've seen that of which She's capable. She hasn't shown Herself yet, but there will be no stopping Her once She does." He took her by her shoulders. "Do you care for the people of Goldenrise or not?"

In truth, Annalais *was* concerned for their welfare. Withal, she dreaded the loss of authority that an evacuation of this magnitude would bring. She looked at Ares. He didn't appear loving or accepting, not at all, but she was looking at him, and that was all that mattered.

"When this is over, may they come home?"

"Of course." Ares let her go. She felt lost. "These are your people, but until Widow is vanquished, they're walking targets in your empire.

Their lives will be spared in Tzapodia. When this war is over, I'll send them home to you."

Trying anything to recuperate, Annalais refilled both of their shells of wine. She hadn't noticed that his was already full, and it spilled. She reached to clean it up, but Ares stopped her and did it himself.

Wiping her tears with the utmost delicacy, she said, "Fine. Do it."

He tossed the wine-soaked rag aside and retook his seat. "Thank you. They will be safe in my kingdom. You have my word."

The Empress watched him drink from his overfilled shell. A new question bit her so hard that she couldn't refrain from asking it. "Is that all you wanted to say? Is that the only reason you came back?"

Ares glanced at her. "Were you expecting something else?"

There were a million and one things that Annalais wanted from the Prince, but she knew that expression. Ares was in no mood for conversations or actions relating to their past, and it was likely that he never would be.

Holding in her yearning, she told him, "No. Nothing else."

After visiting the hot springs, Luxea changed into her nightgown and let her hair loose; the air wasn't too cold in Solissium this time of year, so it wouldn't take long to dry. She made her way down the colonnade and spotted bookshelves through an open doorway.

*A library!*

Her brain ached for books other than the Usinnon. It wasn't that she didn't enjoy her spellbook, it was that it regularly lectured her when she was trying to study.

She darted around like a gnat in a pile of fruit. While she wasn't fond of Annalais — *at all* — she had to commend her for her literary collection. But she suspected these were her family's books, not hers.

Under the windowsill was a shelf of romance novels, Luxea's guilty pleasure. She scampered to it, so hooked on the titles that she didn't notice her foot catching on a sheet of cloth. She steadied herself on a marble bust, and it wobbled; she prayed it wouldn't smash to bits.

The fabric that had snatched her sandal had trailed behind her and revealed a frame. Luxea forgot about the romance novels forthwith, for in the picture was a man in golden armor with fiery hair and blue eyes. He was unfairly attractive with his large hands on the pommel of his gladius — but that wasn't why she was gawping at his face.

This man, this gorgeous, stoic man, was virtually identical to the High Templar of the Order of Stonehall in Cadlespeak.

The Prince strode through the villa with his wineglass, meaning to visit the sea cliffs, but then he spotted the back of Luxea's wavy hair. Swirling his drink, he went into the library and took in her face; her stars were green, the color for deep thought.

"Doing a touch of snooping before bed?" he asked playfully.

Luxea leaped in a start. "Oh, Ares! I hadn't seen you." She glanced at the painting. "Sorry, but do you happen to recognize this man?"

Ares' eyes trailed to the frame, and then his brows twitched. He licked his bottom lip twice before whispering, "Rowan."

*"This* is Rowan Taress? The last Emperor of Goldenrise?"

She held her head to stop it from whirling. She'd seen a bust of Rowan's body in Haven de Asrodisia, but his head had been removed. It was a crime to have broken something so beautiful! It was no small wonder why Estalyn had fallen in love with him.

To their unawareness, Annalais had followed Ares to further their conversation in his bedchamber. Her plans took a turn when he met with Luxea instead. She crouched behind a pillar, holding the tail of her gown to keep it from dirtying. She'd expected them to express adoration for each other, but, no — they talked about her deceased brother. This was as disconcerting as whispers of love or lust.

"Did you know Rowan?" wondered Luxea.

"That's like asking me if I know Peyamo." Ares lined the strokes of paint with his eyes. "Rowan and I grew up together. He was as much my inspiration as he was my friend."

Luxea hoped that this topic wasn't too much for Ares. That being said, she *had* to know if her theories were pure speculation. Rowan's death was a sensitive subject, and talking about Annalais made Ares sick, but it was worth taking the chance.

"Do Annalais and Rowan have a sister? Perhaps estranged, around the same age as you," she suggested.

Behind the pillar, Annalais held her stomach and trembled.

Ares didn't react as negatively as Luxea had thought. "Not at all. It was just the two of them. Alienation is unheard of in this family; the Taresses are close-knit."

"You're entirely sure?"

"Positive." Ares could usually read what Luxea was thinking with fair simplicity, but not right now. "Why the sudden interest?"

She closed her eyes and evoked a clear memory of the high templar's face. When she opened them, the image in her head matched the one in the painting — everything from the self-assured expression down to the last lineament.

"Ares, the High Templar of Stonehall is indistinguishable from Rowan. There wasn't another Taress sister, a bastard child? I'm telling you, that woman in Cadlespeak *knew* you." Luxea tapped the painting. "This is what she looked like. The hair, the skin, the eyes — even the panache! Brielle too said she acted like you. A royal, a politician."

Rowan's blue-green eyes seemed to glimmer, staring from the land of the dead into that of the living. Momentarily, Ares felt as if his friend hadn't taken his own life all that time ago.

He was about to say something, but as if his open mouth had shifted the world, a distant crash came through the window.

Ares and Luxea ducked below the sill, forgetting all about Rowan and the High Templar of Stonehall. They worried that Widow had returned, that She'd come for Luxea once again, but it was merely a vestige of Her wrath.

Through the glass was a silhouette, bent on the sea cliffs. One of the last standing rooms of the northwestern wing had collapsed. Blasting powder streaked up the walls, erasing the serenity that the place had once borne. It was a skeleton where lifeless bodies yet lay in bejeweled gowns and expensive suits. Had it not been for Oscerin, Ares and Luxea would have been among the hundreds of victims.

"It feels like it was all a nightmare," he said as they stood.

"I wish it were."

Luxea blinked. The image of fire and smoke through Oscerin's stained glass face made her flinch. She blinked again. There stood Ares in the rain in Anathema, admitting that those people had died because of her. She tried to keep her eyes open for fear that another guilty reminder would arise.

"Will you be honest with me?" she whispered. "Had I not gone with you to the gala, would Widow have done what She did?"

This was the last question Ares had wanted to hear. His real answer would wound her — but she'd asked him to be honest. "No," he told her. "But if you'd stayed in Tel Ashir, Widow would have targeted you there instead. Oscerin couldn't have protected you . . . nor could I."

It warmed Luxea that he was frank, but it made her twice as cold that her mere existence had stolen away that of so many others.

For an inhale, she felt like disappearing.

On the exhale, she felt like drinking.

"May I have some of your wine?"

His eyes told her, *'I already drank out of it.'* Her eyes told him, *'I'm the last person in the world who would care.'* He handed it to her.

While she supped, Ares relived the wassail of that bittersweet evening. Teaching his date how not to slouch, seeing Peyamo again after so many years, dancing with Luxea — even if she had no idea how to do it . . . and the explosions that had ruined it all.

At his side, Luxea's presence vivified. That girl created a butterfly effect, in every sense of the word.

As selfish as his reason for bringing her had been, what would have been the outcome had he not assigned her to join him in Goldenrise? Unblossomed, Runa, wouldn't be free, he wouldn't have watched Peyamo dance for the first time, and maybe he and his men wouldn't have made it past Blackjaw Hollow or met Brielle and Ruka. If he'd managed to reach Solissium without Luxea, he might've returned to Tzapodia to find her lifeless.

The thought made him sick.

He took back his drink, set it on the bookshelf, and wrapped his arms around her. Luxea kept a gulp of wine in her mouth when her cheek met his chest and swallowed it when his fingers combed through her damp hair.

"May I be honest about something else?" he asked.

She tried to look at him, but he wouldn't let her. "Yes."

"You've changed me in ways I thought I couldn't be changed."

Luxea stepped back and touched his face, urging him to stare at her instead of an unspecific spot on the wall. With some struggle, he met her eyes. Her stars fluttered through novas of vivid pink; he'd seen this color before, but never so brightly.

Maybe he would kiss her.

He tangled her hair around his hand and tilted her head back. The silver ring in his nose brushed her upper lip, and their breaths were shared, but it wasn't until they'd closed their eyes that he had second thoughts. Instead, he softly pecked her forehead.

"Soon, but not in this place," he told her.

And Luxea understood. Ares had too many painful memories here in Goldenrise, in Villa de Taress. Settling for the next best thing, she hugged him.

Behind the pillar, Annalais slid onto the floor and wept.

# To Love a King

## 20.Lightsmeet.26.osc.3
### Villa de Taress, Goldenrise

TODAY, the Mooncallers would leave Solissium, ride along the coast, through Dulcinus, up the Timeless Mountain Pass, and to the gates of the Golden Spire and the Memory Door.

Their dracas were fed and saddled. Avari was ecstatic to ride Elthevir somewhere other than the streets of Tel Ashir, but Oliver didn't feel the same about interacting with Musha. The grumpy dracas glared at him and stood on his foot.

As Luxea fed Velesari snacks, Ares walked by with Pveather. She waved and said, *"Iu lemi thois,* Pveather!"

The Prince's dracas tugged him behind her and nuzzled her snout into Luxea's head. Avari gaped at them. She couldn't count the instances that the pompous, white dracas had nearly champed off her limbs!

"How did you do that, Luxie? Pveather has never been nice to you — hells, she hated you more than me! What'd you say to her?"

Luxea shrugged at Ares. Ares shrugged at Avari.

From the balcony of her sanctum, Empress Annalais watched the Mooncallers ride into the distance. She was equal parts relieved and distraught to be alone again. Curled up on a chaise, she spilled into a journal all that she loved, hated, wished, and feared.

Prior to his visit for the gala, it had been close to a decade since she'd seen Ares. Before that, they'd been together for seven years. Annalais remembered when they'd met as if she were still living it. She'd written about it many times before but could never think about it enough.

She'd been twelve years old, him thirteen.

## 8. Worldbreak.10.0SC.3
### Villa de Taress, Goldenrise

*Ares and Rowan practiced sword fighting in the courtyard. Rowan sent the Prince rolling and aimed the end of his blade at his chin.*

*"Too slow, dragon boy," he said, teal eyes gleaming.*

*Cheeks dimpling mischievously, Ares swung his leg and knocked Rowan off his feet. They wrestled until Isabelia Taress, Rowan's mother, fluttered down the staircase, hand-in-hand with the Queen of Tzapodia Manalaei Lorcé-Lavrenthea.*

*"Up, boys!" said Isabelia. "Rowan, help your father in the study."*

*Rowan kicked the dirt. "But I hardly get to see Ares!"*

*Isabelia smacked her son's bright red head. "You'll be seeing him a lot less if you don't do as I tell you!"*

*Unwilling, Rowan helped the Prince to stand. "Spar later?"*

*"Absolutely," said Ares, shaking out his hair.*

*Manalaei tucked a black tress behind his horns. "Clean up, nach lathene. There's someone your father and I want you to meet."*

*"Who is it?" asked Ares, taking his mother's arm.*

*"You'll see."*

*They followed Isabelia to the sanctum where, by the hearth, sat a girl. Ares had never seen anyone quite as pristine. Her strawberry blonde hair was braided neatly beneath a gold tiara, and her eyes were the color of a shallow sea.*

*Isabelia whispered to her and pulled her up off the chaise. The girl straightened out her silky, white gown, sure not to disturb the rubies lining her waist.*

*"Ares, you know Rowan," started Isabelia, "but I'd like for you to meet my daughter Annalais. Anna, greet His Royal Highness."*

*The young duchess curtseyed and gave Ares a smile for which he would have died. In a voice like pearls, she said, "I'm honored to stand before you, Your Highness."*

*The Prince just stared at her.*

*"Ares," said Manalaei in a hushed tone, "when you're older, you and Annalais will be married."*

*Everyone else in the room looked elated. It didn't take the Prince more than two seconds to realize that he'd been the only one unaware of these plans.*

*The Queen nudged him. "Say hello to her, nach lathene."*

*Wringing his fingers, he stepped forth and requested Annalais's hand. Not meeting her breathtaking gaze, he bowed and made a kissing motion above her knuckles.*

*"A p-pleasure, Your Splendor."*

*Ares practically sprinted back to the door. Annalais giggled.*

*For the next week, the Prince spent every moment with his newly betrothed. Rowan was irritated, but Ares couldn't get enough of his sister. In the evening on the eighth day, Annalais took him to the*

*garden over the sea where they sat on the edge of a fountain with roses pirouetting on the water's surface.*

*Queen Manalaei wandered around a hedge with the purple veil she always wore on her head. "Ares, will you be out much longer?"*

*"Yes. I'll be inside later," he said abruptly.*

*"All right, nach lathene. Sleep sweet."*

*When the Queen left, Ares blew hair out of his face and said, "I'm sorry, Anna. She isn't used to leaving me alone."*

*"It's okay. I like your mother." Annalais fumbled with her satin gloves. "But why does she hide her face? I've never seen it."*

*For the first time in seven days, Ares stared at the ground instead of his promised. "The King hurt her. He scratched her."*

*"Your father?"*

*"Yes."*

*"Why would he do that?"*

*Clinging to his Felastil and praying that Oscerin would be at his side, he whispered, "When I was little, she let me out of the castle when she wasn't supposed to."*

*"Oh. Is she okay?"*

*"No. She can't see anymore."*

*The Queen of Tzapodia couldn't see? How terrible! Annalais stared at Ares' long fingers. "Did the King do it with his. . . . talons?"*

*The Prince nodded. With the fountain babbling in the background, Annalais strained to imagine one of Ares' hands as a claw. The very thought disgusted her.*

*"You won't hurt me like that, will you?"*

*Ares shot her with a pained look. He pulled her into the tightest embrace before he could allow her to see his tears falling.*

*"I'm not like him! Don't ever ask me that again!"*

# Chapter Twenty

## 21.CLAWSGUARD.14.OSC.3
### CASTLE LAVRENTHEA, TZAPODIA

*Years later, Annalais visited Castle Lavrenthea; she'd been looking forward to this trip for moons. Ares had promised they'd spend time together, but he was outside training for combat. From six stories above the courtyard, she could hear the clashing of swords.*

*Time was rushing by. It would be the end of sunrae in three weeks, and then Annalais would return to Villa de Taress to keep up with studies of her own. She retreated to the sofa and wished for the empty space beside her to be filled.*

*That same afternoon, King Naiv Lavrenthea dumped his work onto Wing Regent Isaak. He passed by the Amber Lounge and found his son's promised curled up on the sofa in tears. She was young, no older than sixteen, and her innocence drew him in like a shark to blood.*

*She was delicate; he wanted to break her.*

*"Lemireau lalene, lovely girl, what's wrong?"*

*Annalais shot up from the sofa and fixed her dress. Bowing her head to hide her florid cheeks, she said, "Your Majesty, forgive me. I didn't mean to disturb you."*

*"No, no, I'm worried for you." Naiv sat her down and claimed the space beside her. "Ares has left you alone again. So frivolous, neglecting a flower as she blooms before him."*

*This was the King of Tzapodia? Annalais had been told so many things, none of them positive. "You're so nice, but Ares says you did horrible things to people in Naraniv — to him and the Queen too."*

*Naiv looked like a king then. "Sweet, do you know what happens if you allow others to stand in your way? They will use you, they will*

217

take from you all that you hold dear. If you don't cling to your beliefs, they will be stolen. I've hurt others only because they let me. My son cannot comprehend such a thing. Can you?"

She took his bait but was frequently glancing at the window where Ares practiced below. To pull her mind out of his son's clutches, the King poured her a glass of red wine and urged it into her hand.

Annalais stared into the red. "I don't think I should have this."

"Ares drinks. Why can't you?" The king gleamed. "Take it."

Abiding by his rules, Annalais brought the goblet to her lips. Naiv watched her sip. She'd never had alcohol; it would take effect soon.

"You must regret your devotion to him," he continued. "It's no secret that his love for duty far surpasses his love for you."

It was impossible for her to disagree. "He says he loves me, he gives me things and smiles at me . . . but he then he leaves to spend time with my brother, and, by the time he comes back, is too tired for me."

She finished her glass, so Naiv refilled it. In minutes, red blotches appeared on her chest, and her head tipped slightly. She grinned at all of the King's remarks, having completely forgotten about Ares.

Naiv pinched her bottom lip. "You can't feel it at all, can you?"

Annalais touched her numb cheeks. "No, I can't," she giggled.

"Beaujezel," said the King, meaning 'beautiful.' She reached for her drink, but he stopped her hand. "You've had quite enough, Your Splendor. Let's get you to bed."

He led her down the hall. Annalais couldn't remember what had happened five minutes ago, but she could recognize that the King wasn't taking her to Ares' room — he was taking her to his own.

*It took Queen Manalaei a sennight to hear about the ongoing relations between her husband and her son's betrothed. On the afternoon of Annalais's last day in Castle Lavrenthea, she confronted Naiv.*

*"Your Majesty," she said, feeling her way into the Ruby Bureau.*

*Naiv glared up from his paperwork. "What is it?"*

*Manalaei found her way to his desk. "Annalais will be leaving tomorrow. You must be disappointed."*

*"What makes you say that?"*

*"You needn't hide it from me, Naiv. You've taken her virtue." The Queen whispered next, "When she leaves . . . do not tell our son."*

*The King laughed. "You will lie to him?"*

*"He loves her. It would destroy his heart! I would rather he be as blind as I. Pray do not give him the truth of what you have done — nor what she has done."*

*Naiv wasn't against this; he never interacted with Ares as it was. Manalaei heard his chair creak under his weight as he leaned back.*

*"And you, Mana? How do you feel about it?"*

*"Do not pretend to care for my concerns," said the Queen hatefully. "I will not deny that I'm sickened. The girl is callow, and you have taken all advantage of it!" She inclined over the desk. "But if your bed is open to whomever you please, do not expect me to cater to you exclusively. Shall you defy me, I shall defy you."*

### 3.NIGHTSPEAK.16.OSC.3
### VILLA DE TARESS, GOLDENRISE

*It was Annalais's eighteenth lifeday, and she was running late for her celebration luncheon! She broke into the banquet hall, entirely out of breath — but nobody was at the table.*

A Goldenhand across the room announced, "The gathering has been relocated to the garden, Your Splendor. Happy lifeday."

The last thing Annalais wanted to do was sprint around more, but the Taress family had never been renowned for their patience. She bowed to the Goldenhand and shut the door.

It took only a few minutes to reach the garden by the sea. But when she reached her destination, she didn't find her family. Standing in front of the fountain was Ares. Moons had passed since she'd last seen him.

He was sure not to touch her with his claw when she leaped into his arms. Over the years, she'd only gotten more beautiful. Today, she was the most beautiful he'd ever seen her. Breath hitched, he slipped a ruby ring crafted into the shape of a rose onto her finger.

Carved into the band was 11.LM.17.

"This is me asking, not our families. Marry me on this day, right here," he whispered. "Every time you read this, remember that you're my treasure."

Thoughts of the King and all the others she'd seen in the Prince's absence rotted Annalais's mind. The King was gone, but she saw him in Ares. This was the closest she could get.

With her beloved oblivious to the truth, she accepted.

## 4.Lightsmeet.17.OSC.3
### Castle Lavrenthea, Tzapodia

One year passed. Keen to become the Princess of Tzapodia, Annalais had moved into Castle Lavrenthea. Her wedding ceremony with Ares would be in a week; all of the arrangements had been made.

*That day in Lightsmeet, Ares left the Ruby Bureau early in hopes of taking his fiancee for a walk on the shore. Thinking nothing of it, he opened his bedchamber door.*

*It then felt like all of his bones broke at once.*

*Pinned to the wall by a man was Annalais, her gown and her lover's Tzapodian military uniform strewn across the floor.*

*She shoved the warrior. "Ares!"*

*But he'd already slammed the door and stormed to the Amber Lounge. He paced in fast circles, having forgotten how to breathe or cry or scream. In a fit of some emotion that he didn't recognize, he kicked over a table and threw an ewer down the hallway.*

*Bawling, her gown lopsided, Annalais ran to him and grabbed his arm. He shook her away and shouted, "Get your hands off me!"*

*"Ares, please! I'm so sorry — !"*

*"Don't you dare say that to me!" All he saw in her tears was someone else beneath her. "How long has this been going on?"*

*"It hasn't — !"*

*"How long?"*

*Hands shaking, Annalais held up two fingers.*

*"Two what? Two days? Two weeks?"*

*Annalais cried much, much harder. "Years."*

*That was all it took for every truth that Ares had ever believed to become a lie. All feelings left him. "Two years? With him, a soldier?"*

*She fell to the floor pathetically. "No . . ."*

*Ares laughed but didn't know why. "So more came before him?" Annalais refused to answer. "Tell me who else!"*

*Hiding her face in her arms, she choked out, "The King."*

*Frankly, Ares would have rather been told that he had an hour left to live. With a false smile he couldn't rightly control, he muttered, 'the*

*King,' over and over again. His eyes closed, and when they opened, his irises were violet, and his pupils were in vertical slits.*

*Annalais kicked and screamed down every stairwell. Ares led her to the Kingslane and paid a horse master four times his rate to take her to Solissium that very afternoon. Annalais wouldn't get in the carriage, so Ares lifted her up and latched the door.*

*The last thing he said to her was, "You will never see me again."*

Even after Annalais had become the Empress and a member of The Six, Ares had cursed standing in the same room as her. That had lasted until he'd attended her annual gala. But upon his arrival, there'd been a woman on his arm — that white-haired, starry-eyed woman.

Annalais had a theory that Ares had dragged Luxea along to make her jealous; she was right, but she wouldn't confront him about it.

Now Ares had come back, and so had that girl, the *'Seer.'* Annalais had tried to rid herself of paranoia, but seeing them together that night in the library had broken her heart more than when Ares had left.

The Empress blotted a pretty tear off her cheek and set her swan-feather quill in its ink pot. An icy breeze floated by. What was the matter with this weather? The air had been balmy ten minutes before. She got up to close the balcony door, but then she yelped and fell back into her seat.

Across the sanctum was Widow. She looked . . . different. That night at the gala, the room had rumbled, and metal objects had been drawn to Her magnetic energy. She'd been a spider, a nightmare —

But today She was a goddess.

"You've been weeping," whispered Widow.

Annalais scrambled away. "Yes."

"Because you've been abandoned."

"Y-yes."

The Brood Mother ran Her hand down the back of Her bald head and knelt in front of Annalais. "It's too cruel. Those of us with hearts of glass love the most violently."

Tender, Widow brushed Her cold fingers down the side of Annalais's face. The Empress was startled that Her touch was comforting like a mother's.

"You know that Ares' hatred is warranted, don't you? An affair with the King of Tzapodia, the father of your betrothed. Such a thing is unforgivable," said Widow sternly. "But it was a long time ago, and our blunders do not deem us unworthy of love. I can make him forgive you, I can make him forget it all . . . but you must heed my wishes. Will you allow me to help you, Treasure?"

Hearing that name pass through Widow's serrated teeth brought Annalais to her senses. "No, you're a villain! Leave me alone! If I follow you, Ares and Peyamo will make me their enemy!" Her fingers dug into her gown. "But if I forsake You . . . You will kill me."

Widow drew back. "Kill you? Who told you this? You believe that I would seek your death for simply denying me?"

"I know You would!"

The Brood Mother's smile was as endearing as it was threatening. "I revere you, Annalais, and I don't want you to die. If it is your wish, I will leave you and allow you to find your own path through the labyrinth of lost love."

"You will?"

"You have my word." Widow turned away but halted. "But if I go, the stars will take him from you. He will never be yours again."

Annalais clenched her teeth. "That woman, Luxea Siren?"

Luxea's name cast Widow into hysteria. She whirled around and flashed the line of razors in Her gums. "Sweet, little thing, isn't she? Kind, clever, a sorceress — and she's even *more* special now that Oscerin has chosen her. She's the reason that Ares violated the contract. She told him that, because of you, Goldenrise would fall. She's turning him against you!" Her eight white pupils searched for another argument. "Haven't you heard, Your Splendor? Only moons ago, he flew into Sh'tarr's Iris to save her life."

The Empress looked as if sunlight had never kissed her skin.

"He flew her . . . ?"

"Ares furthered his draconism for her. He fought with Sh'tarr and Alatos by wing, claw, and fire for *her!* Did he ever do that for you?"

"No," said Annalais furiously.

"He shouldn't have done it for her either. Stupid boy," said Widow derisively. "That woman sparkles like the stars — oh, yes — but she's a witch! A demon dressed in white!"

Annalais wiped her fiery tears. "You also resent her?"

Briefly, Widow looked human. "More than you will ever know."

Losing Ares to someone else, to someone so pointless, was indeed the worst of Annalais's fears. She'd thought that if Ares saw her again that he would love her as he once had, and she'd been wrong.

But if Widow could stop Luxea Siren . . .

"How will you help me, and why?"

A smug grin manifested on the Brood Mother's black lips. "Drink me in. When next you see your lover of yore, give him your breath. He will not resist you. You will be the beckoning tongue, the forbidden rose for which he would give his life for a taste. Isn't that what you've dreamed about? Isn't that what has kept you awake at night all these years?

"The *'why'* is simple. I want Ares on the Brood's side. My gifts will establish the divine connection among man, woman, and goddess. You will both be my children when it is done. The essence of the spider from the mouth of the sinner will make him yours *and* mine."

"That would be forcing Ares to be with me," said Annalais at once. "It would make no difference. In the end, it would be of my will, my love — not his own."

"As if that mattered to you when you forced all those courtesans to do the same. That little girl, Runa, ten years old? And you put her in chains!" Annalais lowered her eyes; she had indeed done it. Widow touched her. "But fear not, for I understand. Naiv Lavrenthea made you a victim too. He was not your intended, yet you surrendered yourself to him time and time again because of his coaxing. Oh, but you *relished* it. You do not regret your moments with the King, so why would his son regret his moments with you?"

Annalais's morals burned down quickly. Soon, they were arrantly irretrievable. "If I do this, Luxea can't have Ares?"

"He will never touch her again."

That's right . . . it *was* what she'd dreamed about.

Annalais took the Brood Mother's hand. Widow petted her curled hair and cupped her cheeks, so close that their noses touched.

"Stay very still, Treasure."

The kiss was pleasant until Widow sank Her hidden fangs into Annalais's lip. Venom flowed, and the Empress jolted. It was a jarring, nauseating pain. Something ate at a part of her she couldn't name.

Her soul, perhaps. Yes, that was it.

The pact was complete. Widow wiped a drop of black fluid from Annalais's mouth and sat her down as her body came out of shock. Holding her hand, She said, "Breathe into him, and he will be ours."

# The Memory Door

## 22.Lightsmeet.26.Osc.3
### The Golden Spire

The Dracas were familiar with moors and level terrain, so it took a mere two days for the Mooncallers to reach the Timeless Mountain Pass. On the last stretch of the trail was a guard's post where beyond was a golden gate, and in it was engraved a poem.

*"Time is the loneliest place.*
*I am everywhere and nowhere,*
*Hiding amidst the colors of voices, the heat of sound.*
*I am the seed from which life and death is born,*
*I eat the air, the water, the earth.*
*They say that time fixes everything,*
*But when you are time itself,*
*Who will fix you?"*

Ares drew up by the gate and knocked on the guard's window. As they waited, Avari and Oliver raced down the trail and back.

A Goldenhand soldier swung open the window, and Ares handed him the writ of passage Annalais had given him. "We request access to the Golden Spire," he said formally. "We've been granted passage by the Empress."

The hoplite glanced at the page. "Wonder what you had to do to get this, Your Highness. For what purpose have you come? Giving your friends a tour of the past?"

*How funny.*

"We seek the Memory Door," said Ares briskly.

The Goldenhand cackled. "The Memory Door is a myth."

"Myths are born from truths," said Brielle severely.

"Whatever you say, puppy." Ares had to hold Brielle back from eating the skin from his throat. The Goldenhand scribbled *'approved'* onto the writ and gave it back to Ares. "Best of luck with your door."

After riding twenty reaches, it was apparent that uncovering the Memory Door would be no easy task. The Golden Spire erupted from a crater spotted with broken stones and spindling trees, the redness of the dusty earth muted by thin veils of snow from atop the mountains of rhyolite.

Ruka rounded the Golden Spire, and Brielle ran her fingers along the surface. "We're in the world of the divines. Doors will not look to us as they do to them. They will be hidden, formed only for discovery by those who search in the right places."

Avari groaned and flopped onto Elthevir's neck. Her dracas shook himself and slapped her with one of his spines; she hit him back. "Shir, any chance you can talk to the Golden Spire too?"

The Mythic approached the spire and rang, their tone wavering, trilling, and pulsing. Amazingly, the gold *did* respond. Two children of the earth that had never crossed communicated as if they'd been friends for all lifetimes. The Mooncallers were on the edges of their saddles when Shir stepped away.

"I asked about the Memory Door," said the Mythic.

"What did it say?" asked Luxea.

"It said, *'we are all doors,'*" they replied.

Avari mashed her face into Elthevir's scales. "That's helpful."

"It is. Hildre has never given such a hint," said Shir plainly.

Ares was growing weary of riddles. He rotated Pveather. "Our best chance lies in exploration."

The Mooncallers trotted along. Oliver whistled without rhythm, and Luxea shot sparks into the twilight air to keep herself from dying of boredom. By the time it was dark, there had been no sign of the Memory Door.

The Irestar shone brightly as they pitched camp. Their tents were blankets trussed by twisty branches they'd found buried in the ground, and betwixt them burned an arcanan flame.

Oliver rolled over in the cold, pebbly dirt and stared up the height of the Golden Spire. "Oi. Where'd the spires come from anyway?"

"Anatatri made them," said Shir knowingly.

Brielle marveled. "Did She? How?"

"They were created with Her birth," answered Shir. "Amniven was not always a planet. It was once an egg."

Avari perked up. "An egg, you say?"

"Indeed," replied Shir. "In the time before time, the Sisters of Sun, Moon, and Fire — Tirih, Oscerin, and Ka'ahn — were born. They wished to follow in Their mother Lemuria's footsteps, to become artists of vitality, so They forged Their own world: *'Amniven.'*

"Little had the Daughters known that what They had created was not a world, it was an egg. Amniven was gold, silver, and flame. From that fusion was brought into existence the first divine of the mortal plane, whom They named, *'Anatatri.'*

"At the peak of Her development, Anatatri kicked and screamed within the blazing core. Her limbs cracked the shell of the planet in six places, and the crust spiraled into the clouds. With Her first breath, recorded time began, and thus She became the Goddess of Time.

"Those six breaks in the world became the six spires, and those spires became the wombs that bore the goddesses of the mortal plane. Anatatri, the Golden Spire Hildre. Alatos, the Coral Spire Tsrei. Sh'tarr, the Glacial Spire Tekrah. N'ra, the Crystal Spire Sirah. Daetri, the Steel Spire Nervir. Himhre, the Sandstone Spire Ilsemet. However, Asrodisia, the eighth divine, was instead born from the Bone Spire, the failed frame of the first titan Naolen.

"Together, the goddesses shaped Amniven and built the twelve gods. The twenty-two divines then combined Their essences to form the animals, the plants, the men, the women, and all those in between."

"Has Anatatri ever left the Golden Spire?" wondered Brielle.

"Only once. In the onset of existence, She stepped into the mortal realm, but the very structure of reality crumbled under Her gaze. As time Herself, Anatatri could not enter a plane where a second form of time existed concurrently. Two lines crossed, stable and unstable, and no longer did past, present, or future bear meaning."

"Probably a good thing She ain't never left," gulped Oliver. "Shir, d'you think anyone's ever gone through the Memory Door?"

"No one has. Hildre told me."

Ares sat up. "What? No one has been inside?"

"Only the Goddess of Time."

"Then how do we know we can get in at all?" whimpered Avari.

"The Memory Door exists, but no one has found it."

"Never? Not in three millennia?" asked Luxea.

"Longer," corrected Shir. "The world was not born those thousands of years ago. That is only when you started counting."

"Wonderful," hissed Ares.

"Why's a door got to be such a big secret?" moaned Oliver. "It's a *door.* The entire point's to go through 'em!"

"All existential knowledge lies beyond the door," said Shir sternly. "Had humankind been given the ability to access it freely, time would have ended long ago."

Luxea held her head in her hands. "We may never find it then."

In the dirt, Shir drew two circles. "Time is the embodiment of space, the domain of everything and nothing at all. The Memory Door could be anywhere . . . or it could be nowhere."

Ares' mouth opened. "Is it possible that there *is* no door?"

"There'd better be one." Oliver fixed himself. "I rode all day lookin' for that door, Ares. My gems are hurtin'!"

"But what if we have to make the door?" offered Ares. "Shir, the Golden Spire told you, *'we are all doors,'* didn't it?"

"If we're all doors . . ." Luxea scrambled out of her tent so fast that it collapsed. "Ares, I think you're right! The Memory Door is nowhere because it's everywhere!"

The pebbles on the cracked ground bounced as the Golden Spire roared a message that only Shir could comprehend.

The Mythic strode to the Spire and whispered, "We found it."

The Memory Door had to be created, the riddle had been solved, but the Mooncallers were dreadfully nervous to face an entryway through which not a mortal soul had yet walked.

Ruka trotted to the Spire and started digging; so strongly did he want to go inside and meet another divine. Brielle lifted up his giant paw and rested it on her bent knee. They closed their eyes together and evoked their every memory.

The wolf rider heard a hymn of wind, bells, and ocean waves. Through her danced the souls of all living beings in history as a rift in the gold spread. Beyond it, she and Ruka experienced colors and noises that just couldn't be.

"It's here," she breathed.

Avari peeked past the rider and the wolf. "Where?"

"Right here," said Brielle, pointing at the portal.

But the Memory Door only presented itself to those who'd called to mind their lives from the start. Ruka was too excited to be stopped, so he ran inside. His body disintegrated into a whirl of air as he evanesced into the wall of gold. The Mooncallers feared he'd died, but Brielle was still breathing which meant Ruka was too.

The rider squared her shoulders. "I'm going." And she was gone.

It was Avari's turn. She pressed against the Golden Spire, and Shir, standing beside her, did likewise. Although the Mythic had been alive thousands of years longer, their thoughts translated hundreds of times faster. The door opened for them, and they fazed into Time. Avari sniffled as she recalled her past, and she was lost in the wall.

The likelihood of Luxea entering was slim to none, but it wouldn't hurt to try. She leaned her head against the Golden Spire and remembered everything she could in the order she felt it had happened. The Shadow, her magelas, Cherish, the river, Avari,

Lor'thanin, Ares, Oliver, Brielle and Ruka, Unblossomed, the gala, the Wraiths, Tarot, Mythos, and all that had come to pass since.

But the Memory Door didn't appear.

"It won't open for you?" asked Ares dolefully.

Luxea stepped back. "No."

Frowning, Oliver kicked a rock. "I was hopin' to go in, but I'll stay out here with you, Luxie."

She faced him, pleading, "Will you?"

"Yea, love. You can read to me or somethin'," he said lightly.

Although it eased Ares that Oliver would remain outside with Luxea, he yet worried for their safety. While he gazed up the immeasurable height of the Golden Spire, the Irestar peeked around the edge. His hand snaked to the part in his shirt, and then he found himself removing the Felastil from his neck for the first time in many, many years.

"Keep this, for now, Luxea. Time might translate differently inside, and we may be gone for longer than we mean to. While I'm under Anatatri's protection, I'd rather leave Oscerin with the two of you. You said my Felastil is a communicator, so if you need Her . . ."

Luxea wouldn't take it. "Ares, I can't —"

He urged it into her palm and closed it. "Please."

Saying 'no' would result in further pressing, so Luxea dipped her head through the silver chain and pulled her hair out from under it.

This was a new feeling for Ares . . . he'd never seen his Felastil around another person's neck. Devastatingly slow, he grazed his middle finger over the starry pendant.

Now prepared, he turned away and placed his palms on the Golden Spire. His face twisted as he called forth every pain, every joy and love and hate and empty moment. Sighing, he sank into the wall.

The other side was dark; Ares could hardly see his companions. He'd anticipated lights, echoes of history, and surrealistic visions, but the Golden Spire was barren. The air was temperate, giving no indication of where his skin ended, and the atmosphere began. There were no walls, ceilings, or floors. Nothingness —

But ahead sat a shape, mountain-high and formed of liquid gold.

The Mooncallers drew nearer, and the shape became a faceless woman, seated cross-legged. The Time Goddess' head twitched in their direction; the way in which she moved was jittery like turning through a picture flip-book. When She spoke, Her voice came as static; some words were clear, others were lost in white noise.

"Visitors? Very strange, indeed!"

Anatatri melted and reformed with Her hands and feet sprouting from Her ribs. She scampered forth and coiled Her neck around Her guests. Her head was the size of a watchtower and dripping in viscous gold. They could feel Her drinking in their faces without eyes.

Truthfully, the Mooncallers were scared out of their wits. Even Shir hadn't expected the Time Goddess' form to be so open-ended.

"You came to ask me questions? Very strange, indeed." Anatatri's body morphed until She was seated in front of them. "What is it you want me to tell you? Oh, I have already seen — but I want you to say it! I've not heard voices in sixteen thousand two hundred and eighty-nine years, three moons, three weeks, nineteen days, eleven hours, twenty-six minutes, and forty-two seconds."

Ares choked out, "Um —"

"Yes, yes! Say more!"

Brielle held onto Ruka. "Where is this place?"

"Place? This is a place, isn't it? We are in Time," replied Anatatri.

"And where is *'Time?'*" asked Avari.

"Time is here but also there — and there! Time is inside you, but you are empty. Time is me, but who am I?" chattered the goddess.

Ares was thankful to be Oscerin's Speaker, not Anatatri's. "Those aren't the questions we need to ask You. N'ra told us that You can give us answers about —"

"— a shadow in a blackwood tree," finished Anatatri.

"Yes," said Ares mutedly. "Do You know who she is?"

"She isn't in *your* memories, is she?" giggled Anatatri.

"She's in Luxie's," mentioned Avari, "but she couldn't come in."

"I can tap into memories, but without a link to the brain in which the memory dwells, I cannot speak it," said Anatatri plainly.

"Then how do we learn about the Shadow?" asked Brielle.

"I will tell you," answered Anatatri.

Ares pinched his eyes. "But You just said —"

"Do you have a link? Of course, not. But you do — you must! If you bear something of hers, I can create a link," offered Anatatri.

Avari and Brielle shook their heads, and Shir patted themselves as if they were searching their pockets. This voyage may have been entirely worthless if they couldn't learn Luxea's secrets.

Frustrated, Ares rubbed his neck. He wasn't wearing his Felastil — *Luxea was.*

"What if she has something of mine?"

"Yours? Very strange, indeed. No, no, that . . ." Anatatri's head tipped back to whatever sky lay beyond the veil of emptiness. She held out Her long, shapeless finger. "The Moon Mother's medallion, a relic forged by Oscerin Herself." She snickered almost wickedly. "Oh, my, my! That *will* work!

"My link will ensure your access to her memories, but I must warn you now. Once the link is forged, you will suffer her turmoils, your thoughts and emotions will become indecipherable from the other. When duality is formed within reality, the pages of two stories combine, not to be undone for all lifetimes beyond that in which you currently live. From now until time stops, your lines of individuality will be intertwined. A single block of one will make up the other's existential foundation."

She paused. "Do you still wish to make a link?"

Of course, Ares was hesitant if it meant that his soul would forever be bound to Luxea's. "So this link will allow us to see any memories of Luxea's? Even the ones she hasn't recovered?"

"No. I may see them, but she may not — and neither may you."

"Why? What's so terrible about her memories?" asked Avari.

The question sparked a fit of laughter in the Time Goddess. "Oscerin took them for a reason. If Luxea were to remember her previous life now, she might die of guilt before the Widow has a chance to get to her!"

Ares thought the statement was odd. Guilt? For what? His intrigue grew the longer he dwelled on it . . . and then he found himself *wanting* to be bonded for eternity, no matter what it took. He prayed that Luxea would feel the same.

"Do it. We need the link."

The Time Goddess' fingers branched open over Ares' head and melted, caging him behind bars of gold. "Then it shall be so."

For half a second, Ares felt seven inches shorter and could have sworn his skin was white.

Meanwhile, outside of the Golden Spire, Luxea drew in the dirt with Oliver. She made a line with her left forefinger, but when she blinked, her hand was coated in black scales. She squeaked and rubbed her eyes. Her flesh was white once again.

"What's the matter, Luxie?" wondered Oliver.

She wasn't sure. She kept doodling in the ground.

Ares felt as if he were two people at once. It was complete.

Anatatri raised Her arm, and it began to melt. From Her golden shell, stretching and thinning, was manifested a harp. She strummed a melody using notes that didn't exist on a human tessitura.

The nothingness flashed with images as She conjured Luxea's memories. When the explosion of lights stopped, the blackwood tree in Nav Amani Forest appeared before the Mooncallers.

Climbing up its trunk was a young Luxea, her white hair in braids, her cheeks rosy and plump, looking uncannily like the girl in the family portrait. The Mooncallers witnessed the memory of her and the Shadow playing until Luxea fell out of the tree.

The blackwood bark fluttered into gold flakes. Anatatri shuddered at the blankness where the vision had been. "I have never seen that woman . . . but I have seen everyone . . . everything . . ."

She played the harp again, summoning a second fragment. A child's bedroom materialized this time. The Mooncallers and Anatatri viewed the Shadow, her broken limbs spasming as she crawled across Luxea's bed in the night.

*"Stop scaring her!"* echoed in Time as the past flickered out.

Anatatri's harp dissolved as She shrank into a trembling blob. "No, no, no! I have never seen her! It isn't possible! But it is — it is the only possibility because the time that isn't me says so!" She jerked upright and whispered, "Very strange indeed."

"What's strange now?" groaned Avari.

"Perhaps the Shadow's spool of existence is greater than my own. She has more thread . . . she has more thread . . . than me?"

Ares murmured, "So the Shadow —"

"— transcends Time itself." Anatatri's head regained form. "She was made before reality was in place, back when the light was black, and the darkness was white, when the air, the earth, the fire, and the water were seamless."

Anatatri sat up straight. "There is a final memory. I can see it, I can taste it, but the voices are obscure. Yes, obscure but loud! There is a dent in time — but it isn't *hers*. To whomever it belongs, they never meant for Luxea to hear. Yet it is with her, with *you*. It is a fragment of a stolen consciousness, a remnant of a vile and powerful possession. Interwoven is a stitch that has been unraveled in the wake of a birth eclipsed by a death. Very strange, indeed . . ."

One last time, Anatatri called upon Her harp and strummed it frantically; She wasn't searching Luxea's memories for the Mooncallers anymore, only for Herself. Visions of the past swarmed around them. Once Her song had ceased, and the pictures had faded, the void moved in the way that blackness moved when one's eyes were shut.

Voices filled the air — a whisper, and a child's voice.

*"Wake up . . . wake up . . ."*

*"Who's there?"*

*"A friend."*

*"Why would you be friends with me? No one wants me."*

*"But they could. I can make everyone love you."*

*"Really?"*

*"Let me in, and you will never be alone again. Every wish that you hold within that broken heart will be fulfilled. I promise you."*

*"First, will you tell me your name?"*

*"If I speak it, will you promise never to repeat it?"*

*"Why not?"*

*"All best friends have one big secret, do they not? This is ours."*

*"Okay. I won't tell."*

*"My name is —"*

Anatatri screamed, "The name! The *name!* I cannot hear it! The silence will not leave! It hurts, it hurts! Get it out! *Get out!"*

The Mooncallers clutched their ears and fell to their knees, their bones nearly fracturing from the goddess' tumult. That excruciating quiet soon left Anatatri's mind. With Her head swinging off Her neck from threads of darkening gold, She pointed at Ares.

"You," She growled. "Tell me when this dream took place."

"I-I don't know," panted Ares.

"The essence of that day flows through your consciousness at this very second!" The Time Goddess made shapes with Her fingers. "One. One. Lightsmeet. One. Oscerin. Three."

*But . . .*

"That's the same night Oscerin appointed me as Her Speaker."

"Yes, but this dream came *first,* by a mere minute! Very strange, indeed!" The Time Goddess cackled. "There is something the Moon Mother has not told you! The secret is Hers — it always has been!"

Anatatri laughed and laughed until She curled up and whispered to Herself, "She has more thread . . . she has more thread . . . the thread . . . the thread . . . she has more . . ."

The Mooncallers' feet sank into the black space beneath them. Ruka whimpered and fell, and then Brielle, Avari, and Shir too. Before Ares could be swallowed, Anatatri trapped him in Her hand as if he were Her precious doll.

"There will soon come a day when the past will mimic itself. One of you will die unless the name is spoken," She warned.

Ares was released. As he was devoured by emptiness, he grabbed Her little finger. "Wait, that can't be all You have to say! What do You mean? What name? What is Oscerin hiding? How are the Shadow and Widow connected to Luxea?"

"Only the pages of a mind lost will change the future." Anatatri melted, weeping, "Time fixes everything . . . but what about me?"

# A GIRL WHO DREAMS

## 25.LIGHTSMEET.26.OSC.3
### THE GOLDEN SPIRE

FALLING THROUGH the laces of Time, they were given visions.

The Tehrastar was blotted out by smoke as Avari limped reaches and reaches through the desert. She tripped over shards of bone, and the soles of her boots sizzled in contact with the hot blood on the dirt. In the distance, she saw bronze. Rupturing through a crack in the flaming earth was the arm of Peyamo Nelnah. Avari tugged and tugged until she unearthed the skeleton of the Lady of Tarot, but then she was thrown onto her back. The undead remains of the Lady uncovered a shining needle and sewed Avari's left eye shut.

Light entered through the apex of the collapsed cave in which Brielle sat. A bat flew past her, rustling her red locks, and landed on Ruka's shoulder. As Brielle stood up to approach her brother, he fell on his side, and the bat's black wings splayed on his flank. The closer she came, the furs of the two beasts rotted. Mere steps away, she fell, clutching her throat. Suffocating, she and Ruka turned to ash.

Shir stood beside a throne where atop it sat a phoenix. It rose up and walked onto the sand that swallowed the floor, flaming and staining the grains. The hands of a man sprouted out of its igneous wings, and then it dug where, buried shallowly, was the Moon. The firebird upthrusted a silver dagger and plunged it into the silver light.

Ares' skin tore, his eyes bled, and his mind decayed. Sprawled on the crackling ground not too far off was Luxea, in pieces and slashed by the claws of a dragon. He tried to reach her, but the scalding hot chains binding his neck, arms, and legs hindered him. The other end of the tether was tied to a crimson dragon. Its violet stare told him, *'you are all that I am.'*

Ares, Avari, Brielle and Ruka, and Shir thudded into the dirt. They guessed it was midday, for the Golden Spire shone radiantly.

Avari dusted out her frizzy hair but then recalled her vision. "Did anybody else . . . see something?"

"I did," said Brielle, clinging hard to Ruka's scruff.

"They are glimpses of what may lie ahead," said Shir solemnly.

Shielding her left eye, Avari whimpered, "But . . ."

*"We saw the future?"* Ruka asked Shir.

"Yes," said the Mythic blankly.

Ares couldn't decide whether to worry more about the horror of his own mirage or what Anatatri had told him. 11.Lightsmeet. 1.Oscerin.3 had always been the happiest day of his life because of the Moon Goddess.

*Has that day been a lie . . . all along?*

"Ares?" Avari had been talking to him, but he hadn't heard her.

"Yes," he whispered. "Yes, I'm fine."

Avari fumbled with her scarf. "No, you're not. You must be thinking about that dream. Do you think it was Luxie? Do you think she met the Shadow the same night you met Oscerin?"

"I don't know," said Ares broodingly. "The Moon Mother had to have had something to do with this. She told Luxea She'd planned everything since her birth. I refuse to believe this is a coincidence."

But that wasn't all that harrowed him.

What he'd witnessed . . . he knew he'd been the one to kill Luxea.

After an hour of footing about, the Mooncallers spotted their dracas, but their camping equipment had collapsed and been eaten by sand. As they neared, Luxea rolled over in the dirt. Her clothes were absolutely filthy! What had happened while they were away?

Luxea got up and wobbled. "Where the hells have you been?" Her voice was scratchy as if she hadn't had a drink in a while.

"With Anatatri," huffed Avari. "I've never felt saner after meeting that one."

"What . . . ?" murmured Luxea. "You were in there all this time?"

"All this time? How long has it been?" gulped Brielle.

"Three days," replied Luxea.

"Three — ?" Avari pitched herself at Luxea, embracing her too tightly for comfort. "I'm so sorry! It felt like a few minutes to us!"

"It's all right, but we have to leave soon." Luxea glanced at their ruined campsite. "We're out of food and water, and there hasn't been anywhere for Oliver to keep from the sunlight. He's sick."

In tandem to the dracas lay Oliver under a heap of blankets. He peeked out. As Luxea had claimed, he looked ill. "Blissits . . . took you knobs long 'nough."

Avari and Brielle lifted Oliver onto Musha's back. Fortunately, his scowling dracas didn't try to trample his toes today.

In the meantime, Ares dragged his feet to Luxea. Anatatri's words reverberated in his head as he stared, trancelike, at the Felastil on her neck. Luxea wasn't certain why, but he appeared to be distrusting of it.

"You're awfully quiet," she pointed out.

The Prince couldn't bring himself to meet her stars. "Luxea," he began, "how old were you on 11.Lightsmeet.1.Oscerin.3?"

This was unanticipated, abnormal too. Ares rarely asked her about her past — mostly because she didn't have one. "I'm not sure about my lifeday," she said, "only that I'm under the sign of Wynd, or so Brielle says."

"Yes . . . Lightsmeet."

Luxea nodded slightly. "Why?"

Remnants of the past screamed in his mind. Talking over them, he said, "We saw the Shadow in the blackwood tree and your bedroom, but there was a dream. It occurred the same day that Oscerin came to me for the first time, mere minutes before. The Shadow spoke to a girl and shared her name, but the memory was cut before Anatatri could show us.

"In the Crystal Spire, N'ra swore you knew the Shadow's name. I can't say if it was you in that dream, Luxea, but I have to wonder if there's anything you haven't told me about —"

"I promise you, I have no knowledge of this," she interjected.

Ares attempted to smile, but it fell. "I believe you. I've learned that trusting in what you say is the best course of action. Whether or not it was you, I'm confident that you have some connection with the Shadow and Widow.

"Not only that, but Oscerin has been keeping from us information that stretches back to the beginning of our lives. She withheld secrets from the start and didn't warn either of us of what was to come — She still hasn't! I've asked Her about the Shadow, I've begged Her to tell me about Widow, but She never answers. I feel . . . mislead."

At last, Ares looked at Luxea, but he immediately had to cover his eyes. All he saw were claw marks and dead lips drained of whatever color they had. Meeting her stare was killing him.

Luxea felt small. "What's the matter?"

It couldn't have been harder to collect himself. Ares' mouth was dry as he said, "I saw something when we left the Golden Spire. Shir claims they were glimpses of the future." He crouched, so she did too. "What I was shown . . . I don't know how I would stop it."

"Will you tell me what you saw?"

Ares' claw burned as he said, "I'm going to kill you."

It was a numb tone, deliberately stripped of feeling. Luxea, however, wasn't afraid. Ares had the potential to be dangerous, but the person who'd flown her through Sh'tarr's Iris despite the risk of his own demise and with whom she'd spent so many nights on Mythos, he wouldn't hurt her.

"You can try," she said playfully. "How are you so sure?"

He showed her his talons. "There is nothing like a dragon's mark."

"I'm sure there isn't." Luxea rested her hands on her knees with her palms facing up. "You won't kill me, Ares. Even if it were an accident, you would have to give me more than a few cuts."

She wasn't listening! To prove to her how wrong she was, how quickly her trust in him would lead to pain, Ares snatched her wrist and touched one talon to the tip of her middle finger. Hardly applying pressure, he dragged it to the crease of her palm. A stitch of blood trailed it. He unhanded her and waited for her reaction.

Luxea squeezed her finger, making the red beads grow, and then popped it into her mouth and licked it clean. White brows raised, she asked, "Are you finished being dramatic?"

"I'm not, Luxea. I want you to see how possible it is for me to —"

"You want me to be afraid of you. You want me to be wary of you because you think this vision will come to pass, that I'll die by your hand, and you'll become something you're not. Am I right?"

*Yes, you're right.*

Ares had started this discussion in hopes of changing her mind, but she ended up changing his when she leaned over and kissed his cheek.

In his ear, she whispered, "Monster."

For once in his life, Ares didn't hate the word.

Unlike the first time, Empress Annalais didn't wait for her guests on the front steps. Wonderful news! No one was in the mood for more of her verbal bee stings.

Still feeling puny, Oliver retreated to his guest bedchamber, drew the curtains, and hid under the blankets, far from the sunlight. The others went to wash off in the baths with all speed. It had been so long that they'd forgotten the smell of soap!

As Brielle rinsed her locks, and Avari squeezed hot water out of her lump of hair, they babbled about their visions from Anatatri. It was a dire discussion, at first, but it didn't take long for the seriousness to fade. Soon, they were laughing and dunking each other in the spring.

The ranger burst through the surface and clung to Brielle's muscly shoulders. Luxea, who hadn't spoken since returning to Solissium, smiled at them briefly and turned her attention to Ares' Felastil; she'd forgotten to give it back to him. She rested her arms on the edge of the tub and padded droplets off the starry jewel, unable to tear her thoughts from what Ares had said about that mysterious dream.

From a nearby table, the Usinnon said, "Miss Siren, you're musing again. What is bothering you?"

"It's nothing important, Usinnon."

"My word, Miss Siren. Anything that goes through that pretty brain of yours is of substantial importance to me!"

Luxea giggled, and then her shoulders sagged. "Did you hear what Ares asked me when we left the Golden Spire? He was suspicious that I'd communicated with the Shadow in a dream in year 1. I can't remember that at all . . . but what if it *was* me?"

The spellbook kept an open mind. "It might have been. If you'll allow me to do so, may I make a suggestion, Miss Siren?"

"Of course."

"Recall that man who was once your teacher — Cherish Ven'lethe, a nasty excuse for a magister, if you ask me; I did try to warn you about him. But was Brielle not able to deduce the year of his birth through mere inspection? Mayhap she can do the same for you."

The stars sparked to yellow. "You're right." Luxea sloshed around in the bath. "Brie, may I ask something of you?"

Avari squirted water from her mouth into Brielle's face. Brielle swatted her and said, "Yes, Starlight."

"Do you remember, in Ocaranth's Tears, telling Cherish that he was born in a year when the stars were misaligned? You guessed 87.Tirih."

Brielle pushed Avari again. "I didn't guess, I knew. Why?"

"Can you tell the year of my birth too?" requested Luxea.

The thought hadn't crossed Brielle's mind. She waded closer, took Luxea's hands, and meticulously searched her pale arms. Near Luxea's shoulder was a string of light freckles.

"The stars above L'arneth were arranged like this in the earliest years of Oscerin's century," said Brielle, lining the marks on Luxea's skin. She pinched each of Luxea's fingers, memorizing the contours of her bones. "Which is stronger: your left hand or your right?"

"Right."

Shifting to Luxea's right, Brielle peeked into her pointy ear. "Do you suffer from insomnia?"

"Sometimes."

"Are you color blind?"

"I don't think so."

Brielle blinked at her. "What color are my eyes?"

"Amber?" Luxea hoped she was right.

"Yes," said Brielle with a crooked smile. "Last question: do you often remember your dreams?"

"Almost every night."

Brielle numbered her fingers and frequently shook her head. Her bushy eyebrows joined, and she counted over again until only her forefinger was extended. "Why do you want to learn the year of your becoming?"

"To see if it was me in that dream on 11.Lightsmeet.1.Oscerin.3."

"I imagined as much." Brielle dropped her hands into the water and felt them prune. "Starlight, you were *created* in year 1. It couldn't have been your voice in that dream. You were a newborn."

Curiosity would kill her, not a dragon's claw. After her bath, Luxea went straight to the library to glean information about 11.Lightsmeet. 1.Oscerin.3. From the dozens of shelves, she collected registries, birth certificates, historical documents, and astrological records.

Her wet hair dripped on the tabletop as she read, and the cut on her finger left faint, red streaks on the pages as she turned them, but it still didn't hurt.

Very little was uncovered. Several people had been born or died on this date, but there was nothing of further significance. The only remarkable bit of information was on a sheet that advertised a lunar eclipse that had occurred on the night of 11.Lightsmeet.1.Oscerin.3, one year after the turning of Oscerin's century. Luxea saved the page in her pocket just in case it meant something.

Right as the temptation to give up pricked her, she stumbled upon an account of a different subject that was as thought-provoking: a list of the royal family members of Goldenrise.

Luxea's eyes shot across the room to the uncovered painting and then back to the registry. On the penultimate line was the most recent entry — Rowan Taress.

Male, eight pounds, four ounces. Red hair, blue eyes, birthmark on the right shoulder blade. Son of Isabelia and Genntric Taress.

Lastly —

Date of birth: 16.Duskriddle.94.TIR.3.

"Duskriddle?"

Luxea recalled Brielle calling the High Templar of Stonehall, 'Owl Child.' That meant that the high templar, like Rowan, had been born in Duskriddle under the sign of Ostriseon the Owl God.

She tapped her chin. "So, Rowan . . . you were an owl child too."

# BREATHE ME IN

## VILLA DE TARESS, GOLDENRISE

IN HIS bedchamber, Ares read a book on the divines. He'd memorized this particular volume already but wanted to relearn it after all that Anatatri had revealed.

His eyes lingered one of his favorite stories: Lemuria and the Sisters of Sun and Moon. Involuntarily, he reached for his Felastil.

*That's right . . . Luxea has it.*

Ignoring the emptiness on his chest, he proceeded to read.

> *"The Lemuria created Tirih the Goddess of the Sun to bring light to the universe, but Tirih became lonely. To satisfy Her daughter's needs, the Lemuria formed a second goddess — Oscerin, the Moon.*
> *However, when Oscerin was born, the Irestar would not glow of its own accord. Oscerin wept in darkness for ages until Tirih came to Her and said, 'You are my sister, and my light is Yours.'*
> *Tirih reflected the fire of the Tehrastar upon the Irestar. The shadow of the Moon was then banished, and —"*

A few raps on the door broke his concentration. Regrettably, he answered it. There in the colonnade waited Empress Annalais.

As usual, she looked absurdly beautiful. Her strawberry blonde hair was curled loosely over her breasts, and her lips were painted in a dark red stain.

Raising the gold ewer she held, she asked, "May I come in?"

Of all things, Ares didn't want her company. Despite himself, he let her into his bedchamber. With her backless, white gown twirling, she swayed across the room to the sofa and filled two lover's nautiluses with wine. Ares sat across from her and claimed his shell.

"Did you meet the Goddess of Time?" asked Annalais delicately.

"We did, and it was life-changing," said Ares with a generous gulp. "Anatatri hadn't heard voices for over sixteen thousand years."

"Sixteen thousand? But we're only in Era Three."

"Apparently, that's only when we started counting."

"Incredible." Annalais grinned at him vivaciously. "I surmise She must be somewhat off-kilter, having been alone for so long."

A small laugh came from Ares' throat. "That's putting it mildly."

Their eyes met for a brief moment. Amazingly, there wasn't a hint of desperation on her face. He couldn't say why, but this interaction felt questionably *normal.* All this time, he'd thought they'd never hold a pleasant conversation for longer than ten seconds.

Had she given up on him, at last?

"Did you relive any of the past while you were with Anatatri?" she asked casually.

Her question resurfaced Ares' vision of the future. Crimson scales flashed before his eyes, and Luxea's blood wetted his fingertips. "Not the past," he said under his breath.

The Empress tapped her fingernails on her shell, restless. "Oh. Well, I've been thinking about the past very much lately."

Perhaps she hadn't given up.

Annalais waited for a positive reaction, but Ares didn't give her one. "If you're here to talk about us, don't," he said austerely.

"Please, Ares, lay down your defenses this once!" she pleaded. "So many times have I reached out to you. It would be healthy to put it behind us, don't you agree?"

This was too perplexing. He nibbled his lip. "You want closure?"

"Yes. We've left our wounds open for too many years. I . . . I want to let it go. I want to let *you* go," said Annalais, seemingly earnest.

This sounded like a terrible idea. With his hands steepled in front of his mouth, he weighed the pros and cons. If Annalais complied, he supposed that it would be beneficial to resolve their differences.

"Fine. We'll talk," he murmured.

"Thank you." The Empress cleared her throat as if she were ready to give a speech; Ares hoped she would keep it short. "I'll begin by saying I'm sorry. I've said it before, I could say it hundreds of thousands of times more, but I'll forever be sorry. I hurt you, Ares."

"You did more than hurt me. You betrayed me in the worst, most irreparable way. It's been nine years, and yet the thought of you with the King, of all people —" Ares took a breath and cracked his knuckles. "Why did you do it? Why him, and why, after he was gone, did your disloyalty continue?"

"I was . . . lonely," muttered Annalais.

Ares set down his glass and leaned closer. *"Lonely?"*

"You were always working or studying. No matter if I saw you in Goldenrise or Tzapodia, you would train or run off with my brother to focus on politics," argued Annalais. "You were never there . . . even when I was right in front of you."

"I *had* to work," said Ares reasonably. "I couldn't expect to rule a kingdom one day without the proper knowledge. And when Rowan and I were initiated into The Six, we were overwhelmed. Neither of us had dealt with so much in our lives. I'm sorry you felt ignored, Anna, but I tried my hardest to give you attention."

"It wasn't enough. I thought you wanted me," she sniffed.

"I did."

"But not as much as him!" In her wine, Annalais saw red scales of the same shade. "I gave him my virtue unwittingly, but beyond that, I stayed with the King because he was in love with me."

Nothing about this was comical, but Ares had to laugh. "Is that it? You think he had feelings for you? Gods, no, Anna. He wanted you because you were *mine*. He didn't love you — he didn't love anyone."

"He did!" she shouted at him. "While you left me alone day after day, Naiv always had time for me!"

Ares pressed on his eyes with the heels of his wrists and tipped his head back; his unbuttoned shirt showed a triangle of his chest. "Don't say his name."

"Why not? Are you that afraid of him? So that's why you won't look at me. Because in me you see — !" Her accusing stare was hitched on the opening of his collar. "Where is your necklace?"

His eyes opened to face the ceiling. This wasn't going to be good.

"Luxea has it," he said bracingly.

It was hypocritical of Annalais to be angry after what she'd done to him, but she didn't care. She exploded. "You never let *me* wear it! First, you fly into Sh'tarr's Iris for the whore — gods know how far your affliction has spread — and now she is in my villa with the most important item you own?" She smashed her lover's nautilus on the ground and sobbed, "What is so special about a baseborn spell-flinger like her?!"

Stopping the fire as it sparked, Ares slammed down his drink and stood up. "I knew this was how our conversation would end. We're finished. Please, leave."

As he reached for the door handle, Annalais rushed over, shoved him, and locked it. She beat her fists on his chest and cried, "Why don't you want me?"

"You know why!"

"And you won't ever forgive me?"

"No. I stayed with you after everything you did to me — not only the lying, *everything* — because I thought you loved me. Nothing you say now can convince me that you ever did!"

"I *still* love you!"

Ares moved to unlock the door. Annalais jumped and hung her arms around his neck. He tried to pry her away, but she refused.

"Get off me!" he said through his teeth.

She slid onto her feet and inhaled deeply. When next Ares opened his mouth to tell her to leave again, she exhaled, and a plume of dark smoke shot from her red lips into his lungs.

Instantly, his eyes turned to coals. He stumbled back into the wall, breathing sporadically. Vipers slithered in his veins and leeched every last trace of his self-control. His mind was slipping fast, suffocated by dazzling colors and the pounding of his heart in his ears.

Then the world flipped upside down, and he was calm.

While the soft green gradually returned to his irises, his dilated pupils sailed around the bedchamber. Every glittering stitch in the bedding, slow-motion swell of the curtains, and vivid drop of red wine sliding down the ewer was tempting.

The woman in front of him, however, was irresistible.

He kissed her like he was fighting to survive. In half a minute, their clothes were on the floor, and he was carrying her to the bed.

In the garden, Luxea practiced spells with the Usinnon; she loved to study when it was dark outside because her magick was brighter. This incantation would manifest a spectral blade for close-range battles.

For the tenth time, she upturned her palm and said, *"Ei tensha."*

A strand of light appeared, but it sparked and flickered into a line of blue ash before it could materialize into a sword. Luxea groaned and kicked her legs about.

"This is absurd. I followed the instructions you wrote down to the last letter! What am I doing wrong?"

The Usinnon chuckled, "Your hand, Miss Siren. If you wish to summon a weapon, do you not think it would be wise to position your fingers to hold the grip?"

Luxea blushed. "Oh."

"Your magick is gaining in intensity. Focus, and do not let your innate abilities exceed your knowledge." The book paused. "I think, as you recollect memories, your magick is changing — back to what it was before you lost them."

"Is that why my spells are more potent now?" wondered Luxea.

"Indeed. For that reason, we must keep up with your studies. Power without awareness is the first step to ruin."

Luxea nodded. "All right. Let's try again."

She mouthed the arcanan blade incantation, just to be sure she had it memorized, and shaped her hand into a curl. No matter what, she would hold the grip this time.

But then her eyes rolled, and explosive novas stole her whites.

It felt as if someone had suddenly run into her and fused with her at every contour. All at once, her blood was hot and cold and light and dark, and her breaths were soft and solid and calm and panicked. In a whirlwind around her were shrill, unintelligible echoes, but she could have recognized the voice anywhere.

Oscerin.

## *"QUICKLY, STOP HER!"*

The tie was severed too fast for Luxea to ask the Goddess of the Moon for clarification. She fell out of her chair, coughing and heaving, and her vision doubled as Ares' Felastil swung back and forth below her. If Oscerin had reached out, Luxea had to act now. She scooped up the Usinnon, who was questioning her frenetically, and careened down the colonnade.

"Come with me. Someone is in trouble!"

She found Avari and Brielle chatting in the banquet hall. The ranger was picking from an assortment of Goldenrise's finest cheeses, and the rider was slurping an ale — usual tendencies for them both.

Next came Ruka and Shir in the courtyard. They lay supine, watching shooting stars. The wolf kicked his leg and wagged, and the Mythic rang serenely. This wasn't an emergency either.

The door to Oliver's bedchamber was unlocked, so Luxea peeked inside. Beneath the blankets was the shape of his lithe body, rising and falling steadily. He was still asleep.

That left her last companion. She *hated* running but did so despite that, all the way to Ares' guest bedchamber. At the end of the hall, she panted and held onto her quivering knees.

Her fist raised to knock — but the sounds on the other side of the door forced her muscles to constrict around her bones.

Voices, Ares and Annalais's voices. They weren't talking.

Luxea's face twisted into all kinds of expressions for a split second each. Her ribs bent, her spine crumbled out of alignment, and her stars shrouded themselves in black.

She longed for two things.

First, to destroy something. Second, to destroy herself.

Until now, it hadn't dawned on her that maybe, *maybe* she wanted Ares to want her like that — only her. But she'd woken up from a good dream, one where she'd come to mean something to someone she'd always known she didn't deserve.

Luxea took a deep, stinging inhale and staggered back down the colonnade. On the way to her bedchamber, she took off the Felastil and dropped it into her pocket.

*'Cry,'* her mind told her. *'Endure,'* said her heart.

*Shut up, both of you!*

With her knees on the floor and her arms folded on the edge of her bed, Luxea scolded herself for feeling anything at all. She didn't have the right to be anguished. Why did she care?

*Don't care, don't care, don't care.*

But as much as she tried not to, she cared.

"Usinnon?" she asked breathily.

"Miss Siren?" replied the spellbook.

"May I ask you a question unrelated to magick?"

"Anything, Miss Siren. Bear in mind that I am not only your instructor, but I am your friend all the same."

Luxea rested her cheek on the mattress and lined the stitches in the duvet with her cut-up middle finger. "Have you ever wished it would all stop? That you could go back and prevent yourself from making certain choices or falling into certain situations?"

"I've never known anyone who hasn't wished such a thing," said the Usinnon tenderly. "We are given two choices in life, never more than that. Each achievement, each failure, each gain, and each loss will present a new perception. It is up to us to either accept it as a lesson or a wound. That being said, choosing the wound does not mean you are weak. To hurt is to discover."

Whether it was the words of wisdom or the feeling of deceit in Luxea's chest, it forced tears out of her. The Usinnon was right; first, she would cry, and then she would endure. She climbed onto her bed and curled up with her spellbook held close to her chest.

"Will you sleep with me tonight?" she sniffed.

The Usinnon glinted lovingly. "You needn't ask. I'm always here."

# The Morning After

## 28.Lightsmeet.26.Osc.3
### Villa de Taress, Goldenrise

The Prince stretched his long legs and made a throaty sound. He couldn't remember falling asleep; he must've been exhausted. When he grabbed for the sheets, he touched skin, not cloth. His eyes opened.

Resting peacefully beside him was Annalais, unclothed. Her curled hair was a mess, and her breasts were spotted with blood bruises. The duvet that lay barely over her hip was torn, and the wall above the headboard was decorated with claw marks.

This had to be a nightmare — it *had* to be. It wouldn't have been the first time Annalais had shown up in his sleep as some poisonous reminder.

He rolled onto his back and held his hands open above him. In surreality, there are always too many or too few fingers.

One, two, three, four, five. Five on both hands.

*It's real.*

Ares flew out of bed and into a frenzy. He began to dress but tripped and knocked over the nightstand. The *smash* of wood and porcelain woke up Annalais forthwith. Those tropical eyes opened, and she reached out to him.

"Good morning, my love," she sighed.

"Why are you here?!"

She sat up. "What do you mean?"

He tried to recall the evening before, but something wouldn't let him. Ares slipped on his belt with some trouble, for he couldn't feel his fingers. "How did this . . . I don't . . . I don't remember anything!"

As if it would turn back time, Annalais clutched the pillow. With tears filling her waterline, she whispered, "How do you not remember? You've never wanted me more, you couldn't get enough of me! You told me you loved me, you told me you would make me your queen!"

"I want nothing to do with you!"

That was when Annalais noticed a minor detail in her deal with Widow that she'd overlooked. The promise had been kept, Ares hadn't said no to her — but Widow hadn't specified how long it would last.

"No . . . She said you would . . . Sh-She promised me. . . ."

Ares fitted the pieces together right away. There was only one 'She,' and that was the Brood Mother. He'd been made into a bargaining chip.

"Widow used me as an incentive for you to join Her," he seethed. "That's why you were so calm last evening. You knew that, no matter how I reacted, you would get what you wanted! What the fuck did you give to me? Was it in the wine?"

The moment he asked this question, something happened to Ares that had never happened before. A memory struck him like a blow to the back of his head, but it wasn't his; it couldn't have been, for the hands peeking out of his sleeves were pale and feminine.

Those hands . . . he knew those hands.

But then, through a door of gilded wood, he heard Annalais's voice followed by his own. The worst pain was in his chest, a pain like thorns and stones.

*'Once the link is forged, you will suffer her turmoils, your thoughts and emotions will become indecipherable from the other. When duality is formed within reality, the pages of two stories combine.'*

That's right . . . Anatatri's link. This was his mind calling forth the closest thing it could to an explanation. He was re-experiencing the night before through Luxea's eyes — and that meant she was aware of what had occurred as well.

The reality of waking up next to Annalais became physically painful then. He had to go somewhere, do something! Sick on all levels, Ares tumbled across the bedchamber, swiped his shirt off the floor, and left.

The Prince broke into the colonnade and crashed against the balustrade. A marble vase smashed into the courtyard below where Oliver drank breakfast tea. He yelped, but the instant he saw Ares, his shock was overthrown by concern.

He rounded the courtyard and ascended the staircase to his friend. Ares was mantled with scratches, all of which would heal, but his expression was a mortal wound. Oliver had experienced his fair share of unpleasant flings with women, but this wasn't dissatisfaction or regret — this was outright terror.

"What happened to you, Ares?"

"I . . . I was arguing with Annalais," he shuddered. "I told her to get off me and then . . . nothing. I woke up, and she was with me."

Oliver's wrathful expression was unbefitting of him. He was always brushing things off with a joke, but his next intonation was, as it were, like a leader's.

"I'm assuming she dosed you?"

"She must have." Ares' voice was caught in a three-way chasm of fear, indignity, and fury. "What the hells was I thinking letting her in? How could I have thought she could be trusted? I hate her. I wasn't sure if I ever truly could, but I *hate* her!"

Piteous, Oliver tugged Ares away from the courtyard and offered him a cigarette. They wandered until they ended up at the hot springs. Seated in the shade with their legs hanging over the water, they shared smoke and companionable silence.

Annalais wrecked Ares' bedchamber. Pots were shattered, books were shredded, and priceless paintings were punctured. She tore a banner from above the door and stormed to a wall sculpture of two gold roses crossed. She snapped one of them and almost threw it, but then she noticed that the stem had broken into a point.

Just to try it, she pressed the edge into the back of her wrist. It cut her so, so smoothly. The mild stinging sensation pulled from her a laugh; she nearly made a second laceration for the fun of it.

A smile parted her lips as a streak of shiny droplets formed on her skin. That girl, Luxea, was pure white. It would only take a few stabs to make her red, red, red! The Empire of Goldenrise no longer belonged to Annalais, nor did Ares . . . so why shouldn't she do it?

Cleaning the streaks of kohl from her cheeks, she put on her slip and vacated Ares' bedchamber. On the way to Luxea's, she bid her Goldenhands to leave the villa and not return until the morrow.

The lock clicked, and Annalais peeked inside to find Luxea fast asleep with her cheek pressed against her spellbook. She latched the door and crept to the bed, tapping her fingers on the rose's gold thorns.

As much as the Empress couldn't wait for the sorceress to die, she took in all that she could. She yearned to know what it was that everyone saw in her.

But it was apparent right away that Luxea couldn't have been more unladylike — even in her sleep! Her mouth was hanging open, her hair was everywhere, and her legs were sprawled over the entire mattress.

Who would *ever* love such an unrefined pauper as her?

How dare this starry-eyed freak of magick consider herself worthy of the attention of the royals of Amniven? When the Empress was finished with her, Luxea would be forgotten like the rest of the l'arian elves.

Just then, the Usinnon's gems swirled. "M-Miss Siren? Wake up."

The Empress raised the stem.

"Miss Siren! Open your eyes!"

The spellbook sparked Luxea in the nose, and she jolted awake. All she saw was Annalais lunging at her before the rose's jagged stem scored her ribcage. While her body strove to recall how to move, she received seven more stabs. Upon the eighth, she hurled the Usinnon and rolled off the mattress. The spellbook thumped into Annalais, and a bolt of arcana paralyzed her left arm.

Red leaked down the side of Luxea's pale green nightgown, but there wasn't time to focus on discomfort or anything but survival.

Annalais ran at her with one arm numb and swiped again, cutting Luxea from her ear to her lips.

"What do you have that I don't?!" bawled the Empress. "She promised me, and you ruined it all! He would've loved me again — he *did* love me again! But when morning came, it was all you!"

Without Luxea giving the slightest effort to think this through, a memory struck her. But this wasn't her memory, this wasn't her room, and it wasn't her voice that came from this unfamiliar mouth.

It was Ares'.

*"I want nothing to do with you!"*

*"No . . . She said you would . . . Sh-She promised me . . ."*

*"Widow used me as an incentive for you to join Her. That's why you were so calm last evening. You knew that, no matter how I reacted, you would get what you wanted! What the fuck did you give to me? Was it in the wine?"*

How was this possible? How, so suddenly, could Luxea see Ares' memories? But as perplexed as she was, that ability cleared her head. Yes, she hadn't wanted to think for a second about what she'd heard the last night, but it only took her that long to add up the situation.

Blood rushed heavier and heavier as Luxea's heart rate increased. Her stars turned a dark, hateful scarlet. "You forced him."

Annalais laughed at the remark. "And what if I did? It's already done, so what will you do about it, spell-flinger?"

She swished the rose again. The instant it grazed Luxea's arm, a sparkling, blue hilt appeared in her hand; she gripped it before it could fade away. Thank the gods that, of all times, she mastered the spell now.

The arcanan blade *scraped* the rose stem to a halt. However, Luxea was dizzy, and the magick keeping her sword manifested was flickering. Just before her weapon faded, she picked up a lamp and cracked it against Annalais's head.

She made a break for the door and turned the handle — but it had been locked. Clutching her bruised brow bone, Annalais tripped forth and stuck the gold stem into Luxea's leg, yanked her hair, and cast her down.

Luxea scrambled on her hands and knees, tessellating the tiles with smears of her blood. She managed to unlock the bedchamber door, but then the Empress grabbed her bare ankle to hold her back.

When she did, her hand seared.

Annalais shouted and cried as her palm smoked. A nauseating odor assaulted Luxea's nostrils. The Empress had *burned,* and that determined one thing. It was exceedingly difficult for Luxea to judge the moment, but the loss of blood didn't mean the loss of ideas.

It was a test — a cruel test — but she had to see.

Almost sympathetically, she placed her hand on Annalais's shoulder. From physical contact alone, her skin blistered and smoked.

So that's it. Widow burned when she touched the stars, and so did Her underlings.

With plenty of answers, Luxea let go, picked up the Usinnon, and tumbled out the door. The Empress was left behind to suffer through the anguish of moonlight to shadow.

"Lock her in!" said the Usinnon hysterically.

Luxea glared at the doorway through her strands of bloody hair. From her fingers flared a wall of whistling ice, blocking the door and buying her enough time to escape.

Face twisted, she ripped the rose stem out of her leg and stumbled against the wall, leaving a long, saturated smear of blood on the marble. She fell hard onto her side and rested her head on the floor.

"Please, don't die, Miss Siren," whimpered the Usinnon. "To say the least, I would be upset if you did."

"I'm not dying . . . but this hurts like hells." In the smallest, weakest voice, she said, "C-call for help. . . ."

"At once, Miss Siren." The Usinnon wailed loudly, "Someone, someone help!"

In a lounge down the hall, Avari and Brielle played a game of cards. Brielle had no idea what the objective was but enjoyed the pictures of flowers, animals, and mythical beings in the deck.

Avari untucked a card with a dragon on it and slapped it onto the table. "You're done for. I've got you pinned! Best of luck, Brie."

The wolf rider scowled and searched her hand. She saw a card with a picture of a knight with an axe and put it down. "I win."

"What? No, you don't."

"Historically, men defeated the dragons."

Avari scrunched up her face. "That isn't how you play!"

The echo of a man's panicked voice came from outside the lounge. Avari and Brielle glowered at each other; neither wanted to let the other win, but this screaming sounded urgent.

Stacking her cards, Avari said, "We'll come back to this."

The two trotted around the corner and found Luxea, tipped against the wall beneath a mural of body fluid. Blood dyed her hair, eyelashes, skin, and clothing, and she was only losing more.

Avari ran to her and held her head upright. "Luxie, what happened to you?! Who did this? Tell me. I'll slit their throat!"

"The Empress, Miss Vishera," answered the Usinnon.

The ranger's anger burst into flames. Caring for her best friend was imperative, but this was too infuriating to ignore. She unsheathed two daggers from her thighs and whirled them in her hands. Words eluded her, but her intent was clear. The Empress *must* die.

Brielle corralled Avari back to Luxea. "No, Small One. We must focus on the wounded," she insisted. "Starlight, is the Empress truly responsible?"

Luxea's vocal cords felt like they would melt if she spoke. Instead, she slid the dripping rose stem across the tile.

The rider stole it away and gnashed her teeth. "Devil woman!"

Brielle threw the rose stem on the ground and shut her amber eyes. When next they opened, they were glowing.

In the courtyard, Ruka pranced around in a fountain with Shir. Everything felt peaceful at the Mythic's side, nothing could have hampered the joy he felt —

Until his eyes started to burn.

Ruka whimpered and toppled over, resting his chin on the fountain ledge, and then his vision crossed with Brielle's. He was afeared; his sister had only ever combined their senses in emergency situations. Through her eyes, the wolf saw Avari seated next to a body riddled with stab wounds.

*That's Luxea!*

With a splash, Ruka got to his feet and barked frantically. *"Shir, Starlight is in trouble! She's been hurt really, really bad! You can help her, can't you? Please!"*

The Mythic stood up tall and gazed to the east. Now that they'd been alerted, they could sense Luxea's pain strongly. Calmly, they said to Ruka, "I will go. You collect the others and bring them to me."

The fountain stilled as the Mythic locus-jumped away. Ruka shook out of his coat and sniffed, catching the distant scent of Ares and Oliver. As the wolf galloped up the staircase, he threw back his head and bayed.

Swinging their legs over the hot spring, Ares and Oliver chain-smoked cigarettes. The bliss of a budding friendship couldn't erase his indignity, but Ares felt much closer to Oliver after this morning.

They'd been offloading onto each other since Ares had woken up. It hadn't been intentional, but they'd exposed to each other secrets of their pasts that neither had expected to resurface.

Oliver always surprised Ares when they shared words one-on-one. Like the Prince, the Lord of the Isle of Varnn put up fronts around most people; alone, however, he hardly seemed like the fool he made himself out to be. The potency of his empathy was jarring as if he'd experienced everything in the world and overcome it. In fact, Ares sometimes wondered if Oliver was wiser than himself.

The water in the spring suddenly trembled, and Ruka's howl whirred past their heads with the velocity of a crossbow bolt. Moments later, the wolf skidded around a hedge and scrambled to stand. He snapped his jaws and dropped onto his underbelly, urging them onto his back.

Ares shunted Oliver. "Go!"

He and Oliver doused their cigarettes and climbed onto Ruka. The Prince clung to the wolf, and Oliver clung to the Prince as they bounded into the villa.

Meanwhile, Shir appeared in the colonnade with Luxea, Avari, and Brielle. Two of the three chattered about what had occurred, but Shir didn't need an explanation, they needed space.

"Stay away from me."

All too reluctant, Avari left Luxea. Brielle crouched behind her and petted her fuzzy hair. The Mythic found Luxea's energy seeping out of nine places: her cheek, her thigh, and seven in her abdomen.

They reached for her middle where the threat to her life was the most severe. Light trickled from their fingers into her skin, sending her into a trance of sensuality, peace, and enlightenment. The mending took longer than it would have had there been other Mythics present, but after a few minutes, the first gash was fused shut.

Ruka then careened around the corner. Oliver took his time sliding down his pelt, but Ares jumped right off. After the morning the Prince had, he really couldn't handle another crisis. But when he saw Luxea on the ground, bloody and limp, his own wellbeing didn't matter.

He fell to his knees and reached out, but Shir snatched his wrist. "No touching her. Only me." They turned back to seal her wounds.

Luxea forced her eyes to meet Ares'. All she'd been able to hear since the night before was him with Annalais, but those lecherous echoes fell silent at once. He was battered and distraught, and, as far as she was aware, that wasn't how men looked after a delightful evening with a woman. The emotion in his face was impossible to read, a vicious amalgam of hatred, horror, and heartbreak.

One split second told Luxea that the vision she'd been given that morning of Ares speaking to Annalais was real, and her deductions had been correct — he hadn't given himself to the Empress willingly.

"Who did this to you?" asked Ares shakily.

Luxea winced as Shir's hands moved up her scored ribcage. "As it turns out, Her Splendor isn't fond of me. Fortunately, she also isn't educated on where to stab a person if you want to kill them."

Had Ares been told that he'd just been punched in the stomach, he would have believed it. There were few times in his life that he'd been so livid, so poised to detonate.

"It was Anna?" he labored to ask.

Luxea nodded once.

Ares crossed his arms and paced like a lion in a cell, searching for something — *anything* to lacerate, to slash and slash until there was nothing left. He swung his arm and rent the wall with his talons, casting chips of marble far down the colonnade.

The Mooncallers had never seen him so beside himself. No one dared to douse the dragon's fire lest they happened to feed it instead, but Oliver had spent all morning with Ares and been exposed to his anger. That anger couldn't be allowed to transform into something more powerful.

"Mate, take a breath." He touched the Prince's shoulder, but Ares threw him back. Oliver took a mighty risk by grabbing the front placket of his shirt. "Hold off, would you?"

The Prince shoved him once again. If Ares didn't comply by words alone, Oliver would meet him in the middle. Showing his fangs, he reciprocated the thrust with twice the force.

That caught the Prince's attention. Oliver Kross may have looked like a stick-figure, but he was startlingly forceful. Briefly, Ares thought he'd wind up in a brawl. He'd traded punches with friends before, but something stopped him from striking back at Oliver. His pride told him that he would win, but his survival instinct warned him to keep his distance. He stood down.

"Don't you treat me like this!" hissed Oliver. "I get it, I've never hated Annalais more, but it's done! She did what she did, and we can't change anything. You're alive, Luxie's alive. That's it. Breathe."

Every off blink, Ares' eyes flashed from green and round to violet and catlike. Oliver motioned to Luxea with a stare, and Ares followed it. Despite how belligerent he felt after the Empress had taken advantage of him and made an attempt on Luxea's life, Oliver's standpoint was more rational.

It was done. It was done.

Ares wiped back his hair and counted some of the marble chips on the ground until he'd settled down. At that point, he knelt by Luxea. He wanted to touch her, he'd *kill* to touch her, but he respected Shir's space, for that space would decide whether Luxea lived or died.

In a hoarse voice, he said, "I'm sorry. I'm at fault for this."

Luxea blinked blood out of her eyes. "Unless you asked her to kill me, you aren't at fault. But there's something else — something worse. When I touched her, she burned like Widow did on Mythos. All I can deduce is that she's surrendered herself to the Brood."

It wasn't something that needed mention, for they'd been equally aware of what had become of Annalais. The rest of the Mooncallers, on the contrary, perceived the statement to the extremity.

"If the Empress has made such harmful dealings, we may have less time to clear the city than was foreseen," said Brielle fretfully. "We're all angry with that golden snake, but we will let her reap what she has sowed. Let us leave."

The reasons to take revenge were limitless, but the welfare of the Goldenrise population was more outstanding. At half-past noon, the mending was complete; all that remained on Luxea's blooded flesh were faint scars. Shir's presence proved to be more imperative with each passing day.

Once they'd gathered the belongings they could, the Mooncallers hurried to the front steps of Villa de Taress and mounted their dracas. Down the path and across the plateau, they heard Annalais screaming behind the wall of ice that Luxea had erected.

It would melt soon, and they had to be gone when it did.

# RUINOUS SKIES

## SOLISSIUM, GOLDENRISE

THE WOLF, the Mythic, and the three dracas trotted into *Desha Dunali's* station; it had been a pile of plywood a fortnight ago, but now it was a two-story building with seats, desks, and a platform.

On the tracks was Peyamo Nelnah, tinkering with the headlight of her locomotive. She tapped it twice, and it flickered on bright. As the Mooncallers approached, she grinned and hobbled to them.

"My friends are here! How was your visit?" Her lenses pinpointed Ares' bruises and Luxea's blood-drenched clothing. "What's goin' on, eh? What happened to you two?"

"You were right. The Empress doesn't like me," muttered Luxea.

Ares might have added to her remark in any other situation, but he was still fighting to keep himself calm about what Annalais had done. "Amo, we need to get these people out of Solissium today — as many as possible. Is your machine ready for travel?"

"Aye, she's ready. Why the hurry?"

"The Empress is Widow's servant," said Brielle at once. "Starlight locked her away, but it could be mere hours before the Brood Mother comes to her rescue."

Peyamo had never had so many questions. "Starlight did what to the Empress? Er, okay, right. . . . If that's how it is, I can get this done quick n' clean."

The Lady wobbled into the conductor's car and sat. She flicked a telegraph machine in specific intervals, sending a message to *Matha ou Machina* as it hovered far above the station.

*Tap. Tap, tap, tap, press. Tap, press. Press, tap, press, tap. Tap, tap, press. Tap, press. Press. Tap.*

At the helm of the airship, Nika Lecava lounged with his feet up on the control panel, munching on an apple and watching the clouds float by with that northern grace he loved.

A transmission came from below.

*Beep. Beep, beep, beep, beeeep. Beep, beeeep. Beeeep, beep, beeeep, beep. Beep, beep, beeeep. Beep, beeeep. Beeeep. Beep.*

*'EVACUATE.'*

Blue eyes widened, Nika tossed his snack and snapped his red-tinted goggles over his eyes. "Crew, prepare for rounds over the city!"

The sky-sailors had been ready to reel in the anchors for a week. Nika banked left, heeled the airship over the ocean district of Solissium, and set propulsion to low.

Electrical feedback ripped the sky. On the ground, the Mooncallers shielded their ears. Nika's staticky voice came next, loud and clear through the speakers on *Matha ou Machina's* hull.

*"Oops. Ahem — citizens of Solissium! This is a mandatory evacuation warning issued by the Lady Peyamo Nelnah of Tarot and Prince Ares Lavrenthea of Tzapodia! Pray stay calm and gather at the*

*roadway of the Great Bridge, Tarhelen for transport to L'arneth!*
*Bring only what you require! Citizens of Solissium! This is a —"*

Nika repeated the announcement as the airship drifted above the capital.

Peyamo hopped out of the engine car. "See? Quick n' clean. Lecava will cover us from above. All we've got to do is load 'em in."

"Good. We must fill every car to capacity — even cargo," said Ares, eyeing the first throngs of evacuees as they amassed in the street.

Brielle clambered onto Ruka's back. "We should help them. My brother and I will lead the people here."

"I'll go with you," said Luxea urgently.

Ares caught her sleeve. "No, you're staying here, where I can see you. You were almost murdered this morning, Luxea —"

"— but I survived." She backed up toward Ruka. "I wont get myself into trouble. I mean it. I'll see you soon."

With Brielle's help, she climbed onto Ruka. They bounded away, darting past lumps of panicked citizens as they coalesced around *Desha Dunali.* As Avari and Oliver herded them toward the passenger cars, Peyamo trudged to the Prince's side.

"She's a hardy lass, Ares. She'll come back to you." She shook him by the shoulder. "Till then, stop bein' a fusspot n' come help me load these folks, won't you?"

Ares kept his eyes on Luxea until the moment he couldn't.

Downtown Solissium roared with crying children and couples arguing about what to bring. Four blocks from the station, Luxea and Brielle and Ruka found a man shouting to his wife about the inheritance that waited in his father's bank vault. His wife begged him to leave it and run, but her insistence wouldn't convince him.

This wasn't something Ruka couldn't fix.

The man was so absorbed by the debate that he didn't notice the enormous wolf standing behind him — but his wife did. Chattering at the teeth, she pointed at the beast. Her husband turned and caught his foot on his pile of belongings.

Brielle whisked her hand toward the locomotive. "Money can be made again, but life cannot. Go! Get out now!"

The woman tugged her husband's arm; he was so in shock that he nearly forgot to collect his bags before he ran.

Two lives had been spared, but tens of other groups waited down the road that needed to be rallied likewise. What was worse was that the majority of penurious residents refused to leave whatever little they had.

"Go and collect the ones in the street," said Luxea, sliding down Ruka's flank. "I'll gather those on the inside."

"Yes, Starlight." Brielle darted to the next couple.

Luxea ventured toward an opera where outside stood two haggard streetwalkers; they smelled so strongly of cigarettes that Luxea tasted ash. As she approached them, they whirled their constricted hips and eyeballed her bloody clothing.

"You all right, Miss?" asked the blonde. "Got blood on you."

"Thank you for your concern," said Luxea, "but I need you to —"

"— warm your bed?" suggested the brunette. "We're one gold piece each, three for both at once."

*You're one gold — what?*

Through a scowl, Luxea asked, "There's an evacuation warning for Solissium, and you're working? Go to the Great Bridge and get on the locomotive!"

The courtesans didn't move a muscle. One coughed, and the other fiddled with the strings of her corset. Appalling! Had Luxea had more muscles than morals, she would have lugged one woman under each arm to the bridge. But she couldn't, thus leaving her with one choice.

In the pocket of her nightgown were a few flowers, crumpled up spellbook notes . . . and the Felastil. She'd forgotten about the Moon Mother's pendant. There wasn't a reason not to wear it now that she knew the truth, so she put it around her neck and went on scouring her pocket.

Luckily, there were three gold pieces at the bottom; why money was stored in her nightgown, she couldn't say. She handed the money to the courtesans and pointed down the street.

"This is my payment. You can service me by getting to the bridge. I gave you extra, so make it quick!"

The courtesans summoned smug looks and put out their tattleweed cigarettes. As they swaggered down the street to the ocean, the two squabbled about who would get the bonus gold piece.

Two more had gone, and Luxea was drained after her wild morning, but there were umpteen more innocents to spare before she could relax.

Next, she bolted into the opera and across the lobby. Through the crack in the door to the stage came gushing heady scents of perfume and liquor.

The house was full. Nika's evacuation warnings were all kinds of noisy, but the audience and performers hadn't heard them. The opera was dark except for the single lantern on the stage. Violins and flutes quavered from the orchestra pit, and a woman's rich, warbling voice made Luxea's stars spin.

Yes, it was rude to interrupt a performance — but the only alternative was to let these people suffer Widow's wrath. Naturally, that was a pinch more regrettable to her than forcing an intermission. Hoping she wouldn't trip on the way to the stage or be battered by an audience member's pamphlet, she shouldered her way to house left.

"Excuse me! May I have your attention?"

Only a few people in the front row heard her. She called out again and again and jumped up and down to no avail. There wasn't time for this nonsense! She would have to be more assertive — just a tad.

Luxea took off her shoe and threw it at the star of the show. The woman on stage, who wore a ghastly explosion of a dress, squeaked and stopped singing. A couple of violins screeched, and the percussion died down. The audience members gasped and whispered behind their jewel-coated fans about Luxea's bloody nightgown.

A house of drama-lovers staring at her wasn't helpful for her self-esteem, but Luxea managed to say, "I need every one of you to get out immediately! There's a mandatory evacuation for all of Solissium. If you disregard it, you *will* die! Get out while you can! Go to the Great Bridge, Tarhelen!"

There wasn't a sound spoken or sung for a minute until a round, stunted gentleman in a veiled hat and a dickey stood up and clapped rowdily. "Now *this* is acting!"

"What?" hissed Luxea. "No, I'm telling you! Widow is — !"

Other audience members followed his example. While the house delivered a standing ovation for Luxea, the leading lady hustled backstage with a heart full of broken dreams.

All of a sudden, a stagehand popped up behind Luxea and seized her by the arms, babbling, "This is an insult to the fine arts!" She was promptly yanked up the aisle.

All right. Apparently, *normal* words weren't enough to push these people out of the opera. Magickal words, on the contrary . . .

"For the Goddess' sake." Luxea wriggled out of the stagehand's grasp and said, *"Yeth'lavren."*

A wave of blue fire bit at the stage, and the gold-threaded curtain went up in smoke. The stagehand let her go and tried to put it out, but Luxea controlled her flames to jump to stage right.

Audience members screamed and trampled over each other toward the exit, and figures in lavish costumes and masks with various animal motifs shot into the lobby. The musicians followed behind, lugging their instruments.

Luxea guided groups out the door and into the street, shouting at them, "Leave your belongings and get to the Great Bridge! There are people there who will help you. Run, run!"

It wasn't long after that Brielle and Ruka came trotting down the road; they'd evacuated one hundred citizens or more since Luxea had entered the opera. The wolf barked and growled at some lingering men and women as Luxea pulled herself onto his back.

But then someone called to her from afar.

"Is that you, Lady Velesari? Bless, it is! You remember us, don't you? Please, I beg you! Get us out of here, or we'll perish!"

Luxea dropped from Ruka's flank and peered around. A few *clangs* and coughs sounded from down low where, just above the curb, was a jail cell.

Beyond the bars and the thin waves of smoke that surged into it from the opera, Luxea spied the Haven de Asrodisia headmaster, Pertia Voulet, and his superior, Madam Lilivae Alanis.

Oh, Pertia. He'd been the man Luxea had seduced to rent Unblossomed — Runa — for the night. After the gala, the Mooncallers had put him and Madam Alanis into shackles by the charge of enslaving men, women, and children under the employ of Empress Annalais.

If anyone deserved such a fate as death, it was them.

Stomach boiling hatefully, Luxea knelt by the cell and glared at Pertia's callused hands. She could still feel their impatient roughness on her chest and envision how many times they'd struck Runa.

With her one foot that still had a shoe, Luxea nudged Pertia's fingers off the bars and whispered, "No."

After three long hours, the wall of ice that Luxea had summoned in Villa de Taress broke. Outside the bedchamber, Annalais saw Widow. Weeping hysterically, she scrambled over the threshold to her rescuer. The Brood Mother helped her off the ground, frowning at the burns on her neck and hands.

"The stars hurt you," She said sympathetically.

Annalais covered her wounds at once. "She burned me! She's taken it all, there is nothing left for me!" She went positively florid. "But You . . . You *lied* to me! You promised that Ares would love me, but he isn't mine — he never was — and now he's gone!"

"He will not be gone for long. Might I remind you, Treasure, that he belongs to the Brood?" asked Widow soothingly. "This is not the time for tears. Those infidels are intervening, and I cannot let them."

"How will we stop them?" sniffled Annalais.

"I will do it, but you must swear to me that you will not stand in my way," instructed Widow. "You will stay here, safe, and I will bar the path ahead from the falsely righteous."

"But my empire — !"

"There is no empire! There is only the Brood!" thundered Widow. Annalais staggered backward. "With me, you will gain more power than you can fathom, more power than you deserve! You don't need an empire, Your Splendor — not anymore."

Through bleary eyes, the Empress relived her every memory in her gorgeous home. The politics, the firsts, the lasts, the loves, the losses.

Losses . . . she'd lost everything.

Rowan was gone, she no longer held sway over her lands, and, worst of all, Ares resented her. There was nothing left here. Nothing.

Annalais aggressively wiped her tears. "Stop them."

Widow ran Her fingers over Annalais's burned neck. Eight giant, spiny legs broke through Her flesh up the length of Her spine. She skittered onto the roof of the villa where, from such heights, She saw thousands of evacuees swarming the streets of Solissium. Her white pupils darted up to the airship that circled the city, and She grinned.

"A chill is on the wind." She raised Her arms. *"Come!"*

A gust tipped *Matha ou Machina* to the starboard side. With a violent spin of the wheel, Nika leveled out the vessel, poised to proceed with his announcements until a crewman shouted, "Lecava, what in the Trihells is that? There, on the horizon!"

Over Nika's shoulder, a sudden gush of wind battered his face. In absolute terror, he let go of the wheel and toppled back against the control panel.

Swelling over Plateau de Taress were clouds of violet and grey, spilling toward Solissium at feet per second. These weren't any ordinary clouds, they didn't feel like rain, hail, or snow —

They felt like impending doom.

Nika bolted to the intercom and screamed into it, "Fire up the engines — all of them! *Now!*"

Without waiting for a reply from the generator room, Nika sped to the telegraph. Fingers shaking, he sent a message to *Desha Dunali.*

*Tap, tap, tap. Press. Press, press, press. Tap, press, tap. Press, press.*

A transmission blipped from the conductor's car. Peyamo rushed inside followed by Ares, and Luxea who'd returned minutes before. They stood in the doorway as the Lady's face twisted and untwisted.

*Beep, beep, beep. Beeeep, beeeep, beeeep. Beep, beeeep, beep. Beeeep, beeeep.*

Ares asked urgently, "What is it? What did it say?"

Peyamo squinted out the front window. "It said, *'STORM.'*"

Outside of the locomotive, the citizens screamed. Ares and Luxea dropped onto the platform and turned their attention to the northeast where oozing across the plateau were dark, foreboding clouds.

But that wasn't all.

From the mist sprang reaches-long, shadowy hands. The black fingers clutched the cliffs above the capital, and a woman's head formed betwixt them. Ares recognized Her straightaway.

It was Sh'tarr the Goddess of Storms who'd mysteriously vanished when Widow had sailed to Mythos. She'd scared the very breath out of Ares the first time he'd met Her en route to Mythos, but She looked stranger now.

This wasn't Sh'tarr — this was Widow's prisoner.

"Peyamo, we need to leave!" he demanded.

"Aye!" The Lady yanked her levers, ready for departure.

Ares brought Luxea to him. "Help me get these people inside."

Upon Plateau de Taress, Widow outstretched Her hand. "Sh'tarr, show them that this world is *mine.*"

Trapped under Widow's command, the corrupted Storm Goddess swooped into the city and laid a cloak of darkness over the land, cackling as She flew. Beneath Her, all of Solissium turned to ice.

Human shapes were stuck running down streets, reaching for each other with faces hollow. All men, women, and children who hadn't heeded the evacuation warning were taken by death in an instant. Their blood, their hearts, and their minds were frozen, snared within shells of gelid glass.

While the Storm Goddess enacted Her will, Widow honed Her sight on *Desha Dunali.* Thousands of citizens would make it out alive, and that wasn't entirely disappointing. She hadn't expected *all* of them to be eliminated today — but that didn't mean She couldn't have fun in the meantime, did it? The Brood Mother leaped down the cliffs and scampered across the ice.

The Mooncallers crammed evacuees into the locomotive as the storm's reach spread. Sh'tarr was drawing too near, and Ruka's animal instincts were blaring.

The wolf climbed into a livestock car and howled for his sister to join him. Brielle lifted an elderly man inside and eyed the blizzard as it loomed ever closer. A wolf was born for the cold, the snow . . . but not like this. Choosing to save herself, she grabbed Ruka's scruff and took the last space in the car.

Close by, Avari and Oliver hoisted people one by one. Neither had noticed how quickly Sh'tarr was closing in until Her wind snapped the hood off Oliver's head and whipped about his charcoal hair.

He hated the thought, but it was there regardless.

*We can't save everyone.*

Sharing a like mind with Brielle, Oliver wrested Avari off the ground, threw her over his shoulder, and carried her into the passenger car. She kicked and protested even after the door shut.

*Desha Dunali* lurched into movement as Ares and Luxea slid closed a cargo car. They tried to push into the next open space, but a rush of desperate evacuees herded them back. Then the livestock door slammed, and the locomotive was rolling.

He clutched her sleeve and weaved with her through the screaming throngs, but there wasn't a chance. They would never make it. Soon they stopped running, and the tracks were empty.

Ares and Luxea spun around. Sh'tarr was one street away. The cold broke against their skins as they faced each other once more.

They would die, wouldn't they? But, at the very least, they would die together. In that case, Ares would take the brunt of it.

With his back to the storm, he covered her. But as high as a dragon's tolerance was for heat, it was quite the opposite for the cold. His next breath made fog before them, and his lips turned blue.

The cold was so, so sharp. . . .

As sleet shredded the back of Ares' shirt, Luxea shot her arm out past him. The temperature made her fingers go numb in a millisecond, she could see the rime growing on their tips, but she was still able to erect a magick shield. She gave all the energy she had left, but Sh'tarr's frost shattered her barrier.

*So . . . this is the end.*

Her freezing hand fell to her side, and her starry eyes shut. With her head burrowed in Ares' hair, she waited for their breaths to cease.

Ice ate everyone on the platform — except for them.

Long arms wrapped around Ares and Luxea, and suddenly the cold was no more. When next they opened their eyes, they saw nothing but darkness, and the warmth of many bodies was all around them.

But at their side, Shir's smile shone.

At the very last moment, the Mythic had locus-jumped with Ares and Luxea onto a locomotive car with no windows, packed with refugees. They were *safe.*

At once, Luxea released Ares and knelt. The lingering cold in her veins was hardly noticeable in comparison to the shock she felt to yet be alive. She covered her face with her chilled hands, and Ares leaned on the wall, breathing hot air on his fingers. Shir touched both of their heads and sang them a song.

*Desha Dunali* had just passed the gates of the Great Bridge, Tarhelen when the last cars screeched and wobbled on the tracks. Peyamo cursed the mechanics, but this problem wasn't a defect of her making.

This was external.

The passengers in the back of the locomotive shrieked, for staring through the window were four black eyes. Widow rattled around the caboose, and the movement alerted Ruka who was in the second to last car. Brielle slid open the connecting door, and the two were met with the sight of Widow's giant legs across the gap.

It was then that the rider and her wolf made an unforgivable decision. Ruka started gnawing through the coupler. They thought they would be killing everyone in the caboose — but Widow did it first.

One of Her spearlike legs crashed through the window, impaling several bodies. She fit Her bald head through the gap and exhaled. Smoke erupted from Her mouth, filling the car, and clothing, flesh, and muscles melted into a black fluid. In three seconds, the caboose was packed with skeletal remains.

The coupler *snapped.*

The last car was left behind and gaining distance quickly. Brielle moved to close the connecting door, and then Widow glared upward and gave her a falsely friendly wave.

The Brood Mother bent Her arachnid legs, ready to leap, but then a tidal wave slammed into the Great Bridge. In a gush of salt water, She was thrown over the edge and into the ocean far, far below.

This unforeseen tsunami slammed into Solissium and ripped buildings from their foundations, but it was no tragedy. The wave had saved all those on the locomotive.

Looming above the Great Bridge, higher than all mountains, was Alatos the Sea Goddess. At last, She found Her Sister of Storms — but not in the way She'd hoped.

As Sh'tarr froze the seawater and encased the roadway of the bridge in ice, Alatos cast Her down. The Storm Goddess screamed and clawed toward the Sea Goddess, shredding barnacles from Her skin and leaving electric arcs in Her veins. Alatos ignored the pain. Her aqueous eyes leaked down Her cheeks as Her webbed fingers curved around Sh'tarr's face.

"You will leave these mortals alone," She whispered, but Her voice was heard by every ear for reaches around. She choked, "Will I never have my Sister again?"

The Storm Goddess tried to pry Her hands away, but Alatos wouldn't give in. "Release me! I no longer serve nature, I — !"

Sh'tarr's howling trembled. For only a moment, the shadow melted, and She looked like She had since Her becoming. She embraced Alatos and sobbed while She had the freedom.

"Swim, do not let Her touch you! She bears the power of a greater. All that we have known is a lie!" She held Her head to Alatos' and said, "We have not three Mothers, my dearest Sister — we have *four!*"

Sh'tarr was sucked back into shadow. The Sisters of Storm and Sea fought until *Desha Dunali* was far enough from Solissium for Alatos to make Her escape and guarantee the mortals' safety.

When She was gone, Sh'tarr faded into a powerless wisp.

Hours had passed, and not a breath had been taken in Solissium since the city's fall. Cherish Ven'lethe, a l'arian elvish magister, trampled down a dune to the ocean where washed up on the shore was Widow. Panic consumed him. He skidded onto his knees and pulled Her into his lap.

"I'm here. I'm sorry, my promise. I'm here now."

Widow breathed shallowly and cried, "I can't do this anymore! I'm so tired, Cherish . . . I'm so tired."

"You aren't giving up," he said into Her skin. "From the start, you knew this wouldn't be simple. But after all that you've been through, you've never faltered. You can't stop now."

Perhaps Cherish was right. Widow had wanted this for so long, and it was too late to end it. She held onto him desperately. "Never go."

# MOONLIGHT TO SHADOW

## REFUGEE CAMP, THE STORM PLAINS

THE LOCOMOTIVE arrived at the station in the Storm Plains a day and a half later. *Matha ou Machina* descended and idled above ground nearby, releasing Peyamo Nelnah's sky-sailors to assist with moving the refugees out of the cars.

Avari and Oliver were let out first. She'd been bawling since *Desha Dunali* had started moving, terrified for the safety of their friends. Oliver hoisted her onto his back from the steps of the passenger car and whispered hopes as he carried her.

Peyamo hobbled around as fast as her leg would allow. At the last car, she and three crewmen slid open a livestock door where Ruka and Brielle were inside, safe and sound.

Right away, the wolf carried his rider south to the front of the locomotive where they spotted Avari's frizzy bun from a distance. Brielle leaped off Ruka and ran, and Avari abandoned Oliver's shoulders to meet her in the middle. They wept and hugged as Oliver petted Ruka's snout.

A car in the middle was unlatched next. Ares squinted through the light and grunted. Nearly one hundred refugees were packed into their car, so he allowed them to exit first. Once the way was clear, he petted Luxea's sleeve to wake her up; she'd fallen asleep in the corner beside him.

It didn't take long for the Mooncallers to find each other. Avari refused to let Luxea out of her sight — *ever* — and Brielle thanked Oliver every odd minute for having forced the ranger to board the locomotive.

They migrated to the Lady's quarters, the largest establishment in the military camp while the Solissium refugees were herded into smaller registration tents. Having a place to sit and rummage through her belongings, at last, Luxea stripped herself of her ruined nightgown and her single shoe.

Avari, as she'd sworn, was less than two feet away to be sure the sorceress was safe. Luxea pulled on her Tzapodian military uniform, a dark blue pantsuit with a brown leather trim, and pinned her Seer's sigil to the breast. She'd gotten a few splinters from the floor of the livestock car, so she had Avari pluck them from the pad of her foot before changing into a pair of boots.

Later in the day, Peyamo Nelnah trundled around and marked down heads. She'd filled three pages with one thousand five hundred tallies, so far, and hadn't reached the edge of the camp yet. Many of the the Solissium citizens had been spared, but many more had been trapped in ice far across Eternity's Ocean — where they would forever remain.

The Lady tarried, absorbing the broken families with lost purposes under stained blankets. Elders hunched over their packs, repairing rips in their garbs, and children with dirty, swollen faces clung to each other, no longer the sons and daughters of anyone. Aristocrats blotted their painted faces with the last of their silks, and skinny slum-dwellers who hadn't had a single belonging to their name simply adapted to their new circumstances.

Lady Peyamo had been too focused on the construction of the locomotive to think about it, but she wondered now if her nation, Tarot, was secure. Ank'tatra was a war zone, and all that separated Tarot from the icy graveyard of Goldenrise was the swampy Wraiths.

If the land of the seroden elves was overthrown without Peyamo near, she might never get it back. As she continued on, dashing out hundreds of refugees, her longing to return to her volcanic wasteland grew.

"Amo!" called Ares with Brielle and Ruka beside him. Peyamo zoomed in on him. "How many are there? Brielle and Ruka will ride to Tzapodia to pass the word to the council. They're aware of incoming refugees — but not all of them at once."

"Not sure just yet, Ares." Peyamo scratched down another tally. "I've got about sixteen hundred now, but I ain't even reached that area over yonder. By my eye, I'd estimate two thousand."

*"Two thousand?"*

The Prince inspected a nearby group of sobbing refugees and inhaled their melancholy. It wouldn't be simple, but taking them in was his responsibility now.

"Brielle, give those numbers to Keeper Vessias and send for a few council members. I should be the one to explain the turn of events."

"I will." Brielle rode Ruka around in a circle and gestured to the Lady's quarters. "Dragon? I trust you to watch over the others."

With saliva dressing his teeth, Ruka kicked off his hind legs. Brielle flattened to his shoulders, and the trees rustled as they sank into the barrier of the Western Woods.

Although the Mooncallers were sapped of energy, people who were just as weary needed help. They slept in shifts, and those who were awake assisted Shir to mend wounds, count legal names, and ready the refugees for the coming journey to Tzapodia.

After her shift, Avari returned to the Lady's quarters where beds had been arranged. Luxea was awake, lying face-up with the Usinnon on her belly. Avari sat beside her and whispered, "Hey, you, my shift's done. Think you could take over for a while?"

"Yes," groaned Luxea.

Avari flicked her. "Lazy slug."

As Luxea put on more appropriate clothing, Avari crossed her arms on the mattress and laid her head. Reminiscing hurt all of the Mooncallers lately, but sometimes it was a comfort to visit the past.

"Luxie, remember how Chief Demartiet used to crack the whip on us whenever we didn't feel like working?"

"I'll never forget anything the Chief did," said Luxea sadly.

"Me neither." Avari picked at stray fuzzies on the blanket. "Do you think, if he were still around, he'd be proud of us?"

"After all we've done over the past few days? Maybe." Luxea bounced one of Avari's springy curls and recited, "What do the Mooncallers stand for, Vishera?"

Avari saluted enthusiastically. "As the Mooncallers, we must always offer our help to those in need, sir!" she quoted.

They shared smiles. Once she'd fit on her trousers, Luxea sat next to Avari and held onto her arm. "Sometimes, I wish we could go back to the days when we didn't know a thing about Widow. The barracks smelled like sweat and ale, but I miss them. Do you?"

"Of course, you sausage," said Avari. "It's good that we're both humble about moving up though. After you becoming a member of the council, and me living in the castle with you, you'd think we'd be spoiled. But I'm all right no matter where I am — as long as I have you. Even after all this, you're my best friend, Luxie."

"I'd better be," said Luxea kittenishly.

Avari kissed her on the temple. "As much as I love you, it's my turn to get shut-eye. Get on out there, kiddo."

Weary, Luxea brushed herself off and let Avari take her place on the warm but lumpy cot. In a minute's count, she was carried off to dreamland. Her tiny foot was exposed, so Luxea tucked it in.

It was windy outside, but the air was wildfire dry. Luxea shed her coat and threw it on top of a crate before diving into the spread of refugees. Their tattered sheets sheltered their trembling bodies, and the gold trinkets they'd worn had lost their luster. They were patchwork people.

Half an hour passed without an alarming sight or sound, but then Luxea heard shouting from the northern boundary of the camp. As was her duty, she wove past overstuffed satchels and pairs of callused feet to address whatever issue had risen.

In fifty steps, she saw two men tussling over a linen pouch of butter to use on bread for their families. The altercation was violent, kicking, throwing, and punching. The surrounding refugees were frightened.

"You're bothering everyone," said Luxea sharply. She snatched the butter and peeled it open. "This is more than enough for both of you. Can't you ration it? You won't need a whole stick for your children."

"What would you know, girl?" rasped one man. He poked the sigil on her breast. "A member of the Speaker's council must get everything handed to them on a fucking plate of silver. Give it to me!"

The two refugees who'd previously been enemies joined forces to gang up on Luxea. One reached for her again and again, and the other picked up a long, knotted stick. She backed away and held up her free hand, saying, "If you take another step . . ."

*Thump.* She wheeled right into a warm body.

Behind her was Ares, wearing an expression so fierce that the two men instantly groveled on their knees. The Prince, with a second pouch of butter in his hand, requested the one that Luxea held. She gave it to him. He crouched between the aggressive refugees and threw one stick each onto the dirt at their feet.

"Tomorrow," he husked, "you will eat your bread plain."

Ares and Luxea roved to the northern edge of the camp and sat in a barley field. He lit a roseleaf cigarette and collected the sky in his eyes, for the entire universe seemed to be visible above the Storm Plains this night.

Smoke obscured the view as he exhaled. "Luxea, I should have said this earlier, but . . . about what happened with Annalais —"

"It wasn't either of our faults," said Luxea at once. "She's out of her mind, and it isn't up to you to justify it. We're both her victims."

He gave her a weighing look, but her stars were fixed on the ones above their heads. He'd feared that Luxea would never think of him the same after what he'd done with the Empress — had it been in his will or not.

"You aren't upset?"

"Of course, I am, but not with you. I suppose I felt . . . deluded. I heard you two together and didn't understand." She recalled Ares' voice in her head, accusing Annalais of meddling with his mind. "But that morning, I heard you speak and knew it hadn't been your choice. Widow did something to Annalais, and she did the same to you. I can't be upset with anyone but them."

Ares could almost feel the chain of time that bound them. "Yes, you heard that because of me. In the Golden Spire, I had to link us in order to view your memories. It was the only option I had."

"Link us? In what way, exactly?"

"In all ways, and for all time. In spirit, in heart and mind and body. Anatatri wouldn't show me what She knew about the Shadow without it. If that angers you . . ."

Luxea read the sky, some lines of its story blocked out by thin clouds. "I think it I were to have my fate crossed with anyone's . . ." She sighed. "No. I'm not angry at all."

So this conversation held two reliefs for Ares. He stamped out his cigarette with his boot. "After that night, I saw something from your point of view too, and felt . . . heartache."

"Yes, it was something like that." Luxea propped up her head with her hand. "I think Oscerin wanted me to stop Annalais. I'm sorry that I didn't. If She was expecting me to walk in on you two, She was sorely mistaken."

She held onto his Felastil, feeling the dizzying warmth that radiated from the jewel into her fingers, and then inclined her head and took it off. When she offered it to Ares, both the pendant and her eyes were dark blue.

"Will you take it back now? It's bears a much greater weight than I'd imagined," she said mildly.

He smiled for the first time in two days. Naturally, he had doubts about Oscerin, but being the Speaker was his burden, not Luxea's. He scooped it out of her palm but immediately dropped it again.

Pain — the worst he'd ever suffered.

Every one of his muscles tensed so tightly that they neared tearing. He threw his cigarette and fell onto his back.

"Ares?"

Luxea crawled fast across the grass to him, and then it felt as if her ventricles had stopped giving her blood. Something had happened to him when he touched the Felastil, something she'd seen twice before.

The flesh on his fingers smoked and crusted with black burns. But this was his pendant, he'd worn it all his life. How, and why now, did it hurt him?

Sweat pasted strands of hair to Ares' face. His skin was clammy, his head was heavy, and his pupils were contracted to tiny dots even in the dark of night. Over a few minutes, he steadied himself just enough to think.

The Felastil, the relic of the Moon, had burned him. But if he was tainted by Widow, that meant there was another, more treasured jewel he could no longer touch. Not allowing himself the time to reconsider, he cupped Luxea's cheek.

"Agh!"

He reeled onto his side, his palm scored and peeled into fleshy circles, bubbling with blood blisters. Through his agony, he bit his knuckle and shut his eyes.

Ares had never experienced a burn because it took minutes and minutes of heat and flame to affect a dragon. This was the first time, and it hadn't come from fire, it had come from a girl.

"I don't understand!" he panted. "I wore the Felastil, I touched you only days ago — your skin was in my hands!"

Luxea's voice lost power as she said, "Until Annalais . . ."

The emotions that struck Ares then scorched him in an entirely different, more damaging way. But he kept himself under control in front of Luxea; she'd faced enough anger as of late.

"Widow did this," he forced out. "That's why She didn't want me killed all those times, why She made Annalais a promise. So that I would belong to the Brood too."

He lay on his back with his forearm over his eyes for several hours. Luxea sat beside him with her sleeve bundled around her hand, holding his claw as he recovered from the torment of her touch.

# AN INVITATION
### 30.LIGHTSMEET.26.OSC.3
### REFUGEE CAMP, THE STORM PLAINS

AT DAWN, Luxea's head was screaming at her. She and Ares had spent most of the night alone in the field, burns and shadows and moonlight forbidding their eyes to sleep. She trudged out of the Lady's quarter where Avari, Oliver, and Brielle and Ruka, who'd returned from Tel Ashir with some council members, served brown sugar porridge to the refugees for breakfast.

"Mornin', Luxie!" whistled Oliver.

"Mm," she grunted.

"How was your night? You and Ares up and disappeared. Didn't feel like comin' back?" suggested Avari.

"No, we didn't," said Luxea tersely.

Ares came out of the quarter looking just as sleepless. His eyes were red and sunken, and his hair was wrapped in an unkempt bun, strands lacing down his jaw and hooking to his horns in places. Without a *good morning,* which wasn't uncommon, he sat next to Luxea at the rations table and poured a cup of tea. It had been steeped hours ago and tasted like filth.

Oliver tapped his ladle on the rim of the porridge pot and untied his apron. "What's gotten into you two?"

No one said anything until all of them were at the table; this wasn't a topic that Ares and Luxea could shout to their friends in public. He passed a fleeting glance at her, and she nodded. He started to speak.

"As you know, Widow and Her underlings burn when —"

"Isn't the hour a bit early to talk about Widow?" moaned Avari.

"Do *not* interrupt me," said Ares waspishly. "Oscerin had Luxea consume pure moonlight when her soul left her body. Because of that, Widow and Her underlings burn when they touch her."

"Shadow cannot meet moonlight," added Brielle.

Sick to the depths of his guts, Ares raised his right hand. His fingers and palm were swathed in stained bandages where the Felastil and Luxea's skin had wounded him. He'd never thought he would have a reason to be ashamed of both of his hands.

"You're one of the Brood?" whispered Oliver.

"Yes, to my unawareness," murmured Ares.

"Then any one of us could be tainted," said Brielle uneasily.

Avari had kissed Luxea's head the night before, but she wanted to be sure. She pulled off her gloves, determined, and placed her bare hand on Luxea's. She let her breath flow, for she hadn't burned.

More carefully, Brielle tried next. She crept close and bumped the tip of Luxea's nose with her thumb. She wasn't hurt which meant Ruka wasn't either.

Last came Oliver's attempt. Timid, he scooted near and swept his fingers over Luxea's forearm. To everyone's relief, he wasn't harmed by the contact.

"Then it's only me. I suppose that's good news," droned Ares.

"D'you feel any different?" asked Oliver sadly.

"No, not at all."

Brielle aimed her glare at his hand. "How do we get it out of you?"

"If I knew, I would have done it already," said Ares harshly.

"You should ask Oscerin," recommended Avari.

Ares felt even more alone. "I can't."

The Felastil around Luxea's neck tickled the hollow of her chest. She touched the jewel's contours through her tunic. "I can."

As the balmy midday wind fluttered her wavy, white hair around her head, Luxea trotted around the barley field. She'd spent twenty minutes deciding on what to ask Oscerin and how to phrase her questions, but this was only *if* the goddess responded.

Eventually, she walked all the way to the border of the Western Woods where Brielle and Ruka had first met freedom. She sat crosslegged and flopped backward, *thunking* her head against the earth; the grass was itchy, and the damp soil saturated her shirt. She tucked her chin, eyeing the Felastil as she brought it to her mouth.

"Oscerin, I need answers. If you won't give me all of them, fine, but give me one. Just one . . . please."

It was as if the Moon Mother had been waiting to answer the call. Luxea's eyes rolled back, her cosmos expanding and swallowing the whites. Voices swarmed around her, and the air densified, strapping down her limbs.

*"You have the answer, my stars,"* said Oscerin angelically.

"No, Oscerin. You put too much credence in me, and I'm all tired of Your opacity. I need to hear it from You." Luxea raised her inner voice. "Ares belongs to the Brood now, as I'm sure You're aware. Was this all in Your divine plan too? This happened because You've refused to speak plainly!"

Oscerin's tone was bladed. *"I warned you. I told you to stop her."*

"What did You expect me to do? You're not human, I understand, but in our world, we don't go into a room where two people are in bed together!"

*"I enjoy the manner in which you address me,"* chuckled Oscerin. *"It is in disrespect, but that is what I adore about you — you aren't afraid. All that you have said is right, but there are many secrets I cannot yet share."*

"All right, but if you don't show me how to reverse what Widow did to Ares, he won't ever be Your Speaker again," reminded Luxea.

*"As I told you, you have the answer,"* repeated Oscerin.

"Dammit — no, I don't!"

An exasperated sigh rattled the plane between planes. Oscerin was losing patience, but Luxea was pleasantly surprised to see that her impiety had the desired effect on the Moon Goddess.

She offered her a hint.

*"With the birth of time, I gave darkness a name. When I spoke it, the darkness bent to my will. That is how you will spare Ares from the Widow's possession. You have done it before, you have saved yourself, but it is not time for you to remember. When you do, you shall see that the cure is in the name."*

"Whose name?" asked Luxea briskly.

A wind rushed past her, so harsh that she feared her flesh would peel off and leave her as hopeless bones. Beyond the gusts, beyond the scatter of blood in her veins and coils of unreachable recollections in her skull, came a final statement.

*"Cover your ears, Butterfly . . ."*

The connection was slashed. Luxea's eyes flew open, and the dustiness of plains grass threw her into a coughing fit. She flipped over and held her head until her vertigo passed. When her vision steadied, she glared at the Felastil.

"How does Ares tolerate You?"

Becoming Widow's property was killing the Prince slowly. The Mooncaller Council wasn't made aware of his new tie to the enemy; he trusted them but not enough to share such a fragile truth.

Luxea had passed along Oscerin's message, and he was just as frustrated by Her unwillingness to give a straight answer. The more he lingered on it, the more he realized that Anatatri had been right. The Moon Goddess *was* hiding something — She always had been.

After passing out orders to his council members to transport refugees by dracas carts to the city of Tel Ashir, Ares sneaked past his sleeping companions, except for Shir as they never slept, and went out the back door of the Lady's quarter for fresh air.

It was three o'clock in the morning when the Mythic's crystals trembled. A stranger was here, a stranger powerful and beautiful and nefarious. They wanted to warn Ares, but that sinister force was right next to him. They locus-jumped into a nearby pond and camouflaged.

At the same time, Ares tied up his hair for sleep and rounded the building to go back inside. But then he started back into the wall, for blocking the door, Her black robes twisting in the breeze, was Widow.

"Hello, Ares."

"What are You doing here?" he shuddered.

"I came to welcome you to the Brood." Widow took his hand before he could recall how to move. "I should have advised you against touching her. It hurts, doesn't it?"

Ares fell away. "Nothing hurts as much as what You've done!"

"All I've done is help you."

"You've helped no one!"

The Brood Mother pulled Ares' shirt collar aside, admiring his black scales. "Have you used dragon blood since you became mine?"

"I am not Yours."

This was silly to Widow. She shrugged and said, "Try it."

Although hesitant, he listened to Her. His irises enlarged and darkened to violet, and his pupils warped into vertical slits. Widow motioned to the scales on his shoulder. Typically, doing so much as changing the color of his eyes would have caused one or two scales to surface — but not this time.

Putting himself to the test, Ares exhaled a tiny, purple flame. His scales didn't move. He swallowed the fire, and smoke danced down the silver ring between his nostrils. Next, he pulled up his sleeve. His skin cindered as the transformation began, but the scales didn't spread.

It was a miracle. The greatest of fears that Ares had been doomed to face was gone. If the draconism was dormant, he would never lose his mind, he would have a chance at becoming the King of Tzapodia, having a family, and forgetting about the curse in his blood.

"It's relieving, isn't it?" asked Widow affectionately. "Stay with me, and I'll take it all away. That's what I promised you in the beginning, don't you remember? That contract you tore without a second thought. My offer still stands." She looked sympathetic. "Tell me, has Oscerin done so much for you?"

Ares stalked to the edge of the woods and lit a cigarette using his own flame. Widow took a seat on a boulder at his side. He glanced at Her through the purple fire, perturbed by how nonviolent, almost *friendly,* She was being — or pretending to be.

"If all You wanted was me, why did You push Annalais to do what she did?" he asked, eyes flashing back to green.

Astonishingly, Widow answered with full honesty. "Because she wanted you. I don't blame her — you're virile." Ares hated Her. Widow went on. "Annalais was heartbroken over losing you to someone else, and I couldn't have convinced you to join the Brood any other way. While you and your friends paid Anatatri a visit, I told Annalais to give you my breath. Doing so deemed her irresistible for a short period of time, and you as my paragon indefinitely."

"Yet Your promise to Anna was in place for that single evening. How do I know it won't be the same for me?" he pointed out.

"Use your head, Ares. What can the Empress of Goldenrise offer me? Nothing now. All she had was her connection with you, and that served me superbly. Her promise lasted one night because all I needed was one night. But the list of what *you* can give me goes on, and on, and on," said Widow passionately.

"So every choice You make is out of selfishness. It's all for You."

"No. To rebuild the world, you must make choices that don't take others' needs into consideration. When I've gathered all that I require, the Brood will move forth for the goodness of humanity as a whole."

"By chipping away entire cities at a time?"

What a cutting stare She had. "Have you contemplated how overpopulated this world will be if we continue to live the way we have been? More humans are born which means more humans must work to feed the young. Those humans make even more humans, and more cities must be built to house them. Two generations pass, and suddenly there are one hundred thousand new faces, one hundred thousand hungry bellies, one hundred thousand needs to make a profit.

"But what happens when we use up our resources? By Era Four, we will drain this planet, we will live stacked atop one another, fighting each day to keep a place to rest our heads. For what? So that lovers can have the adorable children of whom they've always dreamed? No. *That* is selfishness, Your Highness."

He couldn't believe it, but a part of Ares agreed with Widow. He exhaled smoke and asked, "If that's Your goal, is there no way to reach it without giving rise to such havoc?"

"You can tell me there's an alternative, but there isn't," said Widow bluntly. "The sovereigns have attempted to counteract this outcome throughout history, but have they succeeded? Not in the slightest. I'm taking the necessary actions to do what they were afraid to do: ignite a controlled burn. Do we have an understanding?"

Even if, in truth, Ares did understand Her, he couldn't accede to it. He changed the subject. "And what does Luxea Siren have to do with all of this? Why have You gone so far out of Your way to kill her?"

Widow giggled. "You don't want to answer? Fair." She rubbed Her bald head. "That starry-eyed rat has been gifted the ability to stop me. If she were permitted to live on, her influence over the Brood would worsen. Her life is a mistake, a waste, a toxic and ever-blooming lie!"

Since talking about Luxea, Widow had grown rigid. Ares showed Her a carnassial smile. "You're afraid to say Luxea's name. There's another reason You want her to die, but You won't admit it to me or to anyone. She terrifies You."

The Brood Mother grinned sublimely wide. "You *are* smart, Your Highness. There are many reasons. Do you wish to learn them?"

"That's why I mentioned it," retorted Ares.

"Follow me, and perhaps I will tell you." Widow reached into Her cloak and showed Ares a scroll. "On the eleventh of Clawsguard, the

Brood will gather in Erannor, at the theater. Your old friends will be there, the members of The Six. Val'noren, Ralvesh, Vesas and Levelia, and Annalais too — but she will keep her distance if that is your wish. Will you join us?"

Joining Widow under any circumstance was the last thing Ares wanted, but he'd always excelled in pretending. "What will happen at this gathering?" he asked, acting interested.

"What happens at gatherings of The Six? Nothing has changed, it's all that you're used to but under a different name. We'll have food, drinks, a discussion in the court, and the night will end with a pretty, little performance," said Widow licentiously.

At gatherings of The Six, the members would share plans under confidentiality. If the Brood did the same, Ares thought it might be his one, nonrecurring opportunity to gain information and undermine the Brood's operations — until Widow spoke again.

"If you plan to present yourself only to siphon knowledge about the Brood's stratagems, you *will* regret it," She said grandiloquently.

It was a risk worth taking.

"I'll attend," he said, accepting the scroll.

As sultry as She was barbarous, Widow raised Herself from the boulder. Her white pupils darted around him — the controlled stillness of his honey brown face, how many times his abdomen swelled with a breath, the tension in his shoulders that he consciously relaxed. She searched for untruth, but Ares had played this game and mastered it.

Finding nothing alarming, the Brood Mother picked his cigarette from his lips and swayed into the woods.

"I'll see you soon, dear prince."

# SOMETHING

# OF A PLAN

### 6.CLAWSGUARD.26.OSC.3

### REFUGEE CAMP, THE STORM PLAINS

ARES SUMMONED the Mooncaller Council as well as Peyamo and the others. Luxea sat beside him, questioning his grimace each time he looked at her. With everyone seated, he began.

"We don't have the time for introductions. On the eleventh of Clawsguard, I'll be attending a Brood gathering at the theater in Erannor."

Spymaster Ruri finally showed fear. "What did you say?"

Whispers combusted amongst the council members. Luxea shot into Ares' line of sight and begged him to rethink his choices with a shake of her head. Promising her that he would be unharmed, he touched her sleeve under the table.

"Listen," said Ares sternly. "Widow came to me last night, here at the military camp."

"*My* camp?" Raging, Peyamo hobbled to a barrel and filled an unwashed flagon. "Gods, damn me or bless me, don't give a cat's fat crap which. I need an ale."

Ares assumed she wouldn't return for a while, for she poured herself another cup within a gulp of finishing the first. He went on.

"Since Widow's visit, I've devised something of a plan."

Keeper Vessias nervously tapped his quill on his tablet. "Your Highness, *something* of a plan?"

"I call it that because I can't know what will unfold. The chances of failure are equated with success. If I go inside without drawing too much attention, I can collect information."

"You will go alone?" asked Ruri.

"That's what Widow expects," said Ares judiciously.

The Wing Regent had always been cold, but today he was glacial. He clutched Ares' arm and asked, "What if this is a trap to recruit you to their ranks? We can't lose you, Ares — not again."

The Speaker and the Seer swallowed at the same time. "Please, don't worry about me," he whispered. "Trust that this might work."

Luxea played with the Felastil, now understanding why Ares always held it; he must have been anxious often. "If you're sure about this, I'll be stationed outside. They can't touch me."

"No," said Ares at once.

"It's dangerous, Luxie!" exclaimed Oliver.

"I think she should go," blurted Ruri. Her black eyes drilled into Luxea's, popping the stars like little bubbles. "The Widow and Her servants cannot come in contact with her, Your Highness. She has made many attempts on Siren's life, yes, and knows that she is significant to you and Oscerin. She will expect you to keep her safe from afar, not to bring Her bane so close by.

"I'll lead a troop of rangers onto which you may fall back. We'll be ghosts in the walls, shadows on the floor. If and when you must escape, we will assist you. Vishera, I'd like for you to come too."

The Spymaster had been one of Avari's biggest inspirations over the past fourteen years of living in Tzapodia, and this wasn't something she'd ever prepared herself to hear. Making a face quite like a frightened hamster or gerbil, she accepted.

"Good. Vessias, I'll need you to share with me any documents you have on the Erannor Theater at once," said Ruri sharply.

The keeper's head bounced. "Yes, Spymaster."

"I haven't agreed to any of this!" snapped Ares. "I'm riding to Erannor alone. I'll be safe. Widow doesn't want me dead."

"No, She wants you trapped," said Luxea harshly. "Might I remind you how quickly She threw you into chains on Mythos? Whatever this is, it isn't a visit. Widow could be leading you into a pitfall. This is as much of an opportunity for us to gather insight on the Brood as it is for Her to make you Her tool, Ares."

It started to make sense to Spymaster Ruri why the Prince had made such a seemingly shallow decision to initiate Luxea into the Mooncaller Council. Perhaps she wasn't the air-headed excuse for a plaything that she'd imagined.

Peyamo thumped back into her seat. "I see where Ruri and Starlight are goin' with this, Ares. I'd hide out with 'em, but I've got to get back to Tarot. With Goldenrise gone, there's no sayin' how long it'll be before the Wraiths are taken too. Ank'tatra's right under my country, and I'm feelin' shaky 'bout leavin' it alone." She laughed. "Besides, we couldn't help you in Erannor. We can be sneaky bastards, but my men've got some clunky boots."

"It's all right, Amo. Go back to Tarot," said Ares concisely.

He glared at Luxea, and she glared back. For half a minute, a noiseless battle transpired in the narrow space between them. He couldn't defeat her. Even if he told her, *'no,'* she would come after him with legerdemain and moonlight on her side. He rested his head in his palm, unhitching his breath.

"Ruri, gather your rangers and supply Luxea and Avari with new uniforms. They'll be going with you." The Spymaster's scarred lips split apart in a grin. "Be wary that Widow has eyes everywhere. We cannot travel on the same route — nor on the same day. Do not let a single footstep go heeded."

"How insulting," snarked Ruri. "I am never heeded."

The Spymaster's gusto was damaging, and Ares hoped that Luxea wouldn't look as self-assured; she didn't, she looked promising. He watched his Felastil shine around her neck.

There were two longings. The first was for the Felastil, the second was for the snowy visage of the one who wore it. The latter was a kick in his chest. He closed his eyes and gathered himself.

"You will depart in three days. May Oscerin protect us all."

On the tenth day of Clawsguard, Ruri collected seven rangers, including Luxea and Avari. They were given alternative Tzapodian uniforms for this mission. The standard colors were brown, silver, and blue, but these were completely black.

Nearby, Ares leaned against a tree with his arms crossed, hiding the nervous fiddling of his fingers. Agreeing to dispatch Luxea and Avari with Ruri's rangers was so, so idiotic. He was sending them to their deaths! But here he was, letting it happen.

"Vishera, Siren!" Spymaster Ruri rode by on a dracas, pearlescent black with floppy spines on its cheeks named Torus. "We'll set out in five minutes. Saddle up."

"Yes, ma'am," said Avari, swinging her leg over Elthevir.

Ruri shot her elfin chin at Luxea. "Siren, throw trappings on Velesari. Her scales are too light. What, you wish to be a beacon in the dark? You'll get us all killed."

Luxea nodded but wanted to punch Ruri in the head.

Before she could straddle Velesari, who was now shrouded in boiled, black leather, Ares intercepted and pulled her into the shade of the tree.

"Be mindful, not reckless. If anything seems off to you, I want you to go to Ruri and insist on returning to Tel Ashir instead of the military camp. You'll be protected there."

Luxea relaxed against the trunk, smiling at him mutinously. "We aren't abandoning you, Ares. That's out of the question."

Ares put on that oh-so-frightening, imperious facade. "It's an order, Luxea. I don't want you endangering yourself for my —"

"That's a shame because I will."

Arguing with her was just about as useful as drinking from an empty glass. Ares' scared eyes darted from her tied up hair to her pale face to the twinkling Felastil to the gloves she wore; if something happened to either of them, he would never have the chance to look at her again. But his desire to touch her was a killer greed, an addiction to poison. If only her lips wouldn't rot him. Alternatively, he took her hands in his and kissed her fingers through the fabric.

He'd said it to her before, but never like this.

*"Iu lemi thois."*

"I still don't know what that means," she said softly.

He didn't tell her. He let her go.

The rangers arrived at the Erannor Theater at the Irestar's high. Brood guards were stationed on the streets, their masks with insect motifs mounted on their many heads. The infiltrators stabled their dracas in the hollow of a decaying tree and ducked behind a strand of bushes. The Spymaster tried to scope a route, but it was too dark.

"Move in closer," she whispered. "The night is strong."

"You can't see?" wondered Luxea.

Ruri scoffed at her. "Yes, Seer. The Spymaster can't see."

"It wasn't an insult, it was a question." As Ruri grumbled irately, Luxea sighed held out her hand. *"Amal luciem, th'luneth."*

A small light appeared, in the shape of a firefly, and zoomed ahead, illuminating the area around it. The guards at the theater didn't even acknowledge it. It was merely a bug.

"Where do you want it to go?" asked Luxea, deep in focus.

The Spymaster side-eyed her. *Fine, little sorceress, you win.*

"Take it to the back door." Flitting about her illusion, Luxea brought it to the furthermost left stairwell. On the ground was a Brood guard. Ruri marked his weakest points through his armor. Trapezius would be an easy shot.

"Up," said Ruri next.

Luxea lifted her light to the rooftop. There patrolled a second man with a fly helmet on his head and a broadaxe in his hand. Ruri unhooked a black bow from her back and nocked a silver arrow.

"Keep it there. The one on top is mine. Vishera, when the lower is alerted, cut him deep."

Avari covered her mouth with her scarf. "Yes, Spymaster."

The guard on the roof paid much less attention to his surroundings than he should have. Ruri smirked. What a fool Widow was, entrusting someone so ill of the senses to protect Her territory.

Ruri's black eyes were scopes. The silver arrowhead glinted as she attained absolute stillness. Watching her was like watching a cyclone turn to glass. When the guard was directly above the ladder, she released her shot. The guard's skin was butter, her arrow a hot cleaver. With his vocal cords severed, he fell.

The second guard reacted. "Everything clear up there?"

When there was no answer, he hurried to the ladder and started to climb. Avari plucked two daggers from her thighs and slunk toward him, her head no more than a foot above the ground. He was on the fourth peg when she leaped onto his back, slicing his throat with lethal precision. He struggled more than Ruri's victim, but the kill was almost as impeccable. As he died, she dragged his body into a ditch.

Ruri rallied her rangers. "Go, go!"

Without a sound, they ascended after Avari to the theater roof. Luxea started to appreciate all of the training that Avari had forced upon her; half of her was proud to be as quiet as the rangers, the other half wanted to show the Spymaster that she wasn't a one-trick pony.

As the group headed north to the storage room, Ruri ripped her arrow from the dead guard's neck and slipped his remains in a pipe. It was a blessing that Keeper Vessias had blueprints for the city of Erannor in his stack of files that he carried all places. Because of him, navigating was a breeze.

At the door, Ruri searched the pouch on her belt for a lock pick. Sooner, Luxea touched the latch and popped it open with a single, magickal thought. She caught the lock before it hit the ground and handed it to Ruri. The Spymaster glowered at her through her greasy hair. She wouldn't say it, but she was considering inviting Luxea to her troop permanently; she was useful.

The rangers sneaked inside. Once hidden, they shut the door, and Luxea latched the lock through a crack in the wood.

# INTO THE WEB

## 11.CLAWSGUARD.25.OSCERIN.3
## ERANNOR, SELNILAR

The next afternoon, Ares rode to Erannor, dressed as he would be for any royal event: his black hair lank to his hips, his form fitted by a pewter Tzapodian suit. Pveather too was decorated. Her pierced brows were bedazzled, and her head was adorned by a silver chaplet.

The streets were unsettlingly empty. The Prince sensed he was being watched — and likely targeted. His albino dracas whistled frightfully. Ares stroked her spine and whispered to her, *"Me-thois jadione,"* — *"You're okay."*

In front of the theater were fifty stabled horses and carriages, fifty guards as well. The scintillating, red orbs embedded in their masks made Ares second guess his decision to send the Spymaster's troops.

As he trotted to a post to tie Pveather, a sickening yet familiar face emerged from the double doors of the theater. Cherish Ven'lethe, Luxea's former magick instructor — and the man who'd tried to murder her in Anathema.

When the magister wasn't dressed as a scrappy traveling merchant, he was far more intimidating. His white hair was slicked back, his lithe body was shaped by a scarlet suit with a matching cape, and a devil's mask rested upon his high cheekbones.

"Your Highness, it's lovely to see you again," he purred. "I had a feeling you'd join us eventually."

Ares could have spat in his smug face, but such an action would be a bad idea. He smiled and offered Pveather a comforting scratch under her chin. "And you, Cherish. There are more guests present than I'd imagined."

"The Brood is flourishing." Cherish's pink eyes scanned the trees and buildings around the city square. "You came alone?"

*Not exactly.*

"Yes," Ares lied. "I told the Mother that I would."

"And you kept your word. Fantastic." Cherish held up his hands and shouted, "Stand down, men!"

From the woods and the rooftops, assassins sprouted out of hiding and lowered their poison-tipped arrows. Ares was able to count thirty who'd been aiming at him before Cherish said, "We had to be certain. Pray do not take it personally."

Inside the theater, Cherish swiped a red drink and handed it to Ares. He was wary of consuming; the color was exceptionally vibrant. But everyone around him was imbibing, and he was tainted as it was.

Ares was accustomed to acknowledgment from people he'd never met, but this time, he was a lightning bug in a den of spiders. There were crowds and crowds of unrecognizable faces. Men and women of the nobility strutted around dressed in black and red formalwear, their grace made all the more haunting by their various masks. Inside dangling, steel cages were dancers and sword-eaters, nude except for veiled, black crowns.

Guards stood vigilant at every doorway, their helmets differing depending on their rank. The lowest had bulbous eyes that resembled a fly's. Above them came scorpions with two large, barbed claws. At the top were the spiders, complete with eight eyes and bladed pedipalps.

It was then that Ares realized this was a masquerade ball. On cue, Cherish handed him a mask, one commissioned by Widow that was, to his dismay, fashioned after a dragon's head. It was beautiful, however, boiled leather studded with black diamonds and lined with polished silver. With his frown held back, he sealed it over his eyes.

"The horns help," joked Cherish.

Ares tried his best to smile.

Little after twenty minutes, the Sun Chief Ralvesh un Gatra spotted the Prince of Tzapodia and neared. His chest was bare and decorated with a crimson sash, and a gold emblem of Ank'tatra swung over his rock-hard middle. On his rugged face was a feathered mask representing a phoenix.

At the Sun Chief's side were the Masters of the Isle of Varnn Vesas and Levelia Kross — Oliver's parents — both wearing bat masks.

Vesas was morbidly obese; the buttons on his dress shirt were clinging to their eyelets with all desperation. His flushed cheeks fought with the darkness of his smoky hair, which had so much product in it that it shone. He crammed legs of chicken and livers of lamb into his fanged mouth, oblivious to the world beyond his dinner plate.

His wife, Levelia, could scarcely walk with her corset strangling her ribcage and her heels forcing her feet into vertical angles. Her greying orange hair was doused in perfume, intoxicating Ares more than the wine he drank.

"Oh, you've grown up to be so charmin'!"

Levelia embraced Ares; he returned the gesture but worried her seemingly ribless waist would snap under his hand. It was odd to be held by Levelia Kross. She'd always been quiet, envying Vesas from his side, and had never interacted with Ares. It was as if she and her husband had been switched.

"How've you been? Well, I pray," she chattered.

Ares politely kissed her knuckles. "Thank you, my lady. I've been adjusting. How are you and your beloved?"

The female Master sneered and swiveled her hips away from Vesas. "I've been lovely. My husband is — well — fat."

Cherish chuckled softly. Unsure if he should agree or not, Ares simply raised his eyebrows and glanced at Vesas. The man didn't even seem to care where he was; he was too affixed on his meal.

"It's a wonder that Oliver is so lithe," said Ares lightheartedly. "I suppose he must have gotten your genes."

Levelia's smile froze and melted. "Oliver?" She made a small laugh. "That's right, he's been visitin' you in Tzapodia, hasn't he? I hope the sunlight hasn't hurt him too much." Much less lively, she glued her eyes to the floor.

Ralvesh spoke next, as tauntingly now as in battle. "Your Highness. I hadn't expected the dragon to serve the spider so easily."

"You don't sound incredibly pleased about it," remarked Ares.

The Sun Chief's whiteless, blue eyes roared. "No, I am not. Before you, *I* was Her champion. But what is a lowly rishja like myself against the Last Son of the Dragons?"

Ares leered. "Surely you have a good quality or two."

The Sun Chief curled his pierced lip. Before a brawl could erupt in the middle of the foyer, Cherish patted Ralvesh's naked chest. "Now, now. Run along, *Yaz Magia,*" he said with a paternal undertone.

It was unbelievable, but Ralvesh listened to Cherish's command. Ares hadn't realized that one magister held such a position of power in the Brood. The Sun Chief strutted away, stropping his anger on the Prince's mocking expression.

"Out of curiosity," said Ares when the brute left, "how goes the Brood's ranking system? The crowned of Ank'tatra looks to Cherish as his superior?"

"It depends what you can offer the Brood Mother," said Levelia, leafing over Ares as he sipped.

"Indeed," added Cherish. "Ralvesh is a skilled warrior, and that makes him of importance to Her. But I have pure magick inside me, and that makes me priceless." He searched for the Felastil in the opening of Ares' shirt and was pleased that it was amiss. "But *you,* there is a fire in your eyes, in your flesh and your blood, but most of all, it is in your soul. Not to mention you bear critical knowledge about the Goddess of the Moon . . . and one other."

"The woman with stars for eyes?" asked Levelia.

Ares chased his fear with a gulp of wine.

A strange smile danced across Cherish's lips. "Correct. She was my best student, you know. Pity that she's forgotten all that I taught her." Ares wondered how Cherish would react if he learned that Therasi Direl was Luxea's new teacher. "Is she doing well now that she's survived my attempts?"

Ares had to be careful of his words. "She is as she always is."

Cherish hummed and drank. "Marvelous. How silly that you went through so much for her only to end up on the other side, no?"

"Quite," laughed Ares falsely. He switched subjects. "Is there no one currently above you in the Brood's hierarchy?"

"There's one. Unfortunately, they were unable to attend this evening," said Cherish a bit derisively.

"Em, Your Highness?" Levelia grabbed Ares' arm and tugged lightly. "Wouldn't you offer a lady a dance? I do love dancin', but Vesas doesn't care for it much nowadays."

The Prince looked to Cherish for permission — although it was infuriating to do so. The magister politely stepped back and motioned for his two guests to do as they please.

Levelia, in quite a hurry, urged Ares onto the dance floor.

As the musical piece began, Levelia fell into position for the Wraithian Wisp, the dance most practiced on the Isle of Varnn. She and Ares spun gracefully over the granite tiles, in sync with those tens of couples encircling them.

"You didn't come here to show your allegiance to the Brood Mother, did you?" asked Levelia in her lowest, quietest voice.

Ares met her black eyes; they wavered. "That is as dangerous a question to ask as it is to answer."

"Then you needn't answer, but I beg you to listen." Feigning coquetry, Levelia glided ever closer, breaking the form of the dance just subtly enough to whisper in the Prince's ear; no one other than him could be allowed to see through her act. "The Widow is far more dangerous than meets the eye. She feeds off our sins — Ralvesh's wrath, Vesas' gluttony, my envy of him. Forget what She's told you 'bout cleansin' the world n' makin' it a better place. Her goal is personal."

"Then what is Her true goal, if you'd be so kind?" he asked flatly.

"To be loved, wholly n' unconditionally," she said direly. "Deny Her of love, n' She'll deny us all of somethin' far less renewable. You're not facin' a divine with a higher purpose, Ares. You're facin' a woman who would kill for genuine adoration."

Ares spun Levelia and dipped her back with supreme skill. "And you, Master. Would you too kill for love?"

"I have. So have you," said Levelia knowingly. "Widow *will* catch you in your lie, Your Highness. Make one wrong move, n' this grand game you play will be lost." She gently laid her hand on his chest where she knew the Felastil should have been. "Oscerin is still with you, thus is Her love. The starry-eyed woman . . . her love too. That's what'll spare you, in the end."

As the dance came to a close, Ares couldn't decide whether to be wary or trusting of Master Levelia Kross. But she pestered him no further about his loyalty to the Brood. Instead, she curtseyed to him and asked a delicate question.

"The starry-eyed woman . . . what is her name? The Brood Mother has never said it. I reckon She fears the sound."

The next words Ares spoke were lovely needles. "Luxea Siren."

Levelia's stare trailed to someplace empty. Her lips traced silent words, and then she laughed sadly. "Ah. *'Luxea'* means *'death.'*"

On the rooftop, the Spymaster and her rangers listened as guards patrolled past the storage room. All that separated them from the enemy was termite-eaten plywood; it protected them well until twilight came.

Two Brood officers in scorpion masks ascended the nearby stairwell, each equipped with a bardiche. The rangers weren't concerned, for they'd seen others like them and hadn't faced complications. But as they closed in, Ruri overheard their conversation.

*"Wasn't expecting to run out of wine so quick. Not even eight o'clock yet. Ploughin' drunkards. Where are the casks?"*

*"In the storage room. I've got the key."*

The Spymaster flew to the door and barred it with her shoulder. But the guards opened it too soon, and the Black Ghost of Tzapodia met faces with the Brood Mother's offspring.

Before her foes could strike, Ruri ejected a knife from her vambrace and slammed it into the eye socket of the nearest. As the life left him, she kicked his corpse into the second guard.

He staggered but quickly accepted that his ally had been killed. "Callers on the roof!" he announced. "Callers on the roof!"

Avari silenced him, popping out from behind a crate and putting him into a chokehold. His helmet *clanged* to the ground as he threw the little ranger off him. Ruri was straining to pull Avari to safety when the guard slammed the door on her leg; it hadn't broken until he crushed it four more times, dooming her to immobility.

Ruri had never felt so stupid. *This* was why she worked alone. She should have let Avari save herself! She staggered back into her group of rangers, unable to stand. The guard swung open the door again, bardiche strung back and hungering to dismember.

Luxea had one shot.

She tore off her gloves, ducked under his weapon, and clapped her bare palms around his neck. As she'd hoped, he was tainted by Widow too. His face stretched as his flesh bubbled red and black. With his windpipe exposed, he could no longer breathe or shout for backup.

Before accepting death as his new master, he punched Luxea in the gut and heaved her down the staircase to the ground floor.

"Luxea — mm!" A ranger covered Avari's mouth at once.

More guards climbed the ladder onto the rooftop, responding to the first. On her knees at the bottom step, Luxea shook her head at the rangers. Two were hiding the bodies, two more were wrangling Avari.

Following her would get them killed. If Avari refused to let her go alone, Luxea would have to make that choice for her. With a swish of her hand, she blew Avari back into the storage room. The door was shut and locked from the outside, but the rangers would be able to escape if need be. For now, they had to remain concealed.

At that moment, four Brood officers dashed across the roof to search. Luxea had to draw them away. She slid around the corner of the theater and whistled as loudly as she could.

The guards' armors *clacked* as they marched in an unorganized line away from the storage room. The rangers were safe, but now Luxea was being pursued. She backpedaled under an overhang where, by her feet, a lone basement window was cracked open. As the guards rounded the building, she dropped onto her behind and slipped through the opening.

The fall almost snapped her ankles. She clamped her lips and held her legs until her bones ceased to ache. With her hood hanging down her back, she propped herself up and absorbed her surroundings.

It was a dim corridor with dusty wooden floors, streaked with what looked like electrical burns. From the walls and scaffolds were strung ruffled costumes and broken-down props, and up ahead was a rippling, velvet curtain of washed-out crimson.

She was in the worst place she could have been — backstage.

Measuring her weight in the balls of her feet so the floorboards wouldn't creak, she crept forth and peeked through the curtain on stage right. There she saw the nobility, drinking and making merry; their brouhaha sounded cheerful as if they weren't the guests of a wicked beast. At the far end of the seating area were the shapes of Ares and Cherish, side-by-side.

Just then, a stagehand swished by the curtain and entered backstage. Luxea hooded her head and twirled into a crouch, hiding the light of the stars as he scoured the shelves above her head. He uncovered a container of inky liquid and carried it deeper into the theater. Luxea heard him open a door —

And then came a woman's horrified screams.

It hadn't been Luxea's plan to follow the stagehand, but that woman wasn't safe. She cursed her undying curiosity and sidled into the dark. At the hall's end, she peered through the only door that was slightly ajar.

Her breath went as cold as death.

The shocks on the floor made sense now, for confined in a cage of murky smoke was Sh'tarr the Goddess of Storms. Unlike how She'd appeared in Solissium, She was no taller than Luxea today. She puffed into a plume and slammed the bars so hard that they bent and whined.

The stagehand promptly dipped a brush into the jar of fluid and slathered it on the metal. The bars grew stronger, and Sh'tarr fell to Her sparking knees.

This substance was weakening Her — no — containing Her.

Luxea wouldn't leave Her there. They'd promised Alatos.

She went inside. Hanging from a ring was a heavy iron hook for lifting theater props. She unfastened it and crept up behind the stagehand.

When the Storm Goddess saw her, She ceased Her wailing. The stagehand turned, and all he saw was the hook as it cracked into his skull. He fell unconscious at Luxea's feet, and the jar he held shattered. The contents sizzled and burned holes in the floorboards.

Sh'tarr cowered as a cyclone in the farthest corner of Her cell until Luxea dropped the hook and met Her gaze. The goddess manifested as a woman against the bars, Her coiling, misty hair alighting with bright white static.

"You're that girl. The dragon's burden, the Moon Mother's tether."

"Yes, it's me," whispered Luxea. "What are You doing here?"

"What do you think?!" Luxea urged Sh'tarr to lower Her voice. "I'm a prisoner, an instrument! The Widow is draining me, breaking the storm in my soul!"

"How did She capture You? Alatos came to us and said You'd been taken," said Luxea sympathetically.

The Storm Goddess wept, Her every tear arcing on the floor of the cage. "The Widow can contain us, She can drive us to act on all evils She desires. She bends me, Starlight . . . She steers me to Her will."

"And She can do that because She's a greater divine?"

Sh'tarr laughed maniacally. "She isn't a greater — She isn't even a *divine!*" Luxea wasn't sure she'd heard Her correctly. "Her essence is divine, but Her body is mortal. The Widow is the home of the fourth greater mother, the fourth Daughter of the Lemuria. She is two beings, not one! There *is* a goddess within Her, for She is the vessel. But you have seen Her for what She truly is . . . long, long ago."

Luxea forced her brain into overdrive; there were too many pieces to fit together. Her stars turned green suddenly. "This greater divine that lives inside Widow, have You met Her before?"

The Storm Goddess recoiled to the back of the cage. "Yes, yes. I have, many times! She is darkness itself. She is a devil of wraps and bugs and blackness!"

She had to ask. "Would You describe Her as a shadow woman?"

It started to snow in the cage, fluttering around Sh'tarr as She said gutturally, "If shadow had a form, it would be Her."

One question had been answered, another ten thousand had arisen. If the Shadow was a greater divine, and that greater divine was bound to Widow, why had She tormented Luxea in her childhood? What did she have to do with either of Them, and why, almost twenty years later, were They both after her?

Before she could ask the Storm Goddess anything else, a clamor came from outside the door.

*"Find the intruder. They're here somewhere."*

*"Did you see them?"*

*"Their hair. Long and white."*

Sh'tarr crawled across the cage. "You must go! Hide!"

Luxea glanced at her palms. "I'm not leaving You here."

She couldn't be sure it would work but would never forgive herself if she didn't try. She clutched the shadowy bars and waited. The darkness then crackled, and Luxea thanked Oscerin for the gift She'd given her. The liquid shadow melted to the floor in pools of starlight. In the shapes of her handprints, the steel bars underneath were untainted. Sh'tarr's faith in mortals was reinforced as Luxea wiped away this evil substance effortlessly.

Then it was gone. Clean.

The Storm Goddess verged on the barrier and touched the bars, jolting from excitement, not pain. She cracked into nothingness and reappeared at Luxea's side in a shockwave. Her closeness alone made Luxea's fine hairs float above her skin.

They stared at each other, eyes of sparks and eyes of stars, the Storm Goddess looking as if She'd met a new best friend. Bursting with joyous cackles and squeals, She threw Her arms around Luxea's neck and enveloped her in a swell of lightning.

"I will not forget this," she whispered into Luxea's ear.

Sh'tarr swirled into a disc of clouds against the ceiling and zipped into an air vent — unleashed.

# Last Song

## 11.CLAWSGUARD.26.OSC.3
### Erannor, Selnilar

Cherish led Ares into a meeting room with very few people inside, all of whom he knew; every member of The Six except for Peyamo Nelnah was present. At the far left was *Luciem Salah,* the Light Seeker of Selnilar Val'noren Paah. Sitting beside him was Tree Warden Tani Renayo of Drenut, who hadn't been a member of The Six. In the rightmost seat beside Ralvesh was Annalais. A collar of red fox fur was draped over her shoulders, hiding the burns she'd received from Luxea's hands.

To the left of the southernmost doorway stood a guard in a fly helmet with a dangerously muscular body. Even through his matte black armor, Ares felt like he recognized this person. The fly knew him too. They revealed their face, and Ares' claws lusted for blood.

Beneath the mask was Doryan Skythoan, the War General of Tzapodia that Ares had beaten and fired earlier that year. The ex-general couldn't have been more entertained by the sight of the Prince.

"Your Highness. What a surprise," he taunted.

Ares felt like tearing off Skythoan's face but pretended to be happy to see it. "And you, Skythoan. I'll not burden you with my story, but how did you end up here?"

"The Brood Mother invited me," said Skythoan complacently. "After you stripped me of my title, She heard of my misfortunes. She came to me and said that, if I shared Tzapodia's secrets, She would take me in as one of Her children. It was a brilliant choice on Her part, don't you agree? Reeling in one of the most knowledgeable members of your council for leeching. And now the Prince himself is here. I'd say the Brood mother owes me."

Cherish stepped in. "Do not expect praise from Her or us." Skythoan moused away. "Might I remind you, Doryan, that I am a magister, Ares is a dragon, and you — you are a fly."

Before the meeting began, Ares took the chair next to Cherish; the only other open placement was to Annalais's left.

The chandelier far above the table jingled. They hadn't seen Her, but Widow had been observing them from the ceiling all along. She zipped down from a wiry web that had ejected from a spinneret on Her spine and landed between Ares and Cherish. The Prince averted his eyes as She passionately kissed the magister; he'd been unaware that they were in that sort of relationship and frankly wondered how Cherish hadn't lost his mind.

Wiping Her mouth, the Brood Mother faced Ares next. He swallowed before kissing the back of Her fingers. "You really came. How lovely. Normally, I would introduce our new member, but you're all acquainted. Shall we begin?" A wave of nods circled the table. "Excellent. Let us celebrate our recent victory in Solissium — oh, Ares was our enemy at the time. Be that as it may, you're here now."

The Prince smiled, but all he could see were frozen faces.

"The Storm Goddess' presence that day drew forth my second target — Alatos. Using Sh'tarr as bait, I shall ensnare the Sea Goddess and bind Her to my will," said Widow pragmatically. "Ares, Your Highness, do you think I can do it?"

Every pair of eyes, black, red, blue, pink, and orange flitted to him. He needed wine. He drank the rest of his cup and cleared his throat. "Absolutely. The Sea Goddess is frightened of You but will do what She must to save Her sister. Luring Her out with Sh'tarr would allow You a fantastic window of opportunity."

Widow was delighted with his answer. "Thank you for your insight. I agree." She petted his hair. Such an affectionate touch made him want to puke. "My plans for Sh'tarr and Alatos are simple. Together, they will reign over air and sea with my collar at Their throats. Alatos will send Her waves to the shore, and Sh'tarr will tear down all that remains. First on our list: Tarot."

A chill ran up Ares' back, and his shoulders tightened. Widow leaned closer. "I realize that your dear friend Peyamo is the watcher of Tarot, but she is the last we need to make the *new* Six complete. I'll invite her, of course, she will be granted the chance to spare her country . . . but should she resist me, it will be lost to the sea. She'll have not a moment's notice to get *Thali ou Tirima* off the ground with the Storm Goddess as her foe."

Widow waved to Doryan Skythoan. "Go! Bring me Sh'tarr!"

Skythoan smirked at Ares and left.

"While we await the storm, we shall discuss another matter of dire import," said Widow giddily. "We've addressed it many times ere now, but it has resurfaced — *again*. Can you guess what it is?"

"The starry-eyed woman," spat Annalais.

Ares' heart rose up into his mouth. Levelia wrung her hands.

"That's right, Treasure." Widow sneered as She said this, knowing that *'Treasure'* was once what Ares had called Annalais. "As luck would have it, she trusts someone on our side. She trusts him *so* much that she doesn't care if he's with the enemy." She blinked those black beetle eyes at the Prince. "My, my . . . everything revolves around you today, doesn't it, Your Highness? I've thought about killing her myself, fantasized about it — even acted on it a time or two, as I'm sure you recall. But I have a different plan now."

Her finger traced the curve of Ares' right horn. *"You* will kill her."

The vision Ares had been given after the Golden Spire annihilated the last of his composure. On the polished tabletop appeared the image of Luxea with her pale skin flayed, her lips blue and dry, the stars gone from her eyes — all because of him.

He ignored Annalais's sighs of delight and asked, "Why me?"

"Because if I do it, she will die, and her soul will rise to Eletheon as every soul does." Widow sneered deviously. "But if *you* do it, her spirit will be so deeply marred by your betrayal that it will haunt her for all time."

He couldn't take it. He snapped. "Why do You hate Luxea?!"

Widow pounded the table and screamed, "Why don't you?!" A mad grin stretched over Her face. "Use caution, Your Highness. If you don't kill her by your own will, I'll *make* you."

Giving him an example of Her power over Her children, Widow said to Vesas Kross, "Master, throw a turkey leg at the Sun Chief."

The fat man's eyes glazed over black. From his platter, he picked up a turkey leg and chucked it across the table. It smacked into Ralvesh's bicep and splattered gravy on Annalais's pretty gown.

Levelia passed a look to Ares, saying, *'I warned you.'*

"Val'noren, dear," said Widow next, "why don't you kill that guard with your bare hands?"

Those beautiful pink irises of the Light Seeker's went black too. He walked robotically to the guard by the back door and clasped his throat, making his frightened eyes bloodshot. Once the life had left his victim, Val'noren went back to his seat, and his stare returned to pink.

Widow smiled cheekily. "You've consumed my ichor, and there is no stopping what I can do through you. So, my prince, you may kill the stars and experience the rush or kill the stars and wake up with her dead in your arms. Which do you prefer?"

The world spun too fast for Ares to think. Ere an answer of any kind could leave his lips, the back door swung open. Doryan Skythoan tripped over the dead guard and tumbled inside, his skin colorless.

"Brood Mother, the Storm Goddess is gone!"

"What?!" shrieked Widow.

Between breaths, Skythoan said, "Her cell is empty, Mother, and Her jailer doesn't remember a thing! He was assaulted!"

Someone had to be punished. Widow bounded across the room on Her eight legs and hovered over Skythoan. Her cheeks split and unveiled a chasmic mouth, and then She bit down on his head. Ares held his palm over his mouth; he hated that man, but this wasn't merited.

Skythoan squirmed as Widow locked him in place. His feet then dangled, and She dropped him. The flesh and the muscle on his face was gone, and the eyeballs in his bare sockets swung from his optic nerves.

The Brood Mother darted back to the table, straight to Ares, and ripped off his mask and threw it. The slashes in Her face fused — and She looked furious.

"You've served the divines all your life. How funny that this would happen on the day that you join us." Her fingers snaked up his shoulder to pinch his scales. "I slowed the spread of your affliction, but do you know what else I can do, dragon boy? *Make it faster!*"

His curse was at her mercy. Tens of new scales erupted from his skin, slithering up his neck and making crackling sounds in his ear. He tore away from her and fell out of his chair, bracing himself for the ground with one arm.

"I didn't touch Sh'tarr! I've been with Cherish since I arrived!"

Widow's eight white pupils flickered to the magister, the one man She seemed to trust wholly. Cherish stared down at Ares as his bandaged hand shook against his scales. What the Prince had claimed was correct, he'd been in Cherish's sight all along. Vouching for him, he nodded.

Widow fell back against the table, sweating grey droplets. "If it wasn't you, we must have a *rat* running around." She smiled at Ares balefully. "What a delightful surprise this is."

The Brood meeting was adjourned after the news of Sh'tarr's escape. About to be sick, Ares stepped over Skythoan's body and careened backstage — but he ran directly into someone.

A figure in hooded, black armor held up their hands, and their gloved fingers sparked with blue light. Ares couldn't see their face but had not one doubt about who it was.

As if he hadn't been afraid enough.

He pulled Luxea by the arm into a niche by a rack of theatrical costumes and lowered her mask. After what Widow had said, he wondered if he should be near her at all, but he just had to see her face.

"I told you not to come inside!" he said, grasping the sides of her head. "You *cannot* be here. If they see you, they'll kill you!"

"I didn't mean to," said Luxea breathlessly. "Ruri's troop was discovered. I hid them away, but the theater was the only place I could go." She noticed more electrical streaks on the stage floor. "That's not all. I found Sh'tarr!"

Ares clamped his eyes shut painfully tight. "It was you. You released Sh'tarr from Her cell."

"She didn't belong there, She's a goddess!" reminded Luxea. "But, Ares, I spoke to Her. She told me that Widow isn't a divine."

"What?" murmured Ares. "She isn't?"

"No. Widow is two people — She and the Shadow are the *same* entity. The Shadow is a greater divine, but whoever Widow really is, She's only a mortal tether like Oscerin to me. The girl who spoke to the Shadow in that dream was Widow, not me. *The Shadow* is the one with whom Widow linked the same night the Moon came to you.

"Ares, when I was with Oscerin in my death, She told me that you're the Parallel, and I'm the Divide. That has to be what She was trying to tell me. You're Widow's match —"

"— and you're what guards me against Her," finished Ares.

Footsteps.

Two Brood guards, one in a fly mask, the other in a spider's, strode around the corner. Ares barred Luxea against the wall, stole a strip of red fabric from a costume rack, and wound it twice around her head.

The spider called out, "What are you two doing back here?"

Ares whispered to Luxea, "Don't talk." Over his shoulder, he said lasciviously, "What does it look like? I'm enjoying my evening."

The fly snickered. "Ah. Forgive us, Your Highness."

"Yes, but . . ." The spider squinted. "Who is that?"

"I'm her partner," said Ares snappishly. "Now, if you don't mind."

The fly went on with his patrol, but the spider stayed behind. "I was sure you arrived alone, Your Highness," he said dubiously.

Luxea heard Ares curse. "I did. I met her here. She was alone, so I requested to escort her."

"Did you? What's her name?"

"I don't have a care about her name. I'll never see her again, after tonight," said Ares irascibly.

The guard squared his back, *clacking* the foot of his spear on the stage floor as he closed in. Luxea felt Ares' talons flexing against her waist in readiness to kill if he had to.

"What's your name?" the spider asked her.

A quick brainstorm sent Luxea sailing. She did the first thing that came to mind and made tens of meaningless signs with her fingers. The spider was befuddled, but Ares caught on quick.

"Ah, I'd forgotten to mention — she's mute." He pinched Luxea's chin through her veil. "That's the best kind of woman, isn't it? Their mouths were made for so much more than chatter, after all."

Luxea ground her teeth. Had Ares' chauvinistic act not been necessary, she would have given him *plenty* of chatter later.

The Brood guard glanced between them, and then he playfully punched the Prince's shoulder. "I'll drink to that, Your Highness," he chuckled. "I'll leave you be, but keep it down, don't make a mess, and get to your seats before the show starts. It'll be any minute."

"I'd never miss it," said Ares tightly.

They stayed stock-still as the spider turned the corner, out of sight.

Ares hung his head. "I'm sorry, I didn't mean that. We have to get you out of here. You're in more danger than before we arrived. If you stay, Widow will —"

The lights flickered out, plunging them into darkness.

From center stage, the announcer yelled, "Please, take your seats! The production is about to begin!"

The curtains ruffled, and pattering feet sounded from backstage. As the performers gathered, Ares adjusted the cloth on Luxea's head and stole away with her to the stairwell. He led her past crowds to his reserved loge.

"Stay with me, but I want you to leave during the last song."

"What about you?"

"I'll find my way out."

They dipped into his loge. He pulled a chair for Luxea and claimed the spot next to her. It was impossible for them to breathe in this dark, threatening place; each time one person tried to take an inhale, the other stole it. Across the theater, Ares spotted Widow and Cherish in a box of their own. With luck, the two wouldn't notice that Ares wasn't alone anymore.

The stage curtain swelled open startlingly fast. Organs rattled the walls and portals, making the jewels that hung from them shriek. The first scene began with two bands of acrobats, dressed in blue and swinging from cords. They swayed, representing drops of heavy rain on a frosttear night.

Astonishingly, the performance was sublime. It was an opera featuring a man and a woman who saw each other in secret. She was trapped in a dungeon until he saved her from her captors. When they escaped together, the woman admitted that she was, in fact, a lost princess who'd been secluded all her life.

Time flew by, and soon it was the final act. The stage darkened as the stagehands switched out the props. Ares leaned closer and whispered into Luxea's ear, "Take the stairs to the corridor by the foyer. When you can, cast a shroud and slip out."

"I will." She touched his hand with her glove. "Ares, be careful."

The theater lit up, and the curtains opened again. The backdrop was painted with moonlight and the ocean. In center stage was a woman on a chair with a white sheet tied around her every limb.

Luxea had crept two steps before the male vocalist sang.

*"Xe d-tanou zami ye zael lu zasteaunemme . . ."*

This scene didn't at all fit with the story about the princess and her savior. But there was something else . . . those lyrics . . .

Ares grabbed Luxea's wrist and pulled her back down.

"What are you doing?" she hissed. "What's wrong?"

"This song is in draconic," he said, listening carefully.

The opera went on.

*"Ona ye yumateme il'Clawsguard,*
*Iu-me tu jetienne'ash e Brood remeni'ash*
*vu ye teatre ue Erannor.*
*Tuoix temen thois pavise?*
*Levinne. Widow halier de isu llol neleau,*
*vola ue ye kamian unoie.*
*Nach unoie?*

*Fatuer Widow 'ze sumyet,*
*Iu-za catolier 'za odentoux il e jashile.*
*M-thois Centounali, dentoux il e jashile?"*

The performer circled the woman in the chair and belted words that no one in the theater except for Ares could comprehend. As he translated in his head, his grip constricted around Luxea's fingers, and his burns tore under his bandages.

*"Iu thue sai tielle tumeilla Iu d-peillon naque tuoix mevu pastiel.*
*Ye chetieu 'ze il rajumne mellou aizu 'ze lea asoreceon.*
*Rui Iu kas uejemoix dalusious hesu 'ash dea shonje jacallsious,*
*Iu peillon gainnon estrenemois."*

"Luxea, we have to leave right now."
"Why?"
Ares tried to lift her from the chair. "This isn't a song. This is the conversation we had with the council before we came here. Widow knew all along that you would be here — this was planned!"

*"Thois mevu kas andoille?*
*Men-teille tuoix Widow nalinoue 'ze.*
*Tuoix rui seille menna e raijon de*
*jidaem thois de xelou pashieu 'ze?*
*Veillon, d-tanou fussant onamin isu.*
*Llaisu teille seille mesu pienon.*
*Rui me-thois noune onamin seille, Iu-me tu xulyet 'za oejemoix.*
*Xeli d-peillon lieufres isu* — they can't touch me!"

The performer slit the ropes around the woman's body. The white sheet fell away from her face and rumpled on the floor. Everyone in the theater screamed, including Luxea. Guests tried to flock out of the theater, but the guards held them back.

Seated in the chair on the stage was the Black Ghost of Tzapodia.

Ruri's face was mangled. The only indicator of her identity was the bloodied Spymaster's Badge on her uniform. Her shredded curtain of brown hair swung as her head swiveled back and dangled from the ribbons of flesh on her neck. It cracked onto the stage floor, severed.

"Get up!" shouted Ares, wresting Luxea from her chair.

She kicked away from him. "What about Ruri?"

"Ruri is gone, Luxea. *Get up!*"

With Widow's laughter ringing in his ears, Ares dragged Luxea out of the loge into the hall. Her legs wouldn't work, and his were failing too, but running was all they could do.

Halfway down the steps, Luxea's veil blew off, revealing her face.

At every turn, members of the Brood waited to stop them. A guard intercepted them and tacked Ares to the wall. He couldn't move, so Luxea removed her gloves and stuck them under the guard's helmet. His screams were muffled as his face melted to slop. Although Ares couldn't touch her either, he admired her new battle tactics.

In the main corridor, two more assailants wrestled Ares to the floor with shackles, ready to detain him as he'd been on Mythos. He was Widow's now; they couldn't let him escape. The Prince swiped at the first and sliced his arm into strips. The shackles dropped. Ares wrapped the chain around his hand and swatted the second, winding it around his neck. He tugged the guard closer and kicked him back with the full force of his long legs, sending him rolling into a blathering group of stray audience members.

In the interim, a third guard of unknown rank sneaked up on Luxea. He trapped her arms at her sides and lifted her up with the intent of carrying her directly to the Brood Mother.

Luckily, he wasn't wearing a helmet. A foolhardy choice.

Luxea shunted him to the wall and pressed their cheeks together. His skin blistered. He howled and wailed as he tipped onto the floor.

A sliver of a chance opened before them. Ares yanked Luxea to the foyer while the guards recovered — or melted. At the front of the theater, he shouldered the door, but it was locked tight. She shoved past him and seized the handles to unlock it with magick, but all attempts failed.

"Why isn't this opening?!" she panted.

It was then that they noticed a smug Cherish leaning against the wall, blocking all of her spells. *"Hilien leloh, Luxea'mithan."*

All Luxea could do was wait for her former teacher to strike. He was a spell-eater, one of the last few, making it impossible for her arcana to affect him. However, if he attacked her first, she could deflect his spells back at him.

But Cherish wasn't a fool. He simply stood there, countering Luxea's magick, as the Brood guards marched to the foyer to apprehend Ares and her.

They were running out of time. Ares didn't have a weapon, but he did have a few other things. He ran at Cherish and swung his talons. Cherish calmly erected a barrier and blocked the attack.

But Ares wasn't a fool either; he'd expected the maneuver. While the magister was sidetracked, he head-butted him, slashing his brow with his horns. Cherish reeled backward and sank to the floor.

The counterspell diminished. At last, Luxea unlocked the front door, and she and Ares bolted outside where she relocked it at once. But when they turned around, they were met with the singing blades of one hundred Brood guards. The theater door smashed outward, and more soldiers swarmed out.

Cherish's face appeared betwixt the rocky shoulders of two officers. Blood trickled down his wispy, white eyebrow and into his eye, staining one pink iris dark, furious red.

"Unwise, Your Highness," he hissed.

The magister bid the Brood guards to advance. Ares and Luxea were caught in a tight circle of spears and swords with not an inch's worth of a gap through which to escape. They'd run out of ideas. Spymaster Ruri was dead, and the other rangers were likely dead too or hidden in the forest. No one could help them now.

There seemed to be no hope — but then the wind picked up.

Luxea watched Cherish's visage twist in slow motion. Choking on his spells, he staggered back and held up his hand. A silvery barrier flared out of his palm and enveloped the theater as he retreated into the foyer, stiff from fear, and abandoned his men.

The Brood guards were as puzzled as their prisoners. One of the world's greatest living magisters ran as if he'd been made a target by death itself. His surrender seemed disobliging until a spear of purple lightning smashed the magick shield and obliterated the foyer.

Unhinged laughter slashed the moonless sky. Cyclones like towers darted down from the churning clouds above with such elemental strength that the flagstone streets shattered. Electricity arced, and by the tens, the Brood guards were sucked up into spouts of wind.

Taking up the width of Erannor's skyline was Sh'tarr. The Storm Goddess' mouth sparked as She played with Her victims. But that wasn't why She'd returned. Her savior was there, and She owed to her all the lives She might have lost without her help.

"Run, Starlight! Run fast!"

Although Ares was stricken still by the Storm Goddess, he hoisted Luxea onto Pveather's saddle and climbed on behind her. His talons slit the stable ropes. Screeching, the white dracas bounded through the laces of Sh'tarr's deathtrap and out of Erannor.

Now it was time for the storm to unleash. She hammered the theater with gust after gust, froze the exits, and shocked whoever dared face Her until they were crumbling, soulless husks.

They'd hurt Her for moons, tortured Her, humiliated Her!

On this night, She would make them *all* pay.

CHAPTER THIRTY~ONE

# IMMEASURABLE CRUELTY

## NAV AMANI FOREST, SELNILAR

PVEATHER HADN'T had food or water in hours, and her legs were giving way. Her coordination was thrown off, and the aches in her clawed feet made her growl.

Ares pulled her reins. *"Dosu, lalene."*

The white dracas slowed and folded her legs beneath her, worn to the bone. Ares climbed off and unhooked a beaded canteen from the saddle; it was almost empty because he and Luxea had needed it, but Pveather couldn't go on without hydration. He spilled the last dregs into his palm and fed it to her.

"She needs to rest tonight. We'll continue riding to Tel Ashir in the morning," he said as she lapped up the water.

Luxea stroked Pveather's cheeks. When she was finished with her drink, she laid her head and gurgled. Ares wandered into the shaded woods as Pveather fell asleep to Luxea's touch.

He lowered himself into a tangle of giant tree roots, and his burned hand curled around some missing thing on his chest. Luxea knew what

341

it was. She wished to give him the Felastil, to reverse everything and go back to Mythos and stay there. But it was impossible.

She sat on a gnarl above Ares. Through the nothingness of sound, the last song of the Brood performance rumbled in their heads.

"I should have gone alone," he murmured.

"Alone, you might've been stuck there," she said downheartedly. "If Sh'tarr hadn't helped us . . . I don't want to think about how the night could have ended."

Ares let his hair fall around his face as he held his head. "Yet the Spymaster is gone. Do you understand? Ruri was impossible to kill, but Widow did precisely that. She had her made into the centerpiece for her performance in mere hours. It easily could have been you, and She'd have done much worse.

"Ruri was important to the kingdom and to me. She's spared my life so many times all because I spared hers once. She had sharp edges, but she was the most loyal person I knew. She had no one but the council and me; she never wanted anything else. It was idiotic of me to have involved her — and you. The others, Avari too, there's no saying what fates they met tonight."

Luxea had been praying for the safety of the rangers since the moment she'd locked them in the storage room. There was no questioning that doing so didn't protect them as she'd intended, but in her heart, she held what felt to her like hope on a hopeless eve.

"Widow would have had more than Ruri on the stage if that were the case," she said breathily. "She's aware that Avari was with me in Lor'thanin, that she fought Garamat's men at the gala and interacted with Cherish. If she and the rest had been apprehended, they would have been humiliated in the same way. They're okay."

That didn't change that Ruri had been brutally murdered. The Spymaster had been less than fond of Luxea, but there was some secret friendship they had beneath the feisty quips and flashy tricks they showed off to one another. When Luxea had helped her with magick, she almost seemed pleased with her. *Almost.* That was the closest they ever were before Widow bit through the thread that could have linked them.

But Ares had respected her, and he was hurting.

Gentle, Luxea touched his hair. He flinched, frightened that it would burn him, and then relaxed. He pressed the heels of his wrists to his eyes to quell an ongoing headache.

He hadn't told her, he hadn't wanted to face it, but the war in his head had more than two sides. What Widow had said, that She wished for him to kill Luxea in Her place, it tormented him. He tipped away from her, leaving her fingers hovering.

"Keep your distance from me after tonight."

"No," she said without a thought.

"Widow wants me to kill you for Her."

She wasn't as startled as he wanted her to be.

"That's fantastic since you won't go through with it," she said facetiously. "Does that mean She's done trying to off me Herself?"

Ares had let it go when she'd failed to heed his warnings before, but now the threat was real. He couldn't allow it to happen again.

"Do not trivialize this, Luxea! If I don't kill you on my own accord, She'll make me do it. Whatever Widow's servants and I ingested allows Her to control us. A piece of Her is inside us — inside me. I'm Her possession. I shouldn't be alone with you right now; She could harm you through me at any given time."

Luxea swung her feet, kicking away her unease. "You don't think you'd be able to stop it if She tried?"

"I fear it would be like that night with Anna. One moment, I was arguing with her, the next, I —" Ares unwrapped and rewrapped his bandages. "If that happens again . . . no. I won't be able to stop it."

The two didn't speak for the rest of the night. Ares stayed far from her until they were forced to share a saddle in the morning. After Pveather got the rest she'd needed, she rode fast and arrived in Tel Ashir by mid-afternoon.

Thankfully, the rangers had indeed survived the encounter in Erannor, including Avari. But she was so broken up about losing the Spymaster that she could scarcely pay mind to how distant Ares and Luxea were from each other. Instead of confronting the tension, she explained how Ruri had been caught.

With her leg snapped, the rangers had found a gap in the patrols and carried her down from the rooftop to safety. They'd meant to mend her with herbs from the woods, but at the tree line, a group of Brood soldiers had caught their trail. Ruri had ordered them to drop her and leave her to her own devices. That had been how she'd outrun death so many times before — alone.

It hadn't worked. Thus ended the Black Ghost of Tzapodia.

Four days after the Storm Goddess had demolished half of Erannor, Widow and the Brood migrated to the capital of Selnilar, Lor'thanin, to recover. She and Her seven highest-ranked members had been safe in the cellar of the theater, but the Brood's military had taken a blow.

She gathered them for a conference on the fifth dawn, fury driving Her. "I've had enough of this child's play. Every path we take is a dead end! If Ares refuses to destroy the stars within a fortnight, I'll take the initiative."

"He won't do it," Annalais dared to tell Her. "Ares would sooner deny himself freedom than bring her harm."

Widow rapped Her knifelike fingernails on Her chin, yearning to end this game and win. "In that case, I will make him slay her in such a way that he will *never* challenge me again."

Ralvesh groaned. "Have Ares slit the bitch's throat and be done with it! I grow tired of speaking about this starry-eyed woman."

"The Brood Mother wants her death to be personal, Sun Chief, not simple," pointed out Val'noren.

Vesas was still eating, this time a plate of goose wings and sautéed leeks, so Widow waited for Levelia's suggestion instead. The Master fumbled with the black ribbon in her hair and whispered guiltily, "I s'pose he could drown her."

Widow and Cherish passed looks. "That isn't enough," he said gravely. "We have already attempted to drown Luxea Siren. We dumped her in Tal Am T'Navin River, sure it was the end, but she was discovered in Lor'thanin with her mentor a year later. Her body must be destroyed lest Oscerin returns her to our plane once more."

As the Brood's council pitched concepts on how to slaughter Luxea Siren, Annalais sipped wine. She wished she could have killed Luxea that day in the villa. If only that stupid spellbook hadn't woken her!

The Empress, dreadfully bored, dipped her finger in her drink and admired the color. Liquid was sketched into her print in purple, a royal shade.

*That's it.*

She burst into a fit of giggles. Widow seemed irritated by that giddy din. "Do you have something in mind, Your Splendor?"

"I do," sighed Annalais, "but only if you're feeling *very* cruel."

Widow laced Her fingers under Her sharp jaw. "Very cruel? Not entirely. I'm feeling *immeasurably* cruel."

Annalais twirled her ruby engagement ring around her finger twice. On the third spin, she said, "Make Ares kill Luxea the same way that King Naiv killed Queen Manalaei."

The ribbon dropped from Levelia's grasp. A long time ago, before Widow, she'd been friends with Manalaei Lorcé-Lavrenthea, the late Queen of Tzapodia. She'd mourned her death but hadn't been aware that she'd been murdered.

"Your Splendor, wasn't Manalaei's death accidental?"

"No, Levelia, she was slain by the King. Ares never revealed the facts to the public, but he told *me* what really happened," said Annalais pompously. "Widow, becoming his father is Ares' direst fear. If he ends the stars similarly, he'll give up. There will be no fight left."

Immensely interested, the Brood Mother left Her chair and sat on the table in front of Annalais. She twirled her strawberry blonde hair around Her hand, pampering her.

"Will you tell me how the King ended the Queen, Treasure?"

With a delicate yet vicious smile, Annalais began.

"When Ares was sixteen, Manalaei announced the upcoming of her second child. He couldn't wait to be a brother. The Ashi priestesses swore it would be female, so Manalaei had Ares name her. He chose '*Llaisa,*' which means '*truth*' in draconic.

"He'd just turned seventeen when Manalaei entered her third term. But Naiv's deterioration was moving swiftly. In his last days of sanity, he became desperate. He had to consume the heart of a pureblooded dragon to reverse his affliction. There were three options: Manalaei, Llaisa, and Ares. He chose Ares."

## 4.SOFTSTEP.14.OSC.3
### CASTLE LAVRENTHEA, TZAPODIA

*The Prince was in the middle of his lessons with a l'arian professor when a courier came. His presence had been requested in the King's Court, a place he was rarely allowed. Once he'd rescheduled the meeting with his teacher, he rushed to give his audience to the King wearing an unwilling scowl. He nodded to the sentinels as they pushed open the carved silver door, their gauntlets jingling the garnet beads on the dragon claw handles.*

*The King of Tzapodia was reclined on his throne, his long legs stretched over the dais. He didn't smile when Ares entered; he never did. He picked at the crimson scales on his face, ones bloody and infected.*

*As was required of Ares, he bowed. His hair swooped down, but his eyes remained planted in the King's. "Your Majesty."*

*In his fiery, sonorous voice, Naiv said to his son, "Ares, tell me something. What can a kingdom not afford to lose?"*

*The King hadn't called Ares by his first name in a decade or more, addressing him instead as 'you' or 'boy.' Hearing it now almost gave Ares a feeling of elation. He'd always wanted his name to fall from his father's mouth, but today, it was strange. Something was wrong.*

*Wary of the King's behavior, he said, "The people, Your Majesty."*

*Laughing and laughing, Naiv rose from his throne. "Wrong. What a kingdom cannot afford to lose is its king."*

*Naiv removed the Tzapodian crown and held it out, picturing it fitted to the Prince's head. No. This could never belong to him. It was his, and no one else's! As he stared, Ares staring back, his yellow eyes shifted to violet. Unable to bear it any longer, he adorned it again.*

*Pacing, black hair swinging, he said, "If I wait to cleanse this curse, Tzapodia will lose its king. Tzapodia cannot survive without the King — without me."*

*"Is that not why you have an heir?" asked Ares snidely.*

*"An heir?" hissed Naiv. "You are a replacement!"*

*The King strode across the court, his cape wiping from the floor the little dust it had collected. His irises erratically flickered between yellow and violet, and his lips twitched upward and downward with each conflicting thought he had; his body was indecisive.*

*"You're as tall as me now," said Naiv almost dotingly. His foremost talon marked Ares. "And your eyes . . . they're like your mother's were once. Just as green."*

*"They've been green since my birth. How nice of you to finally notice — when hers are gone," said Ares grudgingly.*

*"You have her sarcasm too," chortled Naiv.*

*Then the King did something he'd never done before — he hugged Ares. The Prince's hands clenched at his sides as Naiv touched his neck, discreetly feeling his pulse. Ares' heart was strong and healthy.*

*He wanted it.*

*"A kingdom cannot afford to lose its king," he repeated in a whisper. His talons scraped along Ares' collar toward his throat. "But a prince? A prince it can do without."*

*Naiv wrested Ares' neck. Ares shoved him away and fell to the ground. Naiv slashed at him with his crimson claw, but Ares sooner*

*swung his leg and flipped him onto his back. But the King wouldn't
give up until the floor was stained with lifeblood.*

Had the door to the court not slammed open at that moment, Ares
would have lost his heart. The Wing Regent burst into the clearing
with Queen Manalaei on his arm, four sentinels following them. The
King spun onto his feet, and his crusted scales stretched to his brow.

"Leave us!" he raged, voice wobbling between man and dragon.

The Wing Regent was avowed to the King and had been loyal for
decades, but not this day. Isaak brandished his broadsword and aimed
the point at Naiv. Watching that crimson beast's slightest moves, he
hoisted Ares off the floor by the coat and stepped in front of him.

"What do you think you're doing?" growled Naiv.

"My position entails the protection of the Lavrenthea family. That
includes your son," said Isaak stoically.

The King chuckled, but it was false. He looked submissive, the
moment could have ended there, but the Queen refused to let him go.
She'd surrendered enough to him! She'd once sworn that if he touched
Ares again, she would kill him.

Her mind had never changed.

She shook the sentinels off her arms and blindly stepped forward,
her husband's hateful wheezing guiding her. She slowed before him
and sank her forefinger into Naiv's middle.

"You have touched my son for the last time. His heart is his own. I
will sooner rip yours from your chest and grind it under my foot than
permit you to lay hands on him!"

"I won't be taken by this curse, Mana!" yelled Naiv. "I refuse to!"

The Queen didn't care what he refused or accepted; it was no
longer his verdict. With his clothes in her fist, she used dragon blood

for the first time; she wasn't afraid of what it would do to her. Scales of shimmering gold layered down her fingers, and from their tips grew bloodletting talons.

With her opposite hand, she unraveled the purple veil from her head. It twirled to the floor. Only when he saw her scars, the scars he'd given her, did Naiv lower his guard.

Manalaei raised her pristine talons to his neck. Ares tried to push past, but Isaak held him back. The King grabbed her wrist, and the feel of his claw stole all civility the Queen had left. If he would be a monster, so would she, for this was the dance of dragons, the courting of death.

Quicker than he could defend, she raked her talons from his brow to his chin. He seized her arm, but she slashed his hand too. He backed away from her fearfully. Holding her belly, she pursued him.

"I need no eyes to see that you will always be cursed!" Her talons uprooted several scales from his cheek. "Beware a mother's love, Your Majesty — THAT will be your undoing!"

If the King didn't run, he would die; he may have had an unsound mind, but that much was clear. Weaving through her thrashing arms, he threw her down. Manalaei fell, her hand guarding her unborn child. She sat up, ready to finish him, but Naiv had fled through an escape route in the wall.

Ares was afraid to approach his mother. What if she mistook him for the King? But Manalaei knew the fight was over. She could no longer feel the hatred that surrounded Naiv. It was gone. It was done.

"Nach lathene," she whispered.

The Wing Regent let Ares go this time. The Prince whisked the Queen's purple veil off the bloodied floor and knelt beside her. He took her claw in his hand and used the front of his shirt to clean her. Then she looked up at him, and it felt as if his heart had been taken after all.

For the first time since his childhood, Ares saw his mother's mutilated eyes. Above her dark, freckled cheeks, her sockets and the scores of his father's punishment were coated in golden scales.

When one dragon harms another by claw, it hardens into scales and forces their affliction to start. While Ares had thought her pure all this time, she'd been as cursed as the King. She'd never wanted her son to see it, but he was old enough now.

The Queen felt what was swimming in his head. Her son was afraid, not of her, not of the King, but of himself. He'd seen now what lay in his nature, that of the dragons'. She cupped his face in her hands, steadying his trembling jaw.

"Listen to me now," she said, her voice in a rasp. "Only the son of the Devil bears the key out of Hell. Whatever he tells you, however much he scorns you, you will be the one to lead our people to deliverance. I've known since the moment I became your mother that your life would mark the end of our pain. I birthed you with a curse, but you are strong enough to defeat it. Your father is not. I want you to remember that you are not him. His blood courses through you, but you will never, ever be him. Promise me you will not forget this."

He couldn't promise. Manalaei shook him aggressively.

"Promise me, Ares!"

"I promise," he forced himself to say.

His mother tipped against him and clung to his waist. "I would suffer for you a thousand times and die for you a thousand more. Iu lemi thois, nach lathene."

Ares held her head to his chest. "Lemi thois jae, Mea."

## 9.SOFTSTEP.14.OSC.3

*King Naiv hadn't left his bedchamber since the incident with the Queen and the Prince. His affliction bordered so close to completion that he couldn't recall the names of colors, what the numbers on the clock meant. But he did know that he had the crown on his head, and as long as it was there, he would remain the King of Tzapodia.*

*After another sleepless night, Naiv stumbled upon a solution. It was unforgivable, unthinkable, but he would do anything to save himself — anything!*

*At noon, he teetered through the Amber Lounge to the last bedchamber over the Porranim Courtyard, meant to be Llaisa's room when she was born. He was sure Manalaei would be there.*

*He creaked open the door, and there she was. His wife, his goddess of a wife who hated him so, was seated by the balcony with her hands on her belly. She turned her head toward the sound.*

*"Ares?"*

*Silently, Naiv rounded the side of the room. If he could reach her without her acknowledgment, this abhorrent decision would be easier on them both. However, Manalaei's senses were acute. When her husband was a foot away from her, she spun around with her claw extended.*

*"Naiv."*

*His shoulders sagged. "It's me, Mana."*

*He held his wife's claw with his, but she swatted him. He then cupped her face, the most loving touch he'd given her since before their son was born. She fell utterly still as he lowered his claw to her belly, rocking her.*

*"The curse will take me soon," he said tensely.*

*"And when it does, I will never tell Llaisa about you. She deserves to think you were a kind man."* The Queen sank her talons into the chipped scales on his hand. *"But Ares . . . you've ruined him. When you are gone, the darkness you've forced upon him will live on. I pray that your transition is agony. I pray that you die knowing your son sits upon the throne of Tzapodia, more of a king than you have ever been."*

Ares, the King of Tzapodia? What a joke. Naiv grinned, but the Queen couldn't see it. *"Nach lemireau Manalaei, my lovely thing, that will not be so, no, no. But for Llaisa, you are entirely right. She should never know me . . . and she never will."*

His talons drilled into her stomach. With dead, violet eyes, he tore through her and extracted the unborn child. He slashed the cord and cradled his daughter in his arms, wiping vernix from her scalp and admiring her motionless face. Llaisa would have grown up to be such a pretty girl.

The Queen's blood pooled on the tesserae. She couldn't make a sound, the pain of her daughter's death and leaving her son to suffer alone was too overpowering. Naiv gazed at her one last time before he pushed her off the balcony.

Meanwhile, Ares walked beside Mother Mollah with a crate of medical supplies in his arms; she was too old to carry them. Mollah propped open the infirmary side door with her slipper, and Ares took a step inside.

Then came screams from the Porranim Courtyard. Ares set down the shipments and sprinted to the racket. At the corner of the castle, he slid in the gravel and shielded his eyes with the crook of his arm.

Surrounded by a group of keepers and sentinels was a body that had fallen from a great height. It was dressed in gorgeous raiments and adorned with priceless jewels. Ares didn't recognize the victim until a purple veil twirled down from the balcony six stories above, one that only a single person in Castle Lavrenthea ever wore.

Tears wet Ares' face, but he couldn't tell what he was feeling — or what he wasn't. It was everything and nothing at all. Manalaei had been his guardian, his sliver of truth and unconditional love in a kingdom where such things couldn't thrive.

The King had done it, Ares knew. He was plunged into a hatred uncharted. He'd never killed, but he would today. He shoved past the throng of onlookers, and a dagger cried as he stole it from a sentinel. Mollah tried to call him back as he disappeared into the castle.

In the Amber Wing, the Prince snapped every hinge and kicked down every door in search of Naiv. Through the last entryway at the end of the hall, he found his father faced away, hunched over a table.

The King turned around at once, his jaw and neck painted in red. In his arms lay limp who would have been Princess Llaisa Lorcé-Lavrenthea. He sank his talons into the child's chest and ate what was inside. With tears of joy streaming from his eyes, one yellow, one violet, he petted her hairless head.

"She's only sleeping," said the King.

Serene, he waited for Llaisa's pureblooded dragon heart to reverse his affliction. Nothing happened. He waited more. Nothing. His scales remained, he was yet cursed as the Queen had foretold. It had all been for naught. Belligerent, he dropped Llaisa's remains.

"It isn't working, it isn't working! The curse — I'm still cursed!"

All Ares could think was, 'Good.' He tackled Naiv to the ground and plunged the dagger into his gut. The King ripped the blade from his middle and threw it far.

*Father and son rolled about on the floor, cutting and punching each other with irises flashing violet. Naiv cracked his horns into Ares' head, and Ares toppled backward. While he was disoriented, the King dragged his talons down his back. From his shoulder blades, around his ribcage, and to his hip was left a fatal wound.*

*But he couldn't die yet, he wouldn't. Ares held his torn skin and stole Sindred from the King's scabbard and slashed. Naiv caught the blade in his claw and threw the Prince onto a table.*

*As his son's skin drained, he husked, "She didn't scream. She let me do it! And you won't scream either."*

*It wasn't worth holding back anymore. Ares grabbed the King's shoulders, and jet black scales surfaced on his left hand. The key to his affliction had been turned.*

*Naiv noticed his actions and laughed, "You've doomed yourself, boy. You will no longer die a man, but a monster. Perhaps I've underestimated you. You haven't given up. You inherited that fire from someone, didn't you? You are just like me! But until you take the head from my neck . . . you will never be a king."*

*With the crown in his hand, Naiv ran to the balcony. He leaped, and crimson wings blotted out the Tzapodian sunlight.*

*The Prince stumbled across the bedchamber, his boots making streaks in his mother's blood. His skin crackled, and his scales crawled over his knuckles. He jumped, becoming the monster he'd always been doomed to become.*

*That was the day marked across Amniven as the Heavens Devil's last flight, and the first flight of the Last Son of the Dragons.*

By the time Annalais finished telling the true story, she regretted bringing it up. Levelia Kross was in tears. Hearing the truth of

Manalaei Lorcé-Lavrenthea's end made her regret joining the Brood more so.

Widow had the wildest, evilest grin on Her face that any of the Brood members had seen yet. Cherish too was fascinated. "The child, Llaisa," he said quietly, "why did her heart not cure King Naiv of his affliction?"

"No one is certain, but I've heard speculations," said Annalais somberly. "Some have said that Llaisa Lavrenthea was illegitimate, that she wasn't Naiv's daughter. He ate her heart, but it wasn't that of a pureblooded dragon's. Thus, his curse endured."

"Queen Manalaei, unfaithful? With whom?" sniffled Levelia.

"Isaak Oelar, the Wing Regent," answered Annalais. "It hasn't been confirmed but isn't far-fetched. Isaak loved Manalaei, she melted him. If it is true, it was kept a secret to protect Ares. Even I think it best if he never finds out."

"And Naiv Lavrenthea, is he dead?" wondered Cherish.

"No. Ares fought him, but he wasn't killed," muttered Annalais.

Widow sighed dreamily. "Perfect. We shall force Ares to end the stars as King Naiv ended Queen Manalaei, and he will serve us with no reason left to resist. My . . . that *is* cruel."

# Exiled

## 17.Clawsguard.26.Osc.3
## The Ruby Bureau, Castle Lavrenthea

Mid-week, Ares sent for the Wing Regent. Isaak entered the Ruby Bureau and claimed a chair without a word. It took one breath to tell that the Prince was devastated, staring blankly at his stack of untouched paperwork, his blistered palm supporting his forehead.

"I've asked this many times as of late," Ares began, "but I must insist that you take up my position indefinitely."

Isaak stiffened. "Indefinitely? Where are you going now?"

"Nowhere. I don't trust myself as the head of this kingdom and can't say when I will again." Ares rubbed his neck, searching for a silver chain. "Please, ask me nothing further. Just do it."

The Wing Regent's stare shot to the Prince's empty chest, feeling empty too then. "The Felastil, where is it?"

Ares' eyes flared to violet. "I said not to ask questions."

It was unusual for Ares to use his dragon blood so freely, even for something so trifling as a change of eye color. His Felastil was amiss, and the relinquishment of his role was too precipitous. But Isaak had been demanded to drop the subject, and he would do so.

"Is there anything else, Your Highness?"

Ares glared at him. "When have you ever called me that?"

"Since you stopped acting like Ares," said Isaak austerely.

If the Prince could tell the Wing Regent the truth, perhaps he would hold a less severe judgment. But he couldn't. He picked at his scales, hoping they would shed and never return. "Have you any news regarding the whereabouts of the King?"

Isaak flinched. This interaction was becoming stranger with each remark Ares made. "No, not that I've learned. You haven't spoken of him since you were — what — twenty? Why ask about him now?"

Ares laid his head on his arms. "No more questions, Isaak, please. I just . . . I have to hear what you've learned."

"We sent out search parties the week he vanished but ceased the investigation when you gave us the order," began Isaak. "Naiv was spotted flying south when we pulled you out of the Kingscore. There's been no trace of him since. You left him lethally wounded, Ares. He may have died that day."

Ares stood up and paced around. "He refused to die by my hand. He willed me to take the head from his neck, and I failed to do it. I should have chased him, I should have finished it. Maybe then I'd have the crown and a chance at keeping my mind intact."

"No, you would have bled to death had you stayed in the sky. I, for one, am thankful you ended the battle when you did." Isaak eyeballed Ares' claw. If he phrased his next question right, it would no longer be a question. "And your affliction, Ares. . . ."

The Prince wasn't oblivious; the Wing Regent was asking without asking. He hadn't revealed the extent of his curse to anyone but Luxea since he'd returned from Mythos — and now it had spread more.

Fine. If Isaak wanted to see, he would. Ares briskly unlaced the front of his shirt and tugged his collar aside. Unveiled were black scales, running up the side of his neck. Isaak's sharp appearance got sharper, but only because they were broken.

"You poor fool, Ares. Why haven't you told us — told me? That's nearly as far as your father's before he turned!"

"Don't you dare compare me to him!" snapped Ares. Isaak hid his tight fists. "I haven't felt any different. Perhaps the external effects move faster than the internal — I can't know." He decided to tell him. "What's worse is . . . Widow can control this. If I serve Her, it stops. If I defy Her, it quickens."

It wasn't said how or why the Brood Mother had a hold over the Prince, but Isaak knew he had to act. He launched out of his chair and flew to the door. "Widow can't use the curse against you if you aren't cursed at all.I will rally a party to disembark this evening. Even if all we find are Naiv's bones, we will get him."

Ares laughed. "I need a dragon's heart, not the marrow." He started to lace his shirt again but stopped. "Isaak, if you do uncover his hiding place . . . don't take action. Killing him is my task. Only mine."

Since the day Ares had dumped his duties onto the Wing Regent, he'd not had a clue what to do with himself. It had been years since he'd been at home without responsibilities. He slugged around the Amber Lounge with a glass of wine, making minor adjustments to decor just to accomplish something.

From the sofa, Oliver asked, "You're drinkin' already? It's nine in the mornin'."

Ares swallowed. "Your point?"

Oliver watched the Prince brush invisible specks off the leaves of a decorative bush. "What're you doin' to that plant?"

"Dusting it."

"It's a plant, mate. It don't need to be dusted."

Ares picked lint off the fringe of a wall tapestry. Oliver worried he was snapping from being unfit to work. As the Prince next adjusted the hundreds of beads on a tablecloth, Oliver threw him a cigarette. He needed it; he needed it a lot. He put it in his mouth, but instead of reaching for his matches, he lit it with an orb of dragon-fire.

"Should you be usin' dragon blood?" murmured Oliver.

"What?" asked Ares, spinning a bead face-up.

"Isn't it not such a grand idea to tap into your dragon-y bits, mate? Considerin' you'll go mental n' all that."

"I didn't use it."

"You lit your dart with dragon-fire."

The beads stopped turning. Ares glanced at the tip of his cigarette. It was glowing purple like dragon-fire. He hadn't realized he'd used it. But what if Widow's gift still applied? If it did, would it matter?

He rushed to the full-length mirror and pulled his hair aside. His eyes flickered to violet, and one fresh scale appeared below his earlobe. The Brood Mother had retaken Her offering. Ares was faced with the curse of draconism once more.

"If you see me tapping into my blood again, stop me." The Prince took a smoky inhale, his eyes passing over his hand. "If I'm not aware of my usage, I'll — !"

Ares dropped his wineglass and stumbled into the side of the sofa. Usually, his left hand was armored in black, but it was fleshed. His right, however, had been eaten by chipped, crimson scales.

He met his reflection. It was almost right, his hair was lank and black, he was tall and toned. But his eyes were yellow, his skin was pale, and his horns shot straight to the back of his head.

No longer was he Ares — he was Naiv.

Oliver's distressed babbling was muted by a tumult of thoughts. Ares hid his right hand and left the Amber Lounge with all speed. He trapped himself inside his bedchamber and shut his eyes.

*Crimson. I hate the color. Go away . . . go away . . .*

"You want it to end, don't you?" asked a familiar voice.

Resting on his bed was Widow. She wasn't here to play, not this time. Her four black eyes were four black nooses around his neck.

"Stop following me!" he hissed.

The Brood Mother strode to him and admired the crimson scales on his hand. "They will spread. I give you five years before you're taken — if you're careful. But you can stop it yet."

Ares whirled away from Her. "I don't want Your gifts!"

"You do! I can smell your desperation. You had one chance and stood upon it!" She then burst into laughter as if She'd been holding it in. "Oh, I won't lie to you anymore. It was an illusion. I cannot stop your curse, Your Highness, for a curse can only be met by its counter.

"What I showed you was merely what you wanted to see. You may not forgive me for misleading you, but no matter what gifts I proffer, I own you. Whether or not your mind is taken, whether you are a man or a beast — *I own you!*"

She came to him, a false pity veiling that odd, disturbing beauty She possessed. "I will have mercy on you if you vow to reverse what you've done to sabotage me. You will follow me, fight for me, capture the divines, and kill the stars. Resistance is in vain, *nach lathene.*"

'*My son,*' She called him. The last time Ares had heard the words were from his mother's mouth. Widow knew; someone had told Her.

"End the stars within a fortnight, and I will make certain that your travels to inevitable insanity torment you not," She offered.

"You think that remaining a slave to a curse is any worse than becoming a slave to You?" rasped Ares.

"It's your decision. Beware that if you forsake my bidding, I'll do it for you. If the stars draw breath by the fourteenth day, you will kill her with or without control." Widow pouted histrionically. "What do you think, Your Highness? A nasty fall from the sixth floor?"

His glassy eyes darted to the balcony, and his heart beat so hard that his sternum cracked. Bathing in his despair, Widow lifted his right hand and touched each scale. She wanted to ruin him, and She would.

"I wonder what Oscerin will think when the Divide dies by the hand of the Parallel." Eight legs sprouted from Her spine. She crawled to the balcony and leered. "Fourteen days — *monster.*"

And She was gone.

Ares' legs gave way. He buried his head between his knees and balled his hair in his fists. The crimson scales had vanished but would return unless he met the Brood Mother's demands.

But he wouldn't do it. Never, no matter how many curses Widow took or gave. Ares made his choice before his reasoning frayed. If his only options were to stop a heart or break one, he was ready to destroy.

In her sleep, Luxea heard a *thump*. She rolled over and engulfed herself in her fluffy duvet. Two *thumps*. She burrowed into her pillow.

*Smash!*

She flew up in her bed, dazed, and watched seven castle sentinels pour into her bedchamber.

*What is this, some hyperrealistic dream?*

The sentinels tore through her wardrobe and stuffed her clothing into a sack. What forced her to realize that this wasn't in her head was the pair of hands that nabbed her out from under her blankets.

"Let go of me! What are you doing?"

The sentinels held her wrists behind her back. One of them announced, "By the order of His Royal Highness Ares Lavrenthea, you are hereby banished from the Kingdom of Tzapodia."

"What? But I live here! I'm a member of the council, I —" A sentinel reached for the Usinnon on the nightstand. "Wait, sir, don't touch that! It will — !"

The spellbook screamed and sparked him, blasting him back into a stack of magick notebooks. A second armored man threw a cloth over the Usinnon, rendering its arcanan pulses ineffective. He tucked it under his arm and went to the door.

Smothered by fabric, the Usinnon yelled, "Miss Siren, what is happening? Give me back to her, you oaf! Unhand me!"

Luxea was dragged into the hallway. She kicked at the sentinels to free herself, but they wouldn't let her go. The nearest door opened, and Runa bolted outside in her rosy nightgown.

"Luxea Siren?"

Estalyn tumbled out after her, just as confused by the sentinels that wrangled Luxea to the floor. Although she was frail, she could still fight for those she loved.

"Get your hands off her!" shouted Estalyn. One sentinel listened, the other proceeded to drag Luxea to the stairwell. Runa's mother shoved him. "You can't take her! This is her home!"

It was useless. Luxea hadn't wanted to give them an taste of her abilities, but she'd had enough of this. She spread her fingers behind her back.

*"Vastal'han ma!"*

The sentinel was slung down the hallway by magick. Luxea fell forward and swiped the Usinnon off the floor. Estalyn clung to her, protecting her with whatever strength she had. Three more sentinels pushed her away and detained Luxea. She almost attacked them too, but then Ares appeared two doors down.

When Runa saw him, she briefly forgot who he was and expelled her anger unto him as if he were an ordinary person. She slammed her fists on his waist and cried, "Don't take her away! I love Luxea Siren, she can't go!" Estalyn dragged her off him.

The Prince stared at Luxea, hurting in all ways, and she stared back with the blackest of black in her eyes. Maybe she would hate him, but he would rather have that than watch her die. Refusing to torment himself any longer, he stormed down the hallway in the opposite direction.

The sentinels escorted Luxea to the vestibule. The serving girls and keepers who'd grown to know her over the past few years gawped as she was disposed onto the Steps of Sevinus. She rolled over in the gravel, her torn elbows and knees stinging. Her satchels of belongings were tossed to her, and the Usinnon was slid down the pathway.

Avari had been shaken awake by screaming in the Amber Lounge and tailed the sentinels unnoticed. But Shir had followed her too with as little heed.

Although she was still in her nightclothes, a flappy, brown tunic with patches in the waist, Avari broke through the wall of sentinels.

"What are you doing to her?!" She planted a punch, and a sentinel fell with his jaw aching. "Don't you dare touch her! Luxie!"

The sorceress sat in the gravel, watching as her livid best friend was intercepted. But Shir couldn't be caught. The Mythic phased through hands as they swiped, avoiding containment, and appeared in a circle of light beside Luxea. They helped her off the ground and brushed her off; she was too numb to feel their energy.

"Shir, what's happening?" she choked out.

The Mythic's crystalline eyes rose to the balcony of Ares' bedchamber, six stories above the courtyard. There were traces of black, festering essence embedded in the stone. They knew why but wouldn't say, not yet. They faced the sentinels, almost looking angry.

"I am going with her. Do not stop me."

It had been ordered by the Prince that Shir was not to be left without protection, but they couldn't keep such a thing prisoner. As three of the five sentinels held Avari to the floor, the other two exchanged nods.

"So be it." One outstretched his hand. "Your sigil, Seer."

As if Luxea had it. They'd torn her out of her bed too quickly for her to even get dressed! "It's in my bedchamber. Suit yourselves. I'm sure His Highness can tell you where to find it."

One sentinel sealed the doors of Castle Lavrenthea, and the other said, "Do not return."

❦

With a pack of castle guards magnetic to her, Avari crashed into the Amber Lounge where sat Oliver and Brielle and Ruka. They'd been woken up too but had refrained from asking questions. Nearby, Ares was reclined on the wall with a cigarette and a wineglass in the same hand.

Avari barreled to him and, with Luxea in her mind, slapped him across the face. His drink spilled on his shirt. "Banishing Luxie from the kingdom? What did she ever do to deserve that?"

The sentinels verged on the ranger as she pushed Ares again and again. There was nothing else to do; she just had to hit something. As gauntleted hands moved in to seize her, Ares held up his claw.

"Leave us!"

Although fearful for their leader's safety, the sentinels marched back down the hall and into the spiral staircase in a single-file line, giving the Amber Wing to those whom Ares deemed worthy.

The wolf siblings growled. Brielle stood up and asked, "You cast out Starlight? But she's a part of our pack!"

If only they could see how difficult this was for Ares. He puffed his roseleaf cigarette and drank with smoke in his lungs. "Because she'll die if I don't. Widow demanded that I kill her within a fortnight. Upon my failure to do so, She'll do it through me."

"What the hells are you talking about?" wept Avari. "Luxea has a life here too, Ares, and we love her! So why did you — ?"

"Because I love her too!"

The confession demolished every wall that Ares had spent the past decade building. He trapped his cigarette in his hand, just to experience some sort of pain worse than this, but he felt nothing. If only flames could hurt dragons.

"You may misinterpret my actions," he whispered, "but if Luxea is anywhere close to me, I'll kill her. I know exactly how I'll do it. It can't happen anywhere but here — in the castle."

Ruka was too depressed about Shir leaving with Luxea to involve himself in the quarrel, but Brielle felt otherwise. She came forth and rested her hand on Avari's head, calming her.

"It's like Gajneva and Veshra in Blackjaw Hollow. Veshra loved her sister like nothing else, but something possessed her that day you and your men came. You're telling us that Widow can force you to act against your will."

Remembering the deaths of the Chieftain of Blackjaw Hollow and her bat counterpart, Oliver frowned.

"Yes," confirmed Ares. "Widow has proven Her abilities to manipulate the minds of Her underlings. I can't stop Her once She's taken control. She gave me two weeks. If Luxea is nowhere to be found by then, she'll be safe."

"No!" Avari wormed out of Brielle's grasp. "Luxie is in the open. What if this was Widow's plan to isolate her? You're throwing her into the Brood's trap, Ares!"

It was becoming a habit for Oliver to step in. He took a stand by the Prince. "I agree with 'im. Think 'bout it. Widow n' Her folks can't touch Luxie. You really think they'll go after her when all it takes is a touch to kill 'em off?"

"Not only that," added Brielle, "but Starlight will fight and prevail against man and nightmare. A dragon, however . . ."

The rider and her wolf maneuvered to Ares' side too. Avari, who was unsure if she would ever let this go, snarled, "If Luxea dies out there, I hope none of you forgive yourselves."

All down the Kingslane, men and women in silver armors shoved Luxea and warned her never to return. She and Shir stopped by the military quarter and sneaked inside with the help of several soldiers with whom she'd once shared a home.

Her old friend, a shieldmaiden named Felitia, led them to the Bay of Farewells. She'd been in charge of heating the pieces in Extreme Dragon Stones, a game involving a lot of fire. Felitia kept watch with her shield and spear held high as Luxea, behind a stack of dinghies, stripped. She reemerged in a cloaked uniform, lacking a sigil, and covered her head of unwashed hair with her fur-lined, black hood.

"Thank you, Felitia."

The shieldmaiden patted her shoulder. "Don't thank me, Siren. If you ever come back, stop for a visit. We'll play a round or two."

Luxea tried to be funny. "I do love third-degree burns."

Once they'd exchanged hugs, Felitia carried Luxea's bag to the corrals and helped her prepare Velesari. When her belongings were hooked to the saddle, Luxea climbed onto her back. Her stars met nothing but the ground as she rode off with Shir beside her.

A desperate screech stopped her. Scratching at the wall of her overdecorated pen was Pveather. Luxea had to force Velesari to get closer. Through the gap in the bars, she stroked the white dracas' smooth, pierced snout.

"*Iu lemi thois,*" she whispered.

Luxea covered her mouth with a veil and cantered away. Pveather slammed her body against the stable wall, shrieking for her not to go. Shir glanced at the white dracas and translated the language of the dragonkin. They smiled and swung their arms, a bit happier.

"Pveather loves you too."

"What?" asked Luxea distractedly.

"You said you love her. She told me she loves you too."

Luxea yanked Velesari to a dead stop. "What do you mean?"

Shir blinked at her questioningly. "You told Pveather, *'Iu lemi thois.'* In the draconic tongue, that means, *'I love you.'*"

All this time, Luxea had thought she'd known heartbreak.

Ares had said he loved her, and now it was too late for her to mirror the gesture. The wind froze the tears she hadn't meant to shed as she stared at Castle Lavrenthea. Through the balcony doors of the Amber Lounge, she saw movement.

*This . . . this is heartbreak.*

Before her sorrows could take hold, Luxea cracked the reins and sped to Riverpass. She didn't look back.

# PAGES OF A MIND LOST

## 22.CLAWSGUARD.26.OSC.3
### NAV AMANI FOREST, SELNILAR

AFTER ONE hour, Luxea and Shir passed the border of Tzapodia and entered Nav Amani Forest where a ballad was played by the legs of crickets and the throats of frogs.

Along the way, Luxea rode by some Tzapodian merchants who'd been harvesting herbs or hunting for meats. They waved and offered her samples as they trotted by. She hadn't met any of them before, but they made her longing for Tel Ashir swell with each stride Velesari took away from home.

At twilight, Velesari slowed. Her flank expanded and contracted as she walked. Every once in a while, Shir picked leaves from bushes and fed them to her.

"Shir," murmured Luxea, "why did Ares send me away?"

The Mythic wiggled their branchy fingers as Velesari lapped berry juice from them. "To protect you."

Even if Shir had told her that Ares had exiled her from Tzapodia to plan a surprise party, it wouldn't have made her feel better. That being said, she would have pushed him away too if she were in his position.

"He's afraid that Widow will make him kill me. But I can protect myself. Neither Ares nor Widow can touch me. I wish he would see that."

"He shall, in time." Shir peered around the woods as the day died. "Where do we go? I can lead us back to Ai Florana. We will be safe."

"No. N'ra doesn't want me there."

"Miss Siren?" coughed the Usinnon.

Luxea clicked her tongue to halt Velesari and unearthed her spellbook from her saddlebag. "What is it?"

"Might I suggest your old manor? It was . . . hideous. But it would keep you from the rain and cold," said the Usinnon. "There's a kitchen too. I have recipes on page five hundred and fifty-nine!"

She smiled, thanking the Lemuria for blessing her with Therasi Direl and the Mythic. "Shir, can you guide us back to the manor?"

"By the blackwood tree?"

"Yes, that one."

The Mythic hadn't enjoyed the atmosphere there, but they would do it for Luxea. Counting the colors in her blood, her mind, and her spirit, they took her hand and absorbed her energy. She dug her feet into the stirrups; the intensity of touching a Mythic had returned.

With rainbow vibrations coursing through their limbs, Shir held out their fingers. From them seeped a stream of white light that snaked through the dirt and the trees, matching the traces of Luxea from reaches away.

"The trail is here," stated Shir.

In two hours, Luxea spotted the blackwood tree in a clearing. She cantered under its branches and saw the Shadow staring at her with each blink.

At the Siren manor, she stabled Velesari by the front door. The thorny vines had flourished since their last visit, so Shir bent them away; the plants bloomed with pink flowers, joyous that the Mythic had come back.

Inside, it was as haunting as it had been moons ago. Had the light from Shir's crown not illuminated the place, it would have been too dark to count your fingers. It was the rainy season, so the floor was saturated. Luxea felt her toes imprinting the waterlogged wood.

The only dry place was the mantle. Luxea set the Usinnon there to keep it safe, but the portrait of the little girl and her faceless parents bothered the spellbook. Shir helped her take down the painting. The Usinnon fell asleep immediately after, less threatened.

Luxea unbuttoned her bag and picked out the three or four articles of clothing for which she cared the least. She shook them out, ignoring the scent of Castle Lavrenthea that had stained them — jasmine and sandalwood. She laid them down, but every time she flattened the corners, some horde of ants or baby moths sprouted from beneath it, or spots appeared in the fabric from the ink-secreting fungi.

She soon ceased her attempts to perfect a sleeping space and alternatively scoured the manor for candles. She uncovered five, including a gas lantern in an office. They only had enough wax and oil left to offer light for one evening.

Without Luxea's realizing, morning approached. She bundled up her bag to use as a pillow and lay on her clothes, which had been soaked all the way through with the runoff on the floor.

This was the exact opposite of what she'd grown used to in Castle Lavrenthea. Even sleeping in the meadow on Mythos had been better; in fact, she'd experienced the best sleep of her life on that island.

*That's right . . . Mythos.*

She scooted on her knees to her second bag and dug through it until she found a black leather journal. She sat back and flipped to the last page, to Ares' sketch of the trees on Mythos.

"Shir?" Luxea tried not to cry. "Do you know what this is?"

The Mythic had been playing with a beetle. They set the creature down and leaned in. "That is the Mythos sky," they said at once.

She cried anyway. Shir wasn't sure why the reminder of their home had affected her so profoundly — or perhaps it was the reminder of peace. They stroked Luxea's back through the robe she used as a blanket as she flattened her face to the journal's pages. She wouldn't rest easily tonight.

However, there was something that might help. She dreaded it, but it was there, up the staircase and down the hall. Although she despised it now, it had once put her to sleep when she was young.

"A music box is up the right stairwell, in the last room — the one with the scratches on the walls. Will you get it for me?" she sniffled.

"Yes," said Shir sweetly.

They locus-jumped out of sight. In less than ten seconds, they reappeared with the wooden box and set it down. Luxea wiped her nose and popped open the lid. She turned the winder on the back and wondered with each tiny tick if she was excited or afraid to hear the music.

The butterfly spun, and the lullaby chimed off the water-laden walls. Stars grey, Luxea pulled Ares' journal under the blanket with her and fell asleep to a lost song in a house she couldn't remember.

That night, Luxea had a dream . . .

*Her arms had been pinned to her bedposts for over a week — nine days, to be exact. Her wrists were raw. At times, she couldn't feel them; others, she felt them too strongly.*

*Those priests from Sirah Temple were back. They always showed up on days when it rained or when the clouds hid the Tehrastar. Their hands were rough, not holy or absolving as they were fabled to be. Yet their fingers shook when they touched her.*

*They saw in her a demon, but she was a child! How could they overlook such an obvious thing?*

*In the doorway stood Luxea's father. He'd always been so loving, so concerned for her growth, but today he was disgusted. Those pink eyes of his, so warm and real, those soft features he had, like those of a healer . . . they were amiss. His gaze spoke malice, and his visage was sharp and poisonous. Had Luxea not memorized his face, she'd have thought he didn't know her at all.*

*She lifted her head off the pillow and screamed, "Appa!"*

*Her father curled his lip and gestured to the temple priests. "This is the last attempt. If you can't fix her by dawn, take her away."*

*Luxea wept as he stalked out of her bedroom. Had he forgotten her, was she no longer of use to him? Was she a monster, one unworthy of his love?*

*Alone with those l'arian strangers, she panicked. They flicked glass syringes and poured liquids from cup to cup, expecting her to ingest it without question.*

*Luxea flailed, and then her bones cracked in the wrong ways. Her knobby knees and elbows switched directions and tugged themselves out of their restraints.*

*This was why her father had sent for the temple priests, to begin with. Luxea had told him time and time again that she wasn't sick, it* was all the Shadow's doing, but to no avail. After all, she was a child, and words by the tongues of the young are paltry to the minds of the grown.

But it was happening again; the shadow was taking control.

A stout priest was readjusting the straps on Luxea's wrists when she spoke to him, although she had no jurisdiction over the curses in her mouth.

"It must be titillating, your fingers on her skin," said Luxea in a voice like rime, utterly not her own. "Tell me, did the other children struggle? When you laid those pestilent hands upon the thighs of the boys in the temple, did they weep for their honor?"

The stout priest recoiled, the core of his horror swallowing his mien. The others ceased their tests and listened, for this was the first time in days that Luxea had made sounds other than whimpers or guttural roars.

Next, Luxea faced the tallest man, standing directly above her.

"And you, Father, have your fellow men of the light learned your secrets?" She sneered, and her lips cracked. "You were the one responsible for that innocent woman's death, you were the one in the seat, steering the white horses as their hooves flattened her to the stone. You told them all that your brother held the reins. That Snowhowl day, in the plaza of the Holy City, which was sweeter? The fruition of your lie, or watching his neck snap at the end of the rope?"

A third priest, the only one who hadn't been targeted by his sins of yore, pressed a needle to the crook of her arm where her skin was red and pocked with puncture marks. The point sank in, stinging as severely as all of the injections that had been inflicted upon her.

And then Luxea lost consciousness.

*That was the only remedy now. If whatever curse or demon or beast within her wouldn't leave, all the priests could do was steal away her senses.*

*Late in the night, utterly without rest, she swiveled between freedom and possession. Strapped to her four-poster bed, she did the one thing that gave her peace: dreaming beyond the windowpanes.*

*The Irestar was full and, for once, not hidden away. Luxea loved the Moon and felt as if it loved her too. It had been so long since she'd seen that silver light, the light that, tonight, seemed to speak.*

*It was then that she heard voices from far, far away. She hoped that the Moon really was reaching out to her, that it would save her from the darkness — but it was the Shadow.*

*No . . . this time, it was different.*

*This wasn't unintelligible, it wasn't hissing or wailing, it made sense. Whispers, a child's and a woman's, sharing secrets as friends. It was hopeful, lovely and promising like a favorite memory; however, it wasn't Luxea's memory.*

*A name was spoken. That was all she could recall. A name.*

*But whose?*

It took a week and a half to fix up the abandoned manor to somewhat livable conditions. The floors were eaten through by mold and bugs, and plants cracked through the ceiling and snaked down the walls, but they'd cleaned the kitchen and the main room.

Each morning, Luxea ventured out to hunt. She'd never liked gathering meat, out of pity for the animals, but she had to eat. Although Avari had taught her step-by-step how to trap, she found a better way to do so. She set the Usinnon on the ground and hid in a bush. Therasi Direl made animal sounds until some beast came along for Luxea to stick with a spectral blade.

Shir couldn't kill without dying, so they sat in the garden and called forth the liveliest of vegetables and herbs.

Whenever Luxea brought home a bundle of rabbits or a fox, she cut the meats and soaked the bones in water with Shir's plants to make stock. Soup, roast meats, and eggs were all she could cook anyway.

On the night of the thirteenth day, after a supper of steamed asparagus and scrambled quail eggs, Luxea tore through the old study upstairs to see what she could find.

With a heap of far too many books in her arms, she descended the staircase. At the bottom step, her leg plunged through the rotten wood. The journals and tomes, including the Usinnon, who screamed, flew across the room.

The splinters tore open her leggings as well as her knee and shin. Luxea spewed about thirty curses as she extracted her leg from the hollow.

Shir locus-jumped to her at once with the Usinnon in their hand. They set the spellbook beside Luxea and said, "You are hurt."

"I'm fine, Shir," she grunted. "It's just a scrape."

The Mythic insisted on healing the abrasion, for it was small and wouldn't drain them of energy. As their crystalline hands made contact, Luxea pushed them away and shifted onto all fours.

Below the floorboards, the staircase continued going down.

The pain no longer mattered. Luxea tugged the fringe of the rug and peeled it back to reveal a hatch that had rusted to the crease of the base of the stairs. There was a feeling that she'd never seen it, not even in her past.

"Will you help me lift this?"

Together, she and Shir snapped the fused metal. The hatch slammed onto the main room floor and dented the decayed wood beneath it. Beyond was a lightless passageway leading deep, deep under the manor.

There goes that curiosity again. Luxea scooted down the steps on her behind and stopped when her feet met a floor of lumpy dirt. It was too dark; she almost bolted right back up the stairs. Her hand shot up, and she spat a light spell.

*"Amal luciem!"*

The light didn't come.

She shook her hand and repeated, *"Amal luciem!"*

Her magick wasn't working? But she'd just used it upstairs! To test her abilities, she climbed up a few steps and raised her arm into the main room.

*"Amal luciem!"*

An orb of light sprouted from her hand and drifted about. She squinted into the waiting darkness below. Something in that hidden cellar prevented her from using magick.

"What's stopping my spells?" she asked the Usinnon.

"This is a magister's work, but the foundations of their arcana are corrupt. Their methods are chaotic, far from what I would ever dare teach you. Whoever sealed this cellar was playing a dangerous game." The Usinnon coughed a blue orb into the darkness, but it died quickly. Its pages ruffled in a snit. "Why, even *my* magick — !"

Therasi Direl's confidence had been shot. Luxea comforted her spellbook with a stroke. "Shir, can you light the way for us?"

But another light came first — from Luxea's chest. She gingerly reached inside her blouse and uncovered the Felastil. It was glowing brightly, and, in that moment, Luxea was certain she'd heard Oscerin's voice coming from deep within the cellar. She prayed she was right. Led by moonlight, the three descended into the dark depths.

Luxea clung to the Usinnon and held the Felastil steady. Shir's footsteps usually never made a sound, but it was so airtight that Luxea could barely hear their toes crunching in the grains.

This tunnel was formed of dirt, built not for the eyes of guests like the upper levels. Luxea covered her nose with the crook of her arm, fighting what smelled an awful lot like death.

The way was bare until a ramshackle doorway came into view at the end. Luxea scurried to it and brightened the surrounding area with the Felastil.

The door was shut tight — but the latch was on the outside. Who would ever build this? Unless . . . unless this entry was meant not to keep something out, but to keep something in.

Luxea spun the lock and budged the door with her shoulder. Her feet left grooves in the earth as she applied her whole weight to the barrier. It skidded over a lump and flew open, and the Felastil's light went out.

The entire manor was chilly, but this room was the coldest. There were no windows or doors save for the one through which they'd entered. With Shir's glow, Luxea saw, along the uneven walls, inches-deep scores, unreadable messages, and, in some places, blood smears.

"Is this what all cellars look like?" asked Shir.

"No," breathed Luxea.

In the corner of the room was a candle that hadn't burned to the holder. Luxea lifted it and shuffled in her trousers for a match. She scratched the igniter on a rock in the wall and sparked the wick.

With the candle in her hand, she began lining the boundaries with her eyes. She then noticed that Shir was cowering in the doorway.

"What is it, Shir?"

"The energy in this place is agonizing," said Shir frightfully. "There are imprints of you . . . but also Her."

"Who?"

"Widow."

The warmth of the candle became sacred. "Here? In my house?"

"All over this room."

Luxea took her candle to the far side of the cellar, uncovering bits and pieces of obscure history. She found scraps of clothing, broken feather quills, and a few teacups shards.

But then her foot trod upon unpacked ground. She stepped back and knelt by a dirt pile no larger in circumference than a soup bowl. She dug, cringing at the soil that crusted under her fingernails.

There was something in there.

She uncovered a ruined notebook that had been buried a long time ago. "Shir, look at this!" she called out.

The Mythic crouched next to her. Luxea cracked open the front cover and let dust sprinkle out from between the sheets. On the first page, in her handwriting, was a eulogy.

"Here lies Hannir O'dalar Siren, loving son of Asla and Thaldira Siren,
husband of Iodere Siren, father of Luxea Siren.
Born 14.Blackomen.42.TIR.3.
Died 26.Clawsguard.24.OSC.3.
I love you, Appa.
I'll miss you."

"26.Clawsguard.24?" Luxea felt cold water rushing around her, soaking her clothes and filling her lungs. "Then . . . my father died one week before I was found in Tal Am T'Navin River."

She had a feeling there was something else in the hole. She shoveled the dirt with her hand where not far down awaited a bundle. With the candle positioned beside the journal, she started to unwrap it. Once she'd pulled apart the cloth, she threw it and backed into the wall.

"Th-there's a skull in there!"

Mortal anatomy didn't bother Shir, alive or dead. They collected the fabric where within was indeed a skull. The flesh had long since decomposed, but when they held up the remains and lined it up with Luxea's profile, the lingering traces of life within it matched hers perfectly.

"This is your father." The Mythic wrapped up the skull. "Hannir O'dalar Siren had planned to live long. His end was unexpected."

"How did he die?" whimpered Luxea.

"I cannot say." Shir reached for her. "I feel your loss. You cannot be created again like my kind. I am very sorry."

Luxea's knees swiveled inward and outward. "It's okay. I don't know my father beyond the glimpses I've recovered. I wonder why I can't remember my mother . . . Iodere. All I've seen of her face is in that portrait upstairs. She's gone too, I'm sure."

She gathered the journal and turned the page. A mere three had been filled, but here, in this forgotten, evil place, she uncovered more about herself than she had anywhere.

These entries weren't bragging about past loves of complaining about lessons. These were real, full of fear and angst and hate.

"I've been here for days. It was a week ago that Magister Cherish collected me from my cottage and brought me here. I don't know how he found me. Appa and I were being followed by a strange figure. He seemed to recognize her. Appa insisted we change our names and leave our manor. Appa even had our records burned so we could never be tracked, but Cherish found us anyway. I've been alone since then, but Cherish finally gave me a journal to pass the time. My days are numbered. I can't say how many entries I'll be able to make before then. Maybe I won't finish this one."

~

"This is a cage. The walls and floor are earth, but I hear footsteps and voices above me. Yesterday, Cherish was speaking to someone. He wants to drown me in Tal Am T'Navin River. So I was right, I'll die soon. I've tried breaking out with magick, but I can't use it anymore. I think Cherish sealed the room, or maybe it's in the tea. I would stop drinking it, but I don't get anything else. Cherish always makes it too hot."

~

"I think it's morning, I can't tell. It's dark all the time. I sang myself to sleep last night, my lullaby. Someone sang it back to me through the door. I'm imagining things, aren't I? I don't know what's real anymore."

~

"When I woke up, I saw a spider crawling on the wall. I smashed it. Father used to tell me that a spider would come for me one day. Before sleep, he would have me say, 'The Butterfly mustn't meet the Spider's eyes.' Maybe it's because of him that I hate those creatures."

~

"I can't stop crying. I have to get out. I have to get out. I want to sleep and forget. There was a gift left for me, wrapped in sticky fabric. I opened it but wish I hadn't. It was Appa's head. There were black worms under his skin. He'd been rotting. They killed him. They killed him. They'll kill me next."

Instead of pleas for safety or wishes for something other than a prison beneath the ground, the last entry was a collected, structured thought — a message from past to present.

"Today, the Shadow came through the doorway. Seeing her reminded me of sixteen years ago when I got sick. Appa didn't know how to fix me, and neither did the priests from the Crystal Spire. I was kept in my bed for moons but only got worse. But then I heard crying in my sleep, some sort of memory or echo in my head. It was a name. In the morning, I said it aloud over and over again, and I was released. The Shadow's name is —"

"— Anzthoraz."

The name was a paralytic venom.

Luxea saw herself from an outside perspective. That Nightspeak day on Peyamo's airship, she was dying. She'd seen that little girl, spoken to her and trusted her. Ares had held her hand around his Felastil and whispered apologies that only she could hear. But then that little girl broke the space between them. Before she'd pushed Luxea off the airship, she'd screamed that very name.

The Nature Goddess had been right, Luxea had known the Shadow's name. The Storm Goddess had been right, she had known Her for what She truly was. And Oscerin, She'd told her all along —

*The cure is in the name.*

The journal fell. Luxea vaulted to her feet and kicked dirt onto her father's skull. "We're going back to Tel Ashir."

# The Fourth Daughter

## 8.Venomsnare.26.Osc.3
### Castle Lavrenthea, Tzapodia

The fourteenth day came. Castle Lavrenthea was barred at all exits and entrances, and sentinels guarded them with their weapons brandished. Regardless of the heightened level of security, they knew that spears and shields wouldn't be enough.

Although the Brood Mother would surely sense them, Avari and Brielle volunteered to hide out in Ares' bedchamber. With Ruka in the hall, Brielle crouched in a niche against the ceiling with her bow aimed and an arrow nocked. Avari lay under the bed on her belly with daggers in her hands and backup weapons filling the scabbards on her hips and thighs.

All Ares could do was pretend like he'd forgotten Widow's threats. His emotions would only empower Her if he revealed how terrified he really was.

As if it were any other day, he luxuriated on his sofa with his shirt collar unbuttoned and cigarettes, wine, and snacking fruits on the table. He maintained calm until every ten minutes or so when Avari or Brielle would make a remark. He ordered them to shut their mouths.

With her head covered in her black hood, Luxea galloped to Riverpass. She'd fed Velesari vegetables that morning, so the dracas' stamina was refreshed.

Shir darted through the trees at her side. From far off, they read the energy of the sentinels by the gate. There were two; the rest must have been on duty in the castle.

Fifty feet from the city border, Luxea steered Velesari into a grove and hopped off the saddle. Either this plan would work, or she would be apprehended for unlawful entry. In both cases, she would end up at the castle.

She verged on the Riverpass gate, and one sentinel marched to her to inquire about her reason for traveling to Tel Ashir. Sooner than it could be asked of her, she pulled down her hood and exposed her starry eyes.

The closest sentinel pointed his spear. "It's her!"

Luxea wished herself the best of luck.

Without speaking an incantation, she sent the sentinel rocketing backward. His silver cuirass scraped on the stone, and his bejeweled helmet tipped off his shoulders. While he recovered, Luxea slid the broadsword from his scabbard. These weapons were more unwieldy than she'd surmised; she had a newfound respect for the sentinels, carrying these blasted deadweights all over the place.

The second sentinel ran at her with his shield blocking her vision of him — as if that could hinder magick. She summoned a barrier too, stopping his just as he tried to thump her with it.

But this man had been trained to protect Tzapodia well. When her shield crumbled, he jabbed at her with his pike. Luxea couldn't move fast enough — not like Shir. The Mythic locus-jumped in front of her and absorbed the blow. The lethal edge shattered their arm, but it grew back in seconds.

Her foe was too busy processing the miracle of crystal life to notice the pommel of Luxea's stolen broadsword diving toward him. It *thwacked* into his head, and he fell unconscious. So much for those fancy helmets they wore. When this was over, she would talk with Ares about commissioning a more useful sort.

The other sentinel groaned and shifted. His armor weighed him down just long enough for Luxea to get to him first. She straddled him and cupped his rugged face in her hands.

*"Eluva eshas."*

Rippling from her fingers to her toes, her appearance mimicked the sentinel's down to the mole on his upper lip, the rogue hair growing from his left eyebrow, and the scar riding down his square jaw.

The sentinel looked as if he might resign from his position. He gazed into his own brown eyes as Luxea whispered, *"Detho"* — *sleep.*

And he was asleep.

Luxea sat back on his waist and made fists. This man had bone-breaking hands, but she'd mirrored his visage, not his strength. She struggled to drag each body into the forest and tuck them under bushes. One of their feet stuck out, so she covered it with a palm frond. No one would see them until they woke up.

She purloined a spear and shield and lugged them to Velesari. With some trouble, she mounted and held them up high. "How do I look?"

Shir grinned. "Weapons do not suit you."

Luxea agreed. Sweating from the weight of the shield, she said, "I'll ride. Shut the gate and stay concealed until you make it to the castle. But don't intervene if I'm in danger. I can cover myself."

Although worried for her, Shir nodded.

She fitted on her helmet and kicked Velesari's flank. The dracas bolted into the street, destined for Castle Lavrenthea. Once she'd reached the next district, Velous Direk, Shir sealed the Riverpass gate and blended into their surroundings.

Luxea stabled Velesari in the Porranim Courtyard. Her arms were shaking from lugging around the shield and spear, but those around her couldn't hear her panting under her helmet.

The sentinels in front of the central stairwell let her pass when she flashed the Tzapodian salute. She wanted to laugh at their obliviousness, but her voice hadn't been changed, and she couldn't blow her cover by giggling like the girl she really was.

Her arms turned to jelly as she jogged up the spiraling staircase to the Amber Lounge. Through each passing latticed window in the walls, the sky overhead grew darker. She was thankful she'd made it inside before it started to rain.

On the top floor, she wasn't as flippant. The Amber Lounge was teeming with sentinels; there were pairs keeping vigil before every window, balcony, and door, even if the rooms beyond them were unoccupied. She thought she might be able to pass as a patrol, but the other sentinels didn't make it so simple.

A burly man called out. "You, Ondohal! Why aren't you at your post? You're meant to be watching Riverpass with Pendleman."

*So those are their names. I'll write them apology letters.*

Until then, Luxea had to stay in character as this sentinel, Ondohal, and worm her way into the lounge. She hemmed and lowered her voice several octaves.

"I switched shifts, sir."

"Who gave you authorization? And take off your helm, you fool."

Luxea practically dropped her shield as she scrambled to remove her helmet. She blinked at the sentinel and prayed that her eyes wouldn't soak through with starlight. He didn't react, so she assumed that meant her glamour was upholding.

"I was given permission by . . ." *Damn, who could give the sentinels permission?* "General Claymore, sir."

"Claymore?" murmured the sentinel. "He's off duty today."

This was going nowhere. Luxea wanted to smack herself until an idea came. Of all times, this wasn't one to lack ingenuity. She almost told him a sob story about Ondohal needing to work overtime to feed his seven adopted children, but a blessing sooner arrived in the form of a little girl in her nightgown.

Runa emerged from her room to request a glass of cold milk. She rubbed her puffy eyes with the sleeve of her red nighty and almost went the opposite way down the hall. The mussed, peachy curls on the back of her head gave Luxea the thought fuel she'd been searching for.

She thumped the foot of her spear and shouted, "Miss Faust!"

Runa turned around. "Yes?"

In the form of Ondohal, Luxea beckoned her. Runa feared men, especially ones she didn't know, but she was used to abiding by them. It almost saddened Luxea when she neared without question.

"Your mother —" Luxea's voice cracked, so she hemmed again. "Your mother requested that I come and read to you. May I?"

"Mama did?"

Runa wrung her fingers and refused to look into Ondohal's eyes. But this wouldn't work unless they met their gazes.

"Young women are meant to keep their chins up when speaking to others. Can you do that for me?" asked Luxea in a whisper.

The little girl could but didn't want to. Her feet shuffled as her hazelnut eyes raised up. It was too brief of a moment for the commanding sentinel to catch, but when Luxea showed the stars in a blink, Runa knew who it was. Her lips opened wide; she'd lost a tooth since Luxea was exiled two weeks before.

Runa noticed the hard expression of the sentinel beside them; he wasn't falling for Luxea's excuses. But she'd learned the art of false fronts in her time spent in Haven de Asrodisia. She held Ondohal's arm and tugged.

"I'm sorry, sir, I didn't mean to be rude. Come on! I have lots of books you can read to me. Mama likes them too!"

Luxea followed her. Over her shoulder, she gave the sentinel a Tzapodian salute and a devious smile. He grumbled and returned to his duty as Runa shut the door with this supposed Ondohal.

Inside, Estalyn was in the middle of dressing herself. She wasn't as startled to be exposed as she was disturbed that a full-grown man was holding hands with her daughter.

"Runa, who is this?" she asked, taking on a mother bear's tone.

It was safe to drop the act. Luxea set down her spear and shield, and her mirror image enchantment twinkled away from top to bottom. First was revealed her white hair, and then her starry eyes, finished by her black uniform and her spellbook on her shapely hips.

"Next time, leave me in the saddlebag," coughed the Usinnon.

Estalyn fixed her straps and undergarments. "Miss Siren, you're here? You shouldn't be! The Brood Mother could arrive any minute!"

"I know, Estalyn, and that's why I have to get to Ares as soon as possible," said Luxea, hiding the shield, spear, and Usinnon under their bed. "I can break Widow's control, but I have to get to his room."

"No, I cannot let you!" said Estalyn mournfully. "His Highness told us why he sent you away. If you go near him . . ."

"He may kill me, I'm aware. But I have the remedy for all of this."

Luxea hurried to the balcony door and slipped; it had started raining. She threw up her hood and veiled her eyes with one hand. Ares' balcony was about twenty feet from Estalyn's. Between them was a ledge barely wide enough for her to scale. She peeked over the railing and let a breath leak out.

*Six stories . . . that would hurt.*

"I'm going. Thank you, Runa, for letting me in."

"You shouldn't, Miss Siren!" Estalyn pulled her back from the railing. "If you stay with me, hidden, the Brood Mother may not find you. Perhaps She will leave knowing there's nothing She can do!"

"That isn't like Widow. If She can't harm me, She'll harm Ares and many more." Luxea clutched Estalyn's hands, and her stars shimmered to rose. "If it were Rowan's life, wouldn't you go to such lengths for him? Please . . . let me."

Luxea was right. If Estalyn held her back, she might face the same grief that tore her down when Emperor Rowan had died. Estalyn could never wish such anguish upon anyone, especially not the woman who saved her and her daughter.

She took a weighing breath and let her go. The rain streaked her golden hair down her shoulders as she nudged Luxea outside.

"Go to him."

A spark of gratitude lit up Luxea's smile. She swung her legs over the railing and steadied out as she fit her feet onto the ledge. Runa and Estalyn wished her safety as she sidled forth, her back flat to the wall, darts of water beating her skin, her boot soles slipping.

But she would be there soon.

The cure was in the name, and she had it.

Ares' hair fluttered; this wind was much too cold to be from a tropical storm. Ten seconds passed before a figure appeared on the balcony. With her grey skin dripping wet, Widow crawled to him.

"How sad," She mewed. "Are you going to tell me that the stars aren't here? That I cannot take action now that she's amiss?"

Swallowing a draft of wine, Ares said, "Yes. Luxea is gone. You can't tell me that You expected anything else. I won't kill her."

Widow's legs retracted. She sat on the table before him, and Her knees brushed his through Her scrappy robe. "Do not play dumb with me, Ares. You honestly believed that distancing yourself would spare her? That she would survive in the wild with no one but that gangling hunk of crystal to protect her?

"And better yet, you were mindless enough to station your friends in your bedchamber." Her white pupils switched between the niche in the ceiling to the valance beneath the bed. "A rider and a ranger. Both are skilled. You choose your guardians well. Maybe I'll kill them too. I'm sure that starry-eyed brat will be delighted to hear that two of her friends are dead, three with the wolf. I can't wait to tell her."

Panic took over Ares. "Tell her? You found Luxea? What did you do to her?!"

Widow grinned impishly. *"There's* an honest reaction. We have detained her. She is alive but wishes she weren't," She lied. "The Parallel will yet slay the Divide."

Avari couldn't hold in her sobs. Although Widow had already uncovered her presence, she refused to sit idly by after this demon had hurt her best friend. Screaming and weeping, she slung herself out from under the bed and jumped onto the Brood Mother's back.

"Avari, don't!" shouted Ares.

She was too fast. She slashed Widow's throat again and again until Her bald head dangled back on Her neck. Her body dropped onto the floor, twitching and gurgling as She suffocated.

The ranger's blades fell from her hands. Brielle leaped from her hiding place and held her near. Ares stood from the sofa and inspected Widow's corpse. Her eyes were lifeless, and She wasn't breathing.

Brielle exhaled and hung her bow on her back. "She's . . . dead? Go, Small One. We'll tell the others. This is a day of victory!"

He said nothing, but Ares felt this wasn't the end.

"We still have to save Luxie," sniffled Avari.

"And we will, Small One." Brielle guided Avari out the door. "Dragon, stay where you are. Reinforcements will be sent."

They left. Ares, still speechless, watched Widow's black blood as it pooled on his floor and traced the outline of his boots. It was viscous and smelled like hot, wet rot.

It had to be a dream, it just had to be. That was it? All it took to end the Brood Mother were daggers to the throat?

It seemed too good to be true — and it was.

The blood that rode the tiles turned back to the body from which it had drained. Ares stumbled into the sofa as Widow's skin rejuvenated, Her circulatory system reformed, and Her muscles lapped over Her bones and wove together.

The Brood Mother took a deep, gasping breath as Her legs sprang out of Her spine. She lifted Herself with those eight spears and snarled at Ares, Her head barely stitched to Her shoulders by the tendons.

"A knife, a knife? That's what you expected would kill a greater divine? *A knife?!*" She cracked Her neck as it healed entirely. "Well, so long as those other two are gone . . ."

One of Her legs slammed into Ares. He crashed against a full-length mirror, and it rained shimmery glass onto his head. Widow bounded across the bedchamber and crawled over the door, secreting webs. They hardened, and the way was sealed.

The handle jiggled. *"Ares? Open the door!"*

Cackling like a maniac, Widow drug Her fingernails over the wood. "His Highness is occupied! Come back another day!"

Through his dizzy spell, Ares heard the banging of feet and fists and the clash of weapons on the latch. Then came Ruka's snarling. He rammed his skull into the door and scratched the posts, but it wouldn't break down. The Brood Mother's webs were impenetrable.

Without the slightest gentility, Widow twisted Ares' hair around Her hand and forced him to stand. "Do you see it now? You stare into the face of a *goddess!* The Moon Mother has watched over you since that fateful day — one, one, Lightsmeet, one, Oscerin, three — but the age of light has ended. She cannot save you now!"

There wasn't a point in catering to these sick games any longer. Remembering what Levelia Kross had told him, Ares shook the double vision from his head and clutched Widow's clammy hand.

"You're no divine, you pathetic fabulist! What demon You harbor, She is only a piece of You as Oscerin is to Luxea and me. You want to be worshiped like the real divines, but there's nothing about You worthy of love. Your army follows You because You bribe them into it. You mean nothing to them! All You are is a storyteller. Whether You spare this world or destroy it, Your people, Your *'children,'* as You call them, never have and never will love You."

*"But I do,"* said a whisper.

The room rumbled, and cracks branched out from under Widow's feet. The metal trinkets and artifacts around the bedchamber rattled and clunked off the shelves, rolling toward Her. From within Her came the screams of every soul She'd claimed.

A lanky, mummified figure crawled out of the shadow She cast and stood tall, Her weightless, black hair brushing the vaulted ceiling. She smelled like a crypt, like dusty bones and stale air and decaying flesh. Her magnetic energy drew in the rods of the curtains and slid out the handles on the dressers.

Ares had met a number of divines recently, but this one's presence crushed him, it turned him into a pitiful, breathless insect.

Widow clung to Her like a lost child. "You're here."

Never was there an instance when Ares had been so confused. Before him stood a greater divine, but never in all history had a fourth daughter of the universe been listed; even the goddesses of the mortal plane hadn't known Her. And Widow, the most relentless villain that Amniven had ever seen, was loved by Her like a pet.

"Who are you both?" he shuddered.

The Shadow brushed Her scraggy fingers over Widow's scalp, permitting Her to speak. Widow rested against Her guardian and said,

"I am Her anchor, Her speaker, Her seer, and blade and shield and progeny. I am the body suited for divine infusion, the soul worthy of worship. If only Oscerin held in you as much faith as my shadow holds in me. Maybe then this world would still be under your control."

"And Her . . ." Ares gestured to the shadow, ". . . what is She?"

The Shadow approached Ares, walking stiffly as if consumed by rigor mortis. He no longer possessed his Felastil, but the Goddess of the Moon was within him, deep in an unreachable, unchangeable chamber. She would tear it out.

"You must wonder why Oscerin has withheld from you the secrets She has." The Shadow's voice was frost on glass, nails on metal, as penetrating and inescapable as a plague. "Never did She warn you, never did She share with you the reason She chose you. It is because She wished for none but the three greater and the forgotten fourth to see the truth of Her origination — *our* origination."

She recited the story Ares knew so well, but it wasn't the same.

"The Lemuria created the Goddess of Sun to bring light. Her second child, the Moon, was born in the dark. Oscerin wept for eternities unremembered until Tirih, the Sun, said to Her, *'You are my sister, and my light is Yours.'*

"Tirih set fire to the Irestar, and silver did burn the core of the Moon. Oscerin became the Mother of the Night then, the loved, the praised, and the holy. But the shadow of the Moon was banished. From that forsaken darkness was born the fourth Daughter of the Lemuria. She was kept a secret by Her fellow greater, omitted from the scriptures of man and god. Forever was She doomed to bear alone the verities of Her twin, Oscerin."

Moths and scarabs clicked around the Shadow's face, unraveling Her bandages slightly. Liquid shadow spilled from Her hollow eyes onto the floor, burning a hole in the tile at Ares' feet.

"I am She — the Dark Side of the Moon."

# A Cure of Names

## Castle Lavrenthea, Tzapodia

SOMETHING WAS coming. Someone was here.

The Shadow fell away from Ares and swung Her head to the right. Through the wind and the rain, a figure climbed over the railing and tumbled onto the balcony. Widow glowered at Ares, sure he'd called for help, but even he hadn't expected company.

The intruder wiped their shrouded face and hurried out of the storm. They didn't notice that the room was occupied until they looked up and blenched.

Ares mouthed, *'No . . .'*

Luxea had been relieved to have made it to Ares' bedchamber without falling, but the image of Widow and the Shadow almost made her wish she had.

The Brood Mother snickered as the stars turned to a sulfurous, frightened black. "What impeccable timing, Butterfly."

Ares had really thought that the Brood had detained Luxea and would have been thankful to see that she was unharmed if she hadn't just walked into Widow's trap. He backed into a corner, staying as far away from her as he could.

"Luxea, get out! Don't get near me, don't let me touch you — or Them! Go while you can. The shadow is Oscerin's other half!"

The idea of ripping off the Felastil and throwing it out the window was alluring, but as furious as Luxea was with Oscerin, there wasn't time to dwell on it. Perhaps the Moon Mother had kept from them a terrible secret, but She hadn't lied. She'd been obscure but given Luxea the one answer she'd needed.

The Shadow came forward. Her joints twitched, Her knees buckled under Her weight, and Her fingers dragged on the bloodied, rifted floor. The magnetized knickknacks rolled across the ground after Her, growing hungrier as Her polarity shifted with each step. She was so close that Her whirling, black hair sailed on either side of Luxea's head, but Luxea didn't move.

"Get out of here!" Ares tried to run to her, perhaps to push her out of the way, he wasn't sure, but Widow held him back. Struggling, he begged her, "Please, Luxea, run! Please!"

Silently, the Shadow covered Her face with Her hands as She'd done in the blackwood tree. She lunged closer, again and again. Luxea couldn't hear Ares' screams anymore; she was deprived of her senses, floating, floating, numb and cold and hot and empty.

The Shadow hid Her face one last time. When next She lurched, Her bandages unwound, and Her giant mouth opened to show festering gums, lined with teeth like the bones of a child's fingers.

*Please, please work.*

Luxea whispered, "Anzthoraz."

The Shadow staggered, bemused and weakened. Her bandages shrank against Her body, strangulating Her. She scratched the sides of Her head, trying desperately to peel away the burden of Her name.

Louder this time, Luxea repeated, "Anzthoraz."

"Stop . . . stop it!" squalled the Shadow.

Ares couldn't grasp what was happening as Widow let go of him and ran to Anzthoraz. They clasped to each other, and Widow pressed Her palms to the Shadow's ears.

"Anzthoraz!" shouted Luxea.

"Shut up, shut up! It's our secret — *ours!*" screamed Widow.

With her eyes flaring up in determined yellow, Luxea called out to Ares, "The cure is in the name. Say it!"

*"No!"*

Widow reached out to the Prince. At Her behest, his eyes turned black, stealing from him the ability to say a name or anything at all.

Furious and aching, Luxea stepped closer. Ares was unresponsive. The emotion had gone, leaving not a speck of anger or fear or sorrow in its wake.

"Ares?" she whispered.

Cackling madly, Widow said, "Kill her — don't let her speak!"

The response to the Brood Mother's order was almost too quick. Ares snatched Luxea's arm and threw her down. Her head thudded against the wardrobe, and a vase from the tabletop smashed next to her. Ares slashed at her with his claw with merciless strength.

*"Sheishan'in!"*

Her magick barrier appeared right in time. Ares' talons scraped the globular surface, but then he swung again. Luxea's fingers stretched to a shard of the broken vase and, hoping Ares would forgive her, slammed it into the soft spot above his kneecap. He faltered, and she squirmed away.

Widow laughed hard, enjoying the show put on by the dragon and the butterfly. "Now, *nach lathene!* Cut her open! Steal her breath!"

Luxea's hair was wrested so hard that she was on her feet in an instant. But in the next, she was slammed against the wall and choked through the neck of her uniform. The blankness of Ares' expression was as startling as the ache of his talons digging into Her belly. Thinking of nothing but survival, she clutched Ares' wrist.

Both his skin and Widow's burned. In the same moment, She wailed in agony, and Ares let go of Luxea. His eyes briefly flickered back to green, and he was himself again.

"I'm so sorry, Luxea," he said brokenly. "I can't stop Her — !"

As Widow made him Her puppet once more, Anzthoraz grew in size; She was regaining force. Luxea dodged another one of Ares' killer swings and yelled, "Anzthoraz!"

The name ravaged the Shadow. She collapsed and hugged Her head between Her knees. If Luxea could hold off Widow and Anzthoraz's power in time for Ares to say Her name, they might live through the encounter.

But Widow wouldn't give in so soon.

The Brood Mother willed Ares to trap Luxea's arms, making it impossible for her to touch him. If moonlight couldn't break the link of shadow, the shadow would prevail.

Locking her wrists behind her back, Ares dragged her to the balcony. The wind raged, the rain tore the sky, and the chill of impending failure turned Luxea's bones to thin sheets of ice. She sparked Ares with magick, but it didn't break the trance. All she was doing was worsening the agony he'd feel if and when he was freed.

"Wait, Ares! You have to hear me. Don't let Her — !"

He kicked the railing off the balcony. Luxea's shoes slid as she listened to the metal *clang* into the courtyard six stories down. With no barrier left, she was starting to think she'd been too confident.

"Turn her. I want to see her face," said Widow lowly.

Ares spun Luxea around and held her over the edge. Widow limped to the doorway and drilled Her eyes into the stars. That same feeling came back to Luxea then, the one she'd experienced on Mythos when she'd first encountered the Brood Mother.

This stare was the most hateful thing because it was serene. It wasn't one of malevolence or chaos, it was a romantic, emotional, fulfilled look. To Widow, Luxea's death would mean a happy ending. The sudden light in Her four black eyes was true, so true that it made Luxea wonder if she did deserve to fall.

But then she heard pounding on the bedchamber door, Ruka's whimpers, the screams of Avari and Brielle, Runa and Estalyn and Oliver begging for their safety.

And Ares . . .

If Luxea allowed herself to die today, she would give reason to his fears. He would never consider himself anything but the monster he'd never been. That was enough for her to keep fighting.

She tried to brush her skin against Ares', but all that stopped her from the drop was his claw around her wrists. There was, however, something she could reach. It would doubtlessly hurt him, but —

There was no pain worse than her kiss.

From his lips to his cheekbones, Ares' skin scorched away — and so did Widow's. She screamed and knocked over tables and chairs, reeling and flailing blindly.

Ares was in shock. His teeth and muscles were exposed, his left iris was sapped of color, but he was coherent.

"Say Her name!" shouted Luxea.

"NO! KILL HER!" squalled Widow.

Ares was devoured by Her once more. Luxea's hands were free now, but she kissed him a second time only because she wanted to. He was brought back hardly long enough to recall what had to be done.

Into her lips, he said, "Anzthoraz."

A surge of shadow spilled out of his mouth. He keeled over and clutched his stomach as if he'd been stabbed. Luxea fell beside him and kept his head turned as he choked, and the essence of Widow and Anzthoraz left his spirit. He soon relaxed and opened his eyes. They were green and bright, untouched by that shadow that had caged away their light.

Luxea heard Widow howl as the skin on Ares' face reformed, and his moonlight burns were transferred unto Her tenfold. Melting, She cursed the Moon and the stars and all life for having robbed Her of what She wanted the most.

By Her side, Anzthoraz watched Her dark ichor pool around Ares' head. When he was emptied, it turned to liquid starlight and sparkled into dust.

Although Widow would despise Her for it, Anzthoraz dragged Herself closer and lifted Her tether off the floor. While She was toted to the balcony, Widow cried, "Don't take me away! She has to die! Don't let her go, not again! *No!*"

The greater divine wouldn't let desperation hamper Their efforts. With Widow cradled in Her arms, She turned Her bandaged head to Ares and Luxea.

"Give my Sister my regards."

She and Widow evaporated. The Brood Mother's screams could be heard all the way down as Anzthoraz rode the cracks in the castle walls. Ares and Luxea gazed wide-eyed at the traces of shadow that were laved off the slate by the reborn sunlight beyond the clouds.

The goblets, candelabras, and antique strands of jewelry that had been drawn to Widow and Anzthoraz shuddered to a stop. The cure had worked; They were gone. However, one worry lingered in Ares' head.

Painfully hesitant, he touched Luxea's face.

He didn't burn. He was free.

Her cheeks puffed up as he ran his fingers through her hair. His thumb traced the scar on her cheek that Annalais had given her. He brushed her eyelids and white eyelashes and cupped her pointed ears.

Every inch of her skin was a miracle.

Luxea reached behind her neck and carefully worked out the silver chain from within her collar. She leaned in and draped it over Ares' head. His eyes closed, and gooseflesh rose up on his arms. Oscerin had retained many truths, but he'd missed Her presence.

"Don't ask me to wear that again," said Luxea lightheartedly.

Ares gave her the sincerest grin she'd seen on him, and then he pulled her into a strong hug. Mere seconds later, the webs on the bedchamber door dissolved. The way crashed open, and the other Mooncallers gushed inside with a horde of sentinels.

Letting go of each other was the last thing Ares and Luxea wanted to do, but the patter of feet was closing in. They backed away and prepared themselves for the next step — telling the story.

Luxea had never been called an idiot so much in her life. Even after several days, Avari was *still* scolding her about sneaking into the castle to face the Brood Mother. All she heard was, *'Go take a bath, idiot,'* and, *'Be sure not to fall into a grave on your way out, idiot.'* She didn't mind. This was the first time in a long time that Castle Lavrenthea had felt so colorful.

They'd spent the past four days and three nights recuperating and hadn't addressed what had happened with Widow and Anzthoraz in full detail. On the fourth evening, Ares called the group to the Ruby Bureau for a meeting.

"So, what all went on?" asked Avari, swinging her short legs over the edge of Ares' desk even though he'd asked her not to sit on it. "We know Widow is attached to the Shadow — er — Anzthoraz? But how'd you stop Them, Luxie?"

"I'm also curious," said Brielle broodingly. "If this shadow woman is a greater divine, your hindering of Her and Widow is inconceivable. What is this power you hide from us, Starlight?"

"No power at all," said Luxea honestly. "Anzthoraz has hidden Her name all this time not because She wanted to be forgotten, but because She can be controlled when it's spoken."

"What's so wild 'bout that name?" wondered Oliver.

Ares answered next. "Before time, when only Tirih and Oscerin existed in the spirit realm, Oscerin had a twin. As they were trapped in darkness together, they were, for a time, the same entity, fused by a body neither could leave.

"The Lemuria named Oscerin, but not the shadow. The dark side of the moon was left anonymous for millennia until Oscerin took it upon Herself to give Her a title. But there was a thorn in the rose of such a gift. When Her name was spoken aloud, the shadow no longer held power over the mouth from which it had come.

"Later on, Tirih shed Her warmth upon the Irestar. Moonlight and shadow were split, and the shadow was cast out. That shadow gained its own form over an eternity — whom we now know as Anzthoraz."

"The Shadow . . . She was covered up," muttered Brielle.

"Yes," said Ares almost sympathetically. "Her existence was concealed. Oscerin never wanted Her to come forward as the fourth greater divine, not to Her sisters of the mortal plane or to me."

"But the name, how did you learn to use it as a weapon against Anzthoraz?" badgered Avari. "Either you're really good at guessing, Luxie, or you got some help."

"She never would have discovered the solution had Ares not exiled her from Tzapodia," mentioned Shir. The Prince sank into his chair. "The answers appeared in Luxea's old manor in Nav Amani Forest. She tripped down a staircase and uncovered a hidden cellar."

"You fell down the stairs?" snickered Oliver.

Luxea sliced him with her eyes. "That's beside the point. This cellar was more of a dungeon. There was a door with a lock — on the outside."

Avari shivered. "What sort of family did you used to have?"

That was a question Luxea wanted to find the answer to as well. She went on. "Inside, Shir and I found a journal I'd written in a long time ago . . . as well as a skull I'd buried myself. Shir says it belonged to my father. I wasn't sure how he'd died until I read the passages in the journal. Widow and Cherish killed him."

"Cherish?" hissed Ares.

Luxea nodded. "Cherish helped Widow contain me in that prison. He gave me tea that inhibited my magick, and the cellar was sealed as well. They didn't want me to escape because I was meant to die, or so they thought. What I deduced from the dates in the journal leads me to believe that the memory I had of him in Anathema happened just before this.

"In year 24, my father insisted we flee because we were in danger. He had our records burned so that we could never be tracked." Luxea nodded at Avari. "That's why we couldn't find evidence of my existence in Tzapodia's registries when I first woke up, Avari. They were destroyed on purpose. But, somehow, Cherish found me hiding out in a cottage, stole me away, and locked me in the cellar of the manor where I grew up.

"My journal mentioned that I'd heard him talking to Widow about drowning me in Tal Am T'Navin River. I think that's what happened before I was found and brought to Tel Ashir. I was killed but somehow came back, memories gone, stars in my eyes."

"You're kidding," gushed Avari. "So not only was Widow around for longer than we thought, but She and Cherish were the ones to put you in the river?" She bristled and then laughed. "Maybe I should thank those lunatics. They gave me my best friend."

A smile stung Luxea's cheeks. "Some good came from it."

Brielle pointed to invisible spots on the table, counting a timeline in her head. "Starlight, you say you learned the name *'Anzthoraz'* from this journal of yours?"

"Yes," confirmed Luxea.

"How did you learn the name the first time?" wondered Brielle.

"I can answer this," said Shir collectedly. "Most of you may recall the words of Anatatri in Time. She said that Luxea's last memory, the dream, did not belong to her. It was a stolen recollection, a remnant of possession. I believe that Luxea was never intended to hear the name 'Anzthoraz,' but since Anzthoraz lived within her then, their lines of consciousness crossed unexpectedly.

"That dream between Anzthoraz and Widow occurred in year 1, long before Luxea suffered her sickness. What Luxea heard that night in her sleep was a memory bleeding through the veil of Anzthoraz's control over her." Shir grinned at Luxea, their crown glinting. "I am sure Anzthoraz had not expected you to heed it, to learn Her name. It was meant to be a mere voice in your head, an echo of torment, but it was one to which you were clever enough to respond."

Luxea smiled, but then her expression plummeted. "But I yet have so few answers. Why I saw Anzthoraz growing up, why Widow resents me, and why Cherish helped Her to lock me away when he'd previously been my teacher. It doesn't add up.

"What puzzles me most is something only Ares will understand." Their eyes pinned each other. "When Anzthoraz was sure that She and Widow had lost the battle, She didn't come after us. Widow begged Her to go on, to kill me, but Anzthoraz wouldn't do it."

"Yes, I thought that was odd." The Prince massaged his chin. "Widow said She wishes for you to die because you bear Oscerin's light, and that allows you to stop the shadow. But if that were the true reason behind Her attempts, Anzthoraz Herself would have been far more eager to end you. She didn't seem threatened by you at all."

"You lot think Widow's got some, eh, ulterior motives?" offered Oliver. "I wouldn't put it past Her. Think we've all seen how outta Her skull She is by now."

"There *is* another reason," added Ares. "Widow is terrified of you, Luxea. There's something deeper than all of this, something about who you once were that Widow knows and we don't."

Avari hopped off the desk, and her belt dragged a stack of papers off the edge. Ares jolted to catch them. "Well," she groaned with an over-the-head stretch, "we'll have to figure out Luxie's secrets. But not tonight, pretty please. My tum's been rumblin' for hours."

"You were eating on our way here," pointed out Brielle. But Ruka was hungry too; it was time for his evening meats. "Dragon, let us adjourn. Mayhap we should throw a feast in celebration of our victory. Kross is a wonderful chef. His talent is absurd, really."

"I've got plenty o' rabbits in this hat, love," purred Oliver. Ruka licked his muzzle at the mention of rabbits. "I'll make somethin' you lasses'll never forget. A pot pie sounds droolin' good, donnit?"

The group left before Ares could agree to put the meeting on hold. If there was to be a dinner, he supposed he should be present so that Oliver wouldn't blow a hole in a wall.

But as he stood up to leave, he noticed that Luxea was still there.

She was flat against the closed door with a thousand words written on her face. All of them made Ares smile.

"Yes?" he hummed.

Luxea was practically chewing off her lower lip. Ares worried that she'd broken something valuable; it wouldn't have been the first time.

"Well," she began timidly, "I wanted to apologize for having hurt you. For stabbing your knee, but mostly for burning your face. I'm sure it was unpleasant — more than unpleasant."

Ares arched his brow. "I forgive you, but when did that happen?"

"What? Just the other day when I . . . ."

"When you . . . ?"

"You don't remember?"

"I can't say I do."

Luxea had spent the past couple nights playing out this conversation in her head, but she hadn't once imagined an instance where Ares didn't recall kissing her.

"Never mind, it's nothing," she laughed. But her second question wasn't any less nerve-wracking. Her pink stars searched for an escape route perchance this didn't go well. "Next, could you help me with a translation?"

"Most likely," said Ares indifferently.

Luxea took in a breath and mouthed 'okay' to herself. "How would I say 'too' in draconic? The sort of 'also' too, not the number. Oh, and not the preposition either."

"I'm not unfamiliar with the language arts, Luxea. You don't need to explain homophones to me," said Ares roguishly. She grimaced. "In draconic, 'too' — the 'also' kind — is said as, 'jae.'"

She muttered to herself. Ares flicked his cigarette and waited for whatever thought train she was driving to pull into the right station.

When next she spoke, she looked as if she might faint. "So would it make sense to you if I were to say, 'Iu lemi thois jae?'"

Ares dropped his cigarette but swiped it off the floor as if it hadn't fallen. He fumbled with it before pressing the butt into a white gold ashtray. He'd smoked less than a half, but he only wanted one thing now, and it wasn't roseleaf.

With his expression as unreadable as ever, he leaned back on his desk and beckoned her with a curl of his talons. Luxea's feet were anvils as she wobbled to him. She was suddenly very interested in the designs woven into the rug and might have stared at them for the rest of her life had Ares not lifted her arms around his neck.

He smiled at her. It was a laughing smile.

"I lied. I do remember," was all he said before he kissed her.

First came the kiss of a man, calculated and careful, slow and promising, but then awoke the dragon, wild and dominant, possessive and torrid.

Every stolen glance, unspoken word, and missed chance was redeemed in a flurry of hungry lips and wandering hands. She was his favorite story, and she let him read her and read her.

He loved her in a way a monster could never love. And that, for the first time in all this cursed time, made him feel entirely human.

Far, far away, bathed in the light of the Irestar, the Moon Mother felt a change. It had been many years since Her Speaker's heart had been unchained. She'd wanted this for Ares, for Luxea too.

It wasn't the sole center of Her purpose, but Oscerin had known when Luxea Siren was born that she would become the counterpart of Ares Lavrenthea in more than one way. They'd uncovered two, but there were more — many more.

Then the Moon Mother's pleasure faded. She'd felt hated by Ares and Luxea ever since they'd learned about Her lost twin. Like Oscerin, Anzthoraz knew They'd been separated for a good reason. It was torture to keep it unsaid, She wished She could reveal the truth to Ares and Luxea, but they weren't ready.

No one, not even the Moon or the Shadow, was ready.

Oscerin had waited to tell Luxea about her journal in the cellar because, had it been found any earlier, Luxea wouldn't have gone to the Brood gathering and freed Sh'tarr. Ares wouldn't have learned the truth of Widow's gifts and may have been tempted by pretty lies later in his life.

All She did was for a reason. They would see that someday.

The next task for the Parallel and the Divide would soon arise. The Moon Mother allowed Her chosen to bask in the moment of delight they'd earned, but it wouldn't last.

Love cannot prevail in this world — not yet.

# References

# PRONUNCIATION KEY

(Italicized syllables represent stress.)

## PRIMARY CHARACTERS

Luxea Siren — *Loo* · shee · uh *Sy* · ren
Ares Lavrenthea — Ah · *raze* Lav · *ren* · thay · uh
Avari Vishera — Uh · *var* · ee Vish · *air* · uh
Oliver Kross — *All* · ih · verr Cross
Brielle — *Bree* · ell
Ruka — *Roo* · kuh
Shir — Sheer

## BROOD MEMBERS

Annalais Taress — *Ann* · uh · lie Tarr · *ess*
Ralvesh un Gatra — *Ral* · vesh Oon *Got* · ruh
Val'noren Paah — Val · *nor* · en Paw
Vesas Kross — *Vay* · sauce Cross
Levelia Kross — La · *veel* · ee · uh Cross
Tani Renayo — *Tonn* · ee Ren · *eye* · oh

## MINOR CHARACTERS

Peyamo Nelnah — *Pay* · om · oh *Nel* · nuh
Therasi Direl — There · *ahh* · see Duh · *rell*
Elthevir — *Ell* · thuh · veer
Velesari — *Vell* · uh · sorry
Pveather — Feather
Isaak Oelar — *Eye* · sick *Oh* · lar
Cherish Ven'lethe — *Chair* · ish Venn · *leeth*
Doryan Skythoan — *Door* · yen *Sky* · thohn
Ruri Nairn — *Roo* · ree *Nay* · ern
Mollah Felloen — Mall · *uh Fell* · oh · enn
Claymore Urius — *Clay* · more Yer · *eye* · us

# Pronunciation Key

Hanalea Moots — Haw · nuh · *lay* · uh Moots
Kalo Moots-Urius — *Call* · oh Moots Yer · *eye* · us
Vessias — Vess · *ee* · oss
Daiada — Die · *add* · uh
Salae Haviel — Suh · *lay* Haa · vee · *ell*
Doremi — *Doe* · ray · mee
Hannir O'dalar Siren — *Ha* · neer Oh · *duh* · lar *Sy* · ren
Asla Siren — *Azz* · luh *Sy* · ren
Thaldira Siren — Thall · *deer* · ah *Sy* · ren
Iodere Siren — Eye · oh · *dair Sy* · ren
Nika Lecava — *Nick* · uh Lay · *caw* · vuh
Estalyn Faust — *Ess* · tuh · lin Fost
Runa Faust — *Roo* · nuh Fost
Naiv — Nyv Lav · *ren* · thay · uh
Manalaei Lorcé — Man · uh · *lay* · ee Lore · *say*
Llaisa — *Lie* · suh
Isabelia Taress — Izz · uh · *bell* · ee · uh Tarr · *ess*
Rowan Taress — *Row* · enn Tarr · *ess*
Yerris Raleen — *Yair* · iss Ruh · *leen*
Samsamet — *Sam* · suh · met
Vasna Lorreen — *Vass* · nuh Lore · *een*
Omnia — *Om* · nee · uh
Rosamie — *Rozz* · uh · me
Urcyn Jjolenvaar Haldentred — Urr · *sine Yo* · lenn · var *Hal* · den · tred
Ondohal — *On* · doe · hall

## Remarkable Objects

Usinnon — *You* · sin · on
Felastil — Fell · *ass* · teel
Sindred — *Sin* · dread

## Locations

Amniven — Am · *nee* · venn
Lemuria — Lem · *yer* · ee · uh

Eletheon — Ell · *eth* · ee · un
Sithe — *Sy* · th
L'arneth — Larr · *neth*
Anunaru — Ah · new · *nar* · oo
Mythos — *Mee* · thos
Tel Ashir — Tell *Ash* · eer
Tzapodia — Zuh · *po* · dee · uh
Lor'thanin — Lore · thuh · *neen*
Selnilar — Sell · nil · *arr*
Solissium — Soul · *iss* · ee · um
Erannor — *Air* · enn · or
Aratoia — Air · ah · *toy* · ya
Ai Florana — Eye Floor · *on* · uh
Ank'tatra — *Onk* · ta · truh
Tarot — Tar · *oh*
Irestar — *Eye* · er · star
Tehrastar — *Tair* · uh · star
Cadlespeak — *Cay* · dull · speak
Drenut — Dreh · *noot*
Dulcinus — *Dull* · kin · us
Tarhelen — *Tarr* · ell · en
Tal Am T'Navin — Tawl Am Tuh Nav · *een*
Thali ou Tirima — Thall · *ee* Oo *Teer* · ee · muh
Matha ou Machina — *Moth* · uh Oo *Mosh* · een · uh
Desha Dunali — *Desh* · uh Doon · *all* · ee
Avi Tulani — *Aw* · vee Too · *law* · knee
Orchiris — Ork · *iris*
Calpher's Mount — *Cal* · furs Mount

## SPIRES

Hildre — *Hill* · druh
Tsrei — Sray
Tekrah — *Tek* · ruh
Sirah — *Seer* · uh
Naolen — *Nay* · oh · len

# Pronunciation Key

Nervir — Nair · *veer*
Ilsemet — *Ill* · sem · et

## Ethnic Groups

L'arian — *Lair* · ee · en
Seroden — *Sair* · oh · den
Draconic — Drake · *on* · ick
Aestof — *Ay* · stoff
Rishja — Rish · *jhuh*
Felenoe — *Fell* · en · oh
Sil'simani — Sill Sim · *on* · ee

## Magick Clans

Hantilad — *Hon* · till · add
Pea'natia — *Pay* · uh *Nay* · she · uh
Xexa — *Zex* · uh
Encurio — En · *cure* · ee · oh

## Goddesses

Tirih — *Teer* · ee
Oscerin — Oh · *sair* · in
Ka'ahn — Kawn
Anatatri — Ann · uh · *taw* · tree
Alatos — *Al* · uh · tose
Sh'tarr — Shuh · *tarr*
N'ra — *Neer* · uh
Asrodisia — Ass · row · *dizz* · ee · uh
Himhre — *Him* · ree
Daetri — *Day* · tree

## Gods

Wynd — Wind
Ganra — *Gonn* · ruh
Sithess — Sith · *ess*

# PRONUNCIATION KEY

Nall — Nawl
Ostriseon — Oss · *triss* · ee · on
Raveth — *Ray* · veth
Theryn — *Thair* · in
Mamaku — Mom · uh · *koo*
Ocaranth — *Oh* · car · anth
Rin — Rin
Varnn — Varn
Fenne — Fen

## WILDLIFE

Weorem — *Way* · oh · rem
Fenlaig — *Fen* · lyg
Yulacai — *You* · luk · eye

## UNKNOWN

Anzthoraz — *Annz* · thor · azz

# Amniven Timeline

Months:
1. Lightsmeet (LM)
2. Clawsguard (CG)
3. Venomsnare (VS)
4. Worldbreak (WB)
5. Duskriddle (DR)
6. Blackomen (BO)
7. Kingsreign (KR)
8. Softstep (SS)
9. Riverspell (RS)
10. Redtail (RT)
11. Nightspeak (NS)
12. Snowhowl (SH)

Seasons:
1. Frosttear
2. Wolfswake
3. Sunrae
4. Redrift

Centuries:
1. Tirih (TIR)
2. Oscerin (OSC)
3. Ka'ahn (KHN)
4. Anatatri (ANA)
5. Alatos (ATS)
6. Sh'tarr (SHR)
7. N'ra (NRA)
8. Asrodisia (ASR)
9. Himhre (HRE)
10. Daetri (DTR)

Each month (moon) follows Earth's breakdown. There are 365 days in Amniven's year. To understand the date, take into consideration these factors.

Day (day of the month.)
Month name (as listed above.)
Year (number of the year 1-99 in a century.)
Century name (as listed above.)
Millennium number (Era 3 = 3,000 years.)

EXAMPLE:
11.LM.1.OSC.3 = 11 January, 3201
11 (Day) . LM (Month) . 1 (Year) . OSC (Century) . 3 (Millennium)

# GLOSSARY

## A

Aestof - The people of The Isle of Varnn.

Ai Florana - Domain of N'ra the Nature Goddess. Located in the heart of the Crystal Spire.

Alatos - The Goddess of the Sea. Second goddess born to the mortal plane.

Amal Luciem - Translates in l'arian to "give light."

A'maru Mountains - Mountain range in Selnilar.

Amber Wing - Royal living quarters of Castle Lavrenthea.

Amniven - The world.

Anatatri - The Goddess of Time. First goddess born to the mortal plane.

Anathema - Capital of the Wraiths.

Ankle Biter - The name of Oliver Kross' tiny knife.

Ank'tatra - Nation in southern Anunaru. Primarily deserts. One of the six most prominent territories. Brood territory.

Annalais Taress - Empress of Goldenrise. Youngest member of The Six.

Anunaru - The eastern continent that makes up the Joined Hands.

Anzthoraz - (See the chapter A Cure of Names for more information.)

Aptuli - The orchard on Castle Lavrenthea's property.

Aratoia Desert - A desert in Tzapodia.

Arcana - The essence with which sorcerers are born.

Arcanan - Dead language used by spellbooks and magisters.

Arcanan Reservoir - Naturally occurring pool of arcana.

Arcanan Translator - Device used to translate arcanan created by Therasi Direl.

The Architect - Common title for the Usinnon and Therasi Direl. (See Therasi Direl.)

Ares Lavrenthea - Prince of Tzapodia. Speaker of Oscerin. Member of The Six. The last remaining cursed child of Samsamet.

Ashi Priest - Priests of Tzapodia.

Asla Siren - Luxea Siren's grandmother.

Asrodisia - The Goddess of Fertility. Fifth goddess born to the mortal plane.

Avari Vishera - Seroden ranger of Tel Ashir. Mentor to Luxea Siren.

Avi Tulani - Landlocked nation in L'arneth.

Avi Yeromin - Landlocked nation in L'arneth.

## B

Bay of Farewells - Bay in Tel Ashir located by the military quarter.

Black Ghost of Tzapodia - (See Spymaster Ruri Nairn.)

Blackjaw Hollow - Home to the Riders of the West.

Blackomen - Sixth month of the year. Sign of Raveth.

Blackwood tree - Tree with black bark and purple and white leaves.

The Blightwater - The sea separating Tzapodia and the Isle of Varnn.

Blissits - A slang Varnnish phrase to express surprise.

The Bone Spire - Sacred tower of bone in Emeraldei in the Greatgrace. Formed from the first titan Naolen, a failed goddess.

Brielle - Wolf rider of Blackjaw Hollow. Sister of Ruka.

The Brood - Widow's army.

The Brood Mother - (See Widow.)

# C

Cadlespeak - The capital of Elder's Expanse.

Caldavaan Cove - Cove located south of Tel Ashir. Location of the Tzapodian royal harbor.

Calpher's Mount - Mountain in Northreach.

Castle Lavrenthea - Home of the Lavrenthea family in Tel Ashir.

Cherish Ven'lethe - L'arian elvish magister. Once Luxea Siren's instructor. Brood servant.

Chief Demartiet - Previous Chief of Border Patrol in Tel Ashir. Killed in Lor'thanin.

Clawsguard - Second month of the year. Sign of Ganra.

Claymore Urius - Lieutenant in the Tel Ashian army. Member of the Mooncallers Council.

The Coral Spire - Sacred tower of coral in the Undercrown Ocean. Also called Tsrei.

Court of Light - Plaza in Tel Ashir.

The Crystal Spire - Sacred tower of crystal in Selnilar. Also called Sirah.

Crawler - Skinny, quick-moving creatures that serve the Brood.

Crypt of Beasts - Home to the Riders of the East. Located in Tarot.

Crystal Strangers - (See Mythics.)

Daetri - The Goddess of War. Seventh goddess born to the mortal plane.

Desha Dunali - Locomotive built by Peyamo Nelnah. Translates in seroden elvish to "Iron Dart."

The Divide - Oscerin's title for Luxea Siren.

Division Magick - Branch of the arcana for splitting the soul.

Doremi - Goat-faced faerie minion of N'ra the Nature Goddess.

Dracas - Horselike lizards ridden in Tzapodia.

Draconic - The language of the dragons.

Draconism - Curse placed upon the first people of Tel Ashir. Drives the afflicted to insanity. Eventually traps them in the body of a dragon.

Dragon Stones - Board game won by tossing a bloodstone into the center.

Drenut - Southernmost nation in Anunaru. Primarily rainforests. Brood territory.

Dulcinus - City in Goldenrise.

Dundis Angle - Forest in the Storm Plains.

Duskriddle - Fifth month of the year. Sign of Ostriseon.

Ei tensha - Translates in l'arian to "my blade."

Elder's Expanse - Nation in L'arneth.

Eletheon - The realm of light where souls venture after death.

Elthevir - Dracas belonging to Avari Vishera.

Eluva'eshas - Translates in l'arian to "mirror the face."

Emerald Wing - Sect of Castle Lavrenthea for conferences and the library.

Encurio - One of the four magick clans. Origination unknown. Renowned for silent magick.

Era - Millennia. Currently Era Three.

Erannor - City in Selnilar. Brood territory.

Estalyn Faust - Mother of Runa Faust.

Eternity's Ocean - Ocean between L'arneth and Anunaru.

Felastil - Moon-forged pendant belonging to Ares Lavrenthea. Also a communicator. The second is owned by Oscerin.

Felenoe - Catlike inhabitants of Drenut.

Felitia - Shieldmaiden in the Tel Ashian military.

Fenlaig - Spherical pigs who have a very hard time escaping predators.

Fenne - The Wolf God. Twelfth god born to Amniven.

Filannia - Western nation in L'arneth.

Firelily - Curled, orange lilies. Used for mourning a Tzapodian royal's death.

Flame Gardens - Royal gardens of Castle Lavrenthea.

Frosttear - First season of the year.

Gajneva - Previous Chieftain of Blackjaw Hollow. Killed by her bat counterpart Veshra.

Ganra - The Bear God. Second god born to Amniven.

Garamat un Gatra - Previous Sun Chief of Ank'tatra. Killed by the Mooncallers at the Goldenrise gala.

General Doryan Skythoan - War General of Tzapodia. Member of the Mooncaller Council.

Genntric Taress - Previously Emperor of Goldenrise. Father of Annalais and Rowan Taress.

Given - Nation in the Greatgrace.

The Glacial Spire - Sacred tower of ice in Yriv, the northern pole. Also called Tekrah.

The Golden Spire - Sacred tower of gold in Goldenrise. Also called Hildre.

Goldenhands - The army of Goldenrise.

Goldenrise - Northernmost nation in Anunaru. Primarily moors. One of the six most prominent territories in the Joined Hands. Brood territory.

The Great Bridge, Tarhelen - The largest manmade structure on Amniven.

The Greatgrace - The largest continent on Amniven.

The Grey - The largest nation in L'arneth. Primarily snowy mountains.

Grove Wanderer - Giant, treen beast thought to be extinct.

## ᚻ

Hanalea Moots-Urius - Sage in Castle Lavrenthea's infirmary. Married to Claymore Urius. Savior of Luxea Siren from Tal Am T'Navin River.

Hannir O'dalar Siren - Luxea Siren's father.

Hantilad Conjurers - One of the four magick clans. Originated in the nation of Given in the Greatgrace. Renowned for illusory magick.

Havan'ha neila - Translates in l'arian to "hold him down."

Haven de Asrodisia - The guest wing of Villa de Taress.

Heart of Haven - Previously the den of courtesans in Haven de Asrodisia. Shut down by the Mooncallers.

Heavens Devil - Informal title of Naiv Lavrenthea.

The High Templar of Stonehall - Female knight met by Luxea Siren and Avari Vishera in Cadlespeak.

Hildre - (See the Golden Spire.)

Himhre - The Goddess of Wealth. Sixth goddess born to the mortal plane.

## 1

Ilsemet - (See the Sandstone Spire.)

The Irestar - Alternative name for the Moon.

Iodere Siren - Luxea Siren's mother.

Isabelia Taress - Previously the Empress of Goldenrise. Mother of Annalais and Rowan Taress.

The Isle of Varnn - Island beneath L'arneth. Shrouded in eternal night. One of the six most prominent territories in the Joined Hands. Brood territory.

## J

The Joined Hands - The united continents of L'arneth and Anunaru.

## K

Ka'ahn - The Goddess of Fire who takes on the form of a child. The third goddess born to the spirit plane. One of the three greater divines.

Ka'ahn's Fire - The red dwarf star visible from Amniven once biannually.

Kalo Moots-Urius - Child of Claymore Urius and Hanalea Moots.

Keepers - Accountants in Tzapodia.

Keeper Vessias - Head keeper. Member of the Mooncaller Council.

King of the Abyssal Plain - (See Weorem.)

Kingscore - Flaming canyon created when Naiv Lavrenthea fell from the sky in year 14. Located in Tel Ashir beside Castle Lavrenthea.

Kingslane - Guarded road leading to Castle Lavrenthea.

Kingsreign - The seventh month of the year. Sign of Theryn.

## L

Lady of Bronze - Formal title of Peyamo Nelnah.

Lali - Sage in Castle Lavrenthea's infirmary.

L'arian Elf - The natives of L'arneth. Found mostly in Selnilar.

L'arneth - The western continent that makes up the Joined Hands.

Leitha'maen - Translates in l'arian to "Soul Sword." Army of Selnilar.

Lemuria - The name of the universe.

Levelia Kross - One of the Masters of the Isle of Varnn and member of The Brood. Wife to Vesas Kross. Mother of Oliver Kross.

Light Seeker - Formal title of Val'noren Paah.

Lightsmeet - The first month of the year. Sign of Wynd.

Llaisa Lorcé-Lavrenthea - Would have been the Princess of Tzapodia. Daughter of Manalaei. Sister of Ares. Died before birth.

Locus-jumping - Teleportation.

Lorith - Royal blacksmith of Castle Lavrenthea.

Lor'thanin - Capital of Selnilar.

Lover's Nautilus - Symbolic seashell denoting the Goddess of Fertility.

Luxea Siren - L'arian woman with stars in her eyes. Cannot remember who she was prior to her awakening in Castle Lavrenthea's infirmary. Mortal tether of Oscerin the Moon Goddess.

## M

Madam Lilivae Alanis - Previously the headmistress of Haven de Asrodisia.

Magelas - Arcanan tattoo of a sorcerer's birth-given name.

Magick - (See arcana.)

Mamaku - The Rabbit God. Eighth god born to Amniven.Manalaei Lorcé-Lavrenthea - Previously the Queen of Tzapodia. Wife to Naiv Lavrenthea. Mother of Ares Lavrenthea.

Mandamba - Nation in the Greatgrace.

Maolam - A Tzapodian governess.

Matha ou Machina - Translates in seroden to "Daughter of the Machine." The airship belonging to Peyamo Nelnah.

The Masters - Vesas and Levelia Kross of the Isle of Varnn.

Mollah Felloen - Head sage in Castle Lavrenthea's infirmary.

Mooncallers - The army of Tzapodia and organization founded by the Speaker Ares Lavrenthea.

Mooncaller Council - Members most trusted by Prince Ares Lavrenthea.

Moon Mother - Informal title of the Moon Goddess Oscerin.

Moonpass - The main entryway to Tel Ashir.

Motherpoint - Cliff behind Castle Lavrenthea.

Musha - Dracas gifted to Oliver Kross. Despises Oliver Kross.

Mythics - Asexual beings of crystal. Considered a myth until now. Living purity. Capable of twisting reality.

Mythos - The island on which the Mythics reside. Shielded by Sh'tarr's Iris. Untouched by man.

# N

Nach lathene - Translates in draconic to "my son."

Naiv Lavrenthea - King of Tzapodia. Husband to Manalaei Lavrenthea. Father of Ares Lavrenthea.

Nall - The Mammoth God. Fourth god born to Amniven.

Nan Jaami - Southwestern region of mountain rishja in L'arneth.

Naolen - Failed goddess from the beginning of time. The first titan and supposed mother of Asrodisia. (See the Bone Spire.)

Naraniv - Southern nation of L'arneth that was eradicated by King Naiv Lavrenthea. Has since become territory of Tzapodia.

Nav'amani Forest - Forest in Selnilar.

Nav'in ei th'luneth - Translates in l'arian to "show me my dreams."

Nervir - (See the Steel Spire.)

The Nightingale - Spellbook belonging to Cherish Ven'lethe.

The Nightmare Venom - Incurable poison inflicted upon Luxea Siren. Induces nightmares until death.

Nightskin - Derogatory term for aestof people.

Nightspeak - Eleventh month of the year. Sign of Varnn.

Nika Lecava - Head engineer and helmsman to Peyamo Nelnah.

Novis - The One-Eyed Cat constellation.

N'ra - The Goddess of Nature. Fourth goddess born to the mortal plane.

Ocaranth - The Koi God. Ninth god born into Amniven.

Oliver Kross - Son of Masters Vesas and Levelia Kross. Heir to the throne of the Isle of Varnn.

Omnia - Rider of Blackjaw Hollow. Counterpart to the raven Skye.

Ora Napel - Cafe in Cadlespeak.

Orchiris - The capital of Avi Tulani.

Order of Stonehall - Knights from The Grey.

Oscerin - The Goddess of the Moon. Second goddess born to the spirit plane. One of the three greater divines.

Ostriseon - The Owl God. Fifth god born into Amniven.

The Parallel - Oscerin's title for Ares Lavrenthea.

Pea'natia — Nation in the Greatgrace.

Pearl Alley - Corridor of Castle Lavrenthea.

Pertia Voulet - Previously a headmaster in Haven de Asrodisia.

Peyamo Nelnah - Leader of the nation of Tarot, member of The Six, and mentor to Ares Lavrenthea.

Phoenix Sons - The army of Ank'tatra.

Porranim Courtyard - Courtyard of Castle Lavrenthea.

Priestess Daiada - Head Ashi priestess. Member of the Mooncaller Council.

Pveather - Albino dracas belonging to Ares Lavrenthea. Called "finger-snapper."

Quaritan - City located in northern Tzapodia. Eradicated in year 99.TIR.

Ralvesh un Gatra - Sun Chief of Ank'tatra. Member of the Brood.

Ramenne - Capital of Filannia.

Raveth - The Raven God. Sixth god born into Amniven.

Redrift - Fourth season of the year.

Redrise - Menstrual cycle.

Redtail - Tenth month of the year. Sign of Rin.

The Riddling Roads - Unreliable roads in the Wraiths. Rearranged in Nightspeak by Cherish Ven'lethe to trap the Mooncallers.

Riders of the West - Tribe of riders who dwells in Blackjaw Hollow.

Rin - The Fox God. Tenth god born into Amniven.

Rise of Reflection - Mountain range in The Grey.

Rishja - Half-giant descendants of Xeneda.Riverpass - Gate in Tel Ashir for access to Tal Am T'navin River.

Riverroot - Water-dwelling root used for treating burns.

Riverspell - Ninth month of the year. Sign of Ocaranth.

Rosamie - Oliver Kross' forsaken daughter. Killed by Widow at age five.

Roseleaf - Rare blossom often smoked or steeped for tea.

Rowan Taress - Previous Emperor of Goldenrise. Brother of Annalais Taress.

Ruby Bureau - Ares Lavrenthea's office in Castle Lavrenthea.

Ruby Wing - Sect of Castle Lavrenthea used for archival purposes.

Ruka - Brother and wolf counterpart to Brielle.

Runa Faust - Ten-year-old girl living in Tzapodia. Was previously a courtesan in Haven de Asrodisia, called Unblossomed. Saved by the Mooncallers.

# S

Sage - A nurse.

Salae Haviel - Founding magistress of Sirah Academy. Haunts the academy to this day. Also called "Sweet Salae."

Samsamet - The last dragon. Cursed the people of Tzapodia with Draconism.

The Sandstone Spire - Sacred sandstone tower in Ank'tatra.

The Sapphire Bazaar - Shopping center in Tel Ashir.

Seer of Tzapodia - Formal title of Luxea Siren.

Selnilar - Eastern nation of L'arneth. Primarily forests. One of the most prominent territories in the Joined Hands. Brood territory.

Seroden Elf - Elves renowned for their technological advancements.

Sheishan'in - Translates in l'arian to "shield me."

The Shifting City - Capital of Tarot. Made entirely of machines.

Shir - The last *Sil'simani*. Mythic from the isle of Mythos.

Shrine of Luciem Salah - Home of the Light Seeker. Located within Sirah Temple in the Crystal Spire.

Sh'tarr - The Goddess of Storms. Third goddess born to the mortal plane.

Sh'tarr's Iris - The eternal hurricane in Eternity's Ocean.

Sil'simani - Translates in l'arian to "Sacred children." The Mythics.

Sindred, Tail of Samsamet - Blade of the Lavrenthea family. "Sindred" translates in draconic to "consequence."

Sirah - (See the Crystal Spire.)

Sirah Academy - Abandoned magick academy built into the Crystal Spire.

Sirah Temple - Home to the Light Seeker. Built into the Crystal Spire.Sithe - The realm of punished souls. Also called the In-between.

Sithess - The Serpent God. Third god born into Amniven.

The Six - Organization of the six most sovereign leaders in the Joined Hands.

The Shadow - Mysterious entity who has tormented Luxea Siren throughout her childhood. (See the chapter A Cure of Names for more information.)

Sleepthistle - Herb steeped in tea for stress-relief. Occasionally smoked.

Snowhowl - Twelfth month of the year. Sign of Fenne.

Softstep - Eighth month of the year. Sign of Mamaku.

Solissium - Capital of Goldenrise.

The Speaker - (See Ares Lavrenthea.)

Spell-eater - Sorcerers who cannot be harmed by another's magick.

Spirit Healers of Pea'natia - One of the four magick clans. Originated in Mandamba. Renowned for healing.

The Splinters - Mountain range in The Grey.

Spymaster Ruri Nairn - Head of the rangers of Tel Ashir. Also called the Black Ghost of Tzapodia. Member of the Mooncallers Council.

The Steel Spire - Sacred tower of steel in Janeel in the Greatgrace. Also called Nervir.

Steps of Sevinus - Royal staircase of Castle Lavrenthea. Named after Sevinus Lavrenthea.

Stonehall - The capital of The Grey.

The Storm Plains - Nation on the eastern coast of L'arneth. Always stormy.

Sun Chief - Formal title of Ralvesh un Gatra.

Sunrae - Third season of the year.

Sweet Salae - (See Salae Haviel.)

Tal Am T'navin River - The longest river in L'arneth located in Selnilar where Luxea Siren was found.

Tani Renayo - Leader of the nation of Drenut. Member of the Brood. Formally called the Tree Warden.

Tarot - Nation located in Anunaru. Primarily mesas and igneous rock. One of the six most prominent territories in the Joined Hands.

The Tehrastar - Alternative name for the Sun.

Tattleweed - Hallucinogenic plant often smoked by unruly adolescents.

Tekrah - (See the Glacial Spire.)

Tel Ashir - Capital of Tzapodia.

Titantula - Slow, hulking creatures that serve the Brood.Thaldira Siren - Luxea Siren's grandfather.

Thali ou Tirima - Floating fortress belonging to the Lady Peyamo Nelnah.

Therasi Direl - Era Two magister and professor at Sirah Academy. Was seroden elvish. Inventor of the arcanan translator. Called "the Architect."

Theryn - The Lion God. Seventh god born into Amniven.

Time - Domain of the Time Goddess Anatatri. Accessed through the Memory Door. Location unknown.

Timeless Mountain Pass - Pass leading to the Golden Spire.

Timeless Mountains - Mountain range surrounding the Golden Spire.

Tirih - The Goddess of the Sun. First goddess born in all time. One of the three greater divines.

Tomb of Vasna Lorreen - Crystal tomb within Sirah where hundreds of soldiers were trapped during the eradication of sorcerers in Era Two.

Torus - Dracas belonging to Ruri Nairn.

Tree Warden - (See Tani Renayo.)

Trihells - The three realms of the damned.

Tsrei - (See the Coral Spire.)

Tzapodia - Southeastern nation of L'arneth. Primarily deserts. One of the six most prominent territories in the Joined Hands.

Unblossomed - (See Runa Faust.)

Urcyn Jjolenvaar Haldentred - High King of The Grey. Demigod. Son of the Bear God Ganra.

The Usinnon - Luxea Siren's spellbook companion. (See Therasi Direl.)

Val'noren Paah - Leader of Selnilar. Formally called the Light Seeker. Member of the Brood.

Varnn - The Bat God. Eleventh god born into Amniven.

Vasna Lorreen - Era two Light Seeker responsible for the purge of magick.

Velesari - Dracas belonging to Luxea Siren.

Venomsnare - Third month of the year. Sign of Sithess.

Vesas Kross - One of the Masters of the Isle of Varnn and member of The Brood. Husband to Levelia Kross. Father of Oliver Kross.

Villa de Raleen - The previous name of Villa de Taress.

Villa de Taress - Royal home of the Taress family.

Weorem - The Sea Goddess' first creation. The world's largest marine mammal. Also called King of the Abyssal Plain.

The Western Woods - Expansive forest located in Selnilar.

Widow - Deified woman who is rallying the greatest leaders of Amniven in preparation to recreate the world.

Wing Regent Isaak Oelar - Placeholder of the throne of Tzapodia.

Witchsleep - Settlement in the Wraiths.

Wolfswake - Second season of the year.

Worldbreak - The fourth month of the year. Sign of Nall.

The Wraiths - Nation in Anunaru. Primarily marshes.

Wynd - The Stag God. First god born into Amniven.

Xexa Witches - One of the four magick clans. Originated in The Grey. Renowned for division magick.

Yaz Magia - Translates in rishjaan to "Sun Chief."

Yerris Raleen - The first Emperor of Goldenrise.

Yeth'lavren - Translates in l'arian to "bring fire."

Yulacai - Horselike creature with a mane and a long snout for bug-hunting.

# ACKNOWLEDGMENTS

To my parents: You are the very core of who I have become and am becoming. Without your insight, your support, and your love, this world in my head would never have been born. As I write this series, I pray you learn more about me than I have allowed you to see.

To my friends, Tilly and Ted: In the last six months, we have shared a household. Writing the first book of Mooncallers, I cut off everyone in my life for over a year thinking it was best to dwell inside my head without influence, but you two have proved me wrong.

Ted, you painted the first book cover with your *finger,* and you painted the second better than I could have imagined myself. When I was worried about whether or not I could finish thirty-five chapter headers on my own, you stepped in and did the line art and shading for half of them. I pray that you understand how much I appreciate you, as a friend and an artist, and aspire to, one day, spill from my mind to my canvas the same magic that you do.

Tilly, you have reminded me that I do not need to be alone to see our world through the eyes of a child. At first, I was afraid that I would lose my vision of Amniven with other people around me, but what I have experienced with you has taught me that, without friends, I would never understand the truth of relationships and be able to translate them into another world.

To Losse Lorien: Not only did you give me the most valuable guidance for this book, but you have done so for me in life for many years. You have defied all odds, you have broken barriers and faced demons that most people have not found the courage to face. I know that, for all time, you will glow. You may doubt yourself, you may be

XIX

lost in new lands, but I am confident that you will find the doorway, and that doorway will lead to something more beautiful.

To Kat: I miss you every single day, whether you know it or not. No matter where we go or who we become, you will always be my best friend. You started this, and so many other shenanigans, at my side, and I cannot finish it without you. I pray that you never forget that I love you and always will — unconditionally.

To Max: I was unsure if I would speak to you again after we fell apart, but I could not be happier that you are once again in my life. What I treasure most in this life is knowledge — not the sort that schools can teach, but the sort that comes from someone who has hurt. You have given me that and beyond, and I will forever treasure you.

To my followers: No matter how many times I disappear or for how long, you have remained to support me and all that I love. I wish I could explain my silence, but I will tell you now what I always tell my closest friends: *'We could not speak for years, and I would still be your friend exactly the same.'* Had it not been for all of you, I never would have discovered the key to achieving my dreams or even starting them. You have saved me. Every one of you is my key, and I will always, always love you.

I'd also like to thank Karina, who talked to me for hours on end about book two, asked me all the necessary lore questions, and ended up the first Ares Lavrenthea cosplayer and writing the first fan-fiction of Mooncallers. To Jeff Walden, whom I miss each and every day.

To my four cats: BMO, who ate my entire carpet this year, Xya, who ate everything else, Panks, the sweetest sock-wearing kitten, Courage, who loves dust baths, my fifth half-cat, Mia, the telepath, and my two puppies, Prince, the coolest dog dad, and Loki the coolest son. Also Zant, who is not my dog but should be.

# About the Author

Leda C. Muir was born in 1994 in Santa Barbara, California. Growing up, she chose solitude over socialization. Her best friends were trees in the schoolyard and faeries.

Since she was thirteen, she has been an online entertainer on websites such as YouTube and Instagram — but there was only so much that she could express on those platforms.

At age twenty-three, she published her first book, Mooncallers: Stars Wake. In the beginning, Mooncallers was never meant to be released. It was merely an outlet, but she became attached to Amniven and its inhabitants and thus decided to show her imaginings to the world.

She doesn't know what is to come, but she plans to continue to walk the paths of Amniven — until the end of all things.

Printed in the USA
CPSIA information can be obtained
at www.ICGtesting.com
LVHW021953101123
763491LV00005B/491

9 780578 411965